EEG

Daša Drndić

EEG

*Translated from the Croatian
by Celia Hawkesworth*

A NEW DIRECTIONS BOOK

Originally published in Croatian by Fraktura in 2016
Published in arrangement with MacLehose Press, London

Manufactured in the United States of America
New Directions Books are printed on acid-free paper
First published as a New Directions Paperbook Original (NDP1437) in 2019

Library of Congress Cataloging-in-Publication Data
Names: Drndić, Daša, 1946– author. | Hawkesworth, Celia, 1942– translator.
Title: E.E.G. / Daša Drndić;
translated from the Croatian by Celia Hawkesworth.
Other titles: EEG. English
Description: New York : New Directions, 2019.
Identifiers: LCCN 2018046578 (print) | LCCN 2018056251 (ebook) |
ISBN 9780811228497 (ebook) | ISBN 9780811228480 (alk. paper)
Subjects: LCSH: Intellectuals—Croatia—Fiction.
Classification: LCC PG1619.14.R58 (ebook) | LCC PG1619.14.R58 E3813 2019 (print) |
DDC 891.8/235—dc23
LC record available at https://lccn.loc.gov/2017013734

2 4 6 8 9 7 5 3 1

New Directions Books are published for James Laughlin
by New Directions Publishing Corporation
80 Eighth Avenue, New York 10011

For Maša and Gojko

As we endeavor to distance ourselves from our torments, madness is our last refuge.

What saved me was considering suicide. Had I not considered suicide, I would certainly have killed myself. So, the desire to die is my one and only concern; I have sacrificed everything to it, even death.

—E. M. Cioran, *Cahiers 1957–1972*,
Paris, Gallimard, N.R.F. 1997

Of course I didn't kill myself.

Although silent suicides lurk all around. They skulk. Silent suicides are not violent suicides, they are gradual, ongoing. My sister Ada is killing herself silently. And I sometimes kill myself slowly, I go through phases, then I pull myself together, get over it. Eating too much can be a silent suicide, as can starvation, often observed in ambitious and insecure anorexics or old people who have lost their teeth and their place in life, so they stare at the TV screen, eating bananas and ice cream, if they can afford them. But starvation can also be forced, when people are killed by someone else (silent murder), when people don't want to be hungry, but are.

Recently, in a transnational shopping center, a man ran away from a guard with a little piece of steak in his jacket. The guard caught up with him and the packet of meat ended up on the ground. The man, whom the guard called a thief, managed to get away, but without the meat. Maybe he should have settled on a cheaper option, like another man who went for chickens. He slunk into the basement of a family house in Veliki Grđevac and removed from the freezer forty kilos of frozen chickens and ducks worth nine hundred kunas. It was reported in the paper that the owners had not anticipated a thief would steal their chickens and ducks. They probably thought that, in a village of 3,313 inhabitants, 80 percent of them Croats, everyone loved each other, they all had enough to eat.

Maybe it's safer to collect snails and sell them, and then use the proceeds to buy something to eat, polenta for example, or maybe to pay the electricity bill. The "policemen" of the European Union do not prohibit this; on the contrary, they encourage such initiatives. The snails have to be collected in April (that's what T. S. Eliot thinks as well), because it usually rains in April, so snails slide smoothly, they get excited, emerge from their hiding places and then snail collectors can catch them easily. Snail collectors advise taking only adult snails, of thirty-four millimeters or more, because tiny snails are no use. So, snail collectors collect snails, then they sell them to snail dealers who pay half a euro for a kilogram of collected snails, then the snail dealers distribute them through their business partners to the European Union, to restaurants, where the snails, the *escargots*, are taken out of their shells, cooked in butter, wine or stock, along with garlic and other seasonings, then put back into their small houses and served to guests in portions of six to twelve, with little pliers for holding the shells and little narrow forks for removing the snails, and the guests then dunk them in thick aromatic sauces, smack their lips and say *mmmmm*.

Silent suicides visit the young as well. Increasingly. Silent suicides come to those who are isolated, who have become social outcasts, and because they are social outcasts, they often turn to drink, or drugs, whatever, then they get ill and become depressed and sad. I know one (older) man who did kill himself, leaving a little note in which he had written: *I need peace and this is the only way I'll find it*. He was sixty-seven.

It has been scientifically proven that it is common for silent and invisible suicides to be committed by people who cannot accept change, who are a bit inflexible, cognitively rigid, unable to adapt, conservative (they cling to tradition, to the hearth, to the homeland, to the Church, and don't let go), people who are obedient and emotionally repressed, so emotionally repressed that they forget to laugh, thinking they should mostly be serious; who are disciplined, who allow themselves to be disciplined, because they believe that's the way to heaven. In the end they snap.

But that's not always how it goes. Those whose lungs and brains are constricted by such people, so they can't breathe, they kill themselves too.

> *Listen, get over it. What terrifies us about death is not the loss of the past. Forgetting is a form of death ever present within life.*
>
> Kundera

I have something to say on that topic as well. Death is not an event in life, but is the end of my life. If we take eternity to mean not infinite temporal duration but timelessness, then eternal life belongs to those who live in the present. Our life has no end in just the way our visual field has no limits.

Wittgenstein

So, I didn't kill myself. Nor did I leave. I didn't abandon anything or anyone, everything around me is as it was; here are the books, here is the furniture and my small, select collection of glasses, here are my clothes—worn-out shirts (100 percent cotton), my pictures on the wall and my former self who no longer exists. Everything is here, only the space sways. I moved away to study small dead things, to observe close-up dead things that refuse to die. Arranged in impenetrable cages of milky glass, seen from outside, those dead things appear like quivering figures, opaque and inaudible, but alive. So, on my short journeys, I observed those huge cages, approached them, tapped on them, placed my hand on them to summon those imprisoned within, in case they came close to me, so I could speak to them through that thick milky-white glass, tell them I knew them, those imprisoned people, that I remembered their stories, that I was guarding their lives, but they just danced blissfully, disembodied in the silent vacuum. I remained invisible to them, external.

Then I came back.

There was a time when I had abandoned Rijeka, my language, my body, I was leaking away in droplets. Now I'm gathering up the remnants (of myself), this amalgam resembling the wet sand that children squeeze and make into wobbly figures, swollen, deformed and gray. Now I'm porridge-like, I'm porridge that is curdling, refusing a form, a porridge of squeezed organs, mush. Pith, pulp, formlessness. I glean rinds as well, vestiges of other people's lives, to give them shape, even a distorted, deformed shape which occasionally emits a spark, and then I believe that not everything around me is utterly dark after all.

The town has not changed. People still walk diagonally, with great amplitude. They turn suddenly across my path, they spring up in front of me, making me jump every time. Pedestrians do not stick to their left-hand side; they attack, they leap out, they destroy my rhythm, they move in a crippled, hiccupy rhythm so that my own gait becomes disorderly, jerky and erratic. Deformed. In the street around me people buzz, shout, bump into each other, steal those last remnants of my momentum, then I stop stock-still and let them pass, let them go, let them leave me a little bit of space so I no longer hear their empty chatter that makes my chest tremble and my brain undergo electric shocks that erase my thoughts. A few days ago I sat down to take a break, to have a coffee, to wipe out the remains of my morning nightmares, my swaying dreams. At the table next to mine at the little pavement café, three women were shrieking, grinding words as though rolling small pebbles around with their tongues and spitting degenerate phlegm in all directions, monster spirits that hovered in the air and rolled over the pavement, spreading across the space. What's more, one of them kept hailing acquaintances and comparing her life to theirs from a distance of some ten meters, as though she was in a Neapolitan alleyway.

Once, at breakfast in a hotel, I said to a man who had been carrying on a senseless and repetitive conversation on his cell phone at the top of his voice for a full fifteen minutes, *Perhaps you could continue your conversation outside the dining room*, and he replied: *Have you never been to a hotel before?*

In a café, I once called out to a woman who was shrieking into her cell at the next table: *Could you tone that down a little?* She was stunned, she opened her eyes wide and said, *Get lost, old man, fuck off*, and carried on even more loudly than before.

My friends tell me to calm down, which is a somewhat milder way of saying: You're cracked.

The din all around is appalling, it assaults one shamelessly. I have said before that I don't know a noisier town than this. Sometimes the roar, the racket, the blaring, booming, thudding, rumbling, shouting, yelling, the general bawling—sometimes it's so intolerable one feels like stopping in the middle of the street and screaming. Then maybe someone would pause, stunned into silence. The other day a woman came into the pharmacy, long bleached hair, disheveled, with black grime under her fingernails, wearing flowery harem pants, like pajamas, screeching into two cell phones at the same time, one white and one red, and the whole pharmacy reverberated. When she came to pay she was fifteen kunas short, so she went out but soon came back, still shouting into the little instruments pressed to her ears. Then a nun came in, exceptionally quiet by contrast, to collect her prescription medicine. Her Medazol vaginal suppositories had arrived (for trichomoniasis infection, among other things), but she too was short of some ten kunas. She rummaged through her purse, and the pharmacist asked deferentially (why deferentially?), *Does that seem a lot to you?* and the nun said, now rather more loudly, somewhat brusquely, *One could do without*. What did she mean, *one could do without*, why should it be done without? I immediately imagine this penguin-like believer on a gynecological exam table, is she half-naked or does she open her legs in her bat's habit? There's a story going around Rijeka about a nun who had six abortions. The gynecologist recommended contraceptive measures, but she said, *That's against my religion*. Generally speaking, I have a problem with nuns. Outwardly, they look modest and humble, but they're not. As soon as they're touched (verbally), they become truculent, they raise their voices, sometimes they even become pugnacious, belligerent. Once I was waiting in a clinic, a long line, there was no hope of reading so much as a leaflet, partly because of the miserable light, partly because of the general clamor out of which from time to time someone's penetrating voice emerged as patients described their ailments and exchanged test results in detail, blow by blow, then there she was, the nun: *I'm in a hurry*, she said, *I can't line up*. Everyone fell silent, they looked at her piously, some even crossed themselves, as though the Virgin Mary had wandered into the waiting room. I said, *I hope you won't take long*, and she pretended not to hear and went in. She stayed in the consulting room for forty-five minutes, it became so oppressive to be waiting in that darkness that even the pious grew restive. When she emerged, that venerable nun, I asked, *Have you been getting prescriptions for the entire convent?* She put her hands on her hips and said, *That's right*. And fluttered away. Her glasses frame was more expensive than mine.

*

Then, in that clinic, I got annoyed again, because now it seems even quiet people annoy me, not only loud ones, and that's no good.

When I write and talk about the noise level in this town, some people feel personally affronted, as though they were the town, and in fact they are. But in the mere twenty minutes I spent in the pharmacy, three individuals asked for earplugs, wax ones, they said, we want wax ones because the wax ones fit better, they block the sound best, they said, not the ones for keeping out water, they said, water ones are rigid and they slip out, while wax ones can be molded to fit. There.

> *Listen, a great many people smile at such things, because they are not sensitive to noise; but they are just the very people who are also not sensitive to argument, or thought, or poetry, or art, in a word, to any kind of intellectual influence. The reason of it is that the tissue of their brains is of a very rough and coarse quality. Noise is the most impertinent of all forms of interruption. It is not only an interruption, but also a disruption of thought. Of course, where there is nothing to interrupt, noise will not be so particularly painful. Those sudden, sharp cracks, which paralyze the brain, rend the thread of reflection, and murder thought. On the thinker the effect is woeful and disastrous, cutting his thoughts asunder, much as the executioner's axe severs the head from the body.*
>
> Schopenhauer

Dog owners walking their pets are best, they don't talk, they walk in a straight line and pick up shit.

Writing *Belladonna* was a game. A jerky confession passably shaped by D. D. That had to be mentioned. For the sake of avoiding readers' misconceptions, for the sake of truthfulness. As it is, there have been some misunderstandings, minor misunderstandings, granted, because everything has become minor—conversations, places, contacts, footsteps, time, and I myself—my breathing, my sight, my testes. My lungs feel tight. In any case, confusion has arisen. A confabulation of my life has come about, as though my life could be pressed between the covers of a book. As though I had lived unreality, warehousing other people's stories in my innards, ingesting other people's lives, whose odor, whose sorrow, whose insanity had begun to rot my insides.

People say I have written an autobiographical book, *Belladonna*, or rather they say it is an autobiographical book by D. D., but it isn't. Every novel is a novel about salvation, says Béla Hamvas, there is no novel without confession. So there.

Autobiographical books don't exist, autobiographies don't exist, there are multigraphies, biographical mixes, biographical cocktails, the whole mélange of a life through which we dig, which we clear out, from which we select fragments, remnants, little pieces that we stuff into our pockets, little mouthfuls that we swallow as though they were our own. This trash heap (of lives) has swollen so much over the centuries that already it covers the surface of the globe and nothing in it can be recognized, nothing can be separated from it anymore, no uniqueness, no form, just overcooked husks, a mush which pulsates, barely, shallowly, before its *exitus*.

Now, if one is to write, and what is written is of absolutely no use to the deformed human race, it is best to "invent" a story that has already been told with as many words as possible on as many pages as possible and blend it all into a child's drawing. For the sake of comprehension. For the sake of ease. For the sake of breeziness which will undulate like a current of air above the trash heap of our existence, to drive away (our) stench, so that, at least for a moment, we can believe that we are not ebbing away, that we are not leaking out like black slime. No allusions, heaven forbid, no metaphors or symbols, but sticking one's finger straight into the shit. Make it simple. But I'm not offering "a story," because I write about people who don't have "a story," not about those or for those who are looking for *other people's stories* to find their own.

A critic once wrote that *Ban's discourse is too moralizing. He is an inconvenient writer, he keeps punching the reader in the stomach.*

Celebrated writers can sometimes write truly worthless texts, but since they are held in high esteem, they are not only untouched by critics, but praised to the skies, even so they will be forgotten when they are no longer here, just as some who have been dead for twenty or so years already have. It happens the other way around as well. Which is no comfort, but rather a source of sadness or exasperation. Those who are immediately forgotten—writers, painters, women, men, musicians, scholars—are often all too easily plucked out of centuries-long oblivion and their names are bandied about everywhere by the present, mercilessly magnified after their own present had kicked them into poverty, madness, despair, suicide.

When one writes, it helps to repeat oneself. It's even desirable to transpose whole passages from one book to another, which is what I do from time to time, because people are chronically forgetful. And they are often surprised. When they are surprised, they cry out *Imagine!* The human brain is running out of space, running out of breath, becoming asthmatic, pale, the way the optic nerves grow pale until their final extinction, until blindness. Take music, for instance, the songs known as *turbofolk*, songs bus drivers play maniacally on intercity journeys and which are hummed by passengers who gaze at the loudspeakers, moving their lips in a trance.

Peter, Peter, handsome Pete, buy shoes for my pretty feet, and you'll make my life complete!

My girl's front teeth are missing, oh, there's nothing like her kissing!

I look at the trees above, you are my first true love.

My legs may be bandy, but I'm really handy, give me a try, you'll want me till I die.

I can't wait to bury my old ma, and bring home my little Sara!

Die, my darling, I'll join you in the ground, through our coffins our hands will be bound.

If there is anything good about this yelping and wailing, it's that it blends into an amalgam of linguistic variants, Croatian, Serbian and Bosnian, with even the occasional Slovene or Macedonian word, so that, at least temporarily, for the duration of an intercity bus ride, its insipid sentimentality overwhelms the belligerence of many people in these parts.

Nothing but repetition, all sorts of things are repeated, the worst are TV and radio commercials filled with absurdities, screeching hysterically *Turbolax—for regular evacuation of the bowels!* just when I sit down in front of the screen with a sandwich and a glass of wine. And then:

Lose 100% of your weight in 30 days.

Problems with passing urine? Prostamol Uno—an efficacious treatment for inflammation of the prostate, Prostamol Uno! It's easy to be a man.

Then comes a jingle: 𝄞 ♩ ♪ ♫ then:

Crunchy wafer, Milka chocolate is something special for a bit of good cheer … Milka Crispello, improves the mood, crunchy and light. 𝄞 ♩ ♪ ♫ *Save your memories in a CV photo album. Visit the website www.cv.hr to make your own CV photo album, because our memories are important.* 𝄞 ♩ ♪ ♫ *The best-known international writer has inspired millions throughout the world. Jana, water with a message from Paulo Coelho …*

A few days ago, I asked a shop assistant whether they had a particular cheese and she said, *We had that cheese yesterday, we'll be getting that cheese again in two days, it's very popular, you know, it's a reasonable cheese, sells immediately, if it doesn't come the day after tomorrow, it will come a day later and by evening there won't be any left, because ...*

I said, *Madam, stop*, and she said, *You should see a doctor.*

Now, as I am composing this story, I shall be able to tell my son: Here's a window onto madness. *Our planet is a cosmic madhouse*, said Goethe as much as a hundred years and more ago, to which Nietzsche, while he was still of sound mind, before he was assaulted by *Spirochæta pallida*, lues, or syphilis, added: *With individuals madness is rare; but with groups, parties, nations and epochs, it is the rule.* Like those who spend months camping in tents in the middle of capital cities, because their lives have lost all sense, because there are no more wars, because for them only war gives life meaning, because for them, it is only because of death that it is worth living, that's what the priests who visit them say, but that will pass as well, life will forget them, whatever that life is like, because let me repeat once again what Giono said long ago: *There are no heroes, the dead are immediately forgotten. The widows of heroes marry the living only because they are alive and being alive is a greater virtue than being a dead hero. There are no heroes after a war, there are only the lame, the crippled and disfigured from whom women turn away; only fools are left. After a war, everyone forgets the war and those who fought in it. And that is right. Because war is useless and one should not make a cult of those who dedicated themselves to the useless.*

For this curtailed, mutilated age, there is no point in spreading its image. There is no longer any point in sewing up, patching, joining, putting more fragments into our panoramic frame, because all the components are rotten, in a state of decay, incompatible. The empty spaces are so great that they can be filled only with new empty spaces—which are nothing, an enormous elusive nothing, that *das Nichts* of Heidegger's. *So, yes, let's make it simple.*

It is good that books are disappearing, they too are getting smaller. Often the fattest books are the thinnest. Ironed, with no creases, tidily folded and put away, they are ready for disuse.

Yes, the cheese seller said, *You should see a doctor.*

I found her in a bad way. Buried in the cellar of the family house we had sold for peanuts in the early 1990s to some Italians. That's what prices were like then, pitiful. Probably because of the war. The house is worth twenty times more today. And even if it had been left the way it was, with rickety old windows, a half-rotten wooden floor, a bathroom hastily put together right beside the kitchen, decorated with bright-red oil paint, that house would be worth twenty times more today (and it is). Foreigners became greedy, because foreigners like small Mediterranean towns, especially if they're run-down by capitalist standards—they think they're exotic. Like the people who live in them, also run-down, that is to say branded with the seal of socialist poverty. It's a bit different nowadays. Tattoos are fading. Life in these little Mediterranean towns was cheap for foreigners. Back then. Some twenty years ago.

Today, the house is a renovated, expanded, serious house on the top of a hill, some hundred meters from the sea, with a view of the sea. That's worth a lot. A view of the sea drives people crazy—in a positive sense, it calms them, but it disturbs them too. There must be some atavistic link between the eye, the soul and water, extensive waters of mystic depths and an inaccessible, dark bottom. Some connections quiver, are inexplicable.

The house is dry (apart from the cellar), in a small town sometimes steeped in dampness, it is a sunny house, several centuries old, made of stone and tall—the tallest on the street, with a terrace that looks out over the town, the bay, the islands and the open sea, with windows on the street side as well, so it's a house with both outdoor and indoor space. It would be simple and in literary terms banal to say the house is like a person, because just as there are different houses, so there are different people, then one would have to describe the person whom this house resembles. There's no time for that here, and no need. This house also has attic windows through which the bell tower of the church is visible, so close that one could ride on it. At night, when it's hot, the maestral blows in from the sea and lights tremble on the water, it creeps in through all the cracks (for no house can be completely sealed) and gets under the skin of the house, and the house breathes. And it is quiet.

The basement in which my sister Ada Ban lives does not look out at anything, in fact it looks at used-upness and tedium. At the occasional roof in the distance, somewhere down there, at the occasional façade in the distance and at other people's illegally grafted-on terraces and balconies, and, although the basement has a concrete yard, my sister hardly ever spends time in it, because she is surrounded by tourists who from on high look down at Ada, buried there. And the owners of those old houses are all inland owners from the new Croatia who do not know how the little town breathes, or how it dreams, or what it remembers, not to mention its crannies or its secrets. Like aggressors, like bandits, the new arrivals invaded the town and set about wounding it, tearing at its tissue, rummaging through its organs and its languages, so that today in summer the town becomes a blown-up, botoxed puppet, submissive and dumb. In winter, thank God, the town awakes from its summer stupor, from this drugged state, embraces its in-laws and, somewhat heavily, stretches and smiles, not thinking of the ordeal that awaits it the following summer.

One of these people exploited a three-meter gap between his

hovel and that yard of ours, paved it over and built a kitchen and toilet there. In the stone wall that separates his place from ours he made an opening for extracting the human bodily stench, which was then wafted through the Ban family's garden and settled on the table where we ate. Later that man, who died recently, covered over his toilet ventilation with an ordinary white ceramic tile, and that little tile now stands out among the huge, centuries-old gray blocks—upright marker stones with weathered edges.

We sold the house because we had nothing to live on. In the new Croatia. My father, Ada and I. Our mother Marisa had long since turned into dust and was now seeping out of her corroded tin urn in Belgrade, instead of in Split.

It used to be lively in that house, it was noisy and cheerful. People ran up and down the stairs that cut through the three levels of the building, quarreled over the use of the single cramped, ugly, socialist-style bathroom with tiles that kept falling off; people shouted, dried cod was beaten flat, black risotto cooked, fritters fried, bean pasta was prepared in a large pot on a worn stove-top with burnt, rusty rings, and carried down into the garden, which was then not paved, it was overgrown with weeds, but with a white early summer fig tree in the lower right-hand corner and an old loquat planted in the center. (The fig was cut down and the loquat died, one summer it dried up and, cracked with age, bent over and collapsed.) Dozens of liters of Teran wine from Motovun and Istrian Malvasia flowed, there was singing, there were a lot of people of all kinds, from fishermen and politicians to doctors and chess players, there were writers, the only people who didn't come were those (few) city slickers from Zagreb, from the top of Rovinj hill. Because that house at 31 Bregovita (Hill Street) in Rovinj was the demarcation line between two worlds, and has remained so to this day in a somewhat impoverished, lopped, insignificant and already worn-out way.

On the terrace, shoddily built—everything about this house was largely improvised and botched—we played preferans until dawn ("we" being three close water polo friends, one of whom was Adam Kaplan), then we went for a night swim, and at dawn for warm meat pie. When our parents were not about we'd bring home women for a night, and Ada the occasional lover, in the morning the house quivered with unfamiliar footsteps, bent under the warmth of naked bodies, supple and sunburned, wanton.

Now, the house is old. A tired house, restored, but worn out. The Italians on the upper floors are old, their guests are old, Ada, down in the cellar, is old. Upstairs, the walls have been spruced up, new bathrooms built, the electric wiring replaced, the house has been made up, a gaudily dressed lady past her prime, and so few know what her pulse is now like, what (if any) memories haunt her and in what dust they disperse.

Somehow it happened, not at all by chance, I believe, that this visit of mine to my sister Ada and the stump of our outlawed house coincided with the publication of a book about tranquil days in Rovinj by the excellent writer Bora Ćosić. The book mentions this same little Rovinj street, Bregovita, which, it is very important to mention, because of history, because of the past, because of remembering, because of the people in that little town who do not live on the hill, but down below, in the belly of the old town, where the sun often does not reach, where there are no gazebos or verandas, where mold settles on the lungs, where cats yowl at night and sometimes rats gnaw at the trash, it is important to mention that this steep, stone street is also called via del Monte, just as for decades all the streets in this town have had two names, which used to grate on the ears of some people in power at the beginning of the 1990s, so there was almost a premiere here of the chiseling away of street names, but that was left after all for the appalling Vukovar performance twenty years later. In those days

Istria shouted, *Tudjman go home!* and thus saved the streets and identity cards and Italian schools and Italian kindergartens and Marshal Tito Square. Those up there, intoxicated with stinking Croatdom, persevered in carrying out "small" corrections, so they changed the name of the heroine Roža Petrović (whose eyes were gouged out by Italian Fascists, but nevertheless, blind as she was, she carried on knitting socks for the Partisans, including a pair for our father) to Ruža Petrović, so that now the little street that bears her name is somehow additionally crippled, blinded even though that little alley is indeed short and blind.

There's a constant palaver with streets, with their naming and renaming. In the small town of Rovinj, before this last war, the main street was called Beogradska, and the only cinema the

"Beograd." Now Beogradska is called what it should be, Carera, because Rovinj is really Rovigno, and there's no cinema, all that remains is the modified name of the little café, Cinema Café, beside the place where the cinema once was, while the building itself has been adapted to house a German bank. Films are shown in the little baroque theater built way back in 1854, when it bore the name of Antonio Gandusi, then a famous actor of the Novecento, born in Rovinj.

All right, we won't go on about history now. Although history, that of Rovinj for example, is very rich and fascinating, but quite unknown to many of its perennial (uninterested) summer visitors.

The top of Bregovita, here, the top of via del Monte, is occupied in summer by members of the old Zagreb (Agram) elite, which in my opinion is no longer any kind of elite because it has grown moldy. That elite almost never talks about the history of Rovinj, or of Istria, just as it doesn't talk about the inhabitants of Rovinj who live (or lived) in this little town, although they include internationally famous painters, there are also writers, there are doctors, architects, dozens of scholars, so the "elite" (on the hill) would be able from time to time to invite them to their tables (if only metaphorically), for otherwise they are "profiles" which interest the "elite" (on the hill) à la Madame Verdurin, more as profiles than as people. However, since that elite has degenerated with time, becoming hidebound, it increasingly eavesdrops on what is happening in that artistic field, while it hears and sees ever less, and ever less well. During the tranquil days in Rovinj, there live what could be called colorful—quite unusual—judges, fishermen, shopkeepers, custodians, and so on, unknown to the "elite," for them nonexistent.

For instance, that "crazy, brilliant painter" who moved from one abandoned Rovinj house to another, the painter Bora Ćosić wrote about in his book as having left a house that he bought in chaos and tatters. Yes, she left paints and a mess after her, the confusion and disorder of a wild nature, cosmic and human. In his book about the tranquil days of Rovinj, Bora Ćosić mentioned "my friend," but without calling the painter by her name. Now that painter is dead, so she can't tell her friend that all her disorder, in life, in space, internal and external, all her painterly disorder, was in fact what Bora described in the catalogue of one of her exhibitions: a dread of the whole of existence. My friend, the joyful Zora Matić.

The fact that in his book about the tranquil days of Rovinj Bora Ćosić forgets to mention the names of people (who had been) close to him upset me, because I now name people fanatically, too weightily for literature, that is, unnecessarily, obsessively, because I see more and more clearly that this, their name, is perhaps the last cobweb thread that separates them from general, universal chaos, from the cauldron of turbid, stale mash.

So, in that book, a little essay about three small wooden horses waiting in vain for the day when they will be able to leave the wall in Bora's porch and trot off to freedom, is a touching and charming little essay, but there is no mention in it of Ljuba Gamulin, who brought him both the horses and the story about them one summer evening and built them into the wall. I was there and I remember that enchanting moment.

Yes, Zora Matić lived in Bora's house, in the house into which he had imported an aesthetic of order, an aesthetic of controlled civilization, while hers, Zora's, was an expressionist aesthetic, distorted and at times painful. Zora Matić lived in our house after it was abandoned at the end of the 1950s by Bruno Mascarelli. In that house, our parents' former home, there wasn't a single beam into which Zora had not hammered at least a hundred nails. She hung her own and other people's lives from them. In that house at 31 Bregovita, Bruno Mascarelli left a whole wall covered in a charcoal drawing—of an Istrian fireplace, and it kept Zora warm in winter. Zora's story is long and this is not the place for it, or perhaps it is, if this is a story, if this is going to be a story of people who fall outside frames.

Ever since she could remember, Zora had wobbled on the edge of that frame, those frames of lives, at times withdrawing—returning—into the picture, and then overflowing out of it again.

Zora Matić came to Rovinj in 1954, from Zagreb. She was thirty-one years old. In Zagreb she had worked as the director of a company, Dekor, which she founded in 1949. The People's Front of Yugoslavia had given her the task of finding premises for the company, which was meant to undertake artistic/crafting activities, on condition that the premises must be in the main, Ilica, street. Given that in Croatia for at least two and a half decades tons of reinforced concrete have been poured over the past, it's likely that few readers know what this People's Front was. So, in brief. The People's Front is the name of the international alliance of democratic parties opposed to the establishment of fascist regimes. The concept came into being in the 1930s, during the period of aggressive politics in Fascist Italy and Nazi Germany. In Croatia those politics were endorsed by left-wing intellectuals (Krleža and co.), and supported by individual members of the Croatian Peasants' Party, so the People's Front is mentioned also in documents of ZAVNOH, the State Antifascist Council of the People's Liberation of Croatia. After 1945, because of its organizational breadth but also its political authorization, it initiated and led all educational projects, and coordinated the work of cultural-educational societies.

Right, back to Zora Matić.

So, at the beginning of the 1950s, Zora goes from building to building (in Ilica), looking for a location for the Dekor company, she peers through keyholes and finally comes to a building housing the Jadran cinema, she goes into the courtyard and on the first floor, also through the keyhole, she sees an enormous hall, with quantities of washbasins. She informs the relevant people in the People's Front and the People's Front requisitions the space, although the owner of those washbasins, Zora tells me, is a friend of the influential communist politician Bakarić, so the decision is to an extent (briefly) held up, on Party instructions. However, the hall is nevertheless "mobilized" and in it all conceivable artists, as Zora puts it, obtain space to work. In the new Croatia, Dekor was privatized, then placed into liquidation, and finally it disappeared.

When I first saw the sea from here, Zora said, *when I saw this red Istrian soil, it took my breath away and I said "This is where I'm going to live."* Because of her inordinate, as she put it, love for Rovinj, Zora lost the right to her apartment in Zagreb, and in Rovinj first slept on a hospital bed in an empty room, *found for me by Bruno Mascarelli. Bruno was already in Rovinj by then.*

Bruno Mascarelli came to Rovinj in 1948. He was twenty-two. He had studied painting at the Academy in Belgrade and later in Zagreb. *Many Italians had left, there were a lot of empty houses*, Bruno said, *then gradually artists began to come. In summer, the Zagreb student Cesco Dessanti used to invite colleagues to his native Rovinj. Their arrival led to the resurrection of the town, material and spiritual. First Ljubo Ivančić, Edo Murtić, Josip Vaništa, Miljenko Stančić and me, then Slobodan Vuličević and Zora Matić. The atmosphere was brilliant*, he said. *We all got on well and we all worked.*

I learned Italian quickly, Zora said—the last time we spoke, at the end of the 1990s, in her last abode, this time outside the old town, in a modern two-room apartment in which there still reigned a divinely elusive, almost abstract, disorder: a bath full of incomplete oil paintings on canvas and hardened, unusable brushes, among which rolled shriveled apples, heads of cabbage and half-squeezed tubes of paint. *It was possible to paint*, she said, *already then, in the early 1950s, it was possible to paint. I have only one socialist-realist oil painting made earlier in Zagreb, some weary fighters,* she said. *Stančić used to come at eleven or twelve at night to see what I was working on. He was a great artist and it's a great shame that he died too soon.*

As there were no museums in Rovinj at that time, a small but select group, initially with the assistance of the Local Council, set up a department for painters and brought paintings from the National Liberation Struggle, and then from the Red Island and Brijuni the works of well-known Italian and German old masters from the collection of the Hütterott family (and the Hütterott family is a special Rovinj story and how could I fit that in now?), works painted between the fifteenth and nineteenth centuries, and a real permanent display. Later, significant exhibitions from the Museum of Art and Crafts and the Yugoslav Academy of Science and Arts were organized, but also many individual and collective exhibitions of painters who are well known today. For two years Zora did all this on a voluntary basis. The Visual Arts Colony of Rovinj was founded, the oldest such colony in Croatia, and it has now been active for more than half a century without interruption. Its instigator was Bruno Mascarelli.

I wasn't any kind of instigator, Bruno said. *It came about of its own accord, the way cells of societies are formed in life in general. I dragged in the artists, writers and painters who came—some because of me, some with me. There were thirty-seven of us then from Zagreb and between eight and eleven from Belgrade. We were young, full of energy, far from the pressures of convention, open to ourselves and the world, in a movingly inspiring atmosphere. Some of us didn't have either electricity or running water, coffee was a luxury, and we sent paintings to Rijeka on a boat that sailed around Istria. These were dreams on the scale of Don Quixote and similar attempts to create something. Dreams are important.*

Soon afterward, Zora Matić began to exhibit at home and abroad. As she got old she appeared less frequently, but she had two exhibitions, one in Rovinj and one in Zagreb, and organized an auction of her paintings, all for the children who had suffered in this last war.

What did Zora Matić paint?

I have phases, she said. *At one time, I did only heads. Those heads and my Istrian landscapes became so phantasmagorical that they began to be entangled with my personal life. I have a lot of expressionist canvases; they were all sold and scattered all over the world, I no longer remember where, nor does that interest me.*

Zora also painted portraits, *but portrait-painting is unrewarding,* she said. *People often don't recognize themselves and get angry. Once I painted the portraits of three children in Germany. The parents didn't want to pay me, because they maintained that the portraits didn't look like their children. When I went back the following year,* said Zora, *they invited me to see how wonderful my portraits of their children were. And how like them the children now were. But still they didn't pay me. When I was working in the Croatian Advertising Agency, immediately after the war, I painted portraits of politicians ad nauseam. We did Tito, Ranković, Djilas, Bakarić, we must have made a couple of hundred large paintings. That's when I got to know Mascarelli. We were both working in the Advertising Agency, in the Yugoslav National Army premises housed in the Dubrovnik Hotel. We painted the leaders and made decorations. We wrote slogans,* Zora Matić said, *political slogans for parades and celebrations.*

I didn't have a place to live then, Bruno Mascarelli interrupted, *so I slept in the larder of the Advertising Agency, with a Yugoslav flag for a blanket.*

As you see, I didn't move much out of Rovinj. Bruno soared to the heights, he traveled the world, he exhibited everywhere, and finally managed to get his life into some sort of order. Now he lives between Paris and Rovinj. Bora doesn't mention him at all in his book, either by name or anonymously.

Yes, they don't know me here, apart from in Rovinj, where I'm looked after and spoiled, Bruno chimed in with a smile. *Rovinj was always special. Unfortunately, it never had its interpreters. What can be put right should be put right, but it's not worth even discussing what cannot be fixed.*

Maybe Bora Ćosić was ashamed of inviting me to share a table with those Agram stiffs, Zora said. *Maybe he wanted to save me from their dumbfounded expressions, their sneering, perhaps even their disguised contempt. My paths never crossed those of that elite.*

I didn't study in Zagreb, Zora Matić says. *I followed only two semesters at the Academy. In Munich I studied for three and a half years without any grant, without anyone's help. That was in '41, when I ran away from Zagreb. Mile Budak gave a speech in the big hall at the old display ground, after which the several hundred people present raised their hands in greeting. I found it comical, so I raised a hand and a foot, first the right, then the left. People around me began to laugh. I was eighteen. I wanted to go to university, but because of that incident, for ages they wouldn't let me enroll. At the University there was a lecture for prospective students. The hall was full, I came in at the end, and the woman who was giving the lecture pointed at me and said, "If you don't leave, I'll have you thrown out." I realized that it was all beyond a joke. I got on a train and went to Leipzig.*

In Leipzig Zora works in a factory (she doesn't say which) as a draughtswoman, and with a painter (she doesn't remember his name) she learns to make landscapes and *pointless flowers*, she says. *It was pointless,* Zora Matić says, and goes off to Munich. *I had a godmother in Munich,* she says, *who promised to give me a scholarship, but when she saw that I wasn't enamored of her Führer, she changed her mind. Then I enrolled in a school for applied art, but since I worked in my own way—the teacher would tell me to draw horses and I would draw my neighbor—they suggested that I go to the Academy. It wasn't easy there because, due to the frequent bombing, we spent more time mending the roof than painting. I came back to Zagreb in 1944, and then the new government almost shot me because of my sojourn in Germany. I was saved by Anka Špalj, a civil servant in the Ministry of the State Treasury of the Independent State of Croatia.*

Zora Matić sang, she sang beautifully, she had perfect pitch.

I don't sing anymore. At one time, when I was with jolly company, I used to imitate the Neapolitans, I'm good at that. I even thought of studying singing at the Academy of Music in Munich, but they said either paint or sing. Now I'm okay. The paintings I left in my apartment have been taken away by some distant relatives, people I don't know. I see that they sell on the internet for a decent price. Someone always comes along to steal your life. Bora could have mentioned my name in his book.

Zora Matić died, as though out of spite, on Republic Day, November 29, 1999. That was her last transgression.

More than ten years ago, a small band of people from outside Rovinj, that is, summer residents, founded the Society of Friends of Rovinj. A statute was drawn up, the Society was registered, and when I saw that the Society was composed almost exclusively of the Zagreb elite, who get together in their town in any case, because they are presumably lovers of that town as well, I did not join the Society. In that Society (in practice, but also according to its statute) there was not and there is still no room for the other lovers of Rovinj, who really exist, for instance Italians, Hungarians, Slovenes, Serbs, Germans and Austrians, who have also been coming here for decades and staying for long periods. Today the activity of the Society is largely confined to excursions round Istria (when it isn't quite the weather for bathing), to shared dinners and collecting membership fees.

When I took that photograph more than thirty years ago, 31 Bregovita was still ours, our family home, as was evident in its shutters, worm-eaten, rotted by rain and baked by sun. Today the shutters are white, freshly painted, the façade plastered, light yellow and almost cheerful. In fact, the whole street has become well mannered, its poverty and the smell of grilled sprats, fried sardines or dried cod steeping in the sun have all ebbed away and boredom has moved in. Tourists thunder down it, they stop by the cellar window behind which is Ada Ban's bathroom (because opposite it there is an elegant shop selling souvenirs, wine, cheese and truffles, a boutique dominated by an old wind-up gramophone, one of those with a horn, emitting Beethoven, Mozart, Rachmaninoff and excellent jazz, and about whose owners a strange and exciting story could be constructed), these tourists who stop, make a racket, yak yak ad nauseam, thinking presumably that Ada's window is the abandoned opening of a storeroom, a dark warehouse, where old junk and rusty odds and ends are kept, which is no longer far from the truth. The guides yell, and one particularly in Russian, so Ada and I (when I'm there) think that she is shouting at the tourists, quarreling with them.

So, one group on the hill, without ever seriously stepping out of their cocoons, visited each other alternately, taking it in turns to treat one another to three-course meals designed to a perverse degree and little glasses of benign gossip with flashes of impatience, so the twittering around the tables would become louder and falsely cheerful, unadulteratedly adulterated. Others, the ones below the visible-invisible demarcation line in Ulica Bregovita/via del Monte, cooked in their unpaved gardens on improvised grills cheap oily fish caught that morning (with the occasional sea bass thrown in), making merry with a guitar, drinking from glasses of various shapes, eating off stained plates from old mismatched sets. All educated plebs. Today, they would be called middle-class losers.

Of course, for the (petty)bourgeois class moored for the summer at the top of Rovinj hill, peaceful days have now arrived.

There are ever fewer members of that class, and so, encircled by the wall of their own vacuity, entrenched in rhetorically saccharine but at times quite bellicose patriotism, they no longer have, as they once did, a group, with whom to spend evenings on the terrace with a view of Mediterranean helichrysum and the starry sky. Some have succumbed to dementia and ended up in hospital or a luxurious home for the infirm and are fading away at last, while their houses are inhabited by new people, unknown to me, among whom can be found the occasional newly fledged Russian tycoon; some of them so old that climbing (and descending) the hill is no longer an option, so instead they spend their summers in apartments in Zagreb, having first dismissed their long-standing seasonal butlers and other domestic help with a humble *adieu, mon ami, adieu*; they remain, once their young swells, now retired, spending their benign days in the languor of their deflated lives. And the "refuge" of Bora Ćosić's house is also deserted. The four-meter-long black table with the four-meter-long black benches in the "reception room" (the veranda) of that house, Scaletta dietro Castello 3b, in which there are now Proustian flashes of Bora's life, that black table is cluttered with objects of short-lived seasonal occupation, the profane everyday: newspapers, read and unread, some foreign, some local, little bottles of body oil, tubes of hand cream and sun cream, spectacles for seeing objects both near and far, an open packet of biscuits, tomatoes of various shapes and sizes, together with grapes, grapefruit, aubergines, red and white onions; the remains of breakfast—melting butter and crumbs, the sad disorder of transience, negligence, which, yes, conjures up tranquil days, but also abandonment, moving backward into selective remembering.

I, Andreas Ban, am familiar with that house and its many cracks. Now, when I visit my sister, I cannot concern myself with the house, with its innards, its organs, its former brilliance and the story of the way the house, hugging itself, has now closed up. There was light in it, *ah, oui*, rapid breathing, the everyday crackled, time changed like gift baskets, but also baubles, trinkets, without which days become dense and gray. I, Andreas Ban, could write about the houses I've lived in for extended periods, there were at least twelve of them, about the houses in which paintings, chairs, files, photographs, antiques, family heirlooms and other objects bought at flea markets, together with all kinds of odds and ends, mark out the footsteps of several generations of my family, not only their steps but also their paths, well-worn roads which history first churned up, and then leveled in a Machiavellian way.

But I stuffed my souvenirs into black trash bags and pulled their plastic strings tight. People tend to collect bits of nonsense to remind them of things because it's easier, there's no effort, they don't conjure up walks, scenery, conversations, aromas and touch, there's no time for that as life flows by, for most people just trundling along. People arrange paragraphs of their lives on shelves and walls, from time to time casting them a frozen smile and saying: *Stay there, wait for me*. When they switch off the lights, people imagine they will all be together again, reunited with their past, by then already rotten, moldy, stale, crammed into lifeless objects, that they will touch one another again, tell one another forgotten, withered tales. Not a chance. Mementoes die as soon as they are plucked from their surroundings, they disperse, lose their color, lose their pliancy, stiffen like corpses. All that remain are shells with translucent edges. Brain platelets, half-erased, are slippery terrain, deceptive. The mental archive is locked, in the dark. The past is riddled with holes, souvenirs can do nothing to put that right. Everything should be thrown away. Everything. And maybe everyone.

I would not, as I climbed the hill (struggling to breathe) toward the amputated remains of our parents' house, I would not have called to mind the many happy days spent in Bora's Rovinj fortress *dietro castello* (because I was being stifled by the hydra, not to say the present, that has adhered to my back like a rucksack) had I not, on that path toward Ada's buried shack, been stopped in my tracks by one of those Madame Verdurins whom Proust made immortal. One of those people, as Bora would say, *of the middle-class milieu, who despite the whirlpools of socialism, published her doctorate, found an academic post and a respected social position, but, for all that, retained a limited range of knowledge, and her conversation was wanting in most intellectual disciplines*, and, I would add, often in ethical-political-national ones as well. So this personage camouflaged in singsong, coming down the Monte as I was panting my way up, said, *You had no business to write a book like that about the town which gave you everything. A home and employment.*

Listen, I exchanged my dolled-up, tucked-in Belgrade apartment (with central heating) entirely legally for this neglected tenement in the small town of Fiume, whose windows don't fit and through which the north wind whistles and where in winter I sit in the half dark dressed for a ski run down some abandoned, neglected little mountain. In this town "which gave me everything," I spent five years without work, because wherever I looked, whoever I asked, I was told that I was either insufficiently qualified, or excessively qualified. In this town "which gave me everything" people listened attentively to my speech and would often label me with an invented, imagined, falsified allegiance, no matter which, religious, nonreligious, national, anational; in this town "which gave me everything," my son's school friends told him that Ban was not a Croatian surname, in this town, where I did all kinds of loathsome little jobs, including writing speeches for the mayor, and when, after all reasonable deadlines had expired, I finally received the most miserable fee imaginable for writing those speeches and took my son out for a plate of ten *ćevapčići* with onions, and my son said, *Thanks, Tata*, my stomach clenched like a pump squeezing out poison, although in fact, ever since coming to this town ("which gave me everything"), my stomach had been in a permanent state of paroxysm. I wanted to tell her all this, that woman, but I didn't, because I am polite, so I shortened my utterance dramatically, so dramatically that even I was astounded by what I said. For years I had been silent, I used to say thank you when acquaintances wished me a Happy Christmas or Easter, about which I don't give a tinker's curse, but that changed as well, and now I wish them the same and with a fixed smile say, *I neither believe nor celebrate*. That way I succeed in deflecting at least a fragment of the everyday aggression of those who attack me.

That was twenty or more years ago, in the course of marking some day or other in that town of Rijeka, there was a celebration to mark it, in the theater, with the so-called (pickled) *crème de la crème* present, I wrote a speech for the mayor in which I said (in which he said) that the situation with unemployed youth and the draining away of their brains was spiraling out of control, as it was with the elderly, retired population (which was already then craning over the edges of large dumpsters and itself becoming trash), and the following day in the local newspaper (with tepid pride) I read my lines out of the mayor's mouth, but right beside those seditious lines, calling for urgent, immediate economic and political changes, there appeared the reaction of the local leader of the right-wing opposition party, in which that commissar pointed out the discrepancy between the words spoken at that theatrical celebration (performance) and the maritime party held by the ostensibly left-of-center party where fine wines and little colorful canapés were served to *la crème de la crème* while cruising around the bay. On the same day, the person responsible for public relations, the mayor's right-hand man one might say, asked me to react in my "sharp style" (not in my name of course, but in the name of the Town) to the opposition leader's "impudence." I merely gave that PR person back this demand/request—correcting its grammatical and syntactical mistakes, which pierced my eyes—with the comment that in fact and unfortunately on this occasion I agreed with the right-wing party leader. That was when my speech-writing activities ended forever.

Then in that town of Fiume (after I had lived there for five years) people suggested that I should secretly replace someone who was working part-time because she was dying of cancer, adding that in the course of carrying out that work I could not possibly write, because in that Local Council, in that Cultural Department, in that town which has interesting misunderstandings with culture, the work was such that it demanded twenty-four seven commitment, and when I said that such secrecy was out of the question, because I did not like secret services, they raised their eyebrows in genuine surprise. Today, when I think back, perhaps that authentic astonishment meant precisely what the teacher with her fashionable foreign name had wanted to say, up there on the hill, there, we offer you a chance, and you reject it.

I no longer remember, nor does it matter, whether that and the other miserable incidents happened before I left Rijeka, before I immigrated to Canada in fact, or after I returned from Canada. When I went away, I left my apartment to a newcomer who became the director of the local theater and who was, of course, received considerably better by the town than I had been, the newcomer had a pedigree in stasis, with the exception of some short-term, high-speed business trips outside the borders of the newly created statelet, unlike me, with my forty-five-year absence from the motherland, my little homeland. When I came back, I found broken windowpanes, a burnt carpet, displaced furniture and greasy marks on the walls, but that, surprisingly, did not bother me. I replaced the windowpanes with new ones, I threw the carpet (four meters square) into the trash and cleaned off the greasy marks with detergent. To this day, all that remains a mystery is how and why my black Bakelite telephone disappeared. But the temporary occupant of my repository moved back to the small town of his permanent residence (the Town could breathe again) and died suddenly, relatively young.

There were issues with the faculty as well. At the beginning, the vice chancellor was a woman who had written a doctorate on the American Beatniks (I leafed through that illiterate little work) and along the way had become fairly active politically in what was at the time the caricature District Council of the Croatian National Parliament, and exchanged the little book of the Communist Party of Yugoslavia for a crucifix around her neck, and Party meetings and constructive criticism for Rules of the Mass with the people, mumbling in rapture: *mea culpa, mea culpa, mea maxima culpa.* Today that former, as they like to say, first female vice chancellor of the university in that little town (which had "given me everything") hangs in a hall there, known as the Rectors' Gallery, while the Lower House of Parliament no longer exists.

For five years I visited potential employers with my neatly typed and pruned life under my arm, but there was no sign of any permanent work. When I got to this vice chancellor I had not even opened my mouth when she asked me, in all seriousness, *Are you Croatian?* I turned and walked out. Multiculti Fiume-Rijeka had barricaded itself and remained padlocked.

To go back for a moment to that chief puppet in the puppet District Council of Parliament, which the nationalist HDZ Party renamed the Croatian State Parliament, so as not to lose continuity with the Independent State of Croatia (NDH). In the *Evening News* of October 29, 2004, Darko Đuretek wrote that he had discovered that the parliamentary president's portrait of Zlatko Tomčić had been finished, but that it would not hang on the wall until Šeks gave the go-ahead, and he also wrote that the only portrait to have been painted twice was that of Nedjelko Mihanović, because Nedjelko Mihanović had objected when he saw how small he had turned out, and was now waiting for the painter to make him bigger, and he also wrote that Katica Ivanišević was not altogether happy because of the brooch on her dress, which she, Katica, said was far more beautiful in the original. Katica Ivanišević was famous for her statement that after renewed elections in the Coastal-Mountain District of 1997 it was not the HDZ that had failed, but the voters. Then they shunted her off to some kind of international society for human rights.

And finally, my scandalous treatment when I was eventually accepted into the faculty, and with time became imprudently courageous and began to say things that were disagreeable for "dirty ears" (in the words of T. S. Eliot), and they kicked me out.

And as for the problems with enrolling Leo in Year Three of elementary school when we arrived in 1992. Some ministry or other required that Leo should first take a test in the Croatian language, Croatian geography and Croatian history (although geography and history do not appear in the curriculum for Year Three, instead there is something called "nature and society"), *Only then will we enroll him*, they said, so I had to ask that ministry whether Leo also had to take tests in Croatian nature and Croatian society which were taught in Year Three. And I asked what we were to do about Croatian math and Croatian gymnastics, whether he would have to pass tests in those, or at least demonstrate them. Fortunately, the head teacher of the nearest school to us was a reasonable man, Professor Merle, a Czech by nationality, and perhaps that was why, as a member of a minority, he was sensitive to our problem, and he immediately enrolled Leo and presumably sent the ministry a favorable report.

Not to mention all the fuss over Leo's enrollment in the first year of secondary school after we came back from Canada. *That* was a comedy, a black one. We were supposed to move from Rijeka to Zagreb. Some kind of more or less permanent work had turned up in Zagreb.

Mrs. Vokić, the then Minister of Education and Sport, was in Norway.

Mrs. Sabljak was with her.

Mrs. Galović had remained in Zagreb.

In Zagreb there was also Mr. Luburić (Deputy Director of the Office for the Advancement of Education) together with Mrs. Grdinić. They were all then responsible for secondary education or the nostrification of school documents.

In May 1997 (precisely when the two of us came back), the Ministry of Education and Sport announced the Competition for the enrollment of pupils in secondary schools, sending it to the press and school head teachers. This announcement served as a joint notice. Among other things, this joint notice included the following: *On the basis of an unnostrified testimonial, judgment or confirmation of completed elementary school signed by a witness and endorsed by a public notary, a school may enroll pupils conditionally ...*

And further: *Without a points system for success in elementary school, the following may be enrolled DIRECTLY in a secondary school:*
  —pupils returning from immigration
  —pupils who have been educated abroad for at least two years because their parents were working in diplomatic capacities or in other Croatian agencies
  —other pupils—returnees
and so on and so forth.

Mrs. Galović (after I had told my story at length and in detail, over my private telephone in Rijeka) put me onto Mr. Luburić. Mr. Luburić was busy. An unknown voice then directed me to Mrs. Grdinić. After I had told the (same) story at length and in detail over my private line in Rijeka (the fifth call), Mrs. Grdinić directed me to Mrs. Galović, who sent me back to Mrs. Grdinić, and Mrs. Grdinić sent me back to Mrs. Galović, who told me that in connection with the direct enrollment of my son in secondary school (that conditional route, without marks), there should not be a problem.

Off I go to the head teacher of the XVI Grammar School in Zagreb, Kata Bolf. The head teacher of the XVI Grammar School in Zagreb Kata Bolf tells me that she will not enroll my son before she receives confirmation from the Ministry that he (my son) is eligible for the first year of secondary school. I submit to Kata Bolf the Competition published by the Ministry and circulated to all secondary school head teachers. Kata Bolf said, *That doesn't concern me.*

I call Mrs. Galović again. (Every conversation involves telling the same story.) I arrange a meeting with Mrs. Galović in Zagreb (my second journey there in a week), so that, on the basis of a request from the head teacher Kata Bolf, Mrs. Galović should give in writing the green light to enroll my son conditionally in the first year of secondary school. Because, as Kata Bolf says, she does not acknowledge telephone calls; she acknowledges only what is written down.

I arrive in time for the arranged meeting.

Mrs. Galović is angry that I am asking for something. Mrs. Galović tells me that I am wasting her time. I say that my time too is worth something, it is worth no less than her own time, Mrs. Galović's time. From the conversation with Mrs. Galović, I discover that the name of Kata Bolf is well known to people in the Ministry of Education and Sport. Whether that's a good thing or not, I don't have time to consider. The name of Kata Bolf, spoken out loud, thudded on the floor of the Ministry room loudly and threateningly.

They walk me through the floors of the Ministry, up and down, no longer on the telephone but on stairs. No one wants to write the confirmation for Kata Bolf. I lose patience and raise my voice.

35

Mrs. Galović suddenly turns from a deputy minister into a human being. Two hours later, the confirmation for Kata Bolf is in my hands, tidily recorded in a protocol, with a seal at the bottom.

I make it to Kata Bolf. For a second time. This is the second time that Kata Bolf does not wish to listen to my story. I take out the confirmation she had asked for. Kata Bolf says, *Come back in two hours, although we have nothing to discuss.* Then she adds, *I shall not enroll your son,* and slams the door in my face. That Kata Bolf.

I go to the nearby II Grammar School. I recite the whole tale from the beginning. The head teacher says, *I have nothing to discuss with you. There is the Chairman of the Enrollment Board, talk to him.* He too slams the door in my face. I tell the Chairman of the Enrollment Board my whole story from the start. The Chairman of the Enrollment Board does not have (or does not wish to have) a clue about anything. He has never seen the instruction from the Ministry, he says. I take out the instruction from the Ministry, which I had got hold of while I was still in Canada and studied in Canada. I present it to the Chairman of the Enrollment Board. The Chairman of the Enrollment Board says: *We have to define what an émigré is. Because an émigré is someone born outside the homeland.*

I say, *This is about returnees, not about émigrés.*

He says, *I must ask the Ministry.*

After that the Chairman of the Enrollment Board calls the Ministry about every paragraph of the Instruction. That takes two hours.

There's no points system, I tell the Chairman of the Enrollment Board.

There is a points system, says the Chairman of the Enrollment Board.

I show him the Instruction again. The Chairman says, *I must check with the Ministry.*

I conclude that the Chairman of the Enrollment Board's problem is a low coefficient of intelligence.

What do we do now? I say.

It all points to the fact that your child does not have the right to be enrolled in secondary school, says the Chairman of the Enrollment Board.

Since two hours have passed, I go back to Kata Bolf. Kata Bolf says, *There are other schools. I shall not enroll your son.*

He has all the required qualifications, I say.

I am not concerned with qualifications, says Kata Bolf. *By the time you collect and nostrify all the necessary documents, all the places in this school will be filled.*

Schools are obliged to keep one place in each class for returnees, I throw down my last card.

I am not obliged to do anything, Kata Bolf says. *Now leave my room.*

Really, who is Kata Bolf? A metaphor?

In Rijeka Leo was enrolled without any difficulty, because in Rijeka we did not come across a Kata Bolf. And so, partly because of Kata Bolf (at the time), we remained in that, in this town.

It is damaging to tie yourself. To a country and a home. Sooner or later both will fuck you up.

But what would have happened, how would it have been, had I been a woman?

Nevertheless, I did manage to acquire something here: my by now loyal companion/suffocatress: asthma; that is something that this country gave me. I collected a few other little ailments in this town as well, except that on the whole they are hereditary deviations or disorders that come with aging, like that carcinoma, or that glaucoma, or that degenerating spine, then the arteriosclerosis of the knees or the ossified neck, perhaps even the blocked carotid arteries, smokers' COPD, and some small kidney stone and little cysts on the liver, that's all baggage, the germs of which are in my DNA, baggage I am destined to drag around through this thing called life. But asthma is not.

There is something else that Rijeka has not (yet) succeeded in taking from me: my teeth.

Today my position in this town is relatively sorted. From time to time Rijeka even lays claim to me and says our writer. Which somehow fits in the same basket as the announcement by that Zagreb elite teacher who spends her summers on Rovinj hill.

This digression, as my editor would say, is not essential for our story. But this is not about me, Andreas Ban, but about those fine Verdurin types as opposed to the multitude of the homeless, displaced and silenced. Because during this new war, those people changed nothing in their lives, not their beds, not their work, nor their friends, nor their country, nor their town, nor food, nor air. Possibly face cream, a dishwasher or a swimming costume. That's why it would be better if those fine Verdurins said nothing, just as they mostly held their tongues during the time of the former state, the way many—in wartime—become dumb, or, if they do speak, they do so, I presume, in a whisper. The displaced who survived this war horror are wrecks, internally destroyed. People who work with their hands did rather better than those who fiddle about with words. People with money did best.

> *Don't upset yourself. In the case of philistinism or triviality, which also lacks possibility, the situation is somewhat different. Philistinism lacks every determinant of spirit and terminates in probability, within which the possible finds its insignificant place.... Devoid of imagination, as the philistine always is, he lives in a*

> *certain trivial province of experience as to how things*
> *go, what is possible, what usually occurs.*
>
> Kierkegaard

When I finally got work at the university, when they had hung that vice chancelloress in the gallery, I believed that I was doing that work, psychological work, because I knew something about that field, and that I was not then eating Croatian bread, as some frustrated anonymous individual maintained on some portal or other, but my bread, however nondescript, moldy and meager. I have already written one book about this town, or rather not about the town, because the town alone is not so crucial as to merit even a relatively slender volume about it; I wrote generally about towns, about small towns that become bewildered, and then revolt when people they do not know, people from somewhere else, from over there, burst onto the scene, neither smiling nor ecstatic. I shall write again and I shall write more, for as long as I can, because twenty-five years have gone by, and still, on some little rocky, hilly lane, out of the blue, there may suddenly come relentless, threatening barking.

It was then, standing face to face with the lecturer, that a situation from some ten years earlier emerged from what I had thought was a sealed chamber of my brain: when I had traveled (by bus) from "my" town Rijeka to the capital city, Zagreb, which people love to call a metropolis, for the opening night of a play. Catching sight of me in the foyer, a half-educated provincial woman, who had wound up in the so-called metropolis by who knows what channels, asked me, *What are you doing here?* Oh, fuck you!

I had (like many others) existed before I came to Rijeka, I had existed for thirty-eight years outside this new country to which I had recently moved and I had existed for forty-five years outside the town in which I had settled (in which I had up to then never spent longer than two days), and now I had been decaying there for twenty-five years.

Perhaps a year had passed since Leo's and my arrival in the country, when, after my six-month supply post in an elementary school, oh, thank you, Croatia, where a job had just been given to Boško, up to then a scientist and "character" in a Novi Sad biological institute, so I was able to sift through our recent past with him and practice the Serbian language, otherwise barricaded in a little mental compartment, labeled "forbidden," when the Society of Croatian-American Friendship opened a kindergarten for the spoiled children of the nouveau riche from around the Kvarner Bay. The Society was run (from its Zagreb center) by Vera Dumančić, presumably to pass the time. Later Vera Dumančić came to her senses and hotfooted it to the United States. Little Dolores came to the kindergarten, she painted everything blue and kept saying, *Blue is elegant, a very elegant color*, and she was afraid of her father, who was excessively agreeable when he came for her at the end of the day. *You're my little Tinkerbell*, he kept repeating, Dolores stiffened and pursed her lips and I, perhaps professionally deformed, immediately imagined that father sexually abusing his little Tinkerbell, *You're my Tinkerbell*, he pants into her neck while he beds her. Little Ameriko came as well, not Amerigo, but Ameriko, whose mother, a talkative worldly lady, had flown off to that country over there, to give birth—for the sake of her son's bright future. There were other children, of all kinds. So, for five days a week, I stood for forty minutes in an overcrowded bus to Ičići, because the same bus was used by students, there is a tourism faculty in Lovran because Croatia nurtures tourism. Then I returned in an equally crammed bus, again standing, by now with swollen legs. During that time, Leo roamed by himself through the deserted neighborhoods near the refinery (where the polluted air means that even dogs don't pee) and wrote poems. He was nine years old.

Today death was in my pocket,
hiding in the shadow behind me,
then it slipped into my hair,
today death was within me.

I remember this as well:

> *My sea is mine alone.*
> *Small, hidden in my pocket,*
> > *it speaks,*
> > *fidgets*
> > *and murmurs.*
> > *On paper*
> > *it makes a picture in the shadow.*
> > *My small sea*
> > *lives*
> > *and sings*
> > *saltily scented*
> > *within me.*

Leo collected his poems under the title *Grain, a Collection of Poems*, and there wasn't a single word about grain. Pockets were the key thing for him.

There weren't any cell phones then, or perhaps there were but I wasn't aware of them. There, in the nursery, I scampered about with the children singing nursery rhymes:

three-four, open the door,
five-six, pick up sticks,
seven-eight, open the gate,

and so on. Then Vera Dumančić said, *And you'll spend the summer with them as well, camping with them on the beach here in Ičići,* and I said, *One-two, fuck you*, and went off to Rovinj with Leo.

I haven't been skiing in all the time I've lived in Croatia. Over there, I used to go with Leo every winter, since he was tiny. I dragged him up the mountains, carried him with all his gear and my own, he would fall over, get up and fall over, and just before we left, when he was nine, we both skied down, smiling. We went to ski centers in Serbia (Kopaonik), in Slovenia (Vogel) and Montenegro (Durmitor), in Bulgaria (Pamporovo) and once in Italy (Dolomites). Now that outdated equipment, Leo's and mine, is rotting in the cellar, unusable, while Leo goes skiing in Switzerland. We missed the snow. Wrapped up, we took the train to Delnice, climbed up a hill and threw snowballs at each other, trying to convince each other that this was the real thing. But it wasn't. We were conning ourselves with a surrogate, a poor, distorted imitation of our previous life.

Maybe, maybe if I had found a more permanent partner, with whom I would have quarreled, a third person for card games, or at least someone else for a game of chess, maybe that whole perspective on my life would have broadened or shrunk, it doesn't matter which, it might have acquired softer outlines, maybe there would have been some of those dull pinkish tones (because that's what's really at stake, in this story the town is just the stage set), maybe. But I'll never know.

A few days ago, at a bus stop, one kid was shouting to another, *I've got a pistol* and I got riled again. *Shove that pistol up your ass*, I told him and his mother went ballistic, *You watch your tongue*, she hissed.

All this, that brief summer encounter with the gentlefolk from so-called high Zagreb society, coincided with the publication of that book of Bora's about quiet days in Rovinj. And, straight after reading the book (in the name of unquiet days in Rovinj), I wondered why the fashionable *salonnier* and excellent writer Ćosić had for years invited those gentlefolk from the hill to his atrium to sit around his four-meter-long black table while he served them three-course meals of this and that, often picturesquely, colorfully and imaginatively prepared with a lot of effort, when Ćosić, that excellent, one could say both Proustian and Bernhardian, even Krležian writer liked stuffed peppers and burgers more than anything. To be fair, in his book, Bora Ćosić does explain that recklessness, when (his) quiet Rovinj days arrived, entirely different from those of Miller and Perlès in Clichy, but that doesn't seem enough to me. Let's just say that Zagreb rabble from the top of Rovinj hill never sat down at our, Ada's and my, summer table. Nor did those Zagreb socialites ever set foot in our house (as long as we had one) let alone in that neglected garden, where, after damp and mold and shoddy works, the thin concrete slabs came up, by now pockmarked and blackened, and dandelions and clumps of weeds grew out of the cracks.

Salons have existed for centuries, everywhere in the world, some are remembered, some not, some were well known and meaningful, and some became a caricature. So many interesting people (along with a few dull ones, even if highly placed on the social-political-artistic ladder) passed through the Rovinj atrium, and through the Berlin apartments, and earlier also through the relatively constrained Belgrade space of the contemporary *salonnier* (and excellent writer) Bora Ćosić that it seems to me that our writer simply did not need this artificial ornament, so like the remarkably lifelike, handmade flowers with which the Comtesse de Beaulaincourt decorated the table for her guests.

In truth, after the meal, our contemporary *salonnier* would move into his Thonet chair and languidly swing his leg from the side, and full of concentration (and critically, à la Marcel), maybe with an inner mocking smile, he would follow the way the conversation round the table became diluted, sinking into profanity, now that the guests were sated and had entered the phase of general regurgitation and digestion. Madame de Caillavet would sit in her bergère, but Madame de Caillavet was not a writer, nor was our writer a *preciosa*. And our writer did not remotely display any autocratic tendencies, such as those of Madame (Lydia) Aubernon de Nerville, who in the course of dinner would ring her little silver bell to indicate that the conversation had taken an undesirable turn. Bora's guests were famous, yes, and some of them even close, one could say friends.

One should nevertheless be careful with the adoration of the famous; all fame is relative, and need not be close either. Among the famous there can sometimes build up a thick layer of emptiness, which the famous crush reciprocally. An acquaintance always greets me with *So, who was there?* whenever I come back from somewhere where he, that acquaintance, was not. *What do you mean, who was there?* I say, always with a hint of irritation. *What famous people, what famous people were there?* insists that former friend, himself fairly well known to the public, and I don't know whether he is thinking of the ordinary people, well known to us, the generally, publicly well-known, or the generally, publicly well-known people he himself knows personally. So I say no one, no one was there. There are famous people who know each other, and they spend time together because they are famous, not because they like each other or miss each other. Those famous people who imagine that they are close to one another do not know much, if anything, about the childhood or youth of the people they know, about their legitimate or illegitimate children, about their aborted children, about who gave them gonorrhea, or who gave the little Ceylonese elephant on their bookshelf, *Elephants must always face the door*, said Laura (Laura who?), what kind of pajamas they wear, which plates they use when they're alone, how they smell when they wake up, whether they have breakfast dolled up or déshabillé.

The famous, what's more, can be scum, useless, so it's better not to know those well-known people.

And now, just in case one critic should appear and start to randomly dish out platitudes, worn-out assertions that a writer should create rounded, living, complex and convincing characters, about the plausibility of the narrative, about the firm or shaky composition of a text, about classifying writing in a genre, so that this critical eye should not be annoyed, I ought to say what I replied on that summer day to the lady who explained to me how and about what I ought to write. But, I won't.

So I found her in a wretched state, buried. She was twenty kilos heavier than when we had last seen each other, a year ago, two, ten, yesterday. She has some teeth missing. From beneath her upper lip jut four canines, she looks like a nursing baby. Her belly shakes when she walks, her hips sway. It's summer. She is wearing sagging woolen knee-high socks with violet stripes, she adores violet. Her eyes are violet too, like Elizabeth Taylor's, in fact she looks like a fat Elizabeth Taylor just before she died, although Ada has better legs. If she was a man, she would resemble Marlon Brando in his old age, she adores Marlon Brando, *He's my type*, she used to say, *Brando in* A Streetcar Named Desire. Lovely Ada, as they called her there. When she was young and later.

The space is dark, it has grown dark, although it is summer. The space is sticky and black with accumulated grease covered with dust, the carpet scorched, cobwebs hang from the walls. At the window a scrap of cloth swings—a red rag faded in the sun. In the bathroom, next to the wall, two mushrooms grow. *It's not mustiness*, I say, *because there is air, it is stasis.*

I go out into the garden. *Where's the loquat?* I say. *It died*, Ada says, *like me*, she says. *It burst, its stem blossomed, I listened to it at night, sobbing, it whined like a sick kitten, then one morning it just folded up.*

It was a beautiful tree, regal. Adorned with golden fruit, little orange balls filled with juice, fragrant, shiny little apricots. Its branches as wide as an embrace, its leaves velvety like kisses. A powerful tree, a generous tree.

I've made pašticada with gnocchi, Ada says, because I like it, because I like pašticada with gnocchi. We eat outside, in that garden without sun. We don't know what to say, how to say it. A fat, swollen silence settles at our table, drilling into us. We are close.

Ada is a biologist. In the family we called her Bubi. Ada sometimes pranced into my life, and after Elvira's death, she was like a little mother to Leo. There, in Belgrade, when life was nevertheless somehow orderly, long ago, twenty or so years ago. That is not the point now. Ada too has been shunted into retirement, here, she too is alone, her partner is no longer here either. So many vanished people. Ada's Gioia finishes her degree, then leaves. *I'm not about to stay incarcerated here*, she says, and flutters out of the country, out of all the new little countries in the region. Now she shifts her sketchpads and drawings, her paints and easel from one little room to another, from Amsterdam to Paris, from Paris to Vienna, from Vienna to Prague, from Prague to Budapest. Ada has not been to Belgrade for twenty-two years. Gioia comes back to Croatia mostly in summer. *You have to let them go.*

As soon as she moves into retirement, Ada moves out of life.

In Belgrade, Ada works for the Galenika company, Dr. Ada Ban researches the influence of estrogen on spatial learning and the neuron morphology of the hippocampus in rats. Within her and around her is order, laboratory precision, cleanliness. She walks briskly, she thinks briskly. Electric arrows whizz from her, and laughter. Now she is puffed out, opaque and unilluminated.

When she moves to Croatia, some time after me and Leo, there is no place for her in Croatian laboratories, because she is too old at forty-nine. She teaches biology in a secondary school in the next little town. She lives in the Rovinj basement, through which underground waters can be heard murmuring and dampening the walls. She is poor. She is fat. She used not to be. She has gray growths. She has four pairs of spectacles, worn-out shoes and felted sweaters.

Where's that vacuum prosthesis? I ask her. *It rubs and sometimes it falls off*, says Ada, *it'll be okay*, she says, and laughs. That's the laughter I know well. There was a time, in our kitchens over there, when Ada and I used to talk well into the night, over fine cheeses and noble wine. We were looking for a way out of the trap.

That was that. A life, lives, can be compressed into a few short paragraphs.

The two of us spent a week in Ada's hole in the hill. And I became anxious.

Ada has no company, whereas she used to have lots of acquaintances, close friends. She no longer reads, *I've given my books to the library*, she says, *they're consumed by mold here.*

Where are your paintings, the oils and etchings? I say.

I sold them, says Ada.

At midday, Ada goes down to the square, has a coffee and leafs through the newspaper. Then she comes back. She doesn't go to the cinema, she doesn't go to exhibitions although invitations still reach her regularly. As soon as she wakes up, she turns on the TV, watches programs about the sea. In the summer she no longer goes to the beach, *It's too hot, it's sweltering*, she says, *and the south wind does me in.* She sleeps a lot, although she maintains that she hardly sleeps at all. When I go to pee at dawn, I almost always find her sitting at the table, sucking bitter chocolate and staring straight ahead. She swings one leg and smokes. Then she goes back to bed and lazes around until eleven. She never used to sleep till eleven, she used to sleep for six hours and get up singing.

I'm hibernating, Ada says, and laughs again.

And so we chat, and then Ada gets upset over some nonsense and starts shouting.

Why are you shouting? I say to her.

I'm not shouting, she says and starts whispering, she becomes small. Toward evening I suggest, *Let's go to the sea, let's go and walk beside the sea.*

I can't, Ada says, *I've got things to do.*

She has nothing to do. Then, suddenly, Ada seems to wake up, torrents gush from her, she talks and talks, repeats herself, sentences whirl around her as though she is stirring porridge or thick dough.

You're talking a lot, I say.

I know, says Ada, *I go through phases.*

Apart from Leo, who is far away, Ada is now closest to me.

Come to my place, I say, *we'll fix that keratosis.*

Keratosis isn't malignant, says Ada.

We'll fix your teeth, I say.

I can fix them here, says Ada.

You could talk to someone, I say.

Maybe, says Ada, *but psychiatrists want you first to tell your life story, and I don't feel like doing that, it takes a long time. And psychiatrists are expensive. Let's play chess.*

At home, when we were all still alive, when we were a family, we had several chess sets, wooden, carved in the folk style, small, traveling, folding sets, with little holes to push the pieces into (ours were red and black), we had one set with hollow pieces made of cheap plastic and one with huge heavy pieces made of white and black ebony, which, of course, disappeared (all the others disappeared as well), because someone sold it. Recently, on one of my pointless journeys (perhaps to Paris, perhaps to Munich, or perhaps in a dream) in the window of a jeweler I caught sight of a chess set with crystal pieces, made by hand by Strass Swarovski, all transparent, enchanting, through which rays of sun were reflected, so the kings and queens, knights and pawns, bishops and castles seemed to be flying toward the sky and there lining up for some ceremonial parade, which would degenerate in universal extermination, in general carnage. I stood like that, in front of that glittering and luxurious army, like a hungry child at a counter full of candy, playing an imaginary, invented duel with Death. The set cost more than a thousand euros.

So, we play chess. For a long time. In the basement in Rovinj's Bregovita/del Monte street, Ada and I play chess, we play our lives away. With little lifeless wooden pieces.

It's dangerous to play too much chess. Chess players say nothing and calculate, they plan annihilation, attacks and defenses on their fields, visible and invisible, sometimes bloody stories develop, terrible slaughter and underhanded trickery. Too much chess drives some people mad. *That's okay*, says Nabokov, *there's nothing abnormal about the fact that chess players are abnormal. It's completely normal.*

Even before he used a razor to slit the throat of his 83-year-old roommate, people used to say of that American international master Raymond Weinstein that he possessed the instinct of a merciless murderer. When he turned twenty-three, in 1964, they shut him up in the Kirby Forensic Psychiatric Center in New York. He's still there, if he hasn't died.

Lionel Kieseritzky died without a coin in his pocket, in Paris in 1853, in the Hôpital de la Charité, insane, in his forty-seventh year. Kieseritzky was one of the greatest chess players in the world. He was born in Tartu, in what is now Estonia, where long ago Ada once attended a scientific conference. When she came back, she said: *They read papers, I studied the Kieseritzky variant of the king's gambit and the way Anderssen defeated him at that Deathless Contest. Do you know* said Ada to the people in the house over lunch, *do you know that Kieseritzky used to play chess in Paris for money, five francs an hour, as Oskar did in Berlin, he was a mathematician as well.* There was silence at the table, because the mathematician Oskar,

Ada's former boyfriend, had also come to an unusual end. First he beat Ada up, giving her black rings around her eyes, then he immigrated to Germany where he married a nun, having first dragged her out of her convent, of course, a certain Esmeralda who sang in church choirs and even made two records, then he made her change from the Catholic to the Orthodox faith, then he gave her five children, whom he regularly woke at four o'clock in the morning to take to swimming and athletics training. For decades, up until today, he sent Ada threatening letters, increasingly vicious, because no one listened to him anymore, his grandchildren ran away from him, he got a dog, an abandoned mongrel, which was immediately taken from him, that is, it was taken by that timid and obedient Catholic-Orthodox Esmeralda, and all his tenderness, if he ever had any, drained away.

I dreamed about Oskar, Ada suddenly announced. *I don't remember what, I just know he was conflict-free.*

I had dreamed that I was doing a radio interview with Kafka, but I didn't tell Ada that.

Kieseritzky was also quite an abrupt, tense person, he used to say *I'm the chess Messiah, remember, I'm the chess Messiah.* He used to say that mostly after his defeat by Anderssen. It isn't known where Kieseritzky is buried, into what pit for the homeless he was thrown, because there were no witnesses, no one came to the funeral, no one from the crowd of crazed chess players who used to hang around the Paris Café de la Régence, racing from one table to another as though they were in a casino. One waiter went, in fact, but presumably he doesn't count. And Ada's former boyfriend Oskar is still alive.

William Henry Russ was only thirty-three when he died in 1866, after a failed/successful suicide attempt. The American William Henry Russ is well known as a fanatical collector of chess problems, which he later published. Nowadays, when people speak about Russ, they rarely mention his chess matches, and often bring up the unrequited love affair that catapulted him into "madness." Chess players can be fairly egocentric, not to say narcissistic, and their anger soon flares when something, anything, often some stupidity, some nonsense escapes their control. But they can also be timorous, like a closed musical box within which a quiet song echoes—unheard by those outside.

The story goes that William Henry Russ adopted an eleven-year-old girl in Brooklyn, to whom he proposed seven years later, and when she said *No, thank you*, he fired four bullets into her head. The young woman survived, which Russ, of course, could not have known because, in a state of mental disintegration, he threw himself into the East River. But it was low tide and Russ did not drown, instead he clambered onto the bank and then shot himself in the head. An ambulance took him to hospital, where he soon died, because, people said, he had lost the will to live.

The international chess champion Wilhelm (William) Steinitz, famous for his attacking style, born in 1836 in Prague's Jewish ghetto, died of a heart attack in a mental hospital in Manhattan in 1900, with empty pockets and decaying brain cells—caused, some sources have it, by syphilis. Steinitz too was a mathematician. But as early as 1897, when Lasker checkmated him in Moscow, Steinitz apparently had a nervous breakdown and spent forty days in a Moscow sanatorium, so-called, in which, triumphantly rubbing his hands, he played chess with the inmates. Afterward he spent months in the Psychiatric Department of the Manhattan State Hospital, where he had been put by his wife and where, in 1900, he died, maintaining beforehand *I am in electronic communication with God, I give Him the white pieces and surplus pawns, to see who is stronger.*

There were years when chess-playing suicides would serially throw themselves out of windows. Which is surprising, such a lack of existential style and imagination in great international masters, those dogged combinator-combatants. And nowadays the chess players who most like to throw themselves out of windows are from Russia and the Baltic states, perhaps inspired by Nabokov's novel about Luzhin, because in that novel the grandmaster Luzhin, obsessed with the violins, tympani and drums of his life, steps out of that life, hounded by objects and phenomena that melt into black and white fields, on which figures dance in attack, in constant movement, and throws himself, grotesquely, squeezing his slack and unhealthy fat body through a small window placed high up in a dazzlingly white Berlin bathroom.

> *Luzhin, preparing an attack for which it was first necessary to explore a maze of variations, where his every step aroused a perilous echo, began a long meditation: he needed, it seemed, to make one last prodigious effort and he would find the secret move leading to victory. Suddenly, something occurred outside his being, a scorching pain—and he let out a loud cry, shaking his hand stung by the flame of a match, which he had lit and forgotten to apply to his cigarette. The pain immediately passed, but in the fiery gap he had seen something unbearably awesome, the full horror of the abysmal depths of chess and his brain wilted from hitherto unprecedented weariness....*

Perhaps Russian and Baltic chess players experience Nabokov (and chess) more intensely and passionately than Americans and others, and that is why they leap to their deaths. To be sure, Nabokov can be suggestive and he was a good chess player. But Nabokov collected butterflies, which he later hung, pinned and arranged mathematically and precisely, on his walls, as though they were voodoo dolls, and perhaps it was thanks to those murdered butterfly ghosts that he survived. Humphrey Bogart did not collect butterflies, but he played chess extremely well, one could say maniacally. Obsessed with the bellicose strategies of silent opponents, he moved chess pieces in breaks between takes, at tournaments, in parks, in cafés, but also by correspondence, so that in 1943 the FBI banned the practice of such entertainment by correspondence, thinking that he was sending secret codes to someone "over there." Bogart played chess even on his deathbed, as he suffocated from cancer of the esophagus.

And here, of course, is Prokofiev, close to Capablanca and Botvinnik and his (Prokofiev's) numerous diaries, in which, in addition to music, he writes passionately about chess.

That is how I feel at the moment, like a chess player pinned like a butterfly, one of a row arranged in a decorative frame on someone(else)'s wall of reality.

All right, the American chess player Henry Pillsbury, crazed with syphilis, tried to jump from the fourth floor of a hospital in Philadelphia in 1905, only to die the following year at the age of thirty-two, and he had definitely not read Nabokov.

Nor had the German chess master Curt von Bardeleben, who threw himself out of a window in 1924, apparently as a result of appalling poverty; he could not have read Nabokov either, since Nabokov did not publish his story about Luzhin in Russian in Berlin until 1930, and in English thirty-four years later, but on the other hand, in all probability it was precisely the life and death of poor Bardeleben that gave Nabokov the story of the fatal obsession with chess that overwhelms his Luzhin to the point of annihilation, just as it psychophysically destroys and disintegrates Stefan Zweig's Dr. B., who, it seems, (fictionally) remains alive, while in 1942 his creator Stefan Zweig, also a good chess player, killed himself, with his wife Lotte, in his home on Petrópolis in Brazil, and they were found, dead, theatrically holding hands:

> *(And) are we not guilty of offensive disparagement in*
> *calling chess a game? Is it not also a science and an art,*
> *hovering between those categories as Muhammad's cof-*
> *fin hovered between heaven and earth, a unique link*
> *between pairs of opposites: ancient yet eternally new;*
> *mechanical in structure, yet made effective only by the*
> *imagination; limited to a geometrically fixed space, yet*
> *with unlimited combinations; constantly developing,*
> *yet sterile; thought that leads nowhere; mathematics*
> *calculating nothing; art without works of art; archi-*
> *tecture without substance—but nonetheless shown*
> *to be more durable in its entity and existence than all*
> *books and works of art; the only game that belongs to*
> *all nations and all eras ...*

On the other hand, Georgy Ilivitsky had certainly read Nabokov because, in 1989, he threw himself faultlessly out of the window, at the age of sixty-seven. Ilivitsky was parrying Botvinnik, Petrosian and Spassky, following in the footsteps of Geller and Smyslov, and preceding Keres and Taimanov. A powerful player with an even more powerful ego. *They've forgotten me,* said Ilivitsky, *so I'll kill myself the way Luzhin did.* Like the unreal, invented Luzhin, the living Ilivitsky couldn't tell chalk from cheese, reality became imaginary for him, while the imaginary became real. So when it happened to Ilivitsky, as to numerous chess players before and after him, that the imaginary that seemed to him real burst into what was for him shaky, elusive reality, all hell broke loose, barely controllable disorder, worlds split open in whose depths the fires of hell burned. Nothing but checkmate nightmares. Nightmares with no way out.

Oh God, even to the present day chess players leap to their deaths or slide into insanity, transform themselves into their horses, springers, hussars, into their knights and steeds, into their infirm pawns and swift hunters who broaden the field of battle in a light charge, rushing headlong from the delimited battlefield into the abyss, sinking into nothingness, while above them, above their graves, lively and perfidious queens and lame kings, those majestic figures in our lives, continue their well-trodden path through time. And so, the checkmate of life carries off its victims. The battles replace one another. Now one, now another wild horde, however robust it may seem, fails to defend the palace of its fortified rulers forever, so the captured empires flicker through existence, through endlessness, and fall, one after the other.

Under a mantle of soundlessness, terrible battles take place, debacles prepared in advance, deceit, substitution and murder above which reigns paranoia, now gentle and serene, now cruel and penetrating. The great game of chess seizes, captures, drags its players away into the padlocked underground of obsession.

In 1989, the Armenian Karen Grigorian, born in 1947, jumped from the highest bridge in Yerevan, and ten years later his friend, copyist and blitz-partner, the Latvian Alvis Vītoliņš threw himself from a railway bridge into the icy waters of the Gauja River. The Estonian Lembit Oll (1966–99) jumped from his fifth-floor apartment in Tallinn, evidently depressed because of his recent divorce. Lembit Oll played his last tournament before his death in Nova Gorica, where he drew with the Bosnian-Herzegovinian grandmaster and champion of the match Zdenko Kožul, who was then playing for Croatia.

There are a lot of them, these chess-playing suicides.

In 1901, the German Johannes von Minckwitz threw himself under a speeding train, losing both arms, and died soon afterward.

In August 1909, the chess master from Leipzig Rudolf Swiderski, just thirty-one, took some kind of poison, then shot himself in the head.

And then, relatively recently, in May 2012, the leading Bengali chess player, Shankar Roy, hanged himself from the ceiling with the help of his wife's long scarf, stating in a farewell letter that he was going in search of God. He was thirty-six.

I'm not thinking about Bobby Fischer, I remember him, I remember his victories and his unappealing, mad, but also sorrowful story.

There have been wealthy chess players, there are more and more of them today, but there were also some who were very poor and who died of disease, cold and hunger, like the Viennese Carl Schlechter (b. 1874), an elegant player, a gentleman of chess as people called him. Not wanting to ask anyone for help, Carl Schlechter closed his eyes forever in a little rented room in Budapest one snowy Thursday in 1918, just before New Year's Eve.

An excess of chess can make some people's hearts burst. Chess can devour a life. Combinations that twine and intertwine seeking a route to an opening. The board closes, the pieces go beserk, the artillery starts scattering shells, chaos ensues on the battlefield, *the center cannot hold* and—*adieu.*

The Englishman Howard Staunton, 1874, in London, heart failure.

The Hungarian Andors Wachs, in 1931, defeats his opponent, falls onto the board and never raises his head again.

The German Paul Leonhardt (1877–1934) dies in the middle of a match.

The American Frank Marshall (1877–1944), heart failure after a chess tournament ends.

The American George Sturgis (1891–1944) dies in Boston of a heart attack after returning from his honeymoon.

Efim Bogolyubov, born in 1889 in Kiev, dies in 1952 of heart failure after playing a simultaneous exhibition in Triberg, Germany.

The Cuban chess champion Juan Quesada dies in 1952 of a heart attack during an international tournament in Havana.

In 1955, in his fiftieth year, the American Herman Steiner also abruptly goes to meet his maker.

And E. Forry Laucks (1897–1965), after the sixth round of the US Open in San Juan, Puerto Rico, collaborates to ensure he never has to return home.

Then the Swedish grandmaster Gideon Ståhlberg (1908–1967) dies of a heart attack while the international chess tournament in Leningrad is still underway.

Also a grandmaster, the Muscovite Vladimir Simagin dies in 1968 of a heart attack during a tournament in Kislovodsk. He was forty-nine.

In 1970, Charles Khachiyan, president of the Chess Association of New Jersey, dies in the middle of a game of chess.

Two years later, on his way to a meeting of FIDE during the Twentieth Chess Olympiad, the businessman and manager Kenneth Harkness (1898–1972) dies on the train to Skopje.

The Ukrainian Leonid Stein (1934–73), the Soviet grandmaster at the height of his career, dies in the Moscow hotel Rossiya while preparing for the European team championship in Bath, Great Britain.

The Australian Cecil Purdy (1906–79), heart failure during a match. It is said that, before collapsing, he announced *The victory is mine, but the game will go on.*

The grandmaster and president of FIDE for many years, Max Euwe (1901–81), heart failure.

The Dutchman Euwe, otherwise a mathematician, an amateur heavyweight boxer in his youth, twice chess world champion, plays the championship in 1948 in gloves because, he says, it stimulates his competitive spirit.

The American Ed Edmondson (1920–82), heart attack while playing chess on a Hawaiian beach.

The Polish-American grandmaster Samuel Reshevsky, or rather, Szmul Rzeszewski (1911–92), heart failure, respectable age. The wunderkind Rzeszewski/Reshevsky sprang into the world of chess at the age of four. A photograph in which he is playing a simultaneous exhibition in France as an eight-year-old, with a crowd of gray-bearded old men and a voluptuous audience in the background, is disturbing. Something isn't right about it, I know what it is, but I can't deal with that now. Manipulation everywhere, always.

What are you talking about? asks Ada. Then we carry on playing.

And the Polish-Argentinian chess player Miguel Najdorf (Mojsze Mendel Najdorf, or rather Mieczysław Najdorf), master of the rapid transit game, has reached a respectable old age when he dies of a heart attack in his eighty-seventh year (1997), but his entire family disappeared in German concentration camps.

In 2000, the Latvian grandmaster Aivars Gipslis collaborates in the course of a tournament and dies of a heart attack or stroke in Germany in his sixty-third year.

In that same year, at a chess tournament in Finland, the grandmaster Vladimir Bagirov, also a Latvian, born in 1936, dies of a heart attack.

Latvia has some excellent chess players, before Tal and after Tal, up until today. And such a small country.

Leila called, says Ada, *move your king, check.*

So many chess players die young, of heart problems, of TB, of hunger, of torture and cold in concentration camps and gulags, I say.

Leila called, says Ada.

During the Second World War, significant chess events waned. Reality was so noisy (and bloody) that it suppressed the imagination, reality imposed its own game, mercilessly and cruelly; reality outgrew itself, like some kind of giant, arms akimbo, legs apart, threatening the passage to the other side, while the other side was suffocating in darkness, madness, and death. But there are always those forever in the shackles of boyhood who crawl through the blacked-out and obscured imagination, who creep through their lairs without looking for a way out. Sometimes a savior appears, sometimes not. One ought to research the connection between the playing styles of individual chess players and the style of their lives, one ought to research the style of life of individual chess players and their attitude to history, to the present, but I am beset by other thoughts, other presentiments, other memories, which, I now see more and more clearly, lead to an inextricable tangle of senselessness.

I was disturbed. Leila had called, Leila had called, and instead of immediately continuing toward points on the journey which I had designated as ways out, toward the points of an ending, toward the tiny scars that ought to bear witness to transience, to the close of day, to days which lie down in their little caskets under those faded wounds waving au revoir or adieu, drawing ever closer to them, I see the way those points of an ending, those points of finality and no return change their shape, change their structure, broaden and contract, change now into troughs, now into slots, which become furrows, then hollows, and grottoes, they change into dens, boreholes and lairs in which my years and the years/lives of those close (and not close) to me lie, years which only down there, in clefts, thrash about, flail and writhe like some unfortunate body suffering from an epileptic fit or they wriggle like hungry worms. And so, in the course of the match I play with my sister Ada, and which, increasingly distracted, I on the whole lose, I begin to examine the lives of chess players in troubled times, which, unexpectedly (who would have expected such a trick of the mind?), start to bring back images from a distant love affair into which I had entered with a certain skepticism and from which I fled, confused and frozen.

Keres. Estonian, a mathematician and grandmaster. Paul Keres, born 1916, dies of heart failure in 1975 in Helsinki. During the war he participates in chess tournaments all over the Reich: 1942 in Tallinn, Salzburg and Munich, 1943 in Prague, Poznán, and then again in Salzburg and Munich, and in Kraków and Warsaw, all led and organized by Ehrhardt Post, the leading light in the Great German Chess Society (Großdeutscher Schachbund). When the Red Army liberates Estonia from German occupation, Keres does not manage to bolt, the NKVD prepares his liquidation, but Botvinnik intercedes with Stalin and Keres spends the rest of his life merrily shifting around little black and white figures all over the world. Unlike, for instance, the Latvian chess master Vladimirs Petrovs from Riga, for whom there is no one to intercede and who disappears aged thirty-five in the Kotlas gulag in the Archangel province, where in winter the dead, heaped into enormous boxes, are carried by sledge to distant empty spaces, and in spring, when the snow melts, are thrown into communal graves. After the German invasion of the Soviet Union in June 1941, Petrovs, who is then playing in a championship in Moscow, is captured because he allegedly criticized the USSR for the decline in living standards in Latvia, and, in keeping with the ominous Article 58 of the Penal Code of the RSFSR on "counter-revolutionary activity," sentenced to ten years of "socially useful labor," which he does not succeed in completing as he dies two years later.

Of course chess then, under the paw of the Third Reich, is played not only by Keres. Unsurprisingly the talented young SS officer Klaus Junge (1924–45) travels from tournament to tournament, but there are others who participate fervently too: the Estonian (later American) Paul Felix Schmidt (1916–84), then the international master, author of a book about chess, chemist and university professor; a German born in Kiev (then part of Russia), Efim Bogolyubov, a zealous (obedient) member of the Nazi Party as early as the 1930s and a committed anti-Semite. It is said that Bogolyubov was the background player (denunciator) in the hunt for Jewish chess players (his rivals), who would then end up in concentration camps.

Others play their hearts out for the Reich: the Swede Erik Lundin (1904–88) and the grandmaster Gösta Stolz (1904–63), then the Polish-American Samuel "Sammy" Reshevsky, in fact the wunderkind Szmul Rzeszewski (1911–92), then the war criminal, the Latvian-Australian Kārlis Ozols (1912–2001), who is directly connected to the story of Leila, with the story of that Leila, who, as Ada told me, had called again, who forty years after we parted is still pursuing me, and the biggest kingpin of chess among them—the famous Alexander Alekhine (1892–1946). Chess tournaments take place between 1940 and 1944 in Munich, Salzburg, Stockholm, Lidköping, at the Bad Oeynhausen spa, but also in the occupied Polish Bydgoszcz (Bromberg) and, most perversely of all, in Warsaw and Kraków (Tournament of the General Government), under the patronage of the great lover of chess, of men and women, Venice, painting and Chopin, fine wine, smoked salmon and game, SS-Obergruppenführer Hans Frank, king of the General Government with some twelve million inhabitants and four main concentration camps, into which he, SS-Obergruppenführer Hans Frank, delivers, in a precisely planned order, the entire Polish intelligentsia and its nobility, artists and priests, athletes, teachers and political activists, entrepreneurs, social workers and judges, Poles and Jews, in a word all educated people racially, nationally and ideologically unacceptable to the Third Reich. Hans Frank is satisfied; the work is going well, according to plan, so he allows himself moments of relaxation. This anti-Polish campaign, AB-Aktion (Außerordentliche Befriedungsaktion), or rather, Operation Intelligenzaktion (carried out by: Einsatzgruppen and Volksdeutscher Selbstschutz), led by Hans Frank as an "initial, mild" action to realize his notion of transforming Poland into "a heap of excrement that will produce bread, wheat and workers," in just a few months, from the autumn of 1939 to the spring of 1940, it produced excellent results: more than sixty thousand Poles were arrested, many ended up in concentration camps, having been tortured, and some seven thousand members of the intelligentsia were secretly massacred in hidden locations throughout the country, a large number in a forest near the little town of Palmiry, not far from Warsaw. The chess player Izaak Appel (1905–41) simply vanishes, as does Izaak Towbin (1899–1941), today probably transformed into the moss of the Palmiry forest. In camps and prisons, in pits, in raids or holdups, in the street, Hans Frank, that crazed lover of chess, that fanatical devotee of beauty, and, in the end, by 1943, that visionary entranced by the Catholic faith had sorted all of Poland, and therefore also its chess players, his potential partners, his "chums." But at that time chess players were disappearing everywhere in the countries of the Third Reich and in the USSR.

Lists, particularly when they are read aloud, become salvos, each name a shot, the air trembles and shakes with the gunfire. Lists of the dead—the murdered—are direct and threatening. They beat out a staccato rhythm like a march, out of them speak the dead, saying *Look at us*. They offer us their short lives, their faces, their passions and fears, the rooms in which they dreamed, the streets they loved, their clothes, their books, their medical records. But, we have our own dreams and our own faintheartedness and a new age, we don't have time to concern ourselves with the dead/murdered. Chess, a game of liquidation, chess-playing liquidators, what irony.

The Holocaust—in addition to the chess players who stand behind me as I play with Ada, who whisper to me *Not that one, not that move,* others too surge into our gloomy Rovinj space, from everywhere, from Poland, from Austria, from Czechoslovakia, from Hungary, from Ukraine and Belarus, and after them come those from Stalin's USSR, oh yes, and then there's a crowd, we're surrounded by statues, granite effigies with living eyes. Those eyes are dry and their gaze is hard, we are surrounded by monuments with lips that move, from which a threatening soundlessness falls like a breeze onto our stone floor. Then there is not enough air. And the light is extinguished.

Here, some chess players, victims of Nazism:

Leon Kremer (1901–40)

Jakub Kolski (1900–41)

Yakov Vilner (1899–1931)

Abram Szpiro (1912–43)

Leon Schwarzman (1887–1942)

Emil Zinner (1909–1942)

Henryk Friedman (1903–1942)

Henryk Pogoriely (1908–43)

Eduard Gerstenfeld (1915–43)

Heinrich Wolf (1875–1943)

Léon Monosson (1892–1943)

Wilhelm Orbach (1894–1944)

Endre Steiner (1901–44)

Izidor Gross, Kislőd, Hungary, b. 25 June 1860, d. transit camp

Jasenovac, 1942, the Croatian chess grandmaster and cantor of the Jewish community in Karlovac.

In 1940, after a police (SS) raid on the Warsaw chess club, the 59-year-old Polish chess champion Dawid Przepiórka is murdered, while other chess masters end their days, some in mass executions, some in concentration camps: Achilles Frydman, Stanisław Kohn and Moishe Lowtzky. Salo Landau (1903–44) also died in the gas chamber of some Nazi concentration camp in Poland, while his wife and daughter disappeared the same year in Auschwitz. Intensive chess playing and the anticipation of feeling Stalin's fatherly hand on one's shoulder, that combination can make a man really go mad. It is said that during a tournament in Łódź in 1938, Achilles Frydman, stressed out by losing matches, and just before his match with Tartakower, who had been waiting for him at the table for fifteen minutes, ran naked through the hotel, shouting *Fire!* After that he was put into a lunatic asylum.

There are too many of them. So many lives of which the center was a small wooden board with sixty-four black and white squares over which they played, as it turned out in the end, their lost battles.

Murderers in the service of the secret police forces, and the secret police themselves, love forests, in forests and woods they love shooting people in the back of the head and letting them topple in free fall into pits, it is such clean work and does not require much commitment. Throughout the world there are many forests through whose beautiful canopies the breath of the dead sways. And the disintegrated bodies of those dead people nourish the soil, where edible mushrooms and asparagus then grow. The soil is moist, soft and supple. In forests.

Chess players.

The Nazis do not only liquidate Polish chess players, not at all, the honor is bestowed wherever the SS boot treads. The famous

Czech chess player Karel Treybal (b. 1885) is falsely accused of hiding weapons for members of the Resistance Movement, and after a brief trial is liquidated in 1941 in Prague. His body is never found. And so on, not to extend the story, which of its own accord stretches in space and time here and there, left and right, forward and backward, endlessly.

As early as 1940, in Kraków, in "his" magnificent fortress-palace of Wawel, Hans Frank played host to the grandmaster Bogolyubov, who was meant to run a chess school with the then world champion Alekhine. Toward evening he would leaf through his rich collection of chess literature and, when his work cleansing terrain (Polish land, of Poles) allowed, he would play a game or two with some invited grandmaster. At the Nuremberg trials, in 1946, Hans Frank was condemned to death and hanged.

That jolly squadron amused itself in the occupied countries of the Third Reich. Frank's chief of police Friedrich-Wilhelm Krüger, when arrests in Poland became somehow routine, indeed tedious, joined the "Prinz Eugen" 7th SS Mountain Division, in which he lived, in which the Volksdeutsche spoke German, even Serbian, would you believe, in which the Croats spoke Croatian, they all understood each other and slaughtered civilians and partisans in unison. All right, in 1945 Krüger killed himself somewhere near Bleiburg, so there's nothing more to say about that. Besides, Krüger didn't play chess.

Krüger was replaced in Frank's group by a tall 47-year-old police commander (Höhere SS-und Polizeiführer), the monstrous Karl Heinrich Wilhelm Koppe, who deported Poles and Polish Jews en masse to camps and, so as not to get irritated in his work by unnecessary delay, liquidated many of them at once, in the open. He was particularly irritated by psychiatric patients, and showered 1,558 of them with gas. He wasn't especially enamored of consumptives either, because they posed a serious threat to the whole pure-blooded German population, so he summarily removed some thirty thousand (30,000) of them from this world. At the end of the war Koppe did not kill himself, no chance, but he did not play chess. Koppe took his wife's surname (so as not to be recognized) and in Bonn managed the Sarotti factory, known for chocolate confectionery, and settled down and grew increasingly fat. The fact that Koppe was arrested in 1960 is irrelevant, because he was released two years later, just as he was two years after his second arrest in 1964, ostensibly because of poor health, when he was accused of collaborating in the mass liquidation of 145,000 people. Poland sought his extradition, but Germany said, *Keine Chance, nein*, and that was that. Koppe died in 1975, in Bonn, blessed, buried and carefree.

Why have I strayed so far? The paths of human thought really are mysterious.

But still, Alexander Alekhine (1892–1946). Alexander Alekhine, born in Moscow, is among the greatest chess players of all time and also among the most loathsome. At the board a fierce, frequently aggressive player, in life an insecure, obsessive conformist who ran around the world like a lunatic, searching for protection under the skirts of various parties and wives/mothers. For him chess was a refuge, a sanctuary, a cocooned personal reality, a salvation and protection from "the slings and arrows of outrageous fortune." Immediately after the First World War, the Cheka arrested him and accused him of counterespionage, that is, for contact with the White Army, and for the nth time he set out his chessboard, fled into its embrace, while it enfolded its child Alekhine on its breast and rocked him, to and fro. In 1920, Alekhine was the star of the First Chess Championship of the USSR, he worked as an interpreter for the Comintern and as a secretary in the Department of Education, he divorced his Russian baroness wife and married a Swiss journalist thirteen years older than him, thanks to her he was granted permission to leave Russia, and then, in Paris, he left her, Annelise Ruegg, too, and flew around the world in pursuit of his obsession, the hard-to-beat Capablanca. Just as many chess players become cunning strategists in their play, elegant or cruel attackers, refined but crude opponents, in reality, which often passes them by, they somehow melt away and life crushes them vengefully. It was the 1930s. Now a Frenchman, Alexander Alekhine, the hero of a tale outside time, swoops down on the politics of the USSR and the Soviets proclaim him an enemy of the people, and since they could not immediately dispose of the World Chess Champion, the NKVD liquidated his brother, Alexei Alekhine, who went nowhere, ran away from no one, just occasionally played chess in his homeland.

Then comes 1933. The Reichstag is burning, the Nazis arrest their political opponents, the National Socialists seize power, Hitler proclaims the Third Reich, Dachau receives its first "guests," the Gestapo is founded, with the help of students and their professors, throughout Germany between eighty and ninety thousand books are publicly burned, *and that is just the introduction, where books are burned, in the end they will burn people*, as Heine warned as early as 1821. In 1933 Heine's books were burned too, but who, in the heat of general euphoria, is going to listen to the voice of reason? Through its history, bit by bit, Croatia too loses its mind and now it is quite mad. The dumpsters from the 1990s full of "undesirable" books, the films about Madonnas, those orthographies and differential dictionaries, that dispersal of the population, that months-long camp for war invalids under a circus tent in the city center and their gliding down the streets like members of some dark sect in black T-shirts, with enormous white crosses on their chests warning of a potential inquisition for the execution of those who think differently—what a show!—people accused of war crimes being greeted euphorically, the paranoia, the songs, the black uniforms, the gravestones glorifying Ustasha criminals, the foreign currency, the checkerboarding of pavements, the yelling and, in the midst of that insupportable din, a general, deadly silence. Okay, that's not the topic now.

What is the topic?

So, in 1933 warning notices are stuck on shop windows, GERMANS, DO NOT BUY FROM JEWS, a law is introduced on eugenic sterilization, the foundation of new political parties is prohibited, Germany announces its departure from the League of Nations. In 1927, Alekhine, having beaten the hitherto unbeatable Capablanca, becomes world champion, in 1934 he is married for a fourth time, this time to the chess player Grace Freeman, sixteen years his senior, Jewish, but with British citizenship, he returns to France from Portugal and, in order to protect his wife and her vast assets (including six cats which laze about among those assets), he begins to collaborate with the Nazis. Alekhine writes anti-Semitic articles in French, Dutch, and German newspapers in which he maintains that the Jews play limply and gutlessly, while Aryans play aggressively and courageously (which did not impress either Himmler or Goebbels, because Mrs. Grace Freeman's château was plundered anyway), and, as a citizen of Vichy France, he participates in tournaments organized by the Nazi chess association, the Großdeutscher Schachbund.

The mathematician and philosopher (and Jew) Emanuel Lasker, who holds the title of World Chess Champion for seven years, flees from Germany to England, from England to the Soviet Union, from the Soviet Union to the United States, a generally maddened, maddening flight (his sister does not manage to flee, her last station is Auschwitz), and there, in New York, Emanuel Lasker dies at the beginning of 1941. Now that there are no active Jewish chess players on the horizon of the caliber of Emanuel Lasker, Alekhine again expects the crown. In September 1941, Ehrhardt Post of the

SS organizes the Munich Europaturnier, at which of course Alekhine appears, on the table beside the chessboard there is a small flag of the great Reich, just to be clear. Present are some of the leaders of the National Socialist Party and individual members of the Wehrmacht, those who like chess. Here too is Goebbels, Hans Frank comes from Kraków, a reception is arranged for the players and important guests. Waiters in white gloves circle with silver platters, oh, what an array: Mumm champagne, Hine, Delamain, Gautier and Croizet Cuvée Léonie French brandies, the most expensive French wines, all in glasses of fine Czech crystal; there are appetizers—pickled artichoke hearts, asparagus tips, little venison balls, steak tartare, foie gras, black and red caviar, there are grilled scampi tails arranged on little rounds of soft white bread, with a thin golden-yellow crust that rustles like silk under the palate. Yes, and strawberries are served, and on low *Serviertischen* lie boxes of Havana cigars and little cobalt dessert dishes filled with candied fruits and chocolate pralines *à la crème au nougat, aux pistaches, napolitain, de dèmes, de brillant à la vanille royale, au sultan,* mostly products of Poland's famous Wedel brand. As he watches Alekhine's match, Hans Frank consumes vast quantities of cognac and waits for a report on the Warsaw ghetto, after which he orders the maximum daily consumption of two hundred (200) calories per head of the population in the "forbidden city."

Seventeen kilometers northwest of Munich, in Dachau, ailing camp inmates, those incapable of work, 3,166 of them, have already been selected and shortly thereafter are moved to Schloss Hartheim, where they are gassed to death.

The second half of 1941. The following year, Alekhine plays at the Europameisterschaft in Munich, at which, let it be known, the colors of the Independent State of Croatia are being defended by the Croat Braslav Rabar. On the other hand, the chess grandmaster and hazzan from Karlovac, Izidor Gross (b. 1860), does not go to any tournaments, but in 1942 straight to Jasenovac concentration camp, where together with his son and daughter-in-law he is treated to the operetta *Mala Floramye*, since they can no longer sing themselves. Meanwhile, when first the Democratic Federation of Yugoslavia and then the Federal National Republic of Yugoslavia come "to this region," Braslav Rabar plays at the Balkaniad in Belgrade in 1946, at the 9th Chess Olympiad in Dubrovnik in 1950 he wins two gold medals, and so on, there are tournaments in Helsinki, in Amsterdam, then comes the Socialist Federation of Republics of Yugoslavia and—oblivion. So, it's all right. So, it might even be possible to turn a blind eye to the fact that while the war is going on Alekhine competes in seven Third Reich chess tournaments. It's just a game, after all. After the war, Alekhine is accused of collaborating with the enemy, he is no longer invited to international chess competitions, but with time the "punishment" begins to melt until it melts right away. At the beginning of 1946, the leaders of the British Chess Federation agree to organize the match postponed before the war between Alekhine and Botvinnik (Capablanca, Alekhine's obsession, dies in 1942), a match for the title of new World Champion, and convey this information to the now seriously penniless and cirrhotic Alexander Alekhine, who is sitting already dead in his room (number 43) in the cheap Hotel Parque in the little Portuguese town of Estoril. In the official report of the Portuguese police, the cause of Alekhine's death is given as choking on a piece of meat, which, of course, sounds naïve. Even now his death has not been explained. Some maintain that Alekhine was killed by members of the French "legion of death," others, such as his son, believe that Stalin's hand of justice came for him. Ten years after his death, in 1956, Alekhine is moved, with the sponsorship of FIDE, from the little graveyard in Estoril to Montparnasse in Paris, where I visited him when I spent time there (at the cemetery and elsewhere) on some other business.

I've wandered somewhat to the east.

While the Nazis are cleansing their territory, somehow at the same time, in April and May 1940, the paranoid NKVD sorts out its own captured territory. Like wild and hungry beasts they decimate Poland simultaneously from left and right, from east and west. In the Katyń forest the NKVD organizes the biggest massacre of Polish officers, but there were in addition many efficacious small executions in various wooded corners and prisons, with some twenty-two thousand liquidated. For decades, right up until its collapse, the USSR falsified the truth about this crime, attributing it to the Nazis, even punishing and pursuing those who tried to speak about it. The strands are slowly unraveling, but there are still secrets, unexplained "coincidences." It is amazing that Poland has any kind of intelligentsia today, it is amazing that it was able to regenerate, because in 1968 there was another, now authentically Polish period of hysteria (again) of driving Polish Jews out of Poland, which almost suffocated in the vomit of its own anti-Semitism.

Коба, зачем тебе нужна моя смерть? Koba, why do you need my death?

Oh yes, then, at the end of the 1930s, the Soviets too, in the general hysteria about alleged internal enemies, which—that lunacy, that senselessness, that madness, like toxic micro-ampullae—still crouches to this very day encapsulated deep in the brain cells of members of all the secret services of the world (and not only theirs), the Soviets too energetically liquidate chess players (et al.), only the NKVD kills its own chess players, Russians, and for a good length of time after the end of the war. All right, some chess players died of hunger during the siege of Leningrad, such as, for instance Alexey Troitsky (1866–1942), but the NKVD would have liquidated him in any case, because he was concerned with problem chess, that is, he composed modern chess matches which the

Russians call études, and for the rigid minds of the USSR, problem chess becomes particularly dangerous, because problem chess is imagination, the negation of rules, the negation of directives, it is art, challenge and autonomy, problem chess is freedom—and beauty. Here the great Botvinnik also plays a dirty game. In 1936, Botvinnik and Spokoyny, editor of the famous journal *Шахматы в СССР (Chess in the USSR)*, otherwise a university professor in the history of philosophy and (for the sake of security in his life) dialectical materialism and, ah, a poor chess player, hopeless, Botvinnik says of him, so, in the journal *Chess in the USSR*, in an article entitled "Confusion in compositions," Spokoyny and Botvinnik write that the basis of chess is a practical game and that one must fight mercilessly against abstract composition, just as their homeland fights against abstraction in art, against all formalism, and a great campaign ensues. Five months later the name Spokoyny disappears from the imprint, and the new issue, apart from Botvinnik's groveling post-Nottingham letter to Stalin, which, for the sake of preserving at least an appearance of the dignity of the human race, it is best not to remember, and of which Botvinnik later maintains that he only signed the letter, he did not write it, so, the next issue of *Chess in the USSR* also carries an article, which not only freezes the blood of many in their veins, but for many it stops their blood flow altogether. It is entitled: "Beware, you enemies of the people." The article promises the swift and effective exposure and punishment of all Trotskyists, counterrevolutionaries and those who oppose the triumphant march of socialism (into a bright future). In August 1936, Spokoyny is arrested, in October shot.

Ideas must be eradicated. The great Union of Soviets rejects problem chess and chess compositions as menacing and malign *l'artpourl'art*-ism, as Western bourgeois nonsense, and determines for chess a strictly defined role—the instruction and strengthening of the masses within given, limited and controlled political rules. No theory, not on your life! Just the practical game, full stop.

Leonid Kubbel (1891–1942), a chemical engineer and one of the greatest composers of chess problems of his time, particularly endgames, for which he obtains international recognition, died in the course of the nine hundred days of the German siege of Leningrad, when temperatures fell to -40°C and when around a million of his fellow citizens quietly expired. Leonid's brother, Evgeny Kubbel, did not manage to survive even when he dug with his bare hands in the frozen earth into which by some error sugar from a store was melting, and put the hard sticky mess of soil and sugar in his mouth, or when he fed himself on sheep's innards, small dead birds, rats and the remains of his pet dog.

The hunger and cold also killed the chess players Abram Rabinovici (1878–1943), Ilya Rabinovich (1891–1942), Samuil Vainshtein (1894–1942) and so on, some died in action, and others by unfortunate accident.

But about Leonid's other brother, Arvid Kubbel (1889–1938), an internationally famous chess composer, specializing in the selfmate and the auxiliary mate, the Soviet government misleads the public for thirty years, stating that Arvid Kubbel disappeared in one of those apocalyptic Leningrad winters, along with his brothers, although he was already accused by the NKVD as early as 1937 of publishing his own compositions in the famous journal *Die Schwalbe*, founded in 1924. As a foreign spy, Arvid Kubbel was sentenced to be shot, the sentence was carried out on January 11, 1938, and he was buried in Leningrad.

> *Куббель Арвид Иванович*
> *Родился в г. 1889, г. Ленинград; латыш;*
> *беспартийный;*
> *бухгалтер спортобщества "Спартак."*
> *Проживал: г. Ленинград, В. О., 10-я линия,*

д. 39, кв. 28.

Арестован 21 ноября 1937 г.

Приговорен: Комиссией НКВД и Прокуратуры
СССР 3 января 1938 г., обв.: по ст. ст. 58-1а-9
УК РСФСР.

Приговор: ВМН Расстрелян 11 января 1938 г.

Место захоронения—г. Ленинград.

Источник: Ленинградский мартиролог:
1937–1938

Botvinnik affirms that Alexander Ilyin-Genevsky (1894–1941) died in the course of the Nazi shelling near Lake Ladoga, in the suburbs of Leningrad, although, according to others, he fell as a victim of the Great Terror.

The Soviet chess master Georgiy Schneideman (1907–41) cheated himself fatally when he exchanged his mother's surname, Stepanov, for his father's German one, which was also the name of an SS general. His colleague, the chess player Peter Romanovski, denounced him to the NKVD as a German spy, after which Schneideman speedily received a bullet in the forehead. Romanovski succeeded in surviving Stalin's terror, that merry-go-round in which those who were up came down, wrote books about chess and died in 1964, one could not say exactly happy, as his wife and three daughters perished in the Leningrad siege of hunger and sickness.

On the other hand, the imaginative and already well-known composer, chemical engineer and, of course, chess player Sergei Kaminer (1908–38) vanished overnight. There is an already threadbare story about the childhood friendship between Kaminer and Botvinnik, three years his junior, which may as well be forgotten, a story with much that is dubious, particularly in view of Botvinnik's character (autistic), particularly in view of his vanity (vast), in view of his insecurity, his blind allegiance to the Party (communist) and the police (secret, the NKVD). Botvinnik didn't play a single chess match, just for the sake of it, for the fun of it, he didn't play a single match with a single friend, because he presumably had no chess player friends, and so, when Kaminer at sixteen beat Botvinnik, then thirteen, three times in a row, Botvinnik never forgot it (until Kaminer was liquidated).

Botvinnik, otherwise a doctor of electronics, prepares for every match in a particular way: among other things, he hangs a photograph on the wall of his impending, not partner, not opponent, but adversary and at first growls at the photograph, then barks. Botvinnik said *I don't remember fury, I record it.* He would set a date until which he would not talk to his future chess opponents, and when the time was up, communication would be "normalized." He had files of players who interested him and he studied their psychological profiles. But psychologists and psychiatrists had probably been making psychological profiles of chess players for centuries, and so, in some file of theirs, in some book of theirs, there is probably a profile of Mikhail Misha Botvinnik.

So, in 1937, in Moscow and Leningrad, at the Chess Championship of the USSR, there is a match between Botvinnik and Levenfish. Into Botvinnik's room at the famous Moscow National Hotel bursts the 29-year-old Kaminer, in a fury, and says, *Misha, they're going to arrest me.*

Botvinnik says, *No, they won't.*

Kaminer says, *Take these notebooks, hide them somewhere, then take them to my family. You don't write problem compositions, Misha,* says Kaminer, *Krylenko will crucify me.*

Botvinnik says, *Calm down, Seryozha.*

Kaminer says, *People are disappearing.*

I don't know …, says Botvinnik.

Kaminer wails, *Come on, Misha. Otherwise all this will go up in smoke, all my work. Take it.*

And so Botvinnik takes Kaminer's notebooks. Botvinnik is himself afraid, many people are having nightmares now, many people's backbones are bending, and the police place the naïve in front of a firing squad or pack them off to Siberia. Botvinnik is afraid, and publicly, along with the chess section of the Central Committee, bossed about by Krylenko, then the Soviet Minister of Justice and state public prosecutor (when the time comes, Stalin will liquidate him as well), he continues to condemn problem chess, *that decadent phenomenon, that sick, bourgeois formalism*, because, see, his star is rising ever higher in the great communist sky and its brilliance must be preserved.

After his meeting with Botvinnik, Kaminer is arrested and disappears forever from reality.

Каминер Сергей Михайлович
Родился в г. 1906, г. Романово-Борисоглебск;
русский; образование высшее; б / п;
начальник технического отдела Главрезины
Наркомата тяжелой промышленности СССР.
Проживал: Москва, ул. 1-я Мещанская, д. 43,
кв. 3.
Арестован 17 августа 1938 г.
Приговорен: ВКВС СССР 27 сентября 1938 г.,
обв.: участии в к.-р. террористической
организации.
Расстрелян 27 сентября 1938 г.
Место захоронения—Московская обл,
Коммунарка.
Реабилитирован 11 июля 1956 г. ВКВС СССР

In Leningrad, Botvinnik, Krylenko's great mainstay, draws with the Soviet champion and grandmaster Levenfish, and loses the title of champion, and is very worked up, as he whispered to someone, humiliated, and that this fuck-up Levenfish was politically, in Party terms, above all in chess terms, completely unexpected, completely unplanned, for the Party was then preparing the 26-year-old Botvinnik for the title of World Champion, and not Levenfish, that contemporary Chigorin, that elegant and refined tactician who beats almost all the top Russian and Soviet players, including the grandmasters Alekhine and Lasker, because for them, for the Party, he, Levenfish, is now an ordinary worn-out chemical engineer, so let him just carry on doing his chemistry in our glass industry, they say (decide); for him, for Levenfish, there are no more stipends, no state support, no traveling to international competitions, let Levenfish freeze in his shabby little Moscow room, let them take out all his teeth, they say, Botvinnik will be our chess Tsar. So said the Party, and so it was.

If Botvinnik gave Kaminer's notebooks to his family, he must have done so after Stalin's death (1953), although this will never be known, for Botvinnik is no longer alive either. It was not until 1981 that the chess player and chess problematist Rafael Kofman published a book containing seventeen of Kaminer's compositions, and in the introduction Botvinnik, three times World Champion, affirms, *I don't remember anything.*

As early as the 1920s, Pavel Efimovich Neunyvako (1897–1940) publishes chess studies and, as president of the All-Ukraine Chess Organization, defends "his" composers, only to be shot by the KGB in 1940.

Неунывако Павел Ефимович
Родился в г. 1897, д. Кюньтауган Евпаторийского
уезда Таврической губ.; украинец; образование
высшее; член ВКП (б);
служил в РККА в Центральном Доме Красной
Армии, на момент ареста учетчик асфальто-
ремонтного завода.
Проживал: Алма-Ата.
Арестован 11 апреля 1938 г.
Приговорен: ВКВС СССР 7 февраля 1940 г.,
обв.: подготовке терактов и участии
в к.-р. организации.
Расстрелян 8 февраля 1940 г.
Место захоронения—Москва, Донское
кладбище.
Реабилитирован 18 апреля 1963 г. ВКВС СССР

The problem composer Lazar Borisovich Zalkind (1886–1945) is arrested by the KGB in 1930, accused of preparing, with the pro-Mensheviks, a conspiracy against the Bolshevik government, and the main prosecutor, Krylenko, condemns him to eight years in prison. Zalkind is released in 1938, but fresh accusations soon follow, and he is sent to five years of "socially useful labor" in some remote gulag, it doesn't matter which, they were all appalling.

Залкинд Лазарь Борисович
Родился в г. 1886, г. Харьков;
Приговорен: ОС НКВД СССР 23 августа 1938 г.
Приговор: 5 лет лишения свободы.
В заключении находился с 23.08.1938, задержан
до конца войны | умер 06/25/1945—причина
место смерти—неизвестно.

Источник: Архив НИЦ "Мемориал"
(Санкт-Петербург)

Not absolutely all the composers cover their ears, they are not all silent. When, back in 1936, Botvinnik and Spokoyny launched their attack on "the decadent formalism of chess compositions, which threatens Soviet society with ruin," Mikhail Barulin takes a stand in defense of his colleagues, oh, what imprudence, what naïveté. Botvinnik and Spokoyny send Barulin that well-known (threatening) response and seek support from Krylenko and the Soviet Chess Organization, and it arrives promptly—officially and unconditionally—at the beginning of 1937. And so Barulin's fate is sealed. First, one by one, Barulin's friends and colleagues, who used to get together in his apartment, over pickled gherkins, the occasional hard-boiled egg and vodka, in clouds of tobacco smoke, believing in some stupid personal freedom, conceiving chess poetry, begin to disappear. Finally, in November 1941, they come for Barulin himself. Barulin refuses to admit to anything, Barulin refuses to denounce his friends, and dies in prison in 1943. That's how it goes.

Until his dying day, Botvinnik does not deny his participation in writing the article that launches, in 1936, the persecution of chess-problem composers, of innocent people, none of them with political aspirations, none of them political activists, indeed taciturn people who glide through imaginary worlds, who participate in invented battles; of those who dream. Even fifty years later, when not a hair on Botvinnik's head would have been harmed had he changed his opinion, he announces, *So what, that article still seems completely reasonable and principled to this day.*

Comrade Товарищ (Stalin) does not arrest only members of the Soviet Chess Organization; a number of interesting Soviet and internationally famous chess "brands" also come to grief.

Paranoid as he was, Koba imagines that the geophysical engineer and one of the strongest Siberian chess players Pyotr Nikolaevich Izmailov (1906–37) is preparing an attempt on his life, and arrests him in 1936 and, less than a year later, shoots him.

Izmailov worked in Tomsk. Tomsk is in the district of Siberia. Tomsk becomes the most important educational center of Siberia, it came to be called the Siberian Athens. Until the Second World War, every twelfth inhabitant of Tomsk was a student. Even today there are recognized institutes and well-known universities in Tomsk. There are a lot of theaters, interesting museums, philharmonic orchestras, and above them, there are churches which were destroyed or turned into mechanics' workshops, but then resurrected to become churches once again, so that now there are a lot of churches in Tomsk. In Tomsk there is a culture that stretches far beyond Tomsk. Today in Tomsk there is also a Museum of Oppression, or torture and tyranny, a former secret prison, in whose dark underground rooms the NKVD settled its scores with thousands of "internal enemies," out of which in the 1930s six hundred thousand (600,000) "kulaks" were driven into the swampy regions to the north, of whom 120,000 died in their first year of exile. Then, in the following years, new ones arrived. Thousands and thousands of new enemies.

Tomsk today has around 500,000 inhabitants, in other words fewer than, for instance, a Zagreb. People know little, very little, about Tomsk, because Tomsk seems far away to them, while they are nearby. Since 1997 Tomsk has hosted a traditional chess tournament, famous even outside the Russian borders. That tournament is called the "Peter Izmailov Memorial." In other words, in Tomsk there is also memory.

This is how it was:

Izmailov wins the First Championship of the Russian Federation in 1928. A year later he checkmates Botvinnik (a fatal mistake). Then, until 1936, he devotes himself to his profession, he researches Siberian forests, makes love and tells his son fairy stories. Izmailov does not have time to wander around competitions, he transfers his attention to reality, to Russian, Siberian reality, and, it could be said, his chess power wanes. But still, life isn't bad. Despite droughts, there is still food, ever less, but some. Perhaps people eat more buckwheat porridge, piroshki, and blini, but Siberia is known for its beef, so there is milk, there is butter, there is cheese. People make pelmeni, *mmmm*, as Croatian television's Ana would say, the one who, as well as cooking, dances with the stars. So, our Izmailov, not exactly a muscle man, fair-skinned and light-eyed as he is, believes in his today and his Soviet tomorrow. Then in 1936 there comes an invitation to participate in an important chess tournament in Leningrad and he says, *I'm going*, never dreaming that he is going to his death.

Badly prepared as he was, Izmailov finishes sixth of the fifteen on the list. That is not good. A red light goes on at the NKVD. The local secret police (NKVD Tomsk) is in a state of readiness. Izmailov is under strict observation about which he has no clue, because, although he may be troubled by some doubts, like many others he sings:

Thank you, Comrade Stalin, I warm myself at your fire.
May you live for a thousand years, tovarishch Stalin,
And however hard the days may be for me,
Statistics will show that we have more iron, more steel per head of
the population.

On September 10, 1936, Izmailov phones his wife from his office in Tomsk to say that he will be late for lunch as the local NKVD people have called him for a short conversation. That conversation consists of police questions: Why did Izmailov play so badly in Leningrad? Why did he travel such a long distance in order to finish only sixth? From that conversation the police conclude: comrade Izmailov, member of a Trotskyist terrorist organization, travels to Leningrad to develop a plan about the liquidation of the chief of the Leningrad Party branch, comrade Andrei Alexandrovich Zhdanov. The trial lasts twenty minutes. Comrade Petr Nikolaevich Izmailov, Trotskyist fascist terrorist, is declared guilty. Petr Nikolaevich Izmailov is shot near today's Museum of Torture. The museum may include a list of the murdered. If I ever go to Tomsk, I'll check.

The wife of Petr Nikolaievich Izmailov, as member of a traitor's family, is shunted off by the authorities to Kolma, to a gulag, from which, eight years later, she emerges, well, a bit broken. Today, in the rooms of the Chess Memorial Center in Tomsk, for the sake of relaxation, the eighty-year-old Nikolai, son of Petr Nikolaevich Izmailov, plays chess with youngsters. If he is still alive.

Измайлов Петр Николаевич
Родился в г. 1906, Казань; русский;
образование высшее; б / п; геологоразведочный
трест, инженер-геофизик.
Проживал: Томск.
Арестован 10 сентября 1936 г.
Приговорен: 28 апреля 1937 г., обв.: троцк.
фаш-терр.
Приговор: расстрел.
Расстрелян 28 апреля 1937 г.
Реабилитирован в сентябре 1956 г.

The problem composer Petr Moussoury (1911–37) was shot by the NKVD, together with his mother, for being a member of a terrorist organization. He was then burned in the first Russian crematorium at the Donskoye Cemetery in Moscow.

Муссури Петр Степанович
Родился в г. 1911, Баку; грек; подданство:
подданный Греции; образование высшее;
внештатный сотрудник редакции
шахматно-шашечной газеты "64".
Проживал: Москва, ул.3-я Миусская, д.4а, кв.5.
Арестован 20 марта 1937 г.
Приговорен: ВКВС СССР г. 1 августа 1937, обв.:
связи с участниками к.-р. террористической
организации и участии в контрабанде и
спекуляции .
Расстрелян 1 августа 1937 г. Место
захоронения—Москва,
Донское кладбище.
Реабилитирован 24 декабря 1957 г. ВКВС СССР
Источник: Москва, расстрельные списки
—Донской крематорий

Here is yet another who created those shameless chess compositions, fatal for the Soviet system: Mikhail Nikolaevich Platov (1883–1938). In 1910, together with his brother, Misha Platov publishes a prize-winning and perhaps the best-known problem composition, which is printed and reprinted numerous times, and of which even the passionate chess player Vladimir Ilyich Ulyanov, known as Lenin, says with rapture, *Oh what a wonderful creation!* But then some zealous apparatchik, some crazed, bigoted policeman, some frightened snoop, discovers Platov's compositions in German magazines and—the hunt begins. Platov is arrested in October 1937, there is no public indictment, no trial, just a free ticket for a ten-year stay in a gulag, in which a few months later Platov gives up his sinful chess player's soul.

Then, here is the young—oh, so many young—the young Nikolai Konstantinovich Salmin (1907–38?), a withdrawn and quiet worker, one of the best Leningrad chess players of his time, who suddenly, just like that, vanishes without trace. Later, when Nikolai Salmin was rehabilitated in the 1950s, '60s or '70s, the traces suddenly surface.

It would be possible to say a lot and at length about the sly fox and good chess player Krylenko, the highly placed prosecutor in the political show trials of Stalin's reign of terror, who (not unusually) himself ended up a victim, a whole book could be written with just a list of the people whose torture and execution he oversaw, but no. Few people today are interested, because nowadays such hideous things no longer occur. On the whole. Then Stalin dies, and Krylenko is resurrected. In the 1960s Krylenko's great contribution to the development of Soviet chess is acknowledged, he is proclaimed its father, and in 1989 he receives a commemorative coin with his image. And then the Soviet Union disappears.

That's how one should look at history. In an easygoing manner. Briefly. By leaps and bounds. After Stalin's death many chess players of the USSR—and hundreds of thousands of people who were not chess players—were rehabilitated. They receive deeds in which it is presumably written that they are rehabilitated, that they were not enemies, that their country now loves them, and some also receive badges. Except that not one of them is still alive.

While Ada and I play chess, images flare in front of my eyes, arrows flash, they lodge in the frontal part of my brain.

Why are you blinking so much? asks Ada.

It's the glaucoma, I say.

There are no symptoms with glaucoma.

Then it's the dark, I say.

I can't tell her: that darkness sticks to my eyelids, life sticks to my eyelids. What's left of it. It would sound inappropriately poetic, Ada isn't the poetic type, she's not an openly poetic type, although there are strings trembling in her that she plucks in her deserted life.

You're blinking because of Leila. Leila is an optical illusion. Listen, says Ada.

Semyon Semyonovich, with his glasses on, looks at a pine tree and he sees: in the pine tree sits a peasant showing him his fist.

Semyon Semyonovich, with his glasses off, looks at the pine tree and sees no one sitting in the pine tree.

Semyon Semyonovich, with his glasses on, looks at the pine tree and again sees that in the pine tree sits a peasant showing him his fist.

Semyon Semyonovich, with his glasses off, again sees no one sitting in the pine tree.

Semyon Semyonovich, with his glasses on again, looks at the pine tree and again sees that in the pine tree sits a peasant showing him his fist.

Semyon Semyonovich doesn't wish to believe in this phenomenon and considers this phenomenon an optical illusion.

Ada is selling Kharms to *me*. Kharms has nothing to do with my case. Has anyone publicly proclaimed me mentally problematic? Has anyone proclaimed me a traitor? Kharms dies, history maintains, in February 1942, of starvation, in his cell in the Psychiatric Department of Leningrad No. 1 Prison, where he was placed by the NKVD.

> *This is how hunger begins:*
> *In the morning you wake lively.*
> *Then weakness,*
> *Then boredom,*
> *Then comes the loss*
> *of quick reason's strength—*
> *Then comes calm,*
> *And then horror.*

I am not Kharms.

> *Хармс Даниил Иванович*
> *(Варианты фамилии: Ювачев) Родился в г. 1905,*
> *г.Санкт-Петербург; образование неоконченное*
> *высшее; б / п; Поэт.*
> *Один из основателей литературной группы*
> *ОБЭРИУ.*
> *Проживал. г. Ленинград.*
> *Арестован 23 августа 1941 г.*

*Приговорен: ВТ войск НКВД ЛВО 7 декабря
1941 г.
Приговор: Направлен на принудительное
лечение в психиатрическую больницу
закрытого типа.
Умер в тюремной больнице 02/02/1942.
Реабилитирован 25 июля 1960 г.*

Leila is not an optical illusion. Leila was a ballerina, now she is old and fat, she has swollen knees and thin hair, probably from having it tugged back into those silly little buns. Like me, Leila sways when she walks. I hadn't seen Leila for twenty years, then I saw her briefly, and then after another twenty years she surfaced again, and it would have been better if she hadn't. When I met Leila, Elvira did not yet exist in my life, I was in the first league, handsome, tall, strong and intelligent. Leila is Latvian, born in Riga. When I met Leila all I knew about Latvia was that it was a part of the Soviet bloc, I presumed that it was all one and the same history. I presumed, logically, that Latvians lived in a poverty entirely similar to Soviet poverty, in shared apartments in which people wait in a queue for the toilet or a shower, and outside in long queues for everything, for cucumbers and bread, even the whole night, drinking tea from a thermos flask, and then after hours and hours have passed, they stand in front of a counter with shoes on it, they grab what they can, often two shoes of different sizes, and then walk with a limp. I hadn't heard of a single Latvian writer, let alone read one. All right, I did know that Latvia has and has had excellent chess players, that I knew, of course. I knew of the great combinator, the offensive and imaginative Tal, although for a long time I had experienced him as Russian because the Russians experienced him as Russian, as their acquisition, while he was in fact called Mihails Tāls, and not Михаил Нехемьевич Таль (Mikhail Nekhemevich Tal), because the Latvians don't use the Cyrillic alphabet, while Russians do. In his youth, Tal beat Botvinnik, who was arrogant and rude to him thereafter. Then, Tal died in Moscow, not in Riga, and relatively young, at fifty-five, because his kidneys failed, in fact everything about him failed, apart from his head.

Today I know of some well-known Latvians, but the majority of them were only born in Latvia and, as soon as the opportunity arose, they scarpered to the West, so that the world does not experience them as Latvians at all, although that is changing now that Latvia has detached itself from Russia, because Latvia is working on its image, on its positive image, hurriedly recalling its great citizens, promoting them *tutta forza*, all those who left long ago and never returned, because they are dead. On that other image, on its dark side, Latvia is not exactly working, like Croatia. It's a con.

I know that Baryshnikov was born in Riga, I know that he was of short stature, that he emigrated from the Soviet Union first to Canada, then to the United States, that he married Jessica Lange and that he has been living for a long time with a ballerina, who is no longer a ballerina, just as Leila is not.

I discovered that the American Mark Rothko was in fact Markuss Rotkovičs, or today in Russian Маркус Яковлевич Роткович, born in Latvia and that he went with his family to America before the Revolution, but he's still American, people like adopting other people's countries, other people's wealth, so why not also other people themselves. So Latvians say today, *Listen, Markuss Rotkovičs, alias Mark Rothko, is in fact* ours, *he's not yours, but in fact ours.* Okay, with the growth of anti-Semitism before the beginning of the Second World War, Markuss Rotkovičs was overcome by a mild panic, although he was relatively well protected in America, so he changed his name to Mark Rothko, to a supposedly unrecognizable Jewish surname, so that he is no longer Markuss Rotkovičs, as the Latvians like to call him. When Rothko came to Europe in 1950, for the first time since he left Latvia, it somehow didn't occur to him to pay a visit to his beloved Latvia, but spent five months enjoying his freedom, visiting museums in England, France, and Italy. Then Rothko became increasingly famous, then ill, then impotent, and in 1970 he cut his veins and died (at sixty-six), and then, in 2003, a fairly ugly, enormous statue called *A Dedication to Mark Rothko* was erected in his native town, Daugavpils, and in 2013 the town opened a gallery, in fact a small museum, called the Mark Rothko Museum, because the economic crisis was unsettling Latvia as well, so hopes were placed in the flowering of international cultural tourism, with the international Rothko at its heart. In the little museum, alongside local painters, there is a modest collection of Rothko's works, donated to Daugavpils by Rothko's heirs. So, as one of the best-known abstract artists of the twentieth century, after immigrating to America in 1913 with his family as a ten-year-old because of Latvia's rising anti-Semitism, Markuss Rotkovičs finally returned home a hundred years later.

Now I know that the British philosopher Isaiah Berlin was also born in Riga. It turns out that in the world there are quite a few celebrated people from Latvia. Such a small country, remarkable.

There's a Latvian called Ernests Foldāts who is among the best-known world specialists in orchids. That is a good life, constantly in the embrace of the queen of flowers, far from people, far from politics, outside history, enchanted, intoxicated by fragrant velvety petals of pastel shades. Do orchids have a scent? Ernests Foldāts studied mostly Venezuelan orchids, probably because he immigrated to Venezuela, and from Venezuela he could not have studied Latvian orchids, if there are such things, he could only study the Venezuelan ones. Ernests Foldāts died in 2003. Today the Latvians are proud of him.

And Walter Zapp, he died in Switzerland, also in 2003, aged ninety-seven.

Walter Zapp created a mini-camera of high resolution, a so-called spy camera that fits in the pocket.

And Eisenstein was born in Riga, but Latvia was then part of the Russian Empire, so that is probably why Eisenstein is considered a Russian, although today the Latvians vigorously oppose such appropriation of their great men.

Rosa von Praunheim was born in Riga at a terrible time, 1942. I know a lot more than many about him, but maybe that's for later.

I met Leila in Rovinj, in the 1970s. I don't want to write about our love affair, because it was just an ordinary love affair, with quite a lot of wine and sex, and when one talks or writes about ordinary love affairs, which are most often boring, standard and in terms of content intolerably repetitive love affairs, which do not entail any drama, no one slits their veins, no one jumps into a bath with a hair dryer switched on, no one shouts, no one fights or swallows tranquilizers, no one even weeps, when one talks or writes about such love affairs, which are refined and restrained love affairs, there is nothing to say, although there is a lot to say, but such content is less and less popular in literature, for such content is more probing than writing about those *herzig*, heartrending love tragedies, bound in cheap paper, sold at kiosks and read by women under dryers at the hairdresser. The majority of today's readers (particularly, unfortunately, women, because women read more than men) like for the most part a superficial (dramatic) blurring of reality, but with time such reality in love is invariably transformed into a heap of debris and trash, into a slimy succession of senseless little movements, rhythmic twitches like barely audible breathing, not to say impulsive copulation. One can talk or write about other people's love affairs, many people adore filling up their spent, moldy spaces, it's possible to talk and write about one's own love affairs, which then serve others, and mostly those who write about love affairs, either as solace or entertainment, or again, as a way of bringing a little (neon) light into the darkness that drums behind our eye sockets, like Knausgaard, who has already written *six* autobiographical volumes, which people devour as though they had been tottering for months in a scorching desert, and in which everything happens in real time, slowly and pallidly, because real time is no kind of time as it doesn't exist. I've read some extracts from those idiocies of Knausgaard's, absolutely intolerable unless the person reading them is riddled with holes, so the cultivation of voyeuristic instincts fills up that inner void. It would have been better for Knausgaard to keep a diary, though the diaries of writers, even great writers, are fairly narcissistic and in fact tedious material (not long ago a well-known writer asked me, almost conspiratorially, *Do you keep a diary?* He, along with others I know, is waiting for the Nobel Prize, which, of course, he will not get, but who knows. Writers write mostly about themselves and their creations, so that history (literary, although they also count on general, world, all-encompassing history), does not forget them, so that the keepers of civilization should have something to refer to when they are no more. Pure, omnipotent delirium, grandomania par excellence.

People talk too much. In addition, they repeat their stupidities tirelessly, sometimes with variants in the scale of intonation, sometimes in a monotonous tone and rhythm, so that the listener feels as though he is being hit with a hammer. *Know thyself,* they say, *know your non-self, your other self, know your collective self, know thyself, thine own self.*

A few days ago some guy hit his close friend of many years on the head with a hammer because the man would not shut up, he kept going on and on, and the evening had started beautifully, with music, sausages and beer. I recently overheard a woman in the square saying, *Who are you anyway, and what right do you have to ask me about my political preferences?* She could have said, *Who are you anyway?* or better still, *Who are you?*, she could also have said, *Fuck off.* There are many possible abbreviations.

It's best not to go out. Every time I go out, I tell myself, earplugs, don't forget your earplugs, then I forget them. I was also advised to do this by a silly woman once when I was traveling on an inter-city bus, for three hours, and she would not shut up, she babbled behind me into her mobile from the beginning to the end of the journey, so I asked her, *Are you going to stop nattering?* And she said, *You can buy earplugs, they only cost thirty kunas.* On another occasion I asked a man, *When are you going to shut up?* He said, *When my battery runs out.*

Subtle distinctions of pronunciation in our language are being lost and words are becoming slimy, spoken often with an idiotic smile as speakers fashionably soften nonexistent consonants. Degenerate. Like children, half-articulate, vacuous, infantile orators roll words around their mouths like hot potatoes, as though they were toothless, they shift them about, squash them, then open their mouths to eject a mash, a sticky pre-masticated porridge, which slides down their chins.

There are zillions of idiocies spurting out of the caricatured off-key pronouncements, doctored like a caricature, which contort both my mouth and my stomach. No one knows any longer what reflexive verbs are for. Or vocatives. Or that a plural verb can't follow a singular noun. There is such great confusion drilling in their heads, conspiring to devour every superfluous thought, it smudges every image into mess, into shit.

What an illiterate, haughty, puffed-up nation.

But, bit by bit, year by year, these monstrous polluters of words and thoughts will succeed in digging tunnels into my brain, and then, like a colony of ants, their acid will poison (devour) my memory.

The language has shrunk. It has become smaller and moved to the suburbs. Now "clash" is all the rage, there are no collisions or conflicts, hell no.

Of all the communicative horrors that get to me here, the worst may be when I'm trying to tell someone something. People just don't listen. While I'm talking, they keep interrupting and repeating *yes, yes, yes, yes, yes*, they say that five times, sometimes six (I count to myself). For some time, clusters of three have been in fashion, *yes, yes, yes*. Generally speaking, it seems that we have entered an age of frenzied repetition. As though the human brain has totally degenerated (perhaps it has), and it has to be told everything several times so that at least something should make an impression.

My irritations are not decreasing, which surprises me. Now I'm also annoyed by the rustling of jackets, which seems always to pursue me. In winter, people in rustling jackets swing their arms wildly, so they rustle as they walk. They swing their arms in summer as well, but summer clothes don't rustle like winter ones, so in summer you don't hear them. And I'm annoyed by women's heels clicking on the pavement, cheap shoes that follow me, beating into my brain. A few days ago, I heard quiet footsteps behind me, those steps dragged, they ground the pavement, and I instantly felt my nerves tingling. That's why now I stop and let all those loud and all those abnormally quiet walkers, their rustling jackets and their brittle heels pass by me. When they are in front of me, I don't hear them at all, I don't get irritated.

I haven't watched TV for ages, especially not in winter, because it's cold in that room. It's not exactly agreeable in that room even in summer, particularly when the announcer greets me like this:

Because of clouds, it was cloudy today in Croatia.

Or, *In today's accident 365 dead perished.*

The Evening News I find particularly irritating, especially since it's got longer. It's full of nonsense, gossip and tedious images of everyday tedious life, so, of course, the announcers repeat themselves, but they can't accumulate enough banality to appear astute. All right, some of the women announcers have stopped fluttering their forearms and upper arms as though they are about to take flight, but some news programs are presented by two people, male and female, never two men or two women, or just one person, and those two people look at each other at regular intervals, as though they were relating (reading) the events to each other, which looks even more stupid. And, on top of that, they smile, and when they are not smiling they remain jovial, even though what they are saying is often neither funny nor amusing, and can indeed be tragic and alarming, hideous murders, heaps of corpses, hundreds of thousands of refugees and innumerable destroyed cities. But I keep paying my subscription because if I get caught by Hanžeković's office for enforcement, it'll be recorded in my bank account and I'll get an automatic fine, which happened once, although that time they were wrong.

I also have problems listening to the radio. It's dangerous to listen to the radio early in the morning, when one is still groggy, because if a song ambushes one, as happened to me once, a song in which some guy was whining "I knew that I would give my love to her—my lovely Croatian land," then some people's blood pressure leaps to abnormal heights, while that of others plummets so that they have to lie down straight away.

I'm getting old. Everything about me and in me is giving way: it's either giving out or not functioning as it should. My eyelids droop, so the ophthalmologists stick them to my eyebrows and only then start looking at the back of my eye and measuring my eye pressure. Then they exclaim, *Oh, how pale your nerves are!* Then I ask, *Are they going to be snuffed out soon?* and they say, *Don't talk like that.* Glaucoma will cost me my sight in due course, I discovered that in Paris. About that, glaucoma and Paris, later. I spend more and more time hanging around clinics, after which my irritation increases maniacally, which is fatal for one's health. My face is sagging. On both sides of my chin, there are now little bags, like a bulldog's. As soon as I can get a bit of money together, I'll go and get those little bags lifted. I know that I'm not alone, some admit it to themselves with difficulty, but publicly— heaven forbid. Men, the more stable of them, leave the situation as it is and act the fool, they grow beards or in public wrap scarves around their necks that reach to their lower lip. Women do that as well. I once watched a colleague of mine reading her works on a TV program. She was wearing a polo-neck sweater that almost came up to her nose, so one could barely hear what she was saying.

When Easter comes, I don't go out. But I get wound up if I turn on either the radio or the TV. At least I only hear words from the radio, while on the screen for three days actors process in heavy, gold-encrusted robes, all deadly serious as they talk about Easter as a festival of joy and good cheer. At the same time, those animators, those performers, frequently repeat to their flock that Easter Monday is a time for remembering Jesus meeting with his disciples after his resurrection, as though all of them, bishops and priests and their entire suite and their believers, had been present at that meeting between Jesus and the disciples, as though they remembered that meeting, and on Easter Monday they must all together devote additional remembering to that meeting.

I produce a lot of trash, it's unbelievable how much rubbish I generate in just a couple of days, and I don't seem to eat anything. I still don't separate my trash. Particularly not paper, and I have an excessive amount of wastepaper. I do not separate paper because they've put dumpsters here with a short, narrow opening and a lid that cannot be lifted, so I would have to insert each little scrap of paper separately, which is truly annoying, especially when people walk past me probably thinking, that guy's lost it. Besides, I've watched, because they've plonked those dumpsters down literally under my window, I've watched: at one o'clock in the morning a truck comes and collects all that trash from the yellow, blue, green and gray dumpsters, all of it, supposedly sorted, all of it is chucked by the garbagemen into one and the same container.

Sometimes I don't go out for three days. Then I go out. Or travel somewhere. Yesterday I went out and immediately stepped in some shit.

Should I leave?

No.

Sometimes nice things happen, they immediately make me stand tall. I go straight for a brandy. For instance, once a large man rushed past me, he can hardly have been thirty, big, muscular, tattooed, with a shaved head, a bodybuilder one would have thought, a bruiser, a bouncer, he was hurrying and shouting to a friend on the other side of the street, *Later, I've got to pee, I need to pee badly*. What tenderness, almost poetic. Then I remember little Dolores from the terrible kindergarten of Croatian-American friendship, who used to shout, *I have to wee!* and I would shudder. So I tell myself external appearance is sometimes misleading, simply in order to restrain these negative passions of mine.

I like to stop by my little market around the corner, somehow shriveled, flattened, deflated between dilapidated, dark, Austro-Hungarian five-story blocks with no lift or heating. There's a little café under an awning on the square, and every time I go I drop in there (although my home-brewed espresso is better), because the people who come are poor, threadbare people, they carry half-empty little bags of vegetables or fruit bought at a reduced price and, strangely enough, their speech doesn't irritate me at all, even though it's rough and stilted, often too loud, so these people remind me of mongrel dogs, which I adore, unlike dogs with a pedigree, which disgust me, all tarted up but degenerate.

I buy beetroot. And broccoli. Marisa used to love beetroot, *Beetroot is refreshing*, she would say, but I can't bear it, it's like chomping on earth. I don't like broccoli either, but both beetroot and broccoli destroy cancer cells, they say (they didn't help Marisa, or Elvira), so I buy them and eat them to prevent the possible renewed crawling of the tendrils of some tumor that is crouching in me, waiting, I know. In that little café they bring me a macchiato with a hideous spoon made of tin, so light and tiny that it would be hard to stir anything with it and every time I remember how we refugees (political and war) were treated in Canada. We were, each and every one of us, given the same cutlery, four knives, four forks and four soup spoons with such a shallow scoop and such a short handle that it was impossible to hold any fluid in them. I don't know why I didn't throw out that cutlery when we left Canada, because here if I happen to pick up one of those pieces, especially a spoon, I move my hand away as though scalded and leave it lying on the bottom of the drawer, where it is now acquiring a green coating, oxidizing. Not to mention the sheets, synthetic, with barely 10 percent cotton, beneath which sweat is abnormally abundant.

I adore croissants. Nowadays you can get first-class ones here, when I first came twenty-four years ago, they were not first-class, but thick and heavy and mushy. Sometimes I go down into the center of town and sit on a terrace on a little side street, drink a short espresso and order two warm croissants. It's quiet all around me, that early morning quiet, a healing quiet that excites and soothes at the same time. Then, only then, do I hear the sea, for no one's shrieking or senseless yelling or hysterical crooked footsteps force it to retire (as they do me), and the sea withdraws from its cover and pours out into the town. Only then is the sea not silent. My asthma vanishes, I breathe deeply and evenly, and at the café table from somewhere, out of some stale, worn-out past, appear memories of waking à deux, beside the Seine, when, after loving embraces and meaningless whispering, a touch is enough for peace, and in that soundlessness we look at one another, my past time and I, and I wonder how it happened that all that is left of us is pure waste. Then I shake myself and think, what stupid sickliness, what shallow, pathetically touching rapture. And I limp off to my lair.

When Leila and I met again after some twenty years, she was entranced by my little market square, here a market square is not called a "pazar" but a "placa," an ugly word, limp, after the sticky "pl" the mouth opens unreasonably wide and the tongue flicks, Leila was so entranced that she made a series of panoramic photographs into postcards, which she sent around as proof of Balkan exoticism, including, quite unaccountably, one to me.

I read about this market square in some book or other, never dreaming that I would be burying myself in its neighborhood. I read that at the beginning of the twentieth century Clara lived near here, a former beauty and nighttime entertainer, seller of flowers and love around numerous bars, cafés, terraces and hotels in Fiume, and that, in more recent times, on this square, with its pavilion for fish, meat and milk products, surrounded by stalls of genetically modified vegetables from Italy and Spain, on this in fact miniature square, huddling in an inner courtyard surrounded by the solid-stone, several-storied houses of former merchants in textiles, leather and silk, Clara sold flowers. Further on, the author of that text wrote, *That little square is like a trap, and behind what is today the noisiest and ugliest street in this town, behind the once fashionable Deák Street, that little square throbs like a hidden life breathing in secret.* Clara, writes that author, Clara died at the end of the 1990s, alone, wrapped in smelly old rags, and beside her desiccated corpse was a cardboard box with wilted flowers she had collected from the cemetery, and used to sell on the square, around the corner. *Toward the end*, wrote the author, *the box became too heavy for Clara, so she tied it with string and dragged it, the way children drag wooden toys which won't go straight, because they are ineptly carved, with a penknife, as homemade craft.* I'm quoting this here because today I feel like Clara, I can barely walk, I breathe with difficulty and totter along, dragging my shabby luggage behind me.

I spoke English with Leila then, long ago, and then, when we met again, so as not to get annoyed. My English is excellent (I was recently asked by a Canadian here, with undisguised doubt in his voice, whether I could read English, so I gave him my book about the time I spent in his wonderful country which discriminates against refugees and in which I describe my scientific psychology lectures), Leila's English is not excellent, in fact it's terrible, so in order to understand one another, when talking with her, I maximally simplify my statements, and therefore also my thoughts. Leila speaks German. Leila also speaks Latvian, but when I got to know her, she didn't have much opportunity to speak Latvian except with her family, because at that time Latvia was a Soviet region, in which most people spoke Russian, while Leila lived and danced in Germany.

So this association with Leila lasted, remarkably, in phases like the moon, for several years. She skipped about and I traveled, so we would meet up for a day or two in hotels, in theaters in the evening, she on stage, I in the audience, then in bars all over the world, in Chicago, New York, Hamburg and most of all in Stuttgart, because Leila's home base was Stuttgart, and then Nuremberg. I met the famous Marcia Haydée, lovely as a goddess, and John Cranko, persecuted in England for his sexual orientation, then director of the Stuttgart Ballet, Cranko who collapsed after an anaphylactic shock several months after we sat together into the early hours in a gay bar whose name I don't remember, after a production which I don't remember either. During the flight back from his successful US tour, John Cranko experienced an allergic reaction to an antinausea tablet and died. I also experienced an anaphylactic shock, completely absurdly, but I didn't die. Until then I had believed that I was not allergic to anything to the extent that it could kill me, but I discovered that all manner of unpredictable things and horrors are constantly lying in wait for us and that the worst are those apparently innocent ones that can prove fatal. I ate a washed, although not peeled, apple, evidently sprayed with some poison, and it activated my asthma in an instant and I couldn't breathe, and my whole body shuddered, and then, I don't know after how long, I came to on the tiles of the kitchen floor, having peed and crapped. Now, of all fruit, I have an indescribably keen desire for apples, which could be interpreted in all kinds of ways.

In the course of my encounters with Leila, I also got to know the blond Danish angel Egon Madsen, the irresistibly attractive Richard Cragun, and Birgit Keil and her dance and life partner, the Czech Vladimir Klos.

I met many people, not just ballet dancers, I had a rich life.

I also met Leila's family, who lived in a dark, dank Bavarian forest south of Munich, in a little house with a lot of rooms and with a lot of little wood-burning stoves. In those rooms Leila's mother knitted multicolored socks for cold days and she gave me a pair of gray and black striped ones, but of course those socks went missing in one of my various house moves. There were some sisters of Leila's and some brothers, and there was Leila's father, a stately man of about seventy, with hard facial lines and grimaces that he kept under absolute control, an astonishingly immobile face on which even the eyes barely blinked. A leaden face, some would say, handsome, but disturbing. I don't remember the name of the place either.

Up until then I knew little about Leila and her family, partly because of our rare and spasmodic, truncated communication, partly because of my lack of interest in Latvia and Latvian history.

Then a hatch opened.

There, in the Bavarian forest, one quiet Bavarian night in which, as my friend the poet Sibila Petlevski says:

Owls hoot and hawks mew, and a fox howls, barks,
Falcons sing as though in a church. The cruel liturgy
Lets you and me know that nothing is any good anymore,

while everyone was asleep, I packed my little suitcase and set off on foot toward the little town whose name I've forgotten, in the middle of which there was a little redbrick railroad station, to jump on a train bound for Vienna at three in the morning, because that town virtually ran into Austria. It wasn't winter, there was no snow, which these days I wish for with such longing, but in vain, because when it snows, silence falls from the sky onto my chest, feathery, tender and soft, a wounding silence, under which all living things collapse, to which all that breathes abandons itself. It was a late rainy autumn, intrusive and threatening.

That was the end of my contact with Leila—until her next visit to Croatia some ten years later and then again, in her and my unsightly old age.

We were supposed to stay with Leila's family for several days, to walk in the mountains and pick mushrooms in the neighboring woods where, they told me, you could find clitocybe, armillaria, marasmius and beech trunks in which there were pleurotus and boletus. We had planned to pickle some of the mushrooms, I said that I would make risotto from others, to which the family, even

Leila's father, responded *Ah, wunderbar*. They had given me a little room which must have served as a small storeroom for rejected objects, a little room with a floral carpet and curtains edged with frills, the bed was from the 1950s, too short for me, and the floorboards had been painted with white oil paint. In the corner, in three open cardboard boxes there were outdated small household appliances—a hand nut grinder, a lead machine for hand-mincing meat, a Bakelite telephone, a few Ronson electric razors, a dozen old lighters into which you placed a tiny flint and into which petrol dripped from plastic ampules, there were worn-out Pelikan fountain pens, one with green and black stripes, like the one with which my grandmother Ana had written letters to Tito complaining of social and political injustice, there were Parker pens, and pen holders, there were old slides in small yellow Kodak boxes, which I didn't open, then some broken glasses frames, there were all sorts of things, narrow metal hair rollers, which you attached with red rubber bands, there was an irrigator pump and necklaces of plastic pearls, little packets of the past, thrown here without order or sense, in which days and years squirmed and collided, little sparks of joy and sorrow, moments of solitude and togetherness, beauty and poverty, sickness and anxiety, some thirty years of some kind of life in the German backwoods below the Bavarian Alps, in a tiny village with fewer than two thousand inhabitants, a past which its owners no longer had any need to conjure up. There were no letters, or documents or photographs, only rubbish, trash, remains, a superfluity of memory that neither upset nor pleased, just a heap of dead objects covered with dust and a thin layer of soot from the furnace on the other side of the room, piles into which new leftovers, new unnecessary things would occasionally leap, because all three boxes were open. And, just as I had begun to put things back into one of the boxes in the same order in which I had taken them out, at the bottom I caught sight of a gray-black case with a swastika printed on the cover. Naturally I opened that little box. In it lay an iron cross of the Wehrmacht covered by a small yellowing note with the seal of the Third Reich. On the note was written the name of Leila's father, Mazais Arvīds, and: 19/44 p. 3-Mr-45 DK II. At the time I understood virtually nothing of what was written, but later I did. At the bottom of the note was a resounding greeting which made the whole room shake: *Heil Hitler!* I did understand that.

I knew that, after the war, when the USSR mercilessly transformed Latvia and the other two Baltic states into its own provinces, and transported many of their dissidents in cattle trucks to gulags, Leila's family had fled to Germany, that they spent two or three years, I've forgotten how long, in some kind of refugee camp there and that after that their life started all over again. A new life blurred by memories in which albums from the past lay stored in a cranny of reality, in an archive, which, as always happens, someone some day would nevertheless open.

For me Latvia became a riddle only some ten years later, when a half truth, long unspoken in my family, acquired outlines, when, like wormholes, those penetrations into space and time, into new spaces and a new time, it began to create shortcuts toward a journey, that often dangerous and destructive journey the end of which cannot be seen. But, some years later, all that rubbish, all that rot and rubble settled and we began to step over it, softly at first, trying not to disturb the dust, then we collected the shards of that past, all those splinters, we buried all that debris and moved on.

My mother Marisa met my father Rudolf in Paris. They were both then living in Split, she at 4 Ulica Matošića, he on Ulica Haj-duk-Veljko, which was renamed, with the coming of the Fascists, via dei Duchi d'Aosta. She was just seventeen and he twenty-one. She was a pupil at the Girls' Real Gymnasium and had a blue clothbound notebook with pages for the timetable, printed in two variants of Serbo-Croat and Slovene, just as today in Bosnia and Herzegovina the identical phrase *Smoking kills* is printed in Latin (Croatian) script, Cyrillic (Serbian) and Bosnian (also Latin script). That notebook, with its blue cloth cover, with the black coat of arms of the Kingdom of Yugoslavia on the first page, was printed in Belgrade at the State Press of the Kingdom of Yugo-slavia in 1933. He, my father Rudolf, was studying Electronics at the Faculty of Electrical Engineering of Belgrade University and in the summer, during the vacation, he went "home" to Split, not knowing in fact where his home or his house was, because after the Fascist occupation of Istria, as a two-year-old, he had left Pazin with his family in 1921 and lived first in Orebić, then in Makarska and finally in Split where he completed his schooling. She, my mother Marisa, had perfect pitch, two brothers and poverty. Many years later, at the beginning of the 1950s, when Marisa was about thirty and I was already born, Zinka Kunc Milanov was perform-ing in New York at the Metropolitan. Marisa and Rudolf arranged a celebratory dinner for Zinka Kunc and some others, the room was full of guests, *pašticada* was served, followed by crème caramel, it was all cooked by Grandma Ana, then Zinka Kunc began to sing, and Marisa joined in. I was five, maybe six, and I was totally fascinated by Zinka's transparent plastic shoes, because she moved as though she was barefoot, as though floating. With their arms around each other, Zinka and Marisa sang "Far away is my Split," then Zinka threw off her plastic shoes, I took one, examined it, turned it around and upside down, Ada (3) came up, put it onto her chubby little foot and started hobbling about, no one took any notice of us, because Zinka Kunc was singing, someone picked the song out on the piano, and the Zinka-Marisa duet draped itself over each and every one of us in the room like a magic mantle. That duet, that "Far away is my Split" sung by Zinka Kunc and my mother Marisa floated for a long time behind me, sending out bright rays into which I would disappear after deaths began to stalk our lives. But, while the two of them were singing, Zinka's brother Božidar went wild over Marisa. Turning to her, he shouted *Excellent, breathe, a little more, more, that's it, inhale, pause . . .*, waving his arms the whole time. So, perhaps my mother Marisa could have become an opera singer, but she didn't, there was no money for singing lessons, for conservatoires, and then war broke out, the family moved to Zagreb, my grandfather joined the underground, Marisa too, Grandma Ana altered old clothes into "new" ones, one uncle sheepishly supported the Independent State of Croatia, while the other gave her a hard time.

And Grandma Ana could have been *al pari* to Coco Chanel or Elsa Schiaparelli, not only did she clothe half of Split, but after the war she sewed evening dresses for opera singers, for painters, for all kinds of high-ranking functionaries, State and Party, and for the wives of diplomats, she made that famous little black dress for Ada when few people in Yugoslavia had heard of little black dresses, because in those days in Yugoslavia girls wore full skirts to below the knee, held up with starched petticoats with a lot of frills, that swayed as they walked.

So, in Split, in her childhood, Marisa did sing. She practiced the piano in the salons of Ana's rich clientele, when she was allowed in; Grandma Ana had a salon as well, but for dressmaking, with fourteen workers, and she cut out, interfaced and pleated day and night so as to feed us all, three children, herself and her dreamer husband, the anarchist Max Osterman, who read Goethe and Schiller in Gothic, if he was not reading Kropotkin and company. When it was really necessary, when the family income diminished, my mysterious grandfather would drag himself off reluctantly to his barber's shop, at 3 Plinarska, quite near the street where he lived, at 4 Matošića, and there in his own barber's salon, he would crossly scrape with a razor the chins of fat gentlemen, for the most part in the late afternoon. And then, with what was then still a jovial step, he would hurry to some theater performance (the theater was nearby as well) or to a secret meeting of anarchists or perhaps to the "'Anarch' Workers' Football Club, known as "Red," but officially the "Split Workers' Football Club," whose president he was from 1919 to 1921, and which was just two doors further down, at 7 Plinarska. Above the door of that building at 7 Plinarska, Split, and, remarkably, still there today, at the time when the blinded, half-educated Croatian right-wingers were fanatically and hysterically hammering plaques (and our heads), there is one with a star carved in the top, with a little hammer and sickle in its center, put up in 1972 by "the members and administrators," on which it says, IN THIS BUILDING IN 1912, THE SPLIT WORKERS' FOOTBALL CLUB WAS FOUNDED.

While your granddad cooled his balls, as Grandma Ana used often to say of her husband, *top models emerged from my salon for the Split gentry to parade them along the Riva*. Even during the war, until things became really bad, probably until 1942, my Grandma Ana used to travel to Belgrade for the latest *Vogue*, in other words, despite the bombs, the trains ran, unlike in this last dirty little war, when all connections, even telephones, between Croatia and Serbia were cut, and when the telephones were not cut, the operators used to interrupt conversations and comment on them or, if they did not like the conversations at all, they would make a threatening comment and abruptly cut them off. So, in spite of our poverty, my mother Marisa was known as one of the most beautifully and fashionably dressed young women in Split, except that her dresses were always "combined," that is they were composed of the leftovers from Grandma Ana's clients. In the years of her elderly nostalgia and mournful loneliness, my grandmother Ana would talk about the way Šimun would suddenly burst into their dining room.

Who's Šimun? I would ask.

Šimun Rosandić, you silly.

> *We pupils of the Boys' Trade School decided to found a football club. We played for fun, but also out of protest against all kinds of evil. We pondered for a long time what to call the club, I was the first to think of the name—Anarchist! Later we shortened it to Anarch. That seemed to me the best name, because it contained in it—something else! What else? Ah, let others work it out!*

Šimun Rosandić, Grandma Ana would say, *used to appear in the dining room, gobble three fritters and ride off into the night with Max. While I sewed.*

After the authorities shut down the "Anarch" Football Club for a second time in 1919 (the first time was after the Sarajevo assassination, because the Anarch supporters refused to display a flag with a black flower), the club "repositioned" itself as the

Yugoslav Football Club "Yug." Over the years, "Yug" too positioned and repositioned itself, it was closed down, its premises burned, it changed names, merged with other clubs, this was all described to me (when my Granddad Max was long gone) in her old age by the new-born football fan, my Grandma Ana. But that's not the current topic.

As Ana's son, my Uncle Karlo, often used to say, *It's not that Papa wasn't exactly overjoyed when I was born five months later*, which meant five months after the two of them, Max and Ana, had *only* had a civil marriage ceremony, and as Grandma Ana bore three children, I believed that between Max and Ana there was, however hidden and disguised, nevertheless passion. What is more, in her already advanced old age, forty and more years since my grandfather Max Osterman had given up his melancholy soul in 1944, in Zagreb, aged barely fifty-six, after watching every match, particularly those of the Split club "Hajduk" (where Max Osterman had been a treasurer in 1920), which Ana would follow regularly and knowledgeably, poor Max would stroll into the room, illuminated by flashes of what had been, until 1941, their happy life. Until recently, when I definitively overtook the age of Max Osterman in years, I believed that, in their small Zagreb apartment under the NDH, the Independent State of Croatia, my grandfather's heart had simply burst with misery and pain—poof!—and that, blissful and finally free, he had joined his cronies, Proudhonists, Kropotkinists, Vanzetti-ists, Durutti-ists and so on, when in fact, I only realized recently (because I hadn't asked earlier, because I didn't care) my granddad Max Osterman died of pneumonia, or perhaps tuberculosis, because then, in 1944, in the NDH, the Osterman family had no money to buy streptomycin, which Dr. Zora Voneš would not give him (she would have sold it to him), with her private practice situated then and many years later in the neighborhood, on Medveščak. Smuggling flourished during the NDH, of course, the black market was lively, while people on the whole were not. The Osterman family had nothing to sell, apart from its good name. Max Osterman could not find a job, he roamed the Zagreb suburbs, went to barbershops offering his services, but his barber colleagues were suspicious: *Where've you been up to now?* they asked, because in 1941 some were already in the underground, many were working for the Movement, some were in prison, like the barber Pavešić, some died in camps: the barber Muharem Grozdanić from Ulica Radićeva, others were arrested and then killed in the Jasenovac camp: Milan Uzelac from Ulica

Preradovićeva, some were already with the Partisans, and Đuro Peška, Drago Gaži, Ankica Urek and Marijan Hebner had never heard, nor did they wish to, of the Split anarchist Max Osterman.

Max Osterman simply didn't belong. He was born too early for the Great War, and came to Zagreb too late. Grandma Ana didn't sew, she just patched what had already been patched, turned other people's rags inside out, ruined her fingers, clicked her tongue, and when her tolerance snapped she made threats, she beat herself in the breast and shouted, *I'll throw myself out of the window!* Then, as the years passed, Grandma Ana, just incidentally, would toss into her story brief episodes from her life, from what was to us a distant time, episodes which now prowl around me, creep into my *Rumpelzimmer*, adding to the disorder still further. For instance, the formal dance that the "Red Devils," as they now call themselves, then members of the "Split" or rather "Anarch" Football Club, already renamed "Yug," organized on Saturday, February 14 (Valentine's Day), 1920, in the Troccoli café, now the Central restaurant on the Pjaca, inviting workers, laborers and lovers of sport to buy tickets for just fifteen kunas for men and five for women. Bit by bit, it was quite unclear why or because of what, days, nights, years would come into Ana's stories, with no connection to her or my reality at the time, with no stimulus or obvious, at least to me, associations, as though within the walls of her skull parallel tales were spinning, detached stories knitted into balls of history that floated through some cosmic, timeless time, colliding occasionally with a bang, at others remaining locked in an undefined embrace of suffering, longing, loss, anger, caprice and emotions.

You know, I didn't just sew, sometimes I'd go out with Granddad.

Yes, I went to the bazaar, shopping, I sewed and fed them all, plus those fourteen little seamstresses, while he read about revolts in America, about Sacco and Vanzetti, about bombings in Milan in the Ho-

tel Cavour, and in Torino, many dead, and he talked, he didn't speak
much otherwise, about the failed attempts at assassinating Mussolini,
all right, I'd join in then, I'd say it was a pity they didn't succeed, and
he would say, a great pity. He read Proudhon, do you have any idea
who Proudhon was? He read Bakunin, in 1921, he wanted to go to
Kropotkin's funeral somewhere near Moscow, I said, either Kropotkin
or us, he read Pensiero e Volontà *by some Malatesta, and when he died*
back in 1932, he said, now I am going to this funeral, Rome was closer
than Moscow. And he went, it was summer, July, my blood pressure
went through the roof and I miscarried. He was obsessed with that
anarchist Germaine Berton, who tried to kill some right-wing jour-
nalist in France, and I was about to give birth to your mama. If it's a
girl we'll call her Germaine, he said, fuck your Germaine, I said, and I
gave Marisa the name Katica, which is just as awful as Germaine, so
we changed it later. Afterward, that Germaine killed herself, you see.
Is there any football on tonight?

Marisa also swam. We were all swimmers. Marisa swam (I had
a photo in which she is smiling while swimming on her back, I
also had a small portrait photo of my grandfather Max Osterman
from that time, from 1940, the grandfather I had never seen, let
alone got to know, now that little picture too has disappeared), so
Marisa swam and competed for the Split club, Jadran, our father
played water polo in the Jadran club, and at the end of the 1960s I
too played for Jadran, until I moved to POŠK, Ada even won some
medals, we all swam and in the end—drowned. In those days, with
the coming of the Fascists, the Jadran members refused to become
part of the Italian league, collectively abandoned their swimming
pool in Zvončac and the club disbanded, many of its members
joined the National Liberation Movement, and some died in it.

In addition to having perfect pitch, or maybe because of it, my
mother learned languages like falling off a log, easily and gaily,

and, as the best pupil of the then Cercle Français in Split, whose classes she attended without charge, was awarded a prize in 1939 of a trip to Paris. In that same year, in the same month, July, in a parallel story similar to those in American films of wide consumption, as one of the best students in the third year of Electrical Engineering, my father Rudolf from Belgrade went on a study visit to France, to Paris. That Paris would later, on several occasions, cost us all dearly, but that's for another time.

And so, in some Society of the Friends of France, a month before the outbreak of war, my mother Marisa sang, probably Dalmatian songs, in Paris, while my father Rudolf drummed with his fingers, trying to accompany her, to which she said, *It'd be better if you didn't do that, you're tone-deaf.* Paris was still joyful, the terraces were full, the bouquinistes sold books, artists painted portraits of tourists, the Latin Quarter throbbed, the days were long, the nights warm, one war, the one in Spain, had just ended, although a little to the east the ground was rumbling hollowly, in concentration camps the profile of the inmates was changing, a terrible storm was building, but Rudolf and Marisa could not now, now when love was growing, they could not think about that as they strolled along the Seine, their arms around each other, or fed each other pieces of quiche. Horace kept pace with them, whispering: *Carpe diem, quam minimum credula postero*, and they said *Yes, oh yes*, and they didn't have time even to imagine that this tomorrow, so unpredictable and terrifying, was already sitting at their table. Less than a year later Hitler visited Paris, swiftly touring the city, and its sights, with the sculptor Breker and the architects Giesler and Speer, they crossed the Champs-Élysées, went down to the Trocadéro and the Eiffel Tower, which now looked different from the way it did when under it, full of hope for the future, my mother Marisa smiled, in love, and in which the French would keep the lift blocked until the end of the war, so whoever wanted to climb up (or hang swastikas) had to use the stairs. Hitler was not interested in the Palais de Justice, he was not interested in the Louvre, or Sainte-Chapelle, but the beauty of the Opéra drove him totally wild. Less than a year later, in the summer of 1940, more than two million people would leave the city, and the Arc de Triomphe would groan under a covering of red and black flags with hooked crosses.

Marisa's mother, my Grandma Ana, did not, of course, let her go on that journey in 1939, alone, *she's still a child*, so in Paris her older brother Karlo snapped at her heels (only for a day or two, thankfully), because in Paris Karlo soon slipped away to follow his own dream, that Académie Diplomatique Internationale, about which in the dark dining room in 4 Ulica Matošića he had been pestering the whole household: *I'll run away if you don't send me to the diplomatic school in Paris*. Karlo Osterman threatened, gabbled, prattled on about a petition for signing the Universal Declaration of Human Rights sent to the League of Nations in 1933, about the Report on the Legal Status of Women in eighty-three states of the world and about the Study on the Humanization of War that had existed for three years already. *That's what I want, can't you see where we're heading?!* yelled Karlo, which Ana pretended not to hear, until finally she burst out, *Fuck off then, child!*, while Max listened, his heart occasionally trembling, his eye glinting, the corners of his mouth almost imperceptibly rising, then he sighed and said, *I'm going to give Meštrović a pedicure.*

After the German invasion of France, the Académie Diplomatique Internationale moved its offices to Geneva, and all that was left of Karlo's dream were two volumes (of seven published) of the *Dictionnaire Diplomatique*, bought on a walk beside the Seine, and the scars of two unrealized loves. Until his unexpected and sudden death Karlo worked as a journalist, in his spare time he went fishing in his small wooden boat, gazing out to sea and picking through images that could have become reality, but didn't.

In 1939 Frida Landsberg was studying violin with Professor Adolph Metz, the only Jew at the Riga Conservatoire, and just beneath her chin, on the left side of her neck, she had a small red patch, something like a scar or a hematoma. The Riga Conservatoire was later renamed the Latvian Academy of Music, but Frida would never know that. Nor would her teacher Adolph Metz. Frida Landsberg went to Paris in that July of 1939 in the hope of arranging a meeting with the violinist and conductor Charles Munch, director of the Paris Philharmonic Society and professor at the Paris Conservatoire. Walking through the town, making their way toward Gare St.-Lazare, Marisa, Rudolf, and Karlo stopped in rue de Madrid in front of the building at number 14, having no idea that this was where the famous Paris Conservatoire was housed, although from the open first-floor windows a cacophony of notes wafted, piano, trumpet and violin. They stood there, enchanted, watching a blue-eyed girl with long, light-brown curly hair playing, playing what?, they had no idea what she was playing, but she played wonderfully and smiling young people gathered around her and threw small coins into the violin case on the pavement. They would discover later, *That's Guy Ropartz*, Frida Landsberg would say, *Sonata number 2, for violin, in E major*, she would say, as the four of them stirred their lemonade in synchrony in a café on Place de l'Europe, because rue de Madrid was somehow gloomy and deserted, locked between two long rows of dreary buildings of the same color and height. Sometime later Karlo would learn who Charles Munch was, but that is not crucial to this story. Several times, perhaps in the moments when he was trying to stifle the sudden attacks of his inner storms, Karlo would say, *While Matačić was strolling untroubled through the ashes of civilization, while he was conducting in Hitler's Reich, Munch did not leave France*, It's wartime and I shall not set foot on German soil, *that's what Munch used to say, he who had previously played and conducted in Leipzig, Cologne, everywhere*, Karlo said. *And I learned*, Karlo said many years later, *that at that time Munch refused to include the works of contemporary German composers in his repertoire. And he protected the non-Aryan members of his orchestra. And helped members of the Resistance Movement. Unlike Henri Rabaud, director of the conservatoire, who as early as 1941 compiled a list for Vichy France of the detailed racial characteristics of all the students.* At that time, of course, I knew nothing more detailed about Frida Landsberg.

She was beautiful, Marisa would say, *we were all in love with her. In the evening we would sit in the Latin Quarter, sometimes on the pavement, more rarely in a café, she would play, I would sing, then Karlo would steal her from us and she would leave an emptiness. And an uncomfortable silence.* It was only many years later, after that episode with Hitler's medal in Leila's parents' house, that I began to do some research. And to call to mind Marisa's accounts, little sparks of information, snippets, fragments in her memory of a faded time or perhaps of a time so festive and relaxed that it had to be hidden from reality, preserved in special little jewelry boxes, in little boxes opened just once—before death. Marisa was no more, and Karlo was no more, and Rudolf's memory in that regard, amorous, Parisian, seemed to lie even more deeply buried in him, hidden under deep layers of political abominations, intrigue and insinuation, which he spent his entire life trying to clear up. There was no one I could ask. As long as the actors in these two love stories were alive, and I still very young, I spent my summers with my Uncle Karlo, I played water polo, and in the evenings at the pool either briscola or chess. Sometimes, largely in fun, Marisa and Rudolf would mention Karlo's former infatuation, his absolute intoxication with Frida Landsberg, then, in Paris in 1939, never mentioning that the "divine Frida" had found Charles Munch, that she had arranged an audition possibly to continue her studies at that famous conservatoire, nor why her liaison with Karlo was broken off, because perhaps they did not know, or perhaps there was no truth, truth had been transformed into possibility, into hope, or because it was so terrible and incomprehensible that it had become unsayable. Essentially, back then in July 1939, in Paris two love stories from my family pulsated, not to go into details now, love is love, touches, whispers, embraces, smiles and glances often obtuse to the onlooker, and all that in a city whose magnificent beauty (because lovers see only that), squares and parks, water, whose breath enslaves reason and common sense.

As the day of their return to Split approached, Karlo said to his sister, *Let Rudolf go back with you, I'm going to Riga.*

From Paris, in 1939, Marisa brought back a copy of *Vogue* for her mother, my grandmother Ana, and, before going to Zagreb in 1941, Ana would use it to sew glamorous outfits for the Split beauties, for daytime and evening outings, and later, on the Riva, some of these outfits worn by merry "Italian girls," often in the company of Fascist officers and soldiers, would be sprayed with hydrochloric acid by "red" passersby, while some of Ana's other outfits would end up in chests in the attics of family houses as mementos of a past age, because the women of Split would exchange them for military uniforms of heavy cloth, with a partisan cap on their heads.

On May 31, 1939, Germany signed a nonaggression pact with Latvia and Estonia. On November 5 of the same year, in Warsaw, Hitler organized a Victory Parade, and that same day the Soviet Union signed a secret Treaty of Mutual Assistance with Latvia (it signed an identical agreement with Estonia a week later, and with Lithuania a week after that). According to this bilateral agreement, the Soviet Union had the right to locate its military bases throughout those then independent Baltic countries, particularly along their coasts. Anxious, the altruistically benign Soviet Union was preparing to "defend" three weak and unprotected little states from a potential attack by Nazi Germany. In fact, in June 1940, Lithuania, Estonia and Latvia, with military marches and brass bands, with the smiles of high functionaries, but also their secret agents, and with the general waving of little paper flags by the people, ceremonially and officially handed their freedom to the Soviet Union, as one might say, be my guest, only for all three to fall later without a murmur. The Soviet Union swallowed the Baltic states. Twenty-two years of Latvian independence were swept away on the wind, its language sank, slunk off into the crannies of consciousness and the subconscious, the frontiers fractured and the country stretched away out of sight; people scattered, fields were appropriated, houses seized, livestock became everyone's and no one's, the NKVD, later the KGB, determined who would go where, when and how. Cattle trucks waited on the secondary tracks of country railway stations. The gulags acquired new residents. The Soviet authorities did not waste time. Before the German invasion, which would happen a year later, in 1941, the Soviet government arrested some 28,000 people in that little country of barely two million inhabitants, more precisely—today we know—27,586 people, without explanation, without trial, and the majority of them were deported to the distant frozen north because of alleged cooperation with the German Army, while 945 individuals were shot on the spot. Those who were then shot, were shot, they disappeared, full stop. If it is of any comfort, of those who were deported at that time, some survived and returned, whereas had they remained in Latvia they would not have returned. If they held out in those gulags until Stalin's death in 1953, there were those who still had time for life, regardless of the fact that that life was lousy—it was life. There was time for new loves, Soviet ones, granted, but love is love, there was time for studying, for sailing, for swimming, there was time for dancing in the rain, there was time for chess, oh, yes, for singing, for violins and croquettes, for traveling, short journeys within the Union, but still, there was time for giving, for dreaming, and even for escape. All that, that future time, Nazi Germany crushed for many in Latvia, in the blink of an eye, in two or three days.

On July 10, 1941, the German armed forces occupied Latvia and it became part of the *Reichskommissariat Ostland*. Those who opposed the German occupation, and those who collaborated with the Soviets, received a bullet in the brow (or the back of the head), or in the best case were shoved into concentration camps. According to Hitler's decree a civil occupying regime was formed, with Latvian paramilitary formations and with Latvian auxiliary police divided into special—Latvian—police battalions and those Latvians, whether by command or voluntarily, zealously embarked on hunting down and killing their former fellow citizens—Jews, Roma and communists—according to the principle of every man for himself. In fact those Latvians were then a bit, as it were, confused—they had had enough of the Soviets and their communism—and calculated that this SS and the Wehrmacht could not be worse than communism, could they? So the German soldiers were greeted by various people, and by beautiful women walking through town, as on another occasion, on April 10, 1941, in Zagreb, except that in Zagreb that took place with a lot more euphoria, with rapture and joy, and in large numbers, although at that time Zagreb was a smaller town than Riga.

A year earlier, in 1940, my uncle Karlo Osterman, returning from Riga, watched the same thing, the entry of the Nazis into Paris—and wept.

The German civil administration was nominally under the competence of the Ministry of the Reich for the Occupied Eastern Territories (*Reichsministerium für die besetzten Ostgebiete*) under the Nazi ideologue Alfred Rosenberg, some say the son of a wealthy trader, others maintain he was the son of a cobbler from Latvia, that Estonian-German born in 1893 in Reval, today's Tallinn, studied architecture in Riga and Moscow, where he gained his doctorate; a philosopher and ideologue of Nazism, the author of theories about race and the persecution of the Jews, fierce opponent of "degenerate" modern art, which he purloined throughout the whole Baltic region and beyond, and sent to Germany, first for himself, then for the Reich, for Hitler's future museum and the musical academy in Linz, for unlike Adolf, Alfred Rosenberg was a man of undoubted artistic talent, but Alfred Rosenberg was also well read, he read Goethe and Balzac, liked art, all art, and so also music, and so in the course of his plunder, his theft, he did not neglect musical instruments, especially violins (for they were easier to transport, as his private booty). That was the very Rosenberg whose mouth smelled, the Rosenberg of baneful breath, once a friend of the debauched pedophile Röhm (whose life Hitler at first spared, *as long as he didn't touch young men and boys*, and then had callously murdered in the Night of the Long Knives, along with another thousand homosexuals, with the explanation that Aryans could not be gay, but in fact because he didn't care for his politics), that Rosenberg, the Führer's delegate, obsessed with the Protocols of the Elders of Zion, who founded the Institute for Researching the Jewish Question, which he affectionately called "Höhe Schule," and into whose library poured books, documents and manuscripts stolen from literally all the countries of occupied Europe. In document 1015-B-PS there is a detailed list of more than twenty-one thousand stolen works of art, and document 188 describes the plunder of more than seventy-one thousand apartments throughout France, Belgium, Holland, Luxembourg, Denmark, Norway (here Rosenberg was helped by his friend Quisling), and then the occupied eastern territories, Estonia, Latvia and Lithuania, and in Hungary and Greece. This is the writer and engineer Rosenberg who adored wearing lilac shirts with a red tie, who in July 1941 had his photograph taken with a young Ukrainian married couple in national dress, whom the young married couple presented with flowers and a cake, and soon afterward they were murdered.

In Spandau and later in the Nuremberg prison, Alfred Rosenberg wrote, on official Third Reich notepaper, his prison diary, memoirs which served as evidence at his trial, while in his defense

Alfred Rosenberg affirmed that he had absolutely no idea what the Holocaust was, *He'd never heard of it,* he said, and then, after Alfred Rosenberg had been executed by hanging in 1946, that diary magically disappeared, but since nothing ever disappears forever, but returns in an altered form or just as it was, sometimes more horrific, sometimes watered down, so too this diary of Alfred Rosenberg's reappeared, after seventy years, it raised its head, woke up, crawled toward the present, climbed onto the stage of history, and in the name of its creator who, in 1946, with a black hood over his head, fell into the "repository" of the gallows, crowed *Here I am again!* Out of that opus of enviable literacy with lyrical passages of restrained sentiment, out of that diary found in 2013, fell the copy of a small yellowed note, a copy of the confirmation of the confiscation of a violin made by Maestro Jean-Baptiste Vuillaume in the possession of a certain F. Landsberg, born in Riga on April 13, 1920, once resident at 99 Stabu iela, but in October 1941 removed to the suburbs, to Maskavas iela. Of course, immediately after the establishment of the SS government in Latvia, Alfred Rosenberg founded *Sonderstab Musik* (A Special Combat Office for Music"), charged with the task of "collecting" musical instruments and sheet music and sending them posthaste to Berlin, but some minor actions, such as this confiscation of the violin belonging to a certain F. Landsberg, he undertook himself. In the hours he spent philosophizing about the modalities of creating a pure Aryan race, in the peace of his elegantly furnished Berlin apartment, whose walls were adorned with degenerate oil paintings, and the rooms with two pianos, one Estonia and one fairly indifferent J. Becker—which his twelve-year-old blonde angel, his Irene, could practice on—there were also several cellos, the makes of which are not listed, and a dozen violins (there are lists of those, but I don't feel like reeling them off now), listening to Borodin and Rimski-Korsakov, sipping chamomile tea, gazing with longing at his insufficiently studied favorite writers, Dostoevsky, Tolstoy and Nietzsche, Alfred Rosenberg was overcome for a moment, only for a moment, by a faint, vague nostalgia, like a little snake, it slid down under his collar and started crawling over his bare chest. A flash—Paris, a little table in Café de la Rotonde, on the corner of Boulevard Raspail and Montparnasse, when over an unsweetened coffee and two brioches he was waiting for his ballerina Hilda; a flash—Riga and its narrow cobbled lanes, a cramped student's room; a flash—Reval, out of which, as from deep black water, faces emerge, dead faces, immobile, gray, and living faces, the smiling faces of his everyday life. And while in 1942 this well-groomed and tranquil fifty-year-old stroked the violin on his lap that had belonged to F. Landsberg, and in the core of which was hidden a label with the name of its creator, Alfred Rosenberg heard himself asking, who was he asking? *Did I have to leave my native land in order to acquire a homeland? My memories are weightless, my memories are empty.* Then he looked again at the beautiful instrument in his lap, smiled, and a quiet joy came over him. *It's good,* he said. *The job is done.*

But it was not good. Before Alfred Rosenberg, before the soldiers of the Wehrmacht, as I've said, the soldiers of the Soviet Union came into Latvia.

Jean-Baptiste Vuillaume was an excellent craftsman, he made more than three thousand instruments, and he created violins in the style of Stradivarius and Guarneri, as well as perfect copies of them. But, Frida Landsberg knew. Back then, in Paris, in the summer of 1939, Frida would sometimes let her violin slip from her hand, but never from her sight, so when Marisa, after she had first eaten the cheap *potage du jour* with Karlo, Rudolf and Frida, and for dessert the famous Chantilly cream in the always crowded Chartier in Montmartre (7 rue du Faubourg), when Marisa asked her, *Is your violin valuable?* Frida said, *No, it's just a good imitation, with an excellent sound.*

Rudolf returned to Belgrade to study, and during the March demonstrations in 1941 he was arrested and beaten up in prison by the police agent Kosmajac, after which he went to Split and set about organizing a rebellion in Istria. In August 1940, Karlo returned to Split from Riga, half-mad. Marisa, who had joined the Split organization of the League of Communist Youth of Yugoslavia as early as June 1941, went with her family to Zagreb, registered to study medicine, plunged into the underground, but the tracker dogs caught her, in the Ustasha prison at 9 Ulica Franje Račkog she was tortured by the investigator Kamber, she was extracted from prison by her other brother, then, according to unverified stories, a Home Guard university employee or member of the University Ustasha Command, as it was already called then, who, again according to the principle of hearsay, used to come to lectures in uniform, the Ustasha one, or perhaps she was saved by an "ustasha," communist youth guard, I don't know.

In 2006 or 2007, I no longer remember which, at the funeral of my cousin Clara, the one who died of glioblastoma, while, over her open grave, the priest performed a playlet, which the audience, their faces long like the chorus in an ancient drama, accompanied with the singsong refrain, *Culpa, mea culpa*, I was approached by an older woman who told me in a whisper, *In 1942, my brother was a Zagreb student connected with the National Liberation Army. He was with your mother in an Ustasha prison, and your uncle and Clara's uncle, the engineer Bruno, belonged to the University Ustasha Command and used to come to lectures in uniform.* So, at funerals you learn all kinds of things. One corpse is laid to rest in the earth, another climbs out.

In the 1960s no one in my family mentioned the wartime and postwar past of Uncle Bruno, later an internationally known scientist, an expert in the biological protection of agricultural and forest cultures, one of the founders of the postwar Agriculture and Forestry Faculty in Sarajevo, a member of the Academy of Science and Arts of Bosnia and Herzegovina, that Uncle Bruno who succeeded in curing his carcinoma of the testis, while metastases crawled through the body of my mother, his sister Marisa, constricting and devouring her to extinction. How come, I wondered, only too late, too late, how come Uncle Bruno was in Sarajevo in 1946, given that my family, on either Marisa's or Rudolf's side, had no connection whatever with Bosnia and Herzegovina.

Grandma Ana had told me that in 1941 Bruno had a fiancée, Judita, who was studying philosophy, that Judita was a Jew and that, through his connections, which I suppose today were Ustasha connections, Bruno secretly moved Judita to Trieste, where all trace of her was lost. No one in our family ever mentioned Judita again.

Recently, an Ustasha pass fell out of my benign notes of that time, from which the name of the bearer had been cut off. Why was this pass amputated? Who did it? Why did I have that pass and to whom did it refer? Did that pass have any connection with Bruno's getting Judita to Italy? I haven't any answers, and I no longer have anyone to ask.

Does that upset me?

No.

Did Bruno collaborate with the Ustasha? I asked my then 92-year-old father, now that it was already too late. My father said nothing, I asked him again, my father said, *Many people collaborated.*

Why did he go to Sarajevo?

I don't remember, said my father.

What happened to Bruno's fiancée Judita? I asked my then 92-year-old father, now that it was already too late.

Who's Judita? said my father.

I read somewhere that wars are an orgy of forgetting. The twentieth century archived vast catacombs, subways of data in which the researcher gets lost and in the end abandons the search, catacombs into which ever fewer people go, buried—forgotten. The twentieth century, the century of great spring cleaning which ended with cleansing; the twentieth century, the century of cleansing, the century of erasure. Didn't Pliny write somewhere that nothing about us is as fragile as memory, that dubious ability that a person constructs and deconstructs? Whom can I ask now? How can I resolve this family puzzle?

Does it matter to me now?

No. It's just interesting.

Four years passed, laden with dreams, deaths, betrayals, murders, political intrigues, poverty and illnesses, four years after which one day on a scrap of newspaper a message from Rudolf arrived in Zagreb, Ulica Medvedgradska: *If you are still with us, get in touch.* Grandma Ana was making a wedding skirt with wide shoulder straps for Marisa out of my grandfather's, the by-now-late Max Osterman's gray, shabby woolen trousers, on her old Singer (there it is, at Ada's), and turning the collar on a worn-out shirt, which she had bleached, for Rudolf. A new life was beginning.

Why did Karlo Osterman come back from Riga in 1940 half-mad? No one in our family ever spoke about that episode from his life, probably no one knew anything, if they did know, it was a fairly limited knowledge. In any case, after the war Karlo Osterman established one family, then divorced, then he established a second family, while I played water polo, read philosophy, mercilessly expended my youth and was sufficiently uninterested not to ask. But, after that nocturnal stress that occurred to me forty years ago in the dark Bavarian forest in the house of the Latvian Mazais family, I began to compose a picture, bit by bit, not exactly with dedication, I had my own life, and many parts of the puzzle were missing, in fact my jigsaw was full of holes, so that I could not "round off" the figure of Uncle Karlo, let alone that of Frida Landsberg, and so not their truth either, the way stupid written and unwritten literary laws demand. Am I "rounded," existentially and artistically, intimately and publicly? Who is ever and anywhere rounded, and is it necessary to be "complete" and rounded in order to exist—to live—in a complete and rounded way? Unbelievable idiocies.

When I began to look into it, of the older Ostermans, only my grandmother Ana was still alive. Karlo died when I was not yet twenty, my other uncle lived far away, then Marisa died, and Rudolf hadn't a clue about any of it, he barely remembered Paris in 1939, its image having been clouded by the approaching war. After she had buried two of her children (Karlo and Marisa) in the space of a few years, Grandma Ana lived with me for two spells, dejected and impossible, first after Karlo's death, before our parents were in the earth, and then after Marisa's, when she was no longer at home, when my father had married again.

After Karlo:

She woke early, later she realized there was no need, so she woke increasingly late. She made coffee, washed and went back to bed. She left the bath dirty, because, spherical as she was, she could not bend over the edge. *You fix the bath*, she would say, *I'll make you stuffed squid*. She followed me around, she accompanied me through the apartment, talking the whole time. She had a strong voice, piercing, her sorrow notwithstanding. To start with, she drank coffee with real French cognac, the brand wasn't important, then she moved on to coffee with local brandy. Then she developed a mild jaundice, so didn't drink anything, not even wine with water. She ate a lot of soft cheese, the fattiest one, from Srijem, along with dollops of yoghurt with a soft roll crumbled into it, because of her teeth. She couldn't chew very well, she mostly sucked her food, mashing it against her palate. I don't know why, she had perfectly decent false teeth, which gave her a natural smile. *My body needs calcium*, she would say. Then she'd launch into the story of her impoverished childhood, of her mother who remarried and died young, of her miserly aunt with whom she later lived, of having to muck out the donkey and eat stale bread, always the same, as though I were listening to the fairy tale of Cinderella.

She put carrot into everything she cooked, and sometimes sugar as well, so her dishes were orange and sweet, and greasy, she used an unimaginable amount of oil. Neither she nor I needed those lunches, but she had to amuse herself with something, so she cooked, crocheted, and sometimes she would sew, small things, little cushions.

She had attended an Italian school. She read *Grazia*, *Grazia* was fashionable at that time, then she would relate the international gossip in great detail. She had been to America, seen the Empire State Building and Niagara Falls. She had been in Egypt, in Luxor and at the Aswan Dam, from where she had brought back little models with the marble head of Nefertiti, which she later gave to the doctors. But she did keep one head. *Put this model on my grave*, she said. We put the model on her grave and later someone stole it, of course, because we had just put it there, we hadn't secured it.

Grandma Ana had bought that grave when Max Osterman died back in 1944. *Everything I have, including that grave, has been made by my hands, my needles and my ten fingers,* she would say. It's a nice grave, in the middle of Mirogoj Cemetery in Zagreb, 128-II-297, with a respectable black marble slab, an elegant and serious grave, which is no longer ours, which was stolen by Magda from Medvedščak.

When my grandfather, the barber, wigmaker and anarchist Max Osterman died in Zagreb in 1944, Grandma Ana sold his wigs. *So they don't fray, so that moths don't nest in them,* but she kept some of his books, which later I took. For example Hamsun's *Hunger*, bound in white leather.

Ana's other son, the one who went on living for a long time, studied peacefully and obediently during the time of the Independent State of Croatia, nothing could thwart him, no kind of war, nothing could deter him from his scientific path. He was the one who buggered up the business with the grave on Mirogoj.

If I got angry, Grandma Ana would say, *Holy Mary, il diavolo is in your corpo.* She often called on the Holy Mary, although she quarreled constantly with the Church. The older she was, the less she believed, *Oh, those priests, they just pull the wool over your eyes,* she would say, then she'd start enumerating the illegitimate children of well-known priests and lawyers who strolled around Split and saying who resembled whom *like two peas in a pod,* and she'd end every tirade with *If God lies, genes don't.* Then she'd move on to Paganini, she adored Paganini. He also had the *diavolo* in his *corpo.*

Paganini drove his audience wild. He could break three strings on his violin and play on only one. He was as capricious as the capricci *he composed. He did* pizzicato *now with his left hand, now with his right. A great gambler and hothead. And do you know why* il Ponte dei sospiri *is called* il Ponte dei sospiri, *do you know what that means? Answer me!*

She would say that there's also a *Ponte degli Schiavoni*, she mentioned forests chopped down in the time of the Venetian Republic, then she would give me recipes for *brodetto*, for *cremeschnitte*, for black risotto, for floating islands, for boletus mushrooms with cream *Write it down*, she commanded, *it'll come in handy*. When a new woman came into my life, she would sit her down opposite herself and interrogate her for hours, then she'd say: Take care, *tutto ti prometto finché te lo metto*, and when we were alone, she would whisper to me, as if to a confidante, *She hadn't washed her hair*, or *Her skirt is badly made*, or *She has a forced smile, watch out*.

Then there was a phase when she cried the whole time. *Oh, my son, what a life*, she'd whimper, although I wasn't her son. Her hands were as soft as feather pillows, her fingers like jam rolls, and between those fingers she would squeeze her handkerchief, rolled into a ball, wet and slobbery, she never wiped her eyes with it, only her nose. The lenses of her glasses were cloudy and greasy. She rubbed antirheumatic creams into herself and smelled of menthol, then with those greasy hands she'd prop herself against the walls, leaving marks everywhere.

She had unreasonably white skin. White and smooth, she had an excess of skin without any fuzz.

As long as her son Karlo and daughter Marisa were alive, Grandma Ana didn't wear black, she had dresses for going out and a suit of pure silk, blue. She had lilac and green shantung blouses. Gray skirts of thin material. On the left side of her chest, she wore a white-gold brooch with diamonds. Later, when she moved in with me, she waddled through the rooms in a thick, black, synthetic-wool jumper with a lot of little bobbles like burrs. Her wardrobe seemed to have vanished into thin air. What was left were on the whole nightdresses, winter ones—white, light-blue and pink, made of fustian—which she called *baroque*, and summer ones—poplin, edged with lace. She used to relate TV programs to me, especially political and cultural ones. She liked Peter Brook, she followed football, she supported Hajduk Split.

On the anniversary of the death of her son, my Uncle Karlo, she went to the hairdresser, for the first time in twelve months. She had a perm, then she cried. I said, *It suits you, you look tidy*, she went to the bathroom, in front of the mirror she turned her head a bit to the right, a bit to the left, then she announced, *Yes, I'm completely different.*

She was forever writing to someone and she received replies to those letters of hers. She had a Pelikan pen, with thin green and black stripes. One day she said, *Teach me Cyrillic, it annoys me that I don't know it.* She was seventy.

Two summers passed. Then she declared, *I'm myself again now, I'm going home.*

Then my mother's illness and my mother's death happened. Grandma Ana was with us again for a while, with me and Ada, then she went back to Ulica Medvedgradska in Zagreb, but she was never herself again.

It was raining again when we buried Ana. There was mud again, Mirogoj Cemetery mud this time, in Zagreb, not the New Cemetery mud, in Belgrade. There was barely anyone there, the relatives had thinned out. There was just one son left, Bruno, he came. His wife came too, the blonde, blue-eyed Hilda, the sister of Magda from Medvedščak, both half-German or half-Czech, it doesn't matter which. (Neither Bruno nor Hilda is with us now, but Magda still is.) Magda didn't come, why should she? The children of Ana's still-living son Bruno didn't come either. We came, the children of Ana's dead children. The four of us. Hilda organized everything. She gave Ana's furniture to the Red Cross, Hilda arranged the letters written to Ana by her dead children and her living grandchildren in piles and gave them to those who were present, together with postcards. That was all. Someone bought

Ana's apartment and settled in. We dispersed. We spread out through various towns of the former Yugoslavia.

It was a nice apartment, Grandma Ana's, not comfortable, in an unusual building. Strange people lived there, very poor and orderly. They had white linen curtains in their kitchens, and on the walls above their large, wood-burning ranges were pinned cloths with blue or red embroidered sentences such as *Housewife, to gossip less you must learn, so your dinner doesn't burn*, with which the housewives washed and cleaned things or prepared meals. Some apartments had tiled stoves, some didn't. No one in the building had a bathroom, just a toilet. The building had three stories and an attic and nice wooden shutters. On each floor there were two two-room apartments, and in the attic six bedsitters accessed via a kind of dark concrete platform. The rooms in the attic had no water, they had low ceilings and dual-purpose furniture with at least two sofas. There was a tap in the hall over a square white enamel washbasin. The building smelled of *mlinci* and pork fat. It had a circular stone staircase and woodsheds in the communal courtyard, it was enclosed by a wrought iron fence. At the front, beside the entrance, there was a shop selling colonial goods, with silk sweets in tall jars. Mad Emilija lived on the second floor, she sat on her balcony because it was the only apartment that had a balcony facing the street, the other balconies were on the inside, facing the woodsheds and nobody sat on them, they were very small. So, on the semicircular balcony on the street side sat mad Emilija, muttering and pointing at the passersby below. Her feet were wrapped in dirty rags, she was all dirty, disheveled and toothless, but not old, in fact she was young, except that wasn't obvious. Another person living in the building was someone who later became a prostitute, we had gone to the same school. There was also a woman whose son died at roughly the same time as Ana's, so she and Ana mourned together. Later they quarreled and stopped speaking to each other. Mrs. Herman lived in the attic. She had a good-looking husband who collected alarm clocks in that little attic room and who was the train dispatcher with five beautiful railway caps, dark blue. Their little room tick-tocked from all directions, and the window was small, very small. Whenever I came to Zagreb from Belgrade, I went to Ana's grave. Twenty-five years passed. Now I'm in Croatia, I don't need to visit the past, not old buildings, or cemeteries.

I'd sometimes go to a Zagreb funeral, if I had to. Then I'd call on Ana. In the end, I'd just go to that building. Ulica Medvedgradska is completely different nowadays, there are new buildings, there are luxurious shops, Medvedgradska looks like an old lady with ten face lifts, all pulled in and stretched, sick inside. There are no children outside. Ana's apartment has a bathroom now, tiled all over. The range has been destroyed. They've widened the hall. There's a lot of bulky furniture. All expensive and vulgar.

Only one of the former residents is still there, Mrs. Herman, up in the attic, alone. Now she has a telephone. We sat for three hours, we drank five very sweet coffees out of very small cups, with a pattern of women in maroon crinolines strolling through gardens and smelling roses, followed by men in evening dress. Then Mrs. Herman said, *She died in Vrapče Asylum.*

We had believed that she died in hospital, of heart problems, of pneumonia, that's what we were told. That's what we had believed for twenty-five years.

Then Mrs. Herman said, *They took her away by force. She didn't want to go. She pleaded, "Don't, don't."*

Those women on the cups kept on calmly strolling through the scented gardens. There were no clocks anywhere. It seemed that Mrs. Herman had put them away, like the railway caps, they weren't there anymore either.

Then Mrs. Herman said, *Bruno got in touch then. He instructed them,* Take her away. *They shouldn't have taken her, she was in her right mind.*

I thanked Mrs. Herman. It was stupid, but I did. Mrs. Herman gave me her telephone number, I've got it here. *Give me a call from time to time,* she said.

I went to Mirogoj Cemetery, to the office. *To settle the bills, to pay for the grave,* I said. They told me there was no need, that it was no longer the grave of Ana Osterman, but that of Magda from Medvedščak. They said, *Madame Magda pays everything on time.*

I went to the court. They gave me the transcript and the judgment. They were very pleasant. The corridors were crammed with clients, but they took me out of order, which was incomprehensible. They photocopied everything for me, for free.

In the street I studied the papers. The trams had stopped, everything had stopped. The pedestrians had stopped and the noises had stopped. The papers were from the inheritance hearing, somewhat belated, by twenty-five years. Ana's son Bruno, the one who had been alive until two years ago, had given Ana's grave to Magda, he had not called us. No one could have called us because Magda had declared that we did not exist. Magda had declared that Marisa, my mother and Ada's, had never had children, so we had not been born. She did admit that Ana's other son, Karlo, had been born, but his daughters had not been born; one of Karlo's daughters, Clara, worked here in the hospital; she died of glioblastoma. The other is a lawyer and is alive.

So, I said to Clara while she was still alive, when we were eating cakes once in that café with gray armchairs, *we don't exist.*

When my mother Marisa died, the send-off, as some like to call it, was large, a lot of people pushed their way into the chapel of the crematorium at Belgrade New Cemetery and threw themselves onto our chests and spattered us with sticky spit mixed with tears, while we just stood there. In fact, when the body is burned, it's better to say leave-taking than cortège, because the deceased is not carried anywhere; the chapel is usually right beside the crematorium, a few meters away. When you say send-off, it's as though the person is going on a journey from which they will return, and a crowd of people is standing on the platform, waving, smiling, sending kisses and waving.

With a cremation, there are no long processions meandering through the paths of the graveyard, swaying with the whispers of acquaintances from whom a little laugh or a little sob occasionally escapes, above whom fear and unease hover, there is no solemn walking through the city of the dead in which around every corner wait engraved shadows, calling. The speeches end, and now ever more frequently that awful church chanting, that collective praying in which the priests call out the name of the deceased as though they were old acquaintances, which of course has nothing to do with common sense, when the visitors, as though catatonic, repeat *Mea culpa, mea culpa,* that hideous amateur performance with elements of Greek tragedy and vaudeville comes to an end and the coffin just sinks, and the assembled don't know what to do with themselves.

But, when we came for the ashes, we were alone, our father, Ada and I. Torrential rain was falling, we waited in the cemetery office for them to bring us Marisa and watched through the window as the graveyard was submerged before our eyes. Grandma Ana didn't come. She sat beside our mother's bed, eerily empty, stroking the pillow. After that, Grandma Ana became ever smaller, ever rounder and ever blacker. She was transformed into a little velvet ball that rolled through the apartment, unable to rebound. Just occasionally, as though she were all made of ashy down, Grandma Ana would rise barely perceptibly off the ground, then she would softly land again and fall without a sound. Like a little bird, she would try to chirp, and a tiny jerky whisper would emerge from her, a general huskiness, a cracking, internal and external. We were afraid that she would go missing somewhere, under the carpet, behind a door, that we would step on her or squash her, she had shrunk so much. Then one day, she said, *I'm going home* and left.

It was only she, only my grandmother Ana who, quite by chance, if there is such a thing, offered me a little proof of Karlo's amorous adventure on the axis Split–Paris–Riga–Split–Riga–Split, on the basis of which I was able to construct this nonconstructable story.

Even though after my flight from that Bavarian village my affair with Leila Mazais was definitively ended, Leila got in touch looking for an explanation, but I was not inclined to elaborate on my discovery, because I had not yet discovered anything. Then, that year when Grandma Ana went back to her Ulica Medvedgradska for the second time, but before they took her away to Vrapče Asylum, Leila asked me to meet her at Pleso Airport and help her find accommodation on one of the Adriatic islands. We went together to Grandma Ana. *Your girl says that she comes from Riga, Karlo was in Riga*, said Grandma Ana, *long ago, just before the war. I've got two of his letters to us in Split and one of Frida's to him here, sent to Zagreb. I'll tell you sometime, I don't feel like it now.*

She gave me the letters, I went back to Belgrade and I never saw her again. She died that winter. In fucking Vrapče. Alone.

From Karlo's meager letters and that one of Frida's I learned little. I learned that at the end of June 1940, Karlo returned to Split, then in the summer of 1941 he traveled to Riga again, but soon came back, definitively, to Yugoslavia. How he made his way through war-torn Europe I don't know, maybe by train, the trains were running efficiently, except that their timetables were adapted to the passengers, of whom there were so many that they brought in cattle trucks for people, in addition to passenger carriages. Karlo was a journalist and perhaps that legitimation gave him some sort of protection, but also his Saxon surname, which probably had a soothing effect on the police of the Third Reich. Although he did not speak German, Karlo spoke French and Italian, which was interesting, but not essential. In short:

It seems that none of the Landsbergs survived the war. That fact significantly impeded my research, not to say that my delving into the small, encapsulated past of a family that was altogether remote from me became an impossible, almost senseless undertaking. It was seventy years and more since that family broke away, like an independently hovering body, detached itself from the earth and soared to the heavens, where it is now floating, roaming, and continues to emit soft, ever-softer wailing, lamentation, dirges like the plucked strings of a violin. But that the story of Frida Landsberg is not finished and that it draws into itself other stories, contemporary stories with deep roots, which, as some historians like to say, branch out like capillaries, that is, their veins weave a network underground, that I know, that I see, that I have discovered in the course of my relationship with Leila. Now I am making connections, I rummage through my sunken memories, my memories blurred by oblivion, my memories, which are hostages to time, coated in mold, my rejected memories, and I summon up encounters, fragments of conversation, passing faces, I seek links, a reason for my fury with Leila. Around me is chaos, within me confusion.

The building at 99 Stabu iela is a fine white or gray five-story house in the art nouveau style in the center of Riga, not far from its old heart. Today it is a private hotel, but then the Landsbergs lived on the fourth floor, Frida's father Benzon and mother Sonja, née Miller, they ran a small shoe factory, and had a shoe shop in the center of town. Latvia has a tradition of manufacturing shoes. I discovered that in 1939 there were eighty-four factories employing fourteen hundred workers. They produced mainly rubber footwear. When the Soviets occupied Latvia for the first time in June 1940, they nationalized Benzon Landsberg's factory, although he continued to work there—only at one of the machines. His shoe shop was also taken from him, the Russians changed its name, its range and its personnel. Frida was still studying at the conservatoire, Karlo sent "Letters from Riga" to the Split local newspaper, which were not published because in 1940, for Split and generally for Europe, there were more important topics; Hitler was marching on Paris, who could be bothered with some Latvia or other, and Poland was more and more in the news.

So, in June 1940, Soviet tanks entered Riga. Life was not immediately turned upside down. During all wars, always and everywhere, people build niches, magic burrows in which they place their everyday lives, their mirages, their illusions of normality, in order to survive. So, Karlo Osterman watches people disappear. Karlo Osterman is horrified, oh, yes, but these arrests, these disappearances, surely they have an explanation, an acceptable explanation, Karlo Osterman consoles himself, well, he's only twenty-two.

Then friends of the Landsberg family vanish, Karlo Osterman had met some of them, he had gone to exhibitions with some of them, he had played chess with some. A frequent guest in the Landsbergs' apartment at the time was the well-known chess player Kārlis Ozols, who would be mentioned—how amazing—back then in the 1970s in that German dump, by Leila's father, except that it took me forty years to drag that encounter back into my memory and place it somewhere. *Kārlis Ozols was a first-class chess player and a great patriot*, that's roughly what Arvīds Mazais said, *We met in 1946 in a displaced persons' camp in Germany*, he said. And Leila added something along the lines of *He was tall and thin, he had a stoop and a shrill voice*. Of course, I knew about the chess master Kārlis Ozols even then, I knew that he had represented Latvia at Olympiads in Munich in 1936 and in Stockholm in 1937, and that in 1958 he became the chess champion of Australia. I knew that much and it was enough. Much bigger and younger names were shaking up the chess world, and Kārlis Ozols had lost his shine, if he ever had any, in fact I had quite lost sight of Kārlis Ozols. I'll come back to that fellow (in the name of textual structure, cyclical, as the critics would say).

In Riga, in 1940, lawyers, doctors, engineers and some of Frida's colleagues disappear, *They must have gone abroad, training,* said Frida, the Russians arrest around five thousand reputable citizens and who knows how many more "disreputable" ones and shove all those people into wagons. The trains are going to Siberia. Karlo Osterman watches as, from one day to the next, the station becomes increasingly crowded, at the station a dense, impenetrable silence reigns. Disquiet slips into Karlo Osterman's breast, and grows.

So, here are the Russians. The changes are swift, abrupt and remediless. The secret police trail many, including artists and writers. The censors have wide-open eyes, unblinking. The state regulates life, private life above all.

And the worst is yet to come.

When Frida Landsberg is transferred in October 1941, as it says on the little confirmation note that falls out of Rosenberg's diary, from 99 Stabu iela to the suburbs, to Maskavas iela, Moscow Street in other words, she is transferred in fact to a Jewish ghetto. I discover this from Frida's letter to Karlo which by some miracle, even if several months late, reaches 24 Ulica Medvedgradska, in Zagreb. Karlo is already working for the underground movement. Karlo Osterman and Frida Landsberg's love is arrested by history; it is kicked into a corner and on it is put a lock with no key. It is not known how long that love thrashes about, how much it twists and howls, kicking and beating its fists against the steel door of the prison, which has no one to open it. Some loves endure even when all that is left of them are tufts, chipped dreams, which rarely occur, and when they do, create chaos. A few days ago, I dreamed of Frida Landsberg, I embraced her and whispered into her neck, *You're killing me*, I feel her body, her cheek against my own. Then, in an instant, her long curly hair bursts into flame and Frida Landsberg burns up. Am I becoming the forty-years-dead Karlo Osterman?

At the beginning of 1940, one still eats well in Riga. Dairy products are first class, Karlo Osterman spreads warm, freshly baked bread with local butter, the cream is thick, the curd cheese better than that in Split, *jana* cheese with caraway is a real delicacy, a lot of smoked fish is eaten, and for a feast day Sonja Landsberg bakes *piragi*, bread filled with onion and bacon, and *klingeris*, bread with saffron and dried fruit. The beer is excellent, the wine mediocre.

Latvians are not loud. They don't shout in the street, they don't wave their arms about when they talk. When they're angry, they're restrained. They accept foreigners with caution until they get to know them, then they relax and embrace them. Their intimate relations are very intimate. In their intimate relations they touch each other constantly and like to use diminutives. It is not known how noisy, explosive Karlo Osterman gets on in that environment.

When Karlo Osterman arrives in Riga in 1939, culture is flourishing. He visits museums with Frida, goes to the Opera, to concerts, to exhibitions, he is delighted by the extravagant Kārlis Padegs, a painter and dandy who walks around Riga in patent-leather shoes, in a long black coat with a red scarf around his neck, with a black hat on his head, swirling a bamboo cane as he walks and whistles. Padegs hangs his canvases in cafés, in the street, in exhibitions at photographic salons and publicly shoots to pieces the hypocrisy of the scandalized bourgeoisie, in whose faces his urban homeless, cripples, prostitutes and alcoholics laugh. Padegs' paintings and his drawings, distortedly expressionist and figurative, full of refined contrasts, seem to prefigure the evil that was coming. Toward the end of his life, and he died at twenty-nine of advanced tuberculosis, in the spring of 1940, Padegs, a loner, became an embarrassment for the terrified Latvians, a thorn in their side, and if he hadn't died, someone would have tried to get rid of him. And so Padegs sinks into oblivion. Then in 1998 that oblivion miraculously disperses, removes its veil and after nearly sixty years here is Padegs again in museums in Latvia and abroad, personified in life-size statues and on memorial plaques on the buildings in which he lived. That's how it goes. Karlo Osterman didn't know what kind of funeral was arranged for Padegs in 1940, because he was getting ready to return to Split. For another month or two he listened to jazz in cellar bars with Frida's friends, and there was a lot of singing of traditional songs and dancing of traditional dances, there were big choirs, mass festivals, which didn't exactly enthrall Karlo Osterman, but he understood the sickness known as stoking up the national identity, watched that pathetic danse macabre that reinforces the inner orientation of all who are caught up in its ring dance, watched that steel fist with its combination of repressed aggression, violence and fascism, that hypertrophied growth of roots whose branches wrap themselves firmly around the homeland, faith and family. Caught in that trap, people believe, *Here, I exist, I am protected.* All that, those traditional dances, that traditional melody, those customs, all that swiftly sinks, and out of the putrid core of identity surface new identities, new monsters, first the Soviets', and then those of the Third Reich.

Before the coming of the Soviets, Latvia exported large quantities of agricultural products and timber, it was technologically advanced, it produced radios and mini-cameras; per capita numbers of registrations at universities were among the highest in the world. The first sound film was made, *Zvejnieka dēls* (*The Fisherman's Son*), which was hugely successful, and after which nothing significant in film was produced for a long time. Karlo went with Frida to the Splendid Palace cinema, built way back in 1923, and was stunned, he had never seen anything like it. Nor would he again. Behind the neobaroque façade there opened up a vast rococo interior with a painted ceiling and more than eight hundred seats. *We've walked into a dream, in two hours we'll walk out of it*, said Karlo to Frida. *Dreams are short-lived. And deceitful*, Frida whispered to him, as though foreseeing the dirty tricks being prepared for them by fickle History. In 1952, the Soviets renamed the cinema the Riga, so that it should fit at least somehow into communist reality, because that "palace," and "splendid" to boot, was a bit much, simply offensive for the little show-off that was Latvia. Today the cinema has risen from the dead and is once again called the Splendid Palace.

But, as early as the middle of 1940, the tramping of encroaching poverty can be heard, there is an odor of fear. Karlo Osterman senses a small yearning that runs through his body like a flock of colorful butterflies, which then fly out into the ever more somber Riga, because, whenever there is no one to hear him, he walks along the shore of the gray Baltic singing "My Split is far from me." But how much Split is changing, and how rapidly, Karlo Osterman cannot surmise. In his imagination, he visits the shops of his native city, including car showrooms, he leafs through film magazines, freshly shaved at his father's barbershop, drowsy, he goes to jazz evenings, looks at beautiful women, he calls in to some of the numerous bars for a glass of wine, plays a bit of briscola and the compulsory *sei-sette*, in cafés he drinks espresso, newly imported from Italy, his step is blithe and life is, ah, good.

Ethnic Germans abandon Latvia. In 1940, fifty-one thousand leave. When Karlo Osterman returns briefly in 1941, a further ten and a half thousand have gone. Many move to so-called Warthegau, to the parts of Poland that Nazi Germany annexed in 1939, many perish on the journey, others join SS military units, and they too perish.

Immediately before the German invasion of Latvia, in the summer of 1941, the Soviet deportations of Latvians to gulags are increasingly swift and massive. Total madness overcomes the secret police. Or more precisely, from June 13 to 14, the secret police arrest people hysterically, they escort them under guard to the railway stations and put them onto what are by then just emblematic cattle cars. With no court order, with no explanation, the secret police burst into apartments in the middle of the night and give their captives sixty minutes to pack the most essential items, the rest is confiscated by Mother Russia: land, livestock, factories, buildings, apartments, shops, savings deposits, cars, boats, jewelry, gold, people. Thus, 19,184 people—8,275 men, 7,168 women and 3,741 children under the age of sixteen—go off to labor camps in the Siberian backwoods, men to some, women to others. On the journey, 43 people die and 700 are shot on the spot, as they are arrested, so they have no chance of ever returning. Some, the survivors, reeducated, would surface some fifteen years later as wrecks, quiet and ill, harmless, that is to say useless. The aim of the NKVD had been to remove families whose members were in leading positions in state or local government, in the economy and in culture. Almost 1 percent of the population of Latvia was wiped out, and of the 126,000 Latvians who found themselves in the Soviet Union, 75,000 were arrested and sent to gulags, while 20,000 were shot.

In 1941, Karlo Osterman is in Split. Since the Soviet authorities had plundered everything from the little Landsberg family, taking their factory, shop, part of their apartment and their renown, they had become a nondescript family, so they were left in Riga. Perhaps it would have been better if they had been deported. Perhaps some of them would have come back. At least Frida.

On June 22, 1941, Nazi Germany attacked the USSR. The NKVD still had time in Latvia to organize the deportation of political prisoners, "enemies of the people," involved in "counterrevolutionary activities," and to condemn them without redress, for "not singing 'The Internationale' on May 1," for "singing traditional Latvian songs," for "exploitation of the working people," for "hiding in the woods," for "membership of a student organization," for "membership of a youth organization," because they were "policemen," because "in the Latvian Army they fought against the Bolsheviks," because "they were anti-Bolshevik," because they had "criticized the Communist Party," because they "ignored soldiers of the Red Army," because they "encouraged hatred toward other nations," because they "read the foreign press and spoke foreign languages," there is no end to the list, the list could have come out of the notebooks of Daniil Kharms, who would also be arrested by the NKVD a few months later, but in his native Petrograd, Leningrad at the time, and placed in a psychiatric hospital, where he soon died of starvation.

The NKVD also had time for arrests and pronouncing sentences without proof or trial, and for murders. Four days later, on June 26, 1941, a total of 3,600 prisoners left Latvia in special trains. Less than 1 percent came back. Those who were not shoved onto trains were tortured by the NKVD, then shot and thrown into shallow mass graves with twenty or thirty other corpses, which were hastily covered with soil and then relatively swiftly, and for propaganda purposes, uncovered by the Einsatzgruppe A (SS mobile unit, the paramilitary detachment of death). In the courtyard of the Central Prison in Riga, and in Baltezers, Rēzekne, Ulbroka, on the aerodrome in Krustpils, in Babīte, Dreilini, Stopini, corpses lay around everywhere, bodies with their skulls shot through, arms tied with wire, maimed, disfigured, their teeth knocked out, their eyes gouged out, some recognizable, others not. The Red Army retreated from the Baltic, and in the NKVD prisons they left a multitude of instruments of torture, those for breaking bones, for crushing testicles, for piercing the soles of the feet and pulling out nails and all kinds of electrical apparatus. Up to the present day, many of those corpses found in the graves have remained nameless. People without a past, nonexistent people.

In 1912, a magnificent Secessionist residential building was erected on the corner of Brīvības and Stabu streets, with shops on the ground floor which did not become shops until the end of the twentieth century. It was first used by the Latvian pre-war Ministry of Internal Affairs, and then in 1940 by the Soviet secret police, the KGB. During the German occupation some youth organizations gathered there, only for it to be taken over again in 1944 by the Soviets, who remained there for fifty years. Although the building itself was not moved, it was then situated on the corner of Lenin and Engels streets, while today it is back on the corner of Brīvības and Stabu, and for the sake of orientation, people call it the Corner House—*Stūra maja*. In the basement of that building, the KGB installed fourteen cells of different sizes, small, with one somewhat larger space—for liquidation. Here, between 1940 and 1941, terrible torture and executions took place, and continued afterward, when Latvia became Stalin's private property. There were milder "treatments" of suspect aliens, summons to a "friendly conversation" and "cooperation." Of course, it was from there that the deportations to gulags were also organized. It was in that street, Stabu iela, that the Landsberg family had lived. From number 99 to the Corner House took some twenty minutes at a gentle pace.

When, a month after the departure of the Soviets, the Nazis, with an already detailed plan for cleansing the terrain, that is, eliminating all undesirable residents—Jews, Roma and communists—and "saving" Latvia from those Bolshevik "barbarians," permitted the public to "visit" the Corner House, to see the underground cells spattered with blood and the collection of instruments of torture, in order to stimulate a desire for revenge among the population, but also allegiance to the new, their own, regime. And it worked. What people had seen was pure horror. Only, to this day it has been impossible to bring to light the documents and notes of the KGB, lists of informers, collaborators and double secret agents, some of whom are still alive, presumably so that the population should not be additionally disturbed. It is all sealed and put away "in a safe place," no one knows where. Perhaps too much truth is bad for the health.

In the collective memory of that small Baltic people, the year 1940–41 is remembered as Baigais Gads—the Year of Terror. That collective memory, like all memory, has holes, and with time experiences miraculous transformations, and there are still those who experience the arrival in Latvia of the Einsatzgruppe A, the SS detachment of death, not at all as the arrival of the Nazis with all that ideology of theirs, but as the "return" of the liberators. Of course, it does not occur to those planning the Nazi occupation of Latvia to restore its autonomy. The orders are unconditional and strict: it is compulsory to wear exclusively German uniforms, which is immediately accepted by members of the Latvian defense, police and paramilitary forces, then race laws come into force and life follows a well-trodden path. As early as July 10, 1941, Latvia is a component part of Nazi Germany, included in the Reichskommissariat Ostland and is called Generalbezirk Lettland, which is to say the State Province of Latvia. Anyone who does not respect the Nazi occupying regime, and those who collaborate with the Soviets, are under a death sentence. Then there are those types whom the Nazis called *Juden*, for whom there are special elimination programs. They are very swift, effective and uncompromising, these new SS arrivals. On Wednesday July 16, an order comes into force according to which Jews are forbidden to use public transport. Armed Latvian police arrest folk on a whim, and ten days later Jews can no longer go to parks, or swimming pools, they may not walk on pavements, they have to attach that star not only to their chests but also in the middle of their backs so they may be immediately detected in a crowd by truculent pure-blooded yes-men, and so on, all those already familiar outrages, which include the sterilization of the undesirable, and, in addition, non-Jews have the right to attack any Jew unpunished, whenever they feel like it, beat him up, snatch his possessions, which some do, completely unrestrainedly, foaming at the mouth and drooling as though they were sick with rabies. That reminded me of an identity card shown to me by a friend, a former volunteer in this last Croatian-Serbian war, which I'm not allowed to call a civil war, but I must stress that it was an aggressive one and, from the Croatian side, defensive, because the judge Turudić, who has ambitions to become the Minister of Police when (if) that right-wing party comes to power again, that judge threatens us with five years in prison, which, if I had wireless internet in that prison connecting me with the world, would be okay for me, electricity and food bills would evaporate and no one would bother me. That friend of mine soon left the unit where he was, he knows why, while I think it was partly because of what that identity card allowed: *The bearer of this pass is permitted, within the conditions of the law, to ask a person for his or her papers, detain and hand them to the appropriate authority, enter another person's apartment and other spaces to carry out a search without written instruction, to take temporarily items that may serve as evidence in criminal proceedings, and to carry out other tasks provided for by the law and other regulations. The bearer of this pass is entitled to carry a firearm and wear police uniform.*

I have to scan this identity card in order to show it to you, because this friend of mine, who has neither apartment nor social security nor a job and who is very thin, is intending to sell it for three thousand euros.

It is interesting that the crest on this pass states: Socialist Republic of Croatia.

So, the SS arrive, the liberators arrive, the people are on the whole delighted and hopes for renewed Latvian independence grow. Briefly. The people, of course, do not know about the secret pact between Hitler and Stalin, because it is secret.

Alfred Rosenberg comes as well. He places his skill as a painter at the disposal of mobilizing the domiciled population and fanning its hatred for the Jews—those "servants of the communist regime"—and creates a series of propaganda posters with which both the Latvians and the SS decorate the town. On these posters, the Latvian SS volunteer force declares: *Toward our common future, forward!* The Latvian legionnaire commands: *To arms, to work! You must fight for Latvia!*

For the realization of their plans of broad—the broadest—dimensions in the Baltic countries, Germany lacked soldiers. Their hopes that there would be "spontaneous pogroms" of Latvian Jews came to nothing, and as early as the autumn of 1941 the Nazis began recruiting Latvians to police battalions, which on the whole operated on the front, but sometimes also behind it, away from the battle lines. They were all local lads under the strict supervision of Heinrich Himmler's secret services. As early as July 1941 the SS founded the Latvian auxiliary security police, the so-called Sonderkommando Arājs under the command of Viktors Arājs, who recruited to his ranks alienated students and former military personnel of radically right-wing orientation, volunteers, of course. And "spontaneous" reprisals began. Under the direction of Reinhard Heydrich, the architect of the Holocaust, who less than six months later presided over the conference at Wannsee where the final solution to the Jewish question was sealed, that imaginative visionary, organizer of the fighting units (Einsatzgruppen) which followed the German troops at the beginning of the Second World War and "cleaned up the territory," that lover and great connoisseur of music, a good violinist even, who grew up and died with music, that son of a composer and opera singer who founded the conservatoire in Halle and a mediocre pianist, that talented athlete, excellent swimmer, pilot and fencer, in his childhood and youth modest, shy and unsure of himself, to the end of his life tormented by doubt over his Jewish origins, that organizer of *Kristallnacht* skilled in creating spontaneous torrents of destruction against that dangerous, treacherous race, the Jews, that "man with a heart of steel," as Hitler called him, so, with the directive of the high-ranking Nazi dignitary Reinhard Heydrich, officially responsible for the elimination of European Jews, "spontaneous" actions in Latvia could begin.

Viktors Arājs and Herberts Cukurs, multiplied horsemen of the Apocalypse, former members of the Latvian fascist party Pērkonkrusts, and their companions, including that chess master Kārlis Ozols, were solidly armed and thoroughly shaved.

Viktors Arājs (1910–88), Latvian collaborator and SS-Sturmbannführer (major), was accused in West Germany of participation in the murder of thirteen thousand people and in 1980 sentenced to life imprisonment. His closest colleague was the chess master, the great patriot Kārlis Ozols. The horrors carried out by his units in the name of the Nazi authorities are among the cruelest atrocities of the Second World War. In the indictment it is stated that between July and December 1941, the paramilitary formation Sonderkommando Arājs alone carried out death campaigns in which thirty-five thousand Jews were killed, first in Latvia, then in Belorussia. After 1949, when he was released from the British prisoner-of-war camp in Germany, Arājs worked as a driver for the British armed forces in Delmenhorst, then, with the help of the London-based Latvian government in exile, he changed his name to Victor Zeibots and got a job at a printers in Frankfurt am Main.

He died in solitary confinement in prison in Kassel.

Herberts Cukurs (1900–65) was a war criminal, a Latvian collaborator, never brought to court. A pilot and designer of aircraft. He was killed by agents of Mossad in Uruguay. He was known as "the Butcher of Riga." Today in Latvia some people are "abridging" his biography, and organizing exhibitions in honor of the "national hero" Herberts Cukurs, and in October 2014, a private company put on a production of a musical celebrating Herberts Cukurs, their Latvian aviation legend, in song and dance. The authorities did not ban that monstrous show, but just gently (and feebly) condemned it. All of this is somehow reminiscent, I won't say of what, when or where, and probably politically correct.

Here's our Kārlis Ozols (1912–2001) as well. He studied law at the University of Riga, but spent his whole life professionally involved with chess, except when he was killing. During the Second World War, he participated in the execution of thousands of Jews, which left some villages without any inhabitants. Like Arājs, Ozols studied the skills of carrying out mass murders in Germany, in Fürstenberg, in some institution there under the jurisdiction of Himmler's secret service. He was a high-ranking official in the Latvian pro-Nazi Army, and with the arrival of the SS, he attached himself to the Latvian security police in Riga. He was accused of numerous monstrous crimes, but never taken to court. When in 1979 the Melbourne court invited him to make a statement under oath about his wartime activities, Ozols said, *I have no idea what you are talking about. I know absolutely nothing about the horrors perpetrated against Jews and Roma.* But it is not exactly the case that Ozols did not then know what he had done (although he really did suffer from dementia in his old age), because when he fled before the Red Army in 1944, with falsified papers, he hid with his wife and child in refugee camps in Windischbergerdorf,

Bamberg, Wildflecken and Delmenhorst, where he occasionally played chess, and that is how he came across Leila's father, that Arvīds Mazais, with whom, incidentally, in a whisper, he evoked his exciting war years spent serving the ideology of blood and soil, while both secretly looked at and twisted between their fingers their iron medals from Hitler, crosses of the second class, Ozols' was a first lieutenant's, KVK II (Kriegsverdienstkreuz), received on June 20, 1944, and Mazais's was the one I had seen, for the infantry, DK II, of March 3, 1945. Since he knew that the circle around him could begin to tighten, Ozols fled to Australia. I don't know in which camp Ozols and Mazais complained to one another of their bitter postwar fates, because there were many such refugee camps throughout Germany, in all three zones. Perhaps it was Wildflecken, because it was from there that many people went by train to Genoa, and from Genoa by the famous ship, *Mozaffari*, to Australia. On the list of passengers I find the happy little Ozols family, Kārlis, Erika and Vita—numbers 568, 569 and 570. In Australia, now tranquil, far away from his past, Ozols returns to chess and becomes the Australian champion. As soon as he reached Melbourne, the executions of Jews that Ozols carried out in 1942 and 1943, some in the open, some in gas vans, with his team of a hundred or so fiery Latvian warriors, were no longer even a bad dream. Perhaps there was a small, pale reminder of the days of his youth in the occasional benign family association with Konrāds Kalējs, a Nazi collaborator from Arājs's units, pursued, but also never indicted as a war criminal. It is true that when he wasn't playing chess, Ozols was fairly active in the Australian branch of the international organization Daugavas Vanagi, that is, in the branch of "The Hawks of the Daugava," a branch which, from the 1950s on, boasted more than twelve hundred members, not to mention the other branches scattered throughout America and in almost all the countries and towns of Western Europe, in Sweden, Holland,

Germany, and in South America—Brazil, Bolivia, Argentina and Uruguay—which former Latvian SS officers and collaborators joined, and who, those hawks, by their very name, even among those who have no clue about that organization, create an image of creepiness and mild horror when you imagine them flying in flocks over the great Daugava River in Latvia, aiming at the heads and eyes of the innocent. Today these hawks, falcons, whatever, have learned manners, and many of the original members of the organization no longer fly anywhere, because they are either senile or under the earth, and so the Daugavas Vanagi is engaged in good works, not exactly unpaid, given that its branches own restaurants and hotels, halls for this and halls for that, all at the disposal of newcomers—Latvians.

I have collected a longish list of those former Latvian SS collaborators, I have a heap of photographs in which they pose in military uniform with little black runes on their collars, in which, in work clothes, they smile as they dig their gardens or dandle their grandchildren on their knees, I have photographs of their weddings, but not one from a courtroom. I have studied their lives, their movements, their flights, and now I don't know what to do with them. They've swarmed all over the place. For example, in 2007 it was believed that there were around a thousand war criminals living in Sweden, like rats they multiplied in silence, as one might say *they keep a low profile*, but they don't hide, not at all, because Sweden says, *The past is the past, and we have more important business*, because Sweden, like Italy, has a law according to which crimes more than twenty-five years old cannot be processed through the courts.

In their new homes, these placid people, former newcomers, do not change their names, they might sometimes adapt them a little to the language of the country that offers them refuge, not to stand out too much, they set up companies, concern themselves with property, and, every March 16, the Latvians visit their beloved Riga to pay their respects to their comrades, members of the Latvian legion, at the time a component of the Waffen-SS, founded by the direct command of Heinrich Himmler. Since 2000, the state of Latvia is no longer the patron of that pathetic mass gathering of jaded wrecks, with shuffling steps, bent backs, mouths full of false teeth, half-blind and maybe with diapers between their legs, but they will not give up their monstrous dream, because they come, they gather, they make their tearful speeches of reminiscence, while here and there past them, past that pathetic assemblage, walks the occasional leftover Jew, the occasional antifascist with a raised placard of protest, and one year a woman even dressed in the concentration camp prisoners' uniform, the one with blue and white stripes, and she placed the appropriate cap on her head, and on her chest and back she attached the Star of David, but who gave a damn, the former Waffen-SS Latvian legionnaires simply glanced at her and said *Some mad old biddy*.

I haven't a single photograph of Frida Landsberg. If I had, I would go from one to the other of the already-threadbare half-SS officers on my list and ask, *Do you remember this girl?*

I could start with Leila's father, but he died. One of the people I put away at the bottom of a drawer must have seen Frida Landsberg, at least in passing, which, judging by how Marisa and Karlo spoke about her, would have been enough to remember her.

Here are some of those grotesque figures, from memory:

Aleksanders Plesners, head of the Latvian SS Legion. Never taken to court. Died.

Kārlis Lobe (1895–1985), organized the Riga police battalions and then became chief of police in Ventspils.

Arvīds Oše (1896–1989), actively involved in the persecution of Jews in Riga, worked in Sweden as a woodcutter, later in a glass factory. Active in that organization of Hawks.

Alfrēds Vadzemnieks, head of the Latvian security service in the region of Ventspils, and allegedly involved in killing civilians.

Boleslavs Maikovskis (1904–96), chief of the police station in Rēzekne. In the USA he worked as a carpenter. In Latvia, then the USSR, he was tried in absentia; he was condemned to death. When things got tough in America, he fled to Germany, where he died. Of old age. Before that he worked for the CIA. One of Hitler's most active lackeys. For his dedication and devoted collaboration in "establishing the new European order," the governor of the East Baltic region awarded him high offices and a collection of medals of the Third Reich. Thanks to him and his companions, who systematically terrorized the local population and sent five thousand people to German labor camps, more than fifteen thousand inhabitants of the Rēzeknes region were wiped from the face of the earth.

Kārlis Detlavs (1911–83), as a member of the Latvian auxiliary security police, killed Jews from the Riga ghetto. As an outcast—a displaced person—in 1946 he fled to America, where he was quickly accused of war crimes. The authorities initiated proceedings for his deportation to Riga, but, despite witnesses, the judges dealing with immigration issues systematically blocked the process, so Detlavs went nowhere. He died in his home in Baltimore.

Konrāds Kalējs (1913–2001), born in Riga, died in Melbourne. An officer in Arājs's death squads and guard-supervisor in the concentration camp Salaspils near Riga, where, it is now reliably known, he participated in the execution of inmates. When, in 1984, the judiciary of the United States, Canada, Great Britain and Australia finally decided to get a grip, Kalējs, thanks to the wealth he had amassed since the war, after numerous demands from various courts for his deportation from one country to another, flew from continent to continent, sometimes hiding, sometimes not, and generally pleading ignorance. On the little finger of his left hand he wore a signet ring, his status symbol. For his defense, Kalējs, who otherwise passed himself off as a farmer, but was in fact heavily involved in property, engaged a crowd of expensive lawyers, who croaked all over the place about the unheard-of shame, the heartless judiciary, witch-hunts, about a process that from America and Great Britain to Australia, from Australia to Canada, from Canada to Australia, and so on, sought the extradition of a sick, infirm, now already blind old man, oh, the heartlessness, and all this, they emphasized, without any justified reason. When the going got tougher, Kalējs suddenly became demented, with the additional diagnosis of prostate cancer, and soon after that died in Melbourne, in a Latvian old people's home owned by those Hawks from the Latvian river Daugava, with an expression of bliss on his face, amidst urine and feces. It was confirmed, incontrovertibly confirmed, because some have nevertheless survived, that the Arājs Kommando, of which Konrāds Kalējs was a devoted and very active member, was responsible for the murder of half the almost eighty thousand Jews liquidated in Latvia, and above all in Riga, between August and December 1941. It is interesting that, even after achieving independence in 1991, Latvia did not prosecute a single one of "its own" Nazi collaborators, but it did pursue and punish several Russians for their anti-Nazi activities during the Second World War. At the urging of the Office for Special Investigations (OSI) of the United States Department of Justice, Latvia, in connection with the case of Konrāds Kalējs (and some other of its murderer-collaborators), affirmed unconvincingly that there was no convincing evidence for bringing charges against "our lads." When, in 2000, under international pressure, Latvia did finally agree to cooperate in the case of Kalējs, Kalējs promptly died.

Boļeslavs Bogdanovs (1917–84) rampaged with Arājs's commandos, participated in the mass murder of a thousand civilians, among whom, in addition to Jews, there were communists, Roma and psychiatric patients. He entered the United States on the basis of a false statement about his past. The process of denaturalization began in 1983, but Bogdanovs died before the court judgment was known, and after he had been carrying out spying assignments for the CIA for several years.

Valdis Didrichsons (1913–95), also a member of Arājs's legion, based in Riga. In 1988, forty years late, for which there is a valid although until recently confidential reason, the US government began proceedings of denaturalization, which it completed in 1990 when Didrichsons was ready to renounce his American citizenship. In view of his poor state of health, the authorities abandoned their decision to deport him.

There are dozens of them in the United States from Latvia alone (not to mention other countries), those peaceful citizens, former murderers with a distorted, hard East-European or German accent, who manage pistols and *kama* knives perfectly, who for sixty and more years stand up obediently when the American anthem is played, who vote, who have hobbies, who go to the countryside, who pay taxes and have children, who gather in their national clubs of still-dubious political orientation, in which they eat their national dishes (which, unlike their own past, they don't forget), who, although proclaimed war criminals, are never tried or deported, and who because of old age and illness gradually drift away, which does not always mean that the air around them is cleared. Because although their children know or don't know, ask or don't ask, the possibility exists that some hidden seed of their habitus should germinate, just as recently, quite incomprehensibly and inexplicably, among the bricks beneath my window, after two years a little plant sprouted when I had thought the north wind, cold and drought had put paid to it forever. That little plant is important to me, I watch it grow, I fear for its life, and when the weather turns cold or when that hideous, merciless wind gets up, I open the window and protect it with my hands, bringing it the little bit of residual warmth that used once to run through me, because it, that plant, which sometimes even flowers, seems to grow out of my skull, then it abandons me, turns toward the dilapidated façades opposite and throws onto them a fine light that flickers even when dense darkness descends.

As long as the Cold War lasted, those criminals were necessary to the USA, and the USA exploited them to the hilt. The arm of the CIA is long and its fingers wrap around our planet, it believes it holds it in its hand like a little ball. When the Cold War ends, these criminals are old, dispensable, but under oath of secrecy, that is, blackmailed that if they squeal, they'll be deported to the USSR, they become harmless and may continue to cultivate their American, Swedish, Finnish, German, etc. gardens in which they bury their filthy Nazi past. Around that buried past now, when (some) CIA dossiers have been declassified, the contaminated soil radiates, and beneath it nestle small, barely visible landmines.

Here they are, some Latvians, spies for the CIA:

Edgars Inde (1909–80), member of Arājs's death squads, assisted the Nazis in the persecution and killing of thousands of Jews and other civilians from 1941 to 1942, never prosecuted, never condemned, his life warehoused in the Central Intelligence Agency.

Tālivaldis Karklins (1914–83), as a member of the Latvian district police participated in two mass executions of his fellow countrymen, Jews and Soviet activists.

Juris Kauls (1912–2008), deputy commander of a concentration camp near Riga, so a Nazi collaborator, in the United States a tax adviser, after a process of denaturalization is set in motion, flees from the USA in 1988 to West Germany. Dies in Latvia.

Miķelis Kiršteins (1916–94), also a member of Arājs's death

units. A process of denaturalization is initiated in 1987 and completed in 1991. Kiršteins renounces American citizenship, and as a reward the authorities (the CIA) do not deport him.

Edgars Laipenieks (1913–98), athlete, represents Latvia at the Olympics in Berlin in 1936. Then, still in good shape, as a member of the Latvian political police, first persecutes Jews and communists, then tortures and kills them. The United States Department of Justice initiates a process of deportation, the CIA intervenes, and one of its officials addresses the spy Laipenieks in a letter, with the intimate *Dear Ed*, apologizes for the awkwardness of the American justice system wandering a little *off limits* and assures him that everything will be *OK, you will stay*. Laipenieks's CIA cryptonym is AESIDECAR-2, and he is included in the project AEBALCONY which uses American citizens with a fluent knowledge of Baltic languages for "legal" operations in Latvia, Lithuania and Estonia.

These CIA spies from Latvia are two a penny:

Waffen-Obersturmführer Pēteris Janelsiņš, member of the SS Latvian auxiliary police that carries out mass killings. CIA cryptonym: AEMARSH-15, in the project AEMARS.

Herberts Žagars, cryptonym AEMARSH-1, alias Herbert Kalniņš, in the Latvian legion from 1943 to 1944.

Elmārs Sproģis (1914–91), assistant chief of police in Gulbene, in the uniform of the Waffen-SS accompanies around 150 Jews to execution sites and observes their execution, with his pockets full of jewels and money previously taken from them.

The Nazi collaborator Freds Launags (1919–91), a lively spy, a fairly active errand boy—until he is pronounced (by other spies) unreliable, in fact mentally ill, so the CIA dump him unceremoniously. Launags had three cryptonyms in three separate projects: AECAMBARO-1, AEHAWKEYE-1 and iCAMBARO-1, and three pseudonyms: Cleveland O. Hahn, Louis G. Goltedge and Raymond S. Churgin.

*

I came across all this human dross, the names and lives of already deceased, spinelessly loyal humanoid lice as I was trying to find any kind of information about the life of Leila's father, Arvīds Mazais, in the hope of discovering at least something about the disappearance of Frida Landsberg, that love of my uncle Karlo Osterman, cancelled by war. I read the facsimiles of several hundred declassified CIA documents, astounded by the perfectionism of their "research" team. Apart from the fact that the CIA had an insight into the smallest details of the past and present lives of those it intended to woo, from the date and place of their birth, from all the addresses at which they had lived, from their married and unmarried partners and their biographies, from the everyday habits and affinities of their future yes-men—what they read, what they ate, whether they smoked and if so, how much, whether they drank and if so, what and how much, how they spent their free time, from which restaurants they frequented to what kind of clothes and hats they wore, what color their eyes were, how high and heavy they and those closest to them were, those reports at times acquired the form of little literary works shot through with a lyrical-sentimental note, a charming modesty. So, as though I was watching a horror film, I saw the faces of those Latvian criminals, I followed their footsteps, listened to their commands, was present at their drinking bouts, their thieving, and I watched their killings, massacres and organized executions. I pronounced their to me complicated names out loud while they burned down first synagogues, then people, in the thousands, and when that wasn't enough for them, they shot them in the back of the head, and in order to save space, they later arranged them neatly in pits, the way sardines are placed in tins. Seventy thousand (70,000) souls. Thanks to the declassified CIA documents these assiduous

Nazi aides rose from the dead, flew into my current life, lithe, hale, young and handsome, belted into their uniforms with the Waffen-SS insignia on their chests and collars, and set off on their bestial campaign.

It was Hāzners, Vilis Hāzners, who brought me to Arvīds Mazais. I had hoped that Arvīds Mazais, now already a dead man with Hitler's medal hidden in the bottom of a cardboard box, a man with whom long ago in the Bavarian backwoods I had played chess, might indirectly, through the only accessible living person connected with him, his daughter Leila, explain how and why Frida Landsberg disappeared. But, Leila Mazais had no idea about anything, or, if she did, her ideas were mixed up. Had I thought of researching all of this earlier, in fact, had Leila hopped back into my life sooner, of which there was no chance as I had fled from her horrified and afraid, and, presumably thinking that nothing mattered anymore, she had reappeared old and fat and constantly drunk, and I had had my own tribulations, my own deaths, my own solitudes, my own wanderings through the world, my own illnesses, and had this all happened forty years before, or at least when I was in Paris thirty-seven years ago with my terminally ill mother Marisa, who, although full of poisonous experimental cytostatics, was fully aware, or had I once, when I had scarpered off to Canada twenty years before, with no work, and with national-fascism knocking on my door every day with the intention of getting me into bed, and had I there asked the chess player Miervaldis Walter Jurševskis, although he was in Vancouver and I was in Toronto, but he had hung around the Academy of Art in Riga, and perhaps also around the Riga Conservatoire so he might have met Frida Landsberg, because he did not leave Latvia until 1945, when some of the horrors, the most appalling, had already passed, and because he had moved around Germany for several years from one camp for displaced persons to another and because, I know, he had played chess with that criminal Ozols, and the Nazi-fan Bogolyubov, I don't know and don't wish to know what Jurševskis was doing during the war in Riga, where he had been born in 1921, I just recently discovered how much he liked art, bowls, yoga, golf, he liked dancing and traveling round the world, he liked seafood and candlelit dinners although none of that is a guarantee of ethical behavior, but rather confirmation that this Jurševskis lived well, partly from his rapid-transit chess games, partly from drawing advertisements for the Eaton Company, partly from restoring antique furniture, had I at least asked him—but it's too late now, because Miervaldis Jurševskis died in 2014, precisely twelve months before the moment when I am writing this.

Vilis Hāzners was born in Latvia in 1905, and died in 1989 in America, never having become its citizen. In 1977 the American authorities initiated a process for his denaturalization, but the OSI—Office for Special Investigations at the Department of Justice—(under pressure from the CIA) quashed the request and Hāzners closed his eyes, with the blessing of the Church and those closest to him. At the court case, evidence did not help, witness statements did not help, Hāzners was protected.

Vilis Hāzners, Waffen-Sturmbannführer (i.e., major), proud owner of four Hitler crosses, was accused of participation in the liquidation of thirty thousand Latvian Jews and, specifically, for leading crazed Nazi scumbags, gangsters and thugs who, on July 4, 1941, set fire to Riga's Great Synagogue at 25 Gogola iela, having first imprisoned twenty people in its cellar. Later, with his crony, that pilot Herberts Cukurs, Vilis Hāzners watched the synagogue burning from 63 Stabu iela, not five hundred meters, a six-minute walk away from the building in which Frida Landsberg was still living with her parents, and the small Landsberg family watched the smoke from behind closed slats, trembling. My uncle Karlo Osterman was there as well. His arms round Frida Landsberg, he stood behind her and whispered into her neck, *Come with me, I can save you.* The situation was clear to Karlo Osterman, for Karlo Osterman it was a reprise, racial laws in Croatia had been in force for more than two months, they were established quickly, perfected, except that the Croatian synagogues would begin to burn somewhat later than these Latvian ones. The Landsbergs were spared then, the rampaging scum of of Arājs's commandos did not come to their door, having collected from the neighboring buildings enough victims to burn—some thirty of them. Witnesses described the people locked in, like burning flares, breaking windows and trying to flee, while Cukurs waited for them outside and practiced shooting at living targets. Then the synagogue at 50 Maskavas iela was burned down as well.

The CIA did not declassify files that confirmed its use of former Nazis and Nazi collaborators—immigrants for its own spying—just like that. And it declassified more than a million digitalized documents, inaccessible until then. When the CIA "knuckled under" and gave in, after lengthy pressure from the legal institutions of government, and then not until 2006, it became clear that this had been a calculated program on a large scale, established immediately after the end of the Second World War. And so for decades the CIA received into its protective embrace Nazis and their standard-bearers, who were fleeing from the not exactly firm hand of justice, believing that it was protecting the world from future evil. Now that piece of theater is at an end. The Nazis of the time are on the whole dead, although some lived astonishingly long. But the secret services always have work to do. And when they don't, they invent it.

For years the United States Department of Justice researched the work of the CIA, and in 2006, on six hundred and twelve (612) pages, it completed its (of course) secret report. That document would no doubt have remained buried in some well-protected safe had it not been unearthed in 2010 by journalists from *The New York Times* and submitted to the public. Good, we know that both the CIA and the "democratic" authorities of the USA recruited notorious Nazi criminals in the interest of the altruistic advancement of humanity, but the scale of those actions and the number of lies connected with them were beyond imagining. That is how I came to Vilis Hāzners, alias Victor Halfond, and through him to Leila's father Arvīds Mazais.

Radio Free Europe and Radio Liberty proved to be a convenient niche for a certain number of war (Nazi) criminals. Both stations, set up in 1950 and 1953 respectively, were financed by the CIA and as well as the United States (Voice of America), they had editorial offices throughout Western Europe. While Radio Free Europe directed its programmatic propaganda toward the satellite states of the USSR, but also toward Yugoslavia, Radio Liberty was aimed at the Soviet Union. That was where "our" Vilis Hāzners made his nest, participating in the AEFLAG, AEBALCONY and AECOB projects, with the cryptonym AEKILO-2, and all under the supervision of the CIA. The task of AECOB was to infiltrate Soviet Latvia and its surroundings. According to available information, Hāzners was still broadcasting his contributions on Radio Liberty in the 1980s. I found a document in which Hāzners recommends Arvīds Mazais to his bosses as a contributor to RFE/RL, quoting details about his life, his address in Germany, his marital status and number of children, his employment and war journey. I cannot show that document here, because Leila and her brothers could sue me, the way a member of a Jewish family attacked me when I suggested that some of its members had also been collaborator members of the great Aryan family of Fascists and Nazis during the Second World War. I cannot risk directly exposing the evidence, because I don't have money for lawyers, I'm already involved in three court cases, which further annoys me and depletes my resources.

Hāzners's reports clarified the meaning of Mazais's SS medal. So, Lieutenant Arvīds Mazais was a member of the Latvian SS Legion, its 19th infantry division, a hot-blooded, voluntary patriotic formation founded on Himmler's unconditional command. Exceptionally impressed by the fighting activities of the Latvian SS Legion, in 1943 Himmler founded within it a special bomber unit, the 19th Waffen-SS Grenadiers Division. Its task was to throw grenades at people, especially communists, but also at buildings. The very thought of communists, generally speaking, probably made the hair on Arvīds Mazais's head stand on end, although none of his family had perished in either the gulags or the prisons of the NKVD. So, Arvīds Mazais was a fairly hotheaded, fiery and vehement man. When I met him, he seemed tame, not at all bombastic. His only obvious passions were gardening and chess, which are seen as harmless, tame passions. Korchnoi stated somewhere that no chess grandmaster is normal, "Chess players only differ in the degree of their madness," he said. It's not important now where and how Arvīds Mazais fought, it's not important whether his fascism was great or small, it existed, his hatred, mild or fierce, existed. But, today it is known that the people recruited to the 19th Waffen-SS Grenadiers Division were members of the notorious Latvian SS Division who had previously actively participated in the mass liquidation of Jews. And it is known, it can be seen, that there are still a considerable number of Latvians who consider those fighters of Himmler's heroes.

Today Arvīds Mazais's children go to Latvia and read books about the heroes, the knights of their country, about the fighters for a free homeland, those with SS insignia on their chests and collars: the image of the little badge on their uniforms . Today, Leila has her own box in the national theater in Riga, and on the door of that box there is a brass plaque with her name on it. I think that it was bought, that box and that plaque, that it was some kind of donation for the promotion of dance and dancing in general. Because all Leila ever did in her life was dance, and when one dances it's impossible to speak, one just listens to the music and dances. In that theater there is no plaque with the name of Frida Landsberg's famous teacher, Adolphe Metz, nor of the great Latvian pianist Katya Abramis (35), because there are none of their violins, nor their pianos, nor their graves, and so none of them either. Perhaps the occasional not yet disintegrated bone deep in the earth, in one of the fifty-five (55) mass graves there in the beautiful Rumbula forest within easy reach of Riga, from which cries still break the silence of the night.

That volunteer 19th Latvian SS division, founded by order of Hitler and the command of Reichsführer-SS Heinrich Himmler, in which Arvīds Mazais also fought, included recruits from among members of Arājs's cutthroats. In 1944 and 1945, all these volunteers attacked the invading troops of the Red Army so intrepidly, fearlessly and unwaveringly that Hitler presented them with more medals than any other non-German Waffen-SS formation. By July 1, 1944, the Latvian legion numbered 87,550 fighters, with a further 23,000 "assistants" in the structure of the Werhmacht. If Arvīds only became "active" in 1943, maybe he has no connection with the disappearance of Frida Landsberg. How could that be? He lived in Riga. He watched, he listened to what was going on. He was against the communists, and officially, all Latvian Jews were proclaimed communist lackeys and traitors of Greater Germany, therefore also of Latvia. The scum.

So, my uncle Karlo Osterman arrived in Riga for the second time at the end of June 1941. The Russians had gone, the Nazis had arrived, rampaging and armed Latvian youths were breaking into apartments and arresting people, there were bodies in the street.

In the first days of July, Jews had their telephone lines cut. *Go*, Frida Landsberg said to Karlo Osterman, *I'll write*, she said. *I can't go with you now, I just can't.* That letter of Frida's, dated November 3, 1941, reached Split, and from Split, according to Grandma Ana's account, it was sent to Zagreb by lame Marko, who could not join the partisans because of his leg and who, on that famous sunny June 3, 1944, full of good cheer, bought the first cherries at the improvised market near St Dominius's, and then the shards of Allied bombs fell on him, the cherries flew into the air like drops of blood and lame Marko, his wide-open eyes staring at the sky, lay dead among all that debris.

That letter of Frida's reached Karlo at the end of December 1941. That was the letter which my grandmother Ana gave me thirty years later and which, of course, got lost, and then, like that Ustasha pass, miraculously resurfaced, written in rudimentary French and glowing with a simple, almost childish language; there is not much emotion in it, it contains mostly facts, in it Frida says that now they've all been moved out, they no longer live in Stabu iela, but in Maskavas iela, in one room, and they will soon be going east, and she says that her professor Metz lives in the same building, *He's got his violin*, writes Frida, *mine was bought by a German, Rosenberg.* Frida also mentions her friend and colleague Sara Rašin, already a famous violinist, born at roughly the same time as her, Frida, in 1920, and also a student of Professor Metz, *She's with us as well*, Frida writes and reminds Karlo of an improvised concert which she and Sara gave *in that gallery, you know, when you were here last year.*

Frida also writes that sometimes, in the basement of the building where they are now living, which has guards and which is, you know, blocked, Professor Metz and Sara Rašin put on little concerts for the people who live there, they play simple melodies, and Sara often plays the "Spanish dance" from the opera *La vida breve* by Manuel de Falla, and every time the professor asks his basement audience not to applaud at the end, *No applause, please, no applause,* he says and, Frida also writes, Professor Metz and Sara sometimes lend her their violins, so that she too plays sometimes and that then she thinks of him, Karlo, and the way he kissed that little red star on her neck, which now, his little star, is becoming ever paler, it is vanishing, because she, Frida, no longer practices, because that Rosenberg now has her violin. At the end, Frida says that every morning she goes to a field, that she digs the earth and her fingers are already stiff, but that when she gets a new violin, everything will be all right again, that they are going to the east from where she will write to him, Karlo, again, because she cannot, she will not believe Manuel de Falla that life really is short. That letter, a note in fact, is written in pencil, and as I read it, the letters in it are barely visible and the little note ends *Ta petite Frida.*

How did Frida Landsberg disappear?

Singing. To a melody she played in her head.

There are a lot of violin stories, and musical ones in general from the Second World War. Some of them are Croatian. Some are hideous, some are sad. That struck me as interesting, that quality of tenderness among criminals. That need for incomprehensible solace among victims. I met Dušan Šarotar from Murska Sobota. In his novel *Billiards at Hotel Dobray* he writes about a violin which now hangs above his desk, which is no longer played, but he talks about the violin as belonging to his grandfather, who was the only one of the family to come home from Auschwitz, on foot.

In the middle of August 1941, in Riga, on Maskavas iela, preparations began for the opening of a ghetto, which was to be completely enclosed, fenced in with barbed wire and guarded by the local police. In October, thirty thousand people were herded into that ghetto, but as early as September the Einsatzkommandos in both small and larger Latvian towns had succeeded in killing thirty thousand Jews. The mass killings in Latvia had begun in July, when my uncle Karlo was back in Riga, when he realized that incomprehensible horrors were on their way and when he said to Frida, *Come away with me.*

The first mass killings of the Jews and non-Jews of Riga began already at the beginning of July 1941. In just seven days Nazis took four thousand (4,000) people by truck from the Central Prison to the beautiful forest of Biķernieki, not four kilometers from the center of town, where they immediately shot them. That practice continued until 1944. Today it is known that there, in the forest of Biķernieki, lie the remains of thirty-five thousand people, some Latvians, some West European Jews, some Soviet prisoners of war, some political opponents of the Nazi regime. Before Latvia erected a memorial in 2001 in the forest of Biķernieki, which was in fact built and financed by the German Republic, the government opened fifty-five mass graves and began to compose a list of those killed, but this list of those killed in the forest of Biķernieki does not include Frida Landsberg, nor her mother Sonja, nor her father Benzon, nor Professor Metz nor Sara Rašin. That memorial in the forest of Biķernieki is surrounded by gentle hills to which nowadays picnickers come in spring and in winter skiers. Like Zagreb's Sljeme.

In October the ghetto in Maskavas iela is ready. Latvian police raid apartments and drag the population of Riga by force into that enormous pen in the center of town. The Nazi authorities immediately confiscate the entire property of the newly imprisoned, both the moveable and immoveable. In the column heading toward Maskvas iela, carrying their bundles, trudges the little Landsberg family. Sonja Landsberg stares at the ground, Benzon Landsberg passes his former shoe shop and turns away his head, Frida walks with her arms crossed on her chest, clutching a dozen sheets of music, which the Latvian police soon take from her and burn on the spot. In November and December the Nazi authorities plan to disperse these people a little further away, to the east, so that, starving and robbed, they should not disturb the carefree, smooth-running lives of the other people in the city. But, at the end of October 1941, Himmler sends SS-Obergruppenführer Friedrich Jeckeln to Riga and the planned dispersal comes to nothing, if it ever existed. Himmler orders Jeckeln, commander and chief of police of the whole occupied region of Soviet Russia, to eliminate the inhabitants of the ghetto in the shortest time. Jeckeln applies himself to the task: he assembles and stockpiles ammunition, compiles a schedule, that is, a timetable of "events" and recruits seventeen hundred German and Latvian soldiers, policemen and civil guards who are to put his commands into practice. Then Jeckeln sets about looking for a suitable location and in a nearby wood, just beside the small railway station of Rumbula, he sees, *Oh, a favorable terrain, perfection, a fine open space surrounded by pines, with beautiful birch trees all around, my enchanting Birkenau in the little birchwood of Birkenwald, that's it!* Jeckeln, the lover of birch trees, smiles, and employs three hundred Russian prisoners of war to dig pits under the strict supervision of the Germans and Latvians. The soil is damp and sandy, so although it is the end of November and the temperatures drop to -7° Celsius, the Russian prisoners dig by night and day and in record time succeed in digging six three-meter-deep and ten-meter-square pits, in which they themselves will end their days. Jeckeln engages a thousand guards and they will accompany the column of those condemned to death the ten kilometers to the killing field, to the clearing on the edge of the Rumbula wood, known also as *Vārnu mežs*, Raven Wood, a wood in which not only do the leaves rustle and the pine branches sway, but a wood out of which come the cries of those intelligent birds, known to be able to foretell danger, the black cries of those black birds break through, like an echo, a refrain, a response to the laments and pleas of a different species, human. Evildoers generally love thickets, scrub and brush, and that is why they make their camps and dig their graves there, because that is where nature is untouched, quiet. They forget that forests have ears, and fields eyes, that nature is constantly awake.

Jeckeln ordered the guards to ensure that no one stepped out of the column, that no one tried to escape, *In which case, feel free to shoot*, commanded General Jeckeln, *but immediately remove the bodies so as not to create disorder*. Three hundred (out of fifteen hundred) of Arājs's commandos immediately made themselves available, *We are ready, we are armed, my commandos and I are ready to defend our homeland from Jews and communists, those shameless, eternal enemies of our wonderful country, Latvia*, yells Viktors Arājs, probably downing a toast in a tavern with his cronies and fellow murderers, Herberts Cukurs and Kārlis Ozols.

On November 27, 1941, from Berlin-Grunewald Station, train number Da 31 set out for Riga. Three days later, the train containing 1,053 Jews arrived at Šķirotava Station, a few hundred meters from the killing field in Rumbula wood. The ghetto in Maskavas iela was bursting at the seams because the "dispersal" of its inhabitants was to begin a few hours later, so all the travelers on train Da 31 were immediately taken to the killing field, where they were executed in short order. The pits began to fill.

At 4 a.m. on November 30, 1941, the German police, Arājs's commandos and eighty local guards began to wake the inhabitants of the ghetto with shouts and threats, giving them half an hour "to get ready." Great urgency reigned. The guards cut the barbed-wire fence to speed up the departure of people from the ghetto and organized a column for the journey to Rumbula. Those who refused to leave got a bullet in the forehead. By noon, in rooms, on steps, on the road, lay around seven hundred dead. At 6 a.m., the first column of a thousand people set off for Rumbula. The action began three hours later. Accompanied by the whistle of whips, groups of around fifty were ordered to undress, some remained in their underwear, others were naked, it was cold, people were shivering. Their clothes, gold, money and jewelry were all immediately sorted for transport to Berlin, in trains which were otherwise returning empty to the Reich. Then came the order, *The first fifty into the pit!* The people went down and lay on their stomachs on top of the previously liquidated bodies. One bullet in the back of the head was enough, contingent after contingent was "dealt with." The three pits filled simultaneously. SS-Obergruppenführer Friedrich Jeckeln stood to one side, satisfied with the way things were going, proud of his "undertaking," of his system of effective liquidation that meant a significant saving of ammunition, but also of space, proud of his *Sardinenpackung*. Jeckeln walked along the pits, supervising the "process," at times contentedly exclaiming, *Ja, Ordnung muss sein!* and here and there taking the occasional photograph, so that it should be known, should be seen, to show Himmler how this was done, to send proof that would bring him another decoration, another iron medal.

A week later, on December 8, 1941, on the plateau outside Rumbula wood, the second wave of Jeckeln's self-burial, or *Sardinenpackung*, took place. In those two daylong actions, Jeckeln's boys managed to "pack" into three pits twenty-five thousand people.

Trains from the countries under Hitler's occupation continued to arrive regularly in Latvia. I have information about a hundred and thirty (130) trains with roughly a thousand "passengers" in each, I have information about the date and place of their departure and arrival, about the number of children and their ages, about the number of women and men and about the number who died on the journey. If I start listing it, someone might think that I am obsessed, ask why I have got so stuck, and say that that does not belong in literature, that those are nothing but the most ordinary defamatory scribblings. So I won't list anything so as not to upset potential readers. Just this: the passengers in those trains were Germans, Austrians, Poles, Czechs, Hungarians, Jews and Roma, political prisoners, homosexuals, psychiatric patients, and so on, a familiar story of horror, one hundred and thirty thousand (130,000) souls. Given that the pits in Rumbula were already full to the brim, and the Riga ghetto closed, or rather "cleansed," because there was no longer any "material" in it, the new arrivals were directed to Kaiserwald concentration camp, on the outskirts of Riga, and Salaspils concentration camp was also opened at the end of 1941, eighteen kilometers southeast of the capital. In order to destroy evidence of the mass liquidations of the innocent, in 1944 the Nazis forced the inmates of Kaiserwald camp to open up the pits in Rumbula and burn the already well-decomposed bodies. Then they liquidated those prisoners as well, thousands of them. The few survivors of Kaiserwald were then transferred to the Nazi Stutthof concentration camp, also situated in a damp, dark wood in reach of Sztutowo, some thirty kilometers east of Gdańsk. When, on October 13, 1944, the Red Army entered Riga, it found fewer than a thousand Jews there. Already by the beginning of 1942, Jeckeln had succeeded in reducing the number of Riga Jews from 29,500 to 2,600. According to the census of the population of 1935, 93,479 Jews lived in Latvia, forty thousand of them in Riga. According to accessible data, around seventy thousand Latvian Jews disappeared in the Holocaust. Apart from the massacre in Riga, that is in Rumbula, terrible, numerous and mass liquidations were carried out in Liepāja and in Daugavpils, also in the open, in winter and summer, on beaches, in squares, in parks, in prisons and in ghettos. Even today efforts are still being made to compile lists of the disappeared, but since whole families perished with their neighbors and friends, few have survived to be asked, to bear witness, to grieve. And so, the majority of those killed in

Rumbula are nameless to this day. That is why there is no evidence about the disappearance of Frida Landsberg, only guesses. I found lists of people who, after the capitulation of Germany, made their way in fishing boats, ships, trains and some on foot, to Sweden and Germany and then to Australia, America, Canada and so on, as far away as possible. Frida Landsberg is not among them either, because those who fled were those who had bloodied their hands, and those who had thrown flowers onto the Nazi tanks, and then those who had later seen the light and those afraid of the Soviets. After the war, Jews mostly did not flee, because mostly they no longer existed. Those Jews who did succeed in fleeing had fled earlier, when Latvia was free and independent, but then there had been no reason to flee, so, again, they did not leave. Those roughly one hundred and thirty thousand who fled before the Russians invaded a second time never returned to Latvia, because they died waiting for the Soviets to stop embracing their country. Now their children and their grandchildren go to Latvia, baffled and broken. After the Second World War little Latvia was left without a third of its population. Today Latvia is crisscrossed with memorials and ardently developing tourism, which is officially called *dark tourism*. This is when people from the West visit killing fields en masse, clutch their hearts and exclaim *Oh my God, unbelievable! Incroyable! Nicht zu fassen!* then they go to dinner in some traditional restaurant to sample national specialties. To feel the pulse of the country they are visiting. Latvia has a lot of forests.

So, for two centuries various dark forces have been kicking Latvia around. And not only Latvia. If it's any comfort, but it's not, that criminal Jeckeln, who fled toward Berlin, was overtaken on April 28, 1945, in Halbe by Soviet soldiers and brought to a (Soviet) military court in Riga. At the trial, Jeckeln was surprisingly calm, one could say he appeared innocent, almost modest, like a man who, after bringing his accumulated dark passions under control, after feeding the wild beast in himself, was left blank and empty, (temporarily) spent.

> *Those operations were part of the plan for the final solution in the aast,* says Jeckeln to the soldier Tsvetaev who is hearing the case. *The shootings were carried out under the direction of Colonel Dr. Lange, commander of the secret police and the Gestapo in Latvia. Karl Knecht was in charge of security at the liquidation sites.*

At which sites?

> *At the liquidation sites. I, Friedrich Jeckeln, took part in the shootings on three occasions; the same holds for Lange, Knecht, Lohse and Lieutenant Osis, commander of the traffic police in Riga. He is not German.*

Who did the shooting?

> *Ten or twelve German Sicherheitsdienst soldiers.*

What was the procedure?

> *What procedure?*

The killing, how was the killing organized?

> *All of the Jews went on foot from the ghetto in Riga to the liquidation site. Near the pits, they had to deposit their clothes, which were washed, sorted and shipped back to Germany. Jews—men, women and children—passed through police cordons on their way to the pits, where they were shot by German soldiers.*

Did you report the execution of the order to Himmler?

> *Yes, indeed. I notified Himmler by phone that the ghetto in Riga was liquidated. And then when I was in Lötzen, East Prussia, in December 1941, I reported in person too. Himmler was satisfied with the results. He said that more Jewish convoys were due to arrive in Latvia, and these were to be liquidated by me also.*

Go into more detail.

> *At the end of January 1942, I was at Himmler's head-
> quarters in Lötzen, East Prussia, to discuss organiza-
> tional matters regarding the Latvian SS legions. There
> Himmler informed me that additional convoys were
> due to arrive from the Reich and from other countries.
> The destination point would be the Salaspils concen-
> tration camp, which lay one and a quarter miles from
> Riga to the southeast.*

I know where Salaspils is.

> *Himmler said that he had not yet determined how he
> would have them exterminated: whether to have them
> shot on board their convoys or in Salaspils, or whether
> to chase them into the swamp somewhere.*

How was the matter resolved?

> *It was my opinion that shooting would be the simpler
> and quicker death. Himmler said he would think it
> over and then give orders later through Heydrich.*

What countries were the Jews in Salaspils brought from?

> *Jews were brought from Germany, France, Belgium,
> Holland, Czechoslovakia and from other occupied
> countries to the Salaspils camp. To give a precise count
> of the Jews in the Salaspils camp would be difficult.
> In any case, all the Jews from the camp were extermi-
> nated. But I would like to make an additional state-
> ment while we are on this topic.*

What statement would you like to make?

> *I would like to say for the record that Göring shares in
> the guilt for the liquidation of Jewish convoys that ar-
> rived from other countries. In the first half of February
> 1942, I received a letter from Heydrich. In this letter
> he wrote that Reichsmarschall Göring had got himself*

involved in the Jewish question, and that Jews were now being shipped to the east for annihilation only with Göring's approval.

This does not diminish your guilt. Describe your role in the Jewish liquidations in Salaspils.

I have already said that I discussed the extermination of Jews in Salaspils with Himmler in Lötzen. That alone makes me an accessory to this crime. Beyond that, Jews were shot in Salaspils camp by forces recruited from my Secret and Security police units. The commander of the SD secret police and Gestapo in Latvia, Lieutenant Colonel Dr. Lange, was directly in charge of the shootings. Other officers who reported to me on the shooting of Jews in the camp were the commander of the secret police and Gestapo in the Baltic States, Major-General Jost; Colonel of Police Achamer-Pifrader and Colonel of Police Fuchs.

Specifically, what did they report to you?

They reported that two to three convoys of Jews were to arrive per week, all subject to liquidation.

Then the number of Jews shot in Salaspils ought to be known too, isn't that correct?

Yes, of course. I can give you the approximate figures. The first Jewish convoys arrived in Salaspils in November 1941. Then, in the first half of 1942, convoys arrived at regular intervals. I believe that in November 1941, no more than three convoys arrived in all, but during the next seven months, from December 1941 to June 1942, eight to twelve convoys arrived each month. Overall, in eight months, no less than fifty-five and no more than eighty-seven Jewish convoys arrived in the camp. Given that each convoy carried a thousand people, that makes a total of 55,000 to 87,000 Jews exterminated in the Salaspils camp.

That figure sounds low. Are you telling the truth?

I have no other, more exact figures. It should be added, however, that before my arrival in Riga, a significant number of Jews in the Baltic states and Belorussia were exterminated. I was informed of this fact.

By whom, specifically?

Stablecker, Prützmann, Lange, Major-General Schröder, the SS and Police Leader in Latvia; Major-General Möller, the SS and Police Leader in Estonia; and Major-General Wysocki, the SS and Police Leader in Lithuania.

Be specific. What did they report?

Schröder reported to me that over and above those Jews who had been exterminated in the ghetto in Riga, an additional 70,000 to 100,000 Jews were exterminated in Latvia. Dr. Lange directly oversaw those shootings. Möller reported that in Estonia everything was in order as far as the Jewish question was concerned. The Estonian Jewish population was insignificant, all in all about 3,000 to 5,000 and that was reduced to nil. The greater part were exterminated in Tallinn. Wysocki reported that 100,000 to 200,000 Jews were exterminated—shot—in Lithuania, on Stablecker's orders. In Lithuania the Jewish exterminations were overseen by the commander of the secret police and Gestapo Lieutenant-Colonel Jäger. All told, the number of Jews exterminated in the actions in the Baltic East reached somewhere in the vicinity of 190,500 to 253,000.

In his reply to telegram no. 1331, from the Security Police of Riga, dated 6 February 1942, SS-Standartenführer Karl Jäger reported the following *from Kovno:* Re: executions up to 1 February 1942, by the Einsatz-kommando 3A: 136,421 Jews. Total: 138,272, of these, women: 55,556; children: 34,464. *Do you have anything to add?*

    No. Jäger is a precise person.

With a few of his other cronies, Jeckeln was condemned to death and on February 3, 1946, he was hanged on Victory Square—Uz-varas laukums—in front of a crowd of some four thousand.

Now in all this madness, in the hope of finding an answer to at least one question, I am obsessed by the thought that the father of Leila Mazais, the already long-dead Bavarian-Latvian with Hitler's medal in the bottom of a cardboard box, directly participated in the elimination of the twenty-year-old violinist Frida Landsberg, the long-lamented love of my uncle Karlo Osterman and, therefore, altogether irrationally, altogether senselessly, I no longer want to see the fat, aged ballerina Leila Mazais, because discussions on this theme are pointless.

Ada's fridge is full of food. There are all kinds of delicacies, small and large. Pieces of first-class Parmesan, dried tomatoes, jars of pesto, various cheeses, pâté (including goose), pickled eels, olives, capers and prosciutto. On a shelf stand a tin of olive oil, a little bottle of thick, aged *aceto balsamico* and a dozen packets of pasta, from farfalle and "elephant trunks" to tagliatelle. All this is brought by the Italians who come in the summer to the upper floors of the house that is no longer ours, then Ada makes it into dinner for them and they all talk about life. Or else Ada goes to the Italians upstairs and on the terrace that was once ours gathers up her past, for a moment cheerfully. Then she stops mumbling and talks clearly, she doesn't close her eyes like that frustrated Rosalina, who first rolls them upward as though she was fainting. They're decent people, those Italians, with them Ada is completely herself, with them, in what is now their house, she is at home.

Well, tell her, tell her once and for all, my sister insists.

So we invited Leila, who was roaming around Rovinj like a deaf dog, summoning up drowned times, for my ratatouille and Ada's crème caramel, our "red" Italians, Sergio and Elena, came down too, there was a gentle breeze in the garden, the swifts foretold rain, we talked about recent films, and about Thomas Bernhard and Robert Walser, then a bit about Ignaz Semmelweis, a bit about Garshin and Zweig, Elena about some psychiatric cases, because

Elena is a psychiatrist and she keeps a whole galaxy of human pain, human sorrow in little bundles, some in her head, some in her chest. Her Sergio talked about the Left in Bologna, because Sergio is a left-winger from Bologna, languages intertwined, wine was poured, then I said, *Leila's father had a medal from Hitler.*

Sergio smiled and concluded bitterly, *That's a nightmare, generations of the dead oppress the minds of the living. Says Marx.*

Then it rained. Terrible, diluvial rain. A torrent of murky swirling water swept down the hill on Bregovita, and drunken Leila had a heart attack.

Into the garden came a large snow-white bird the size of a seagull, only it wasn't a seagull, seagulls are greedy and they scream, this bird strolled regally into our already dark cellar, bearing on its wings light, a heavenly beauty. A caladrius. It was a male, because it had an orange beak on which a little sun flickered. It had orange legs, while the female has black legs and their beaks too are black, so what quivers on them is not the sun, but death. This caladrius had eyes like tar, out of which lightning flashed.

The caladrius raised its head toward the ceiling and—began to sing. It was a song of joy and a song of sorrow too, a strange song, disturbing and mysterious. It walked over to the numbed Leila and climbed onto her chest.

Legend has it that if the caladrius turns its head away from the sick person it approaches, the sick person will die; if it stops and looks them in the eye for a long time, the caladrius draws into itself the sick person's weakness and carries it high above the clouds, where that weakness, that sickness disperses into a million little fragments. The sick person then recovers.

The caladrius is a bird of foreseeing, a prophet bird of unconquerable wildness. Legend also has it that song is life for the caladrius, it sings when it is sad, it sings when it is angry, it sings when it is afraid and when it loves. And when it loses its mate, its companion, its comrade, a vast sadness overwhelms the caladrius, it sings and remains forever alone. It takes others' sins upon itself.

What to do with the lives around us, within us? How to classify them? They are and are not examined lives, monochrome canvases with blots, smudges, freckles scattered over a space made up of shackled time.

Examined lives (canvases), crisscrossed with shallow empty spaces, dappled with little bumps—hillocks—and narrow furrows, cuttings, grooves, many alike, in which slow, stagnant waters swirl. Lives with rounded edges, easily catalogued, easily connected, easily nailed onto the shelves of memory. And forgotten there.

Then, those others: lives crisscrossed, entangled, knotted with veins, scars, clefts which continue to breathe under the gravestones over the little mounds of our being, scabbed-over wounds that still bleed within. Impenetrable lives. They flicker in the darkness, sending out little sparks of light, fluorescent, like the bones of corpses.

Placed side by side, there is no current between them, because both these kinds of life collapse into themselves, silently and menacingly like rising waters.

Kaleidoscopic lives. Like the drawings of schizoid patients.

At secondary school, we developed our sexuality. At university, when there were no lectures, we played tennis. We batted balls about instead of pounding reality. The little balls came back, reality slipped away. We started digging through other people's lives. The labyrinth became increasingly entangled, the dead-ends multiplied. What remained were photographs. Photographs smear over memory. Memory sinks into a chasm of healed pain. There it ferments and finally evaporates. Leaving only a sigh, an exhalation.

I worked as a clinical psychologist at the University Hospital in Belgrade. In the same hospital my friend Adam Kaplan was employed as a psychiatrist. When I left Belgrade I missed Adam Kaplan. The other people's lives into which we had plunged together melted away, drained away, evaporated. Ours ossified. Imprisoned in our bodies, those strangers' lives wandered off, that is to say I, and then Adam Kaplan too, left them to stagger away mindlessly, lost, penalized and alone. Now they come back to me, now after a quarter of a century they fly up like a species of bodiless, transparent, dumb bird, as though they were steam, they creep in through the cracks in my shack and wrap around me. I hear them, I hear them whispering, *Come back, don't let us vanish exiled like this, abandoned. Separate us. We are squashed flat, crushed, stuck together in a mass, in a ball, and we roll through time.*

When I listen to them, to those voices, when they turn up and break through my shield, I breathe with increased difficulty; those lives, those voices suffocate me like my asthma, the silent strangler-murderer, whose transparent fingers I cannot detach from my lungs. That asthma used to be an enigma, not anymore. I know that she, the seducer, sometimes drags herself into the chests of the undesirable and the unwanted, and that, with time, with an increasingly loud whistling, the desire for life of those undesirable and unwanted becomes ever quieter. But, my childhood and youth were good and healthy. I was loved and I loved. I had little stars round my eyes, so what invited, what summoned this twenty-year-long nonbreathing, this suffocation, this airlessness?

Where am I? Into what, over these twenty or so years away from time that crackled, from time at a gallop that imploded, and set about flowing into me, inside, filling me with a kind of destructive energy that, like electric shocks, disorients one, swallows and drags one down, into silty innards—into what have I drained away, in what have I buried myself? In the love-hate clinch of Ameles Potamos and Mnemosyne. What do I do now?

Adam Kaplan visited me two or three times. They were good visits. I have already written about them, so there's no need to elaborate. In my little Istrian town, where I felt until recently like the old Andreas Ban, because, although my home has fallen apart, although I am myself falling apart, in that little town I was at home, because in summer, after the country broke up, as well as Adam, the occasional other old, aging, metropolitan pal, a water polo chum, a preferans companion, a tennis or professional partner would sometimes come to my little Istrian town, and then there would be a celebration, fireworks of conjured-up adventures, an encyclopedia of names would fly open, from my life at nursery, primary school, secondary school, university, from my sporting, love, military, artistic life oh, how many shared circles in whose whirlpools we danced like spinning tops. Then that all came to an end. Little doses of decency filled containers of tolerableness, I placed them on the rubbish heap of my tiny Croatian life, and instead of that past (life), in my head, in my chest stretched a ditch where a mirage moans, light as a ghost.

So, Adam Kaplan came to my coastal town several times, and then it all stopped. Where I often spend the winters, I have nothing to show anyone. It is an ordinary town, on the tedious side, a small town with a big local section in the daily paper. From that section one learns what is essential for this town: who married whom and where, who was born to whom, when the water and electricity will go off, who has celebrated their fiftieth anniversary of finishing secondary school (with a photograph of smiling old people). That local section informs one of the local tourist association's competition for the best-cared-for vegetable plot, balcony, local architecture and regional details, for which, that expert association, awards a first and second prize (and, for the sake of positive discrimination, on the whole to women), but local readers are deprived of local awareness of the content of those local prizes (are they monetary?). From the extensive local columns, one discovers how many people (say, thirty-one) have given blood, although their names remain confidential to protect their privacy. One can learn details of the meetings of amateur harmonica players, then belated news about street entertainers— musicians, acrobats and jugglers—who had once visited the little town, and then it was truly, not just metaphorically, transformed into a somewhat bigger circus than it already is, but by the time the news was printed, the entertainers had already left, entirely in the style of weather forecasts which let people know about past meteorological conditions, and begin with the words, *Yesterday it was cloudy, with outbreaks of rain.* The local news is not always informative, sometimes it commands: *Put on your national dress and dance a* kolo *for Governor Ivan Mažuranić, who was born two hundred years ago today.* Then there is news about school pupils spending time together, having succeeded in parting from their mobile phones for a couple of hours, there is local news, there is no need at all to go into the town or its surroundings. Besides (during the day) the little town is unnaturally noisy, devastatingly noisy and, if you don't have to, why go out?

And, of course, more than anything local newspapers are full of little black-bordered announcements, sometimes accompanied by doleful amateur verses about those who are no more, along with God's blessing and pleas for the intercession of various saints. That's why, whenever I can, I leave this town in winter.

During Adam's short (and rare) visits, we strewed our lives throughout the rooms and rearranged our luggage. That luggage included heavy clothes and fluttery clothes, there was some decay, eroded by damp, a kind of rotting (refuse) that crumbled like ash between the fingers, there were little boxes in which jewels danced.

When was that? Three years ago, ten, twenty? Time has stuck together like the pages of a book steeped in moisture, become a great mass of grayish-black mold, which now sways over my head, emitting airlessness.

Then comes a call. Dominik Marengo, Adam's former colleague, telephones to say, *Adam Kaplan has killed himself. With his father's pistol.*

A link in my innards uncouples. It spins like a small gold coin, then calms and settles.

He left a letter addressed to you, says Dominik Marengo. *A fat letter. The funeral is the day after tomorrow.*

I go to fewer and fewer funerals, although they are increasingly frequent. At funerals ghosts surface, which later cruise about and frighten me. At funerals brittle (burned) bones and rotten flesh, bloodless veins and blind eyes are buried, and out of the grave spring skeletons, rattling and dancing. Priests spread incense, clergymen reel off their prayers, the bereaved cross themselves or clutch fists, the performance generally ends with some deus ex machina souring the play. Like recently when my father died.

So, at Adam Kaplan's funeral, a woman, roughly as old as me, Andreas Ban, in other words a little younger than Adam Kaplan, stood rigid beside the open grave, gazing into space. That woman had gray eyes, glassy as marbles, and on her head a straw hat with a broad brim, black and drooping under its burden of fruit, vegetables and variously colored ribbons. The woman was unwashed, in a black cape, she had pulled deep, worn-out shoes with no laces onto her bare feet. She had dirty nails and red lipstick. Then, in the middle of the sadness and the pointless speeches by Adam's colleagues, that woman unknown to me suddenly fainted. Before she fell, a cry broke from her. The cry flew up to the sky and heavy rain teemed onto the graveyard. It reverberated appallingly, there over that pit around which small heaps of sticky dark earth caught the light. I asked someone next to me, *Who is she, who is that woman?* and that person said *No one knows.* I stand, and in the inside pocket of my jacket I grip Adam Kaplan's "legacy."

Dear Andreas,

See below my truncated family tree with its rotten shoots. That would already be enough for you to learn details about me of which I was myself until recently entirely unaware. Nevertheless, there comes a moment when someone starts probing, and if they don't discover enough, the gaps can always be filled by the imagination. Or by lies.

In my apartment I have the files of some of the people I treated, whose lives I stratified. Today I don't know whether that was necessary. I don't know whether I helped any of them. Take these stories and organize them, they will open up a map of lives on which nothing is definitively drawn, where everything moves and, in that movement, changes. You have your own "histories of illness," if you did not throw them away when you moved. I have tried to make a crossword puzzle and at the very beginning I realized that many of these lives crisscross, that many of them resemble each other, that they are in fact the same life, that is, they could be one single life, of one single person, both male and female, both adult and child, lives—the life of one single time. Then my own family story caught me unawares, which chilled me. I'm leaving it to the end.

It's a long letter, but since it is addressed to me, I can't quote it in full. It's an intimate letter. Overleaf is Adam's family tree and the story it discloses will be told only in hints, perhaps now, perhaps on some other occasion. There are family trees like this all around us. Nevertheless, what is clear at first glance is that Adam Kaplan didn't kill himself with his father's pistol, because it seems that he didn't know who his father was. Nevertheless, by killing himself, he had also eliminated the father who was unknown to him. At least that's what psychiatry tells us.

The Kaplans

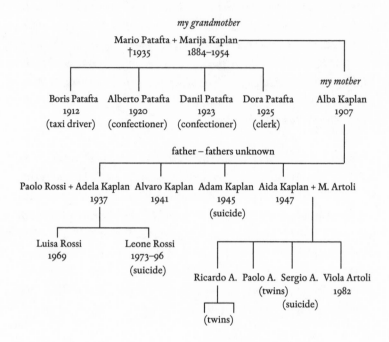

One morning at breakfast at a villa for writers and translators at Wannsee, Stephan, otherwise a graphic designer, said, *I'm from a small town near Leipzig, it's strange that I've forgotten Russian. I learned Russian in school for five years, I had to learn Russian, we all learned Russian at school*, said Stephan, *but now I can't remember a single Russian word.*

Maybe your parents remember? I said to Stephan, but Stephan, who was thirty, perhaps thirty-five, with light-skinned people you never quite know, Stephan said, *They don't remember either, my parents have forgotten everything, and they haven't found their place in the new Germany, either. My parents walk in the air*, said Stephan. Stephan himself is somehow transparent, light as a tiny, hungry cat in one's arms, and he is never in a good mood.

That evening, Stephan, the Romanian poet Nora Iuga and I drank two bottles of red wine, Stephan ate an avocado, Nora asked, *What's that?* and Stephan fed her with a spoon across the table. Nora said, *Mmmm*, leaned toward Stephan and whispered, *Why are you sad, Stephan?* and Stephan let out a wail, *I'm terribly sad. When I come back from Romania*, he said, *I'd like us to talk.* When Stephan came back from Romania, Nora asked me, *What do we do now? Stephan maintains that he had already lived in Bucharest, even though he has never been there.* "I was in Bucharest, I was," Stephan insisted, Nora said, "I was in Bucharest in one of my former lives, but *as a woman, I was a woman in Bucharest," said Stephan*, Nora said.

Then I thought for the first time, perhaps Nora Iuga is not Nora Iuga either, perhaps I am not Andreas Ban, perhaps I am a woman from my previous or future or existing life, or perhaps I am a man whom I have not yet met. Perhaps various people squat inside me, I thought then, and I decided to research it.

In the villa at Wannsee I also met Hans Traube, or rather Antonije Tedeschi, which aroused additional doubts in me, it could even be said (although still mild, but nonetheless) confusion. During a garden party which was, of course, held in the garden, because this particular villa on Wannsee is surrounded by a garden, in fact a very extensive park, and horticulturally astoundingly varied, I will not now list all the cultivated exotic plants that grow there, but later, considerably later, I would come to see the situation with parks as a very significant situation, so, at that garden party I was approached by a good-looking, indeed a beautiful man, well built, tall and gray-haired, around sixty years old, who began to take photographs of everything around him: guests, musicians, vegetation, the tiny windows glittering on the high mahogany doors, while nacreous bubbles burst in the air, filling the park with the scent of painful beauty, like a heavy, mysterious perfume.

Strange, I thought, that man is quite like me.

My name is Hans, said the beautiful man in his admirably tailored suit. *My name is Hans Traube and I come from Salzburg.*

You can't be called Hans Traube, I said, *Hans Traube is an imagined character, Hans Traube from Salzburg was invented by a writer, consequently Hans Traube can't be here, Hans Traube can live exclusively between the covers of a book.* Then "Hans Traube" said, *I'll tell you my life story*, and I said, *Don't. I already know your life story.*

You don't know everything, he said.

Then Hans Traube smiled, displaying his beautiful teeth, his regular teeth, not porcelain, then bowed and disappeared.

*

For two years I sort and classify Adam Kaplan's files and what remains of my dossiers. I travel. I visit cities, people and memories corroded by time. Over the last two or three years I have been in Brussels, in Sarajevo, in Skopje and in Paris. And a few other places, for instance Amsterdam, for a month, or two, or three. I went in the winter, so as not to freeze to death in this tomb here. That whole time I didn't write, I just catalogued. Lives. People. Their little realities and their fragile dreams. Or maybe I didn't go anywhere, maybe I spent the whole time sitting here, wrapped in rags, blowing onto my hands, not knowing where that "here" is.

It sounds feeble, but now, given my advanced years, I have the right to the occasional banal, kitsch utterance, up to a point it's cheering. Life is travel. And traveling, that "small death of departure" as Virilio puts it, reduces the tension of the dead-end and brings (temporary) forgetfulness. So, I travel with suitcases or without them, I go away and I come back, I return through streets and houses—rooms, things, rediscovered and lost friends and books, small objects, toys tucked away, Leo's cardboard boxes with little jumbled cars and Lego bricks, with piled-up LPs containing old hits, but also children's productions, programs and songs, brittle plastic albums with scratched singles; two pairs of skis, two pairs of ski boots, old-fashioned; yellowing bed linen edged with Toledo embroidery and my mother's monogram— I could count until I'm blue in the face everything I encounter on my returns, whether from journeys or simply from sitting in my room. A warehouse, a depository of old things, old people, old days suffocating in a dark, smallish storeroom. I could list to the limits of my memory, which, thank goodness, is contracting, so that I remember less and less of the joy and unease that such moving/unmoving brings, there remain images, blurred images, flickering blots. Were all those journeys, those numerous stirrings and evasions, were they "worth it"? I don't know. Did they bring serenity? No, they didn't. Did they bring pleasure? Sometimes, yes. There were not only suitcases of various sizes, there were also trunks, those transoceanic metal ones, and wooden ones, some of them two meters long, in which drawings and oil paintings wrapped in straw traveled (there are fewer and fewer of them, because I sell them), and in the end, here, as is fitting for endings, a small Chinese suitcase, checked red and black, which holds only the most essential items. The destinations are closer, departures increasingly brief and returns, although I don't know to what or to whom, increasingly rapid.

Some twenty years ago, Leo and I arrived in Toronto from Rijeka with three huge cheap suitcases bought in haste in Trieste, with little wheels that had buckled with the weight, so we dragged our luggage along the ground. What they contained was apparently what we needed for a new beginning. But it wasn't. We bought additional secondhand clothes, secondhand crockery, secondhand books and lived a secondhand life. Two years in Canada brought us nothing, not stability nor a future. Something was missing.

I spent a month in Brussels. I was supposed to write, but I didn't. I could have got to know the city, visited the museums, gone for walks, but I didn't. It was cold, it snowed, there was nothing green anywhere, the café terraces were closed, so I sat in that lovely warm apartment and looked out of the window.

The windows of the study face Oude Granmarkt, a street where wheat was once traded. Across the road is a small Greek restaurant, Menelas, where no one goes, yet candles constantly flicker in its window. There used to be a shooting club in that place. I live in the residential quarter with a mixed population: middle class, artists and writers and—the homeless. As everywhere in the world, the homeless huddle on the pavement, wrapped in rags, holding up a piece of cardboard with *J'ai faim* written on it. In the newspapers I read about shelter for these rejected people and about the fact that such refuges are filling increasingly fast and that all these people and their messed-up, broken lives, their presence, their visibility, is becoming a serious problem for the city of Brussels.

Opposite my apartment is a row of residential buildings with high windows and no curtains. At night I watch what people do there. When they go to bed, when they get up. I see what their pajamas are like, who comes to visit them. I enter their lives obliquely, then I throw my own over my shoulder to roll like a pumped-up ball through the half-empty rooms with their high ceilings and with walls virtually devoid of pictures, and I hear it, that life of mine, bouncing about dully and shallowly.

It's an interesting little street, this Grand Marché/Oude Graanmarkt. Quiet, out of the way, with a small market in its center. On the street that crosses it, which I can also see, there is a secondary school. And those young people who flow toward the school gate every working day at 8:30 a.m. and come out of it around 4 p.m. are all that brings some liveliness outside my window, not to say life. At the weekend, when those girls and boys are not there, I miss them. As I stand glued to the glass during the week, I am beginning to recognize some of them, and I feel like going down to join them.

In a letter, Goran Ferčec writes from Zagreb to describe his visit to Belgrade and he mentions Ulica Gramsci and Ulica Clara Zetkin. In Zagreb there's no Ulica Antonio Gramsci any more, nor an Ulica Clara Zetkin. Others who have disappeared from Zagreb streets (and therefore from the memory) are Karl Marx, the Spanish fighters, Friedrich Engels, Palmiro Togliatti, Che Guevara, Karl Liebknecht and many others from that album. Clara Zetkin and

Rosa Luxemburg held out to the last moment, only in the end to say farewell to the streets of Zagreb too, with a prophetic *Auf Wiedersehen*, I hope.

In Brussels, by contrast, the house where Karl Marx lived and in which he and Engels wrote *The Communist Manifesto* is one of the city's tourist attractions. Even though, in 1848, the Belgian Ministry of Justice accused him of giving financial support to Belgian workers in their preparations for revolution and drove him out of the country, Karl Marx is not dead in Brussels. On the façade of the famous restaurant La Maison du Cygne, on the magnificent central square, La Grand-Place/Grote Markt, there is a plaque recording the fact that this was where Marx and his comrades talked about revolution and the founding of international communist organizations.

The suitcase I arrived in Brussels with is not the checked one, it's large and strong. I filled it with clothes I won't wear. Jackets, trousers, tops, it's all hanging in a large wardrobe, waiting to be crammed back into my only expensive Samsonite, to move on. To go back? Like me, waiting for this journey too to end.

Goran also writes about *the need to flee*, and he's so young. *The world has been completely flattened*, he says, *there's nowhere one can disappear*, he says, then he talks about shoes, which are for him *little apartments*. Many people write or have written about shoes, Hamsun, or let's say Bernhard, but one could write about the shoes of those who did not write about shoes, who died frozen in the snow, like Robert Walser, or in their cold huts, about the shoes of those who languish in madhouses, for instance. Goran sees shoes as a metaphor for constant movement, I see them as a deception. Shoes which pinch or fall off, which wear out, which camouflage or disclose, which are agreeable or disagreeable, which leave marks or cover them over. Which sometimes drive one mad.

One early spring in Rovinj, Goran and I had, as he put it, *a mid-*

night conversation beside the illuminated, blue and empty hotel pool filled with water. He asked me what we, as writers, could offer one another, where writing about the past was leading us, whether writing about the past was like writing about dreams. Who was interested in the past? That's what he asked me.

Then we watched and touched the nocturnal Rovinj silence, sprinkled with the "sweat" of pine trees, as my dead friend the poet Raša Livada would say, and now, as I am writing about this, it ought to be a conversation from the past. How can it be about the past, if I'm writing about it now? If we write about what seems to be past, then what seems to have passed is now, as we are writing, here. Often, while we write about what has recently passed, we write about the present. What is past may be forgotten, and what is forgotten does not exist. But if we think that what is past is forgotten, that means that it is not yet forgotten, because we are thinking about it. The Alzheimer's tangles that we nurture, and on which we hang small decorative antidotes for survival, do not help. They are unexpectedly penetrated by dreams or reality and cause chaos. And people say, *Your past and the past of your characters, that is you, that's who they are now, today and tomorrow.*

In Brussels then, in the apartment, I find an unnumbered issue of a magazine published here by Passa Porta, the Belgian International House of Literature. The theme of the magazine is "Borders." It contains texts by some well-known writers, philosophers and journalists, such as Claudio Magris, Ingo Schulze, Régis Debray and Daniel Salvatore Schiffer. This Schiffer, I discover, is known for being an engaged philosopher of social-democratic orientation, he published a book about dandyism, which immediately reminded me of the late Dragoš Kalajić, also a great champion of dandyism, otherwise a painter and writer of fascist worldview, an emphatic elitist with no funds. Schiffer, his father Italian, his mother of Austrian-German extraction, and he himself a Belgian who lived and taught in Liège, says that it is good that there are no borders within Europe anymore, but *Europe must protect itself from outside elements,* he says. *For example,* adds Schiffer, *I am against the inclusion of Turkey in the European Union. It has no common point of contact culturally or geographically with Europe, apart from that small area west of the Bosporus. Turkey is not Greece. The Turks penetrated into Europe as far as Vienna, but that was an invasion. Unlike Europe, Turkey is a Muslim country. Religious identities also have to be taken into account.*

I "listen" to Schiffer as though I was in Croatia. I would like to say something, to rebel, but Schiffer doesn't let me. Schiffer gets heated and shouts, *Europe must defend itself! Europe must defend its culture and democracy.*

I would like to ask, *From whom must it defend its culture and democracy, how must it defend its culture and democracy, why?* Schiffer doesn't let me, Schiffer is in a trance like Hitler and Mussolini in those old film newsreels, like some contemporary speechmakers, there are some of those in Croatia too. But Schiffer is an educated man, so here and there he produces the occasional stale argument, but he doesn't give up. *We must build our ideas and our reflections on the foundations of national states,* Schiffer waves his arms although he lowers his voice. *I am in favor of a mixture of people, cultures and beliefs, and also cosmopolitanism, an individual must be free, but he must respect the culture of the country that has accepted him. And in order for there to be respect, there must first be a strong identity.*

Instead of reading Schiffer, perhaps when I was in Belgium I should after all have taken a look at the shopping centers or, better still, the museums, especially the Magritte Museum, where René's surrealist works would have made me so cheerful that I would have bought a reproduction of one of them in the museum bookshop and later thought about it, and if *my* tranquil days really do come (wherever I happen to be), which I doubt, as disquiet has so anchored itself in me, so fixed itself in concrete that I don't know whether it is any longer possible to "kill" it, but, carry on, when such days come, I would be able to write the occasional line for the public about my encounter with Magritte. Although I doubt whether such reminiscence would console me, because the way I am, I would immediately connect Magritte's playful pictures with his, Magritte's, life and with the suicide of his mother, who tried several times to disappear, and in the end succeeded, although her husband kept her locked in the bedroom (in those circumstances I would have killed myself too), and in that bedroom she was probably unable to carry on with her millinery, and could only sleep, but, there, she managed to get out and drown herself in some Belgian river. At the time his mother drowned, Magritte was small, only thirteen, and they say, when they found her, Régine Magritte, née Bertinchamps, her wet dress was stuck to her face, and hence, they say, those paintings by her son René, traumatized by the sight, hence those wrapped heads, some of which are kissing. I should have gone to Magritte, I see that now, because I would have been able to tell him about that benighted Schiffer, because René Magritte was an atheist and left-wing, and, unlike bigoted right-wingers, who are always dramatically serious and scowling, as though they were some kind of prophet, he was able to be cheerful even though he may not have been. And we would have laughed, recounting how after the war Magritte supported himself by painting imitation Picassos and Braques, even though in recent years I have been ever less inclined to laugh.

I sit there in that Brussels room, I listen to the maddened Schiffer, and I hear that university bigwig in the Rovinj street on the hill wagging her tongue, *You shouldn't have written that book about the town that gave you everything.*

Belgium is a complicated country. Politically, linguistically and nationally. Its colonial past seems still to linger in nooks of the consciousness of part of her population of burghers, in whose identity (fuck identity) it drills large or small spaces where ideas about "noble masters" may be born. Belgium has a considerable dark-skinned population, descendants of its former colonial subjects, not to say slaves, but today her citizens. These dark-skinned Belgians live for the most part in ghettoized districts and are less well educated.

In Brussels I corresponded with Goran about Danilo Kiš. Goran told me that, for him, Kiš was *distant in time*, which wasn't entirely clear to me, because time is always here, it doesn't go anywhere, it comes, but it doesn't go, it doesn't move further away or come closer, it just flows, and sometimes trickles and drips and one can always plunge into it, one can also drown in it, as Magritte's mother did, and many others, Virginia Woolf for example, but, in the end, one always emerges from it, from time. I don't have a problem with time, I am just ironing my youth.

And Goran Ferčec, with whom I spent time in Brussels, in that Brussels apartment, instead of at least walking and looking into shop windows, actually I did go to a VIP reception where I got drunk and on the way back to the apartment I staggered and vomited, Goran Ferčec also travels. He writes that in Budapest, on the Széchenyi suspension bridge, *which*, he says, *is so massive that it resembles a small town, he saw a man with a beard standing, making comical gestures with his arms, and then starting to unbutton his shirt*, and he says that he, Goran, was watching from the other side of the bridge. *The man catches my eye*, writes Goran, *he starts waving more wildly, then he takes off his shirt and, bare-chested, climbs onto the protective railing and makes faces at me while still waving. If I carry on watching him, he could throw himself off*, writes Goran, *if I stop watching him, he could still throw himself off. And then*, writes Goran, *I turn and head toward Buda without looking round.* I don't know what I would have done, perhaps I would have approached him, and if the man had thrown himself off the bridge, perhaps I would have jumped after him. Or perhaps I wouldn't.

I also attended a celebration for the employees of a company. There, in Brussels. I couldn't spend a month literally confined to the apartment. Everyone had brought some kind of food to that celebration, I contributed two bottles of Croatian wine, from Istria. One employee boasted loudly that *all* the ingredients of her dish were organic, *even the Parmesan*, she exclaimed. That organic dish was, unquestionably, three times more expensive than the same *nonorganic* food, and the person who had brought it did not appear to me any healthier than the other people around the table. Although, I know, that can't be seen just by looking, how healthy a person is, or how sick. Take me, for instance. From the outside, I look like quite a decent container, neither new nor old, while inside everything is just trash. I have reservations about organic food, I'm convinced that it serves to fill the coffers of already wealthy firms.

The theoretical physicist Michio Kaku reflects on whether, in perhaps a hundred or so years, with the help of nanotechnology, that is, thanks to the so-called replicator, the global shortage of food could turn into a great abundance; *That*, says Kaku, *would be the road to Utopia*. Whether that abundance would be organic or not, Dr. Kaku doesn't say.

Then Goran Ferčec spent some time in Moscow, with Bulgakov, and I followed him. *Now we're in the shop known as Torgsin that sells foreign goods*, said Goran. *This shop sells goods to the citizens of Moscow exclusively for foreign currency, and consequently it's a place the majority of Muscovites cannot enter. Azazello and Behemot come without a single foreign coin*, says Goran, *they guzzle international delicacies and create chaos: they toss five or six mandarins into their mouths, with the skins on, the shop assistants are disconcerted, Azazello and Behemot then destroy an Eiffel Tower made of chocolate, swallow a few herrings, set fire to the shop and leave. Moscow burns. There's no longer any freedom of choice, which isn't any kind of freedom, because it's fed with money and power*, says Goran.

It's just as well Bulgakov's dead, not to ruin our shopping.

Goran doesn't give up, he seems to me already a little desperate. He sees charred remnants everywhere. All right, I see them too, but I'm used to them, Goran is young. *It's among those ashes that the man from the Széchenyi Bridge is staggering about*, says Goran, who now recognizes in the look the man directed at him the look of a Holy Fool who gathers up the remnants of the world, and throws those ruins, that charred residue into the Danube (Benjamin and Klee's *Angelus Novus*). I suggest to Goran that he should spend a bit of time in Brussels, although I doubt that this would cheer him up.

Instead of coming to Brussels, Goran goes off, in fact as he puts it, *goes back* to the provinces. *The conditions for alienation are ideal there, but every return to the provinces*, he says, *carries the risk that someone will ask me what I'm doing.* I wanted to suggest that he read Heidegger's essay "Why do I stay in the provinces?" but I don't believe that would have consoled him. I don't have a problem with the provinces, because I am barricaded in, I'm invisible to the provinces and so, I must say, are they to me. No one seeks me out, no one bothers me, no one asks me anything. It's only when I go out that the horrors begin.

I went to have my hair cut, as I have to from time to time. The barber asked me. *What do you do?*

I write, I said.

What do you write?

I write.

For a newspaper?

No.

Some sort of books?

Yes.

For children? I've got grandchildren.
They're not for children.
Are they thin?
No, they're fat.
I don't like fat books, he says.
The Bible's fat, I say.
He wanted to shave me as well, I wouldn't let him.

In Brussels I had a barber on the ground floor. He didn't ask me anything, so I let him shave me.

Goran immediately got the joke. Every question, he wrote, is in fact seeking the answer to just one question: *What are we occupied with? What are we doing? That question recurs constantly in everyday life and its repetition, its concatenation in which I ask you, they ask me, and someone will soon ask them, confirms that there are subjects to which there is no good answer, subjects for which any answer is an unsatisfactory answer. Perhaps then questions are superfluous as well*, says Goran, that is, he concludes, *or simply symbolic.*

I've stopped asking questions. It's enough to observe.

Then we talked a bit about language. I won't quote all that here, because when people talk about language, especially about the Croatian language nowadays, I get irritated, and then it takes me a long time to recover from my irritation.

We talked about other things, that winter, Goran Ferčec and I, we talked for almost a month, he in Budapest, Maribor, Koprivnica, Zagreb and Belgrade, I buried in Brussels. If I were to mention the majority of the subjects we thrashed out, I would do even more damage to the form, the form of this text of mine, wouldn't I? Which would further upset its blinded readers (and critics) who look for a cemented form of regular shapes, harmonious outlines, a form filled with a cascade of connected words, of which it would be possible to say that its characters are nuanced, the relationships, emotions and reflections distinctive, and the style polished;

that the ease of narration comes to full expression (whatever that means), that the characters are alive and convincing and remind us of people we know, we feel close to their doubts, their fears, their expectations and disappointments. What vacuity. So, in the case of a recently published book, the critics repeated, parrot-fashion, that the book was stylistically polished, that it contained powerful poetic miniatures, metaphors even, which revealed the depths of life, but they were all simply nebulous fabrications full of holes with no substance, in fact a manipulative little text by a sad soul flailing about in the cauldron of the writer's own fears, disguised by serving up to readers allegedly profound quasi-philosophical sermons wrapped in crumpled tissue paper. Of one of my books a critic mentioned that its story is presented to us by an omniscient narrator, after which all the other reviewers idiotically referred to this nonexistent omniscient narrator, while I avoid omniscient people in life as in literature. In another book of mine, I wrote that what I was writing was not a diary, nor a travelogue, nor a novel, but something in between, a kind of lame, crippled scampering through condensed time, through particles of time which had become detached from themselves to float through the underpasses of the present, while they, those superficial evaluators, those skiving arbiters, all, without fail, wrote, *This is not a diary, nor a travelogue, nor a novel*, but they didn't say what it is.

What is wanted is a form with continuity.

What kind of continuity? What continuity? Everything around us, including ourselves, it's all in patches, in spasms, in ebbing and flowing, our whole envelope, this whole earthly covering, is crisscrossed with loose stiches, which keep coming undone, and which we keep persistently trying to tighten. Under these unstitched tatters chasms open up into which we don't dare look, into which we don't wish even to glance. We try in vain to sew up and smooth out these seams, the pinpricks remain visible. Scars don't fade. With time, that patchwork of ours, that we, becomes so thin that we forget about it, as though a magic carpet had flown away, and then come back as a huge, heavy cape, covering us.

A life of continuity, how tedious. How monotonous, monochrome. A tepid, limp flow in one direction. Like literary continuity.

Given that I am a small, unknown writer, and what I say leaks away like water through a sieve, and since Hermann Broch is a great and well-known writer, so his words are quoted and remembered, here is Hermann Broch, he may perhaps be believed:

> To write means to endeavor by means of form to arrive at insights, and new insights may only be drawn from a new form. [...] But, a new form is always alien to the public. [...] Fragments are in fact nothing other than the articulated consciousness that there is no wholeness anymore and there cannot be, that it is simply not worth even trying to transform it into a work, that it is simply spurious. All that is left is man and his consciousness of the incompleteness of the world. [...] The possibilities of the novel as form have already been exhausted, and even exceeded by Joyce, and from a sociological standpoint "a good book" would be summer entertainment for a bourgeois woman, therefore it no longer has any function.

I was almost saddened by Goran's search for continuity, which would, as he put it, *accumulate ideas, affirm development*, because in the end Goran concludes, *but we are in a short-term duration, while destruction always finds enough energy to sustain itself continuously*.

Goran writes that he is traveling through the city by tram and *seeing the way the city is falling apart*, and imagines that he is *on a* tourist tour called *"Viewing the Decay."* Then he, Goran, takes up Broch who also says, *A world in a state of decay can no longer be portrayed as a whole.*

Goran also has a story about a grandmother who *refuses to talk about the liberation. Although fifteen years have passed, and almost everyone has left the village. I think, if there are no witnesses, nothing has happened, and I think of that obsessive concern of some writers with apparently the same themes about which almost everyone knows everything and about which no one ever talks. That grandmother, my grandmother,* writes Goran, *is the poeticized embodiment of a wise woman, nevertheless, she was brought up in a society and a system about which talking and communicating was never particularly prized, because if one talked about it, it might be possible, in the end, to say something. And then what? People didn't talk about the last war, and I didn't ask questions.*

Ah, secrets, those troublemakers, swindlers, illusionists, those stirrers and dissemblers, fickle devourers of souls. Seductresses. When they come to us, when they settle in us, they spread like oil slicks, they vomit blackness. They block, suffocate, engulf. They embrace us, press us to their soft, undulating chests and we, their hostages, forever enslaved, reciprocate. We plunge into them and disappear. The outside world becomes a chimera from which we flee. We lower our gaze, whisper, laugh with pursed lips or we cover our mouth with a hand, we tread, stooped, cautiously.

That's a good book, that story of Goran's, because it is not summer entertainment for a bourgeois woman, because it has the function of portraying a world in a state of decay *in* that state of decay, incomplete.

So. He reached mine. Via Broch.

I've written about Amsterdam.

In Sarajevo I alternately died and returned to life.

While I was still at Zagreb Airport, one could have concluded that something in the world, about the world, didn't add up. Flights for Sarajevo, Athens and Frankfurt were scheduled for roughly the same time. At the gate for Germany the queue was so long and drawn-out that it took several buses to carry the passengers to the aircraft, and that took awhile. The queues for Athens and Sarajevo were short, fewer than thirty people in each. Athens was in turmoil, so it could have been dangerous there, travelers like security, playing it safe. By the time I was traveling, the Sarajevo festival was over and there was still plenty of time before the New Year, when inquisitive Western Europeans go off in search of East-European (Balkan) exoticism and bizarre eccentricities.

Although I had been to Sarajevo since the end of the war, this time, when I stayed longer, I met people I hadn't seen for twenty years. I observed faces and tried to guess who had remained in the besieged city and who had left and had now returned. In conversations, twenty years after the war, the war was here, even among those born after apparent peace was established. The Sarajevo director Mladen Ovadija, my friend and former colleague, permanently settled in Toronto, was at that time in Sarajevo. We stood in front of the plaque on Ulica Ferhadija and he said, *This is where*

my friend Mahmut Čikić lost both his legs. He died in Canada. He was
an excellent engineer and first-rate mathematician.

Nedžad Abdija,
Ismet Ašćerić,
Ruždija Bektešević,
Snježana Biloš,
Predrag Bogdanović,
Vladimir Bogunović,
Gordana Čeklić,
Vasva Čengić,
Mirsad Fazlagić,
Emina Karamustafić,
Mediha Omerović,
Bahrija Pilav,
Mila Ruždić,
Mile Ružić,
Hatidža Salić,
Abdulah Sarajlić,
Sulejman Sarajlić,
Galib Sinotić,
Sreten Stamenović,
Srećko Šiklić,
Vlatko Tanacković,
Srećko Tanasković,
Božica Trajeri-Pataki,
Tamara Vejzagić-Kostić,
Jusuf Vladović
       and
Izudin Zukić.

Twenty-six citizens of Sarajevo vanished in an instant. This is just one of the numerous lists of civilians killed during the war in Sarajevo.

On May 27, 1992, in Ulica Vase Miskina, today's Ferhadija, between numbers 5 and 12, near the former Klas shop, people were queuing for bread. At 9:55 a.m. the Serbian forces aimed three 82-caliber mortar shells at that place, and their bursting action massacred 26 civilians and injured another 108 citizens of Sarajevo. This is where that plaque is, and in the pavement in front of it are the shell holes. Beside Mladen and me, in front of the memorial plaque, a twenty-year-old had stopped and said to the girl he was with, *This is where my parents' friends were killed.*

More than twenty years have passed. In sunny weather I stroll along Ferhadija with its European atmosphere; the cafés are full, people sit outside, there are rows of shops of well-known international brands, there is a book fair in the park, pensioners play chess, and stray dogs are everywhere.

They lie motionless, lethargic, curled up in the middle of squares and, on those increasingly cold nights, beside the windows of luxuriously illuminated shops or in the entrances to buildings. These homeless creatures, whose population since the war years has been growing, are surprisingly beautiful, their coats glossy. But people say that when they form packs, they can be dangerous and aggressive.

I read, then, in a newspaper, that according to the most recent census there were 11,168 dogs roaming freely in the streets of Sarajevo. That is the population of a smallish town, Rovinj for instance. I look at those dogs, among which there are some purebreds. I even came across a Tornjak, originally a sheep dog.

A Tornjak, *Canis montanus*, is a reliable, generally even-tempered dog, unbribable and distrustful of strangers.

It is resistant to disease.

It is modest in terms of food and shelter, and on winter nights it is prone to staying out in the snow, which then covers it.

The Tornjak's body is powerful and well proportioned.

They say that the Tornjak is an exceptionally intelligent dog, it learns quickly, makes good judgments and makes decisions.

Tornjaks bark a lot, but they are calm in the house. Nevertheless, if they judge that there is a threat on the horizon, their transformation is instantaneous and they are ready for battle.

Genetically, Tornjaks are a resilient breed.

So, now. There are still discussions about the origin of the Tornjak. Some maintain that their country of origin is Bosnia and Herzegovina, others that the Tornjak is a Croatian mountain dog, whose function since the eleventh century has been to protect flocks from thieves and large predators.

The first descriptions of Tornjaks date from 1067 and they can be found in the annals of the Bosnian Catholic Church, documents which confirm that this is a very ancient breed, raised for a whole millennium in Bosnia and Herzegovina. Others, in keeping with the Iranian theory of the origin of the Croats, endeavor to prove that Tornjaks came to these parts with the Croats from northern Iran, or rather from ancient Persia. Quarrels about whose dog the Tornjak is, Bosnian and Herzegovinian or Croatian, continue to this day. Just as disagreements are still ongoing about which little national state Ivo Andrić came from.

Sarajevans say that on winter nights a large Tornjak lies down on a hungry, freezing homeless man and so protects him from the cold. It is not known whether that homeless man is a Bosnian, Croat, Serb, Jew or member of some other nation, because the homeless man does not say, because he has no one to tell, because he has more urgent concerns, and it is not known on what basis this riddle could be solved from the outside.

I go to Radio-Television Bosnia and Herzegovina to see some old friends. I spend twenty-five minutes in a tram. I look at the buildings. Some have been renovated, some half-patched, pockmarked all over, some are in ruins. And there are graffiti. The most common are graffiti that say: *Watch out for bullets, Sabina, I love you*, and *Why?*

I enter a concrete complex wrapped in the former Socialist age of our shared state, massacred by time. In the huge foyer of the Radio-Television Bosnia and Herzegovina building, which Saraje-vans call "The Gray House," there is a little newspaper kiosk, and on the wall of the kiosk hangs a photograph of Josip Broz Tito. No one gets upset, no one foams at the mouth, nor does anyone exult or pat himself on the back. In that remote kiosk, Tito simply hangs as a reminder, as un-forgetting, he says nothing, he does not give orders, he does not punish, he just hangs, watches and is silent.

When I used to talk to students about Beckett's *Krapp's Last Tape*, 90 percent of them did not know what a tape recorder looked like, that unwieldy contraption with two wheels through which a tape slid. Then someone asked, *Isn't it that machine from George Clooney's film* Good Night and Good Luck? Where does oblivion begin? In childhood?

Teams of horses clopped through towns, with meter-tall alumi-num churns of milk gleaming and clattering on the carts behind them. Women waited at their doors with pots into which the milk was poured. The streets were full of droppings. The little round balls of manure could be kicked as one walked.

Classrooms were heated with "queen stoves," the floors were black, coated with varnish, while homework was written in chalk on little blackboards with golden-yellow wooden frames.

Rag balls and clay marbles and silk sweets.

Games of Chetniks/Ustasha and Partisans, then cowboys and Indians.

Mothers with cold perms.

Russian films, mostly *Stone Flower* and *The Pike's Commandment*.

Shoes, capped, to make them last longer.

Bread-soup and potato stew.

Kekec biscuits.

Bobbed hair, then in 1960 Eton crops, like in Godard's *Breathless*.

Apartments without baths because the Russians took them.

Rest homes for children with TB.

The "Albus" soap of our childhood.

Immediately after the Second World War, for laundry, people first used ash, then "live soda," and only then "Albus" and finally "Plavi Radion" washing powder.

At the end of the 1960s, we were allowed across the state frontiers. We went to Trieste to buy nylon shirts, navy-blue plastic macs, denims, bell-bottoms and winklepickers. And soap.

Then, women teachers had moustaches, joined-up eyebrows and sweaty armpits.

"Rudo" extra-depth orthopedic shoes.

"Black Cat" perfume.

Reversible coats.

Loaves weighing three kilograms.

Boro and Ramiz, the partisan hero "Pinki" and other little couriers.

Tito's collected works.

The film *Walter Defends Sarajevo*.

Postwar poverty turned us into potential members of Mensa. Our eyes were huge. We learned to see the hidden, to read the unwritten, to hear the unsaid. Life became half reality, half myth.

So, while I waited for Miralem Ovčina, editor in chief of the Drama program, and while I strolled through what was now clearly a senselessly spacious and dark foyer, flashes of my past (my youth) erupted, sizzling and crackling. A man approached me and asked, *Didn't you work here once? Might you be Dževad?*

When I was leaving Belgrade, a long-term colleague told me, *The shape of your face is not at all Serbian. You should leave*, she said.

In Rijeka people said, *How did you come by that Serbian accent?*

At the launch of one of my books in London people asked me, *Are you Jewish?*

In other words, my face could have been either a Muslim face or a Jewish face, whatever that meant, and, for Croats, also Serbian. Like the face of that homeless man the Tornjak protects on winter nights.

Whatever, however they look, whoever they belong to, there are faces to be remembered. Because of what those faces say. Or don't say.

For instance, the face of Hasan Nuhanović is a face to remember. Hasan Nuhanović studied mechanical engineering in Sarajevo. His fourth year of studies was interrupted by the war. Hasan Nuhanović survived the suffering in the Podrinje area, after which he fled with his family to Srebrenica, where in July 1995 he began to work for the United Nations as an interpreter. He witnessed the appalling events in which Mladić's forces killed his brother, his mother and his father. He wrote several dozen articles and texts about the murders in Srebrenica. He published a documentary book *Under the UN Flag: The International Community and the Srebrenica Genocide*, followed by a novel, *The Escape: Road to Srebrenica*. The events in this book refer on the whole to 1992, when the genocide began in that east Bosnian town, brought to an ignominious end in 1995.

The novel *The Escape* covers the event in which, in 1992, more than a hundred thousand Bosnian Muslims found themselves in the region of Srebrenica, Vlasenica, Cerska, Nova Kasaba, Konjević Polje, Žepa and Han Pijesak. With no pathos, with no sentimentality, through his literary gift for details and his metaphorical and symbolic images and dialogues, which slip from so-called realistic prose into a nightmare world of the surreal and the magical, then back to reality, Hasan Nuhanović can without hesitation be included among the writers of what may be called Yugoslav literature of the camps. The dead speak, the living speak, those who have yet to come speak.

Then, says Hasan Nuhanović, *we didn't know that we had become refugees. But not any kind of refugees. We had not come to a secure place, or to a third country. We left in order to hide in the mountains of eastern Bosnia. To hide from the war. As though one can hide from war in a forest. War, along with fear, reaches you in an instant. It penetrates walls, it moves over mountains, through rivers. It enters the human mind, human hearts, human souls. It settles there and will not leave.*

Ludwig Wittgenstein's *Tractatus Logico-Philosophicus*, with an introduction by Bertrand Russell and translated by Gajo Petrović, was last published in 1987 by the well-known Sarajevo publisher Veselin Masleša, founded in long-ago 1950. Veselin Masleša, whose publications educated the intelligentsia of the whole of Yugoslavia, is no more; Veselin Masleša disappeared in the war, but its publications resurface here and there, when they are needed and where they are needed.

In the 7th Thesis of his *Tractatus Logico-Philosophicus*, Wittgenstein affirms that what can be said at all, can be said clearly; or else *If something cannot be talked about, one must keep silent*. But, as the colleague who shares my surname, the Brazilian-Hungarian writer and critic Zsófia Bán says, *Seen from the perspective of cultural history, this position represents one of the main sources of cultural neurosis. If we consider, or rather, if a culture considers that we must keep silent about something, it implies that we know precisely what we are not to speak about.* Wittgenstein says, *For an answer that cannot be articulated, the question cannot be articulated either. There is no enigma. If a question can be posed at all, then it is possible also to answer it.*

While Jaspers affirms, *There is no question that should not be posed.*

Wherever I went in Sarajevo I came across new graveyards, and the names of those who, in the course of the four-year siege, were killed by members of the Army of Republika Srpska, the Yugoslav National Army, and paramilitary groups. The graveyards are in parks, right next to houses, on former children's playgrounds, or in stadiums, and there are lists of names on squares, on shops, on memorials, on plaques, in broad streets and in alleyways where there are never any crowds. The names on these signs range from one to a thousand. And in between, among these memorials, life revolves. Everyday, modern European life.

Reminder:

The siege of Sarajevo lasted 1,425 days.

In the course of the siege 470,000 shells fell on the city, on average 330 shells a day.

In Sarajevo, 11,541 people were killed, of whom 1,601 were children. Those children have their own memorial, their names, their square.

In addition to his own active wartime journey, the architect Mirza Fočo also writes about his work on the restoration of monuments of international cultural heritage, which include the Jewish cemetery in Sarajevo. After the one in Prague, this cemetery is the second largest in Europe, and it is situated on a dangerous mudslide site. Presumably seeing it as some kind of no-man's-land, in this last war the Serbian forces covered it with mines. The Jewish cemetery in Sarajevo has a long and rich story, but I won't go into that now. Not to destroy the flow of the narrative, not to stray too far from the theme. What is the flow of my narrative? What is its theme?

Mirza Fočo comes from a well-known Sarajevo partisan family. I ask him whether any of the Sarajevans he knows who crossed onto the side of the aggressor have any regrets, whether any had apologized. *One*, said Mirza. *And he no longer sleeps.*

In Toronto, in 1995, I made a radio documentary for the Canadian Broadcasting Company about people who had fled Bosnia and Herzegovina. In that documentary, the engineer M. B. talked about leaving Sarajevo through the famous tunnel dug under the airport runway. A journalist from Canadian state radio, camped in a completely different world, in a completely different time, asked, *Does the tunnel have a lift?*

What do you mean "a lift"! the engineer M. B. said in exasperation. *It's a hole. It's like going through hell. It's narrow, it's low, water sometimes reaches your knees. It had been raining, and the ground inside is clay, and clay is slippery. I had old shoes on my feet, completely worn out. I kept falling into mud and water. I was carrying two bags. They contained all my belongings. Photographs, documents and diplomas. I set out at four in the afternoon and the following day, around eight in the evening, I left Bosnia.*

Today twenty meters of the tunnel from Dobrinja to Butmir have been restored, and from the house of the Kolar family, which still stands on the Butmir side, riddled with shell-holes, I imagined that military, civilian and humanitarian path through hell toward freedom. The Dobrinja-Butmir tunnel, or rather the city-airport tunnel, is about 800 meters long, one meter wide and a meter and a half high. It was designed by experts, and built by members of the civil defense force and miners from Miljevina and central Bosnia—in catastrophic conditions, with incomprehensible obstacles, using superhuman efforts, in three shifts. Twenty-eight hundred cubic meters of earth was dug out of it, around 170 cubic meters of wooden material was built into it, and about 45 tons of metal. Three months later, in July 1993, accompanied by constant shelling from Serbian positions, people began to move in both directions—out of the city and into the city. An average of four thousand people passed through the tunnel each day. Twelve tons of military material and many tons of food and medicine were transferred through it.

Along with the original section of the war tunnel, known as

the "Tunnel of Salvation," in the Kolars' house there is also a memorial room with photographs and in the cellar an exhibition of items associated with activities in the tunnel—clothes, shoes, trolleys, and later, rails to transport the wounded, children, old people and weapons, rucksacks, and also a film about the shelling of Sarajevo and the building of the tunnel. Visitors sit on military crates, watch and weep.

There is another memorial marking the streets of Sarajevo: Sarajevo roses. Sarajevo roses are the imprints of shells in the asphalt, later filled with red paint. There are large ones, a meter in diameter, there are small ones, hardly visible. There are a lot of them, so simply stepping through the streets of Sarajevo makes forgetting impossible. But individual streets are being dug up, new ones are being constructed, and the imprints are disappearing, so many steps tread over others that the red color is fading. Sarajevo roses in the asphalt, a homage to the dead. But who are the dead? If these red flowers do fade, then disappear, perhaps it would be possible to press into the asphalt beside them small, bright, brass letters, spelling the names, along with the date of birth and death of each individual, so that the steps of walkers would involuntarily polish all those lives over which they would pause, over which they would bow and so pay their respects. The way all over Europe passersby are obliged to stop by Demnig's stone stumbling blocks. Because every name carries a story, and history remembers the names of the perpetrators, not the victims.

Gentlemen!
Lovers of profanation,
of crimes,
of slaughter,
have you seen
the most terrible—
asks Mayakovsky.

About the Memorial Center Srebrenica-Potočari, the monument and *mezarje* for the victims of the 1995 genocide, I cannot write. By 2015, a total of 7,100 of the 8,372 listed had been identified, but this number is not final. On the vast space, which the eye could only encompass from a great height, on the undulating space covered with little islands of green grass, which await new tombs, are row upon row of gravestones. A wall with the engraved names of the killed stretches in a semicircle two meters high and some fifty meters long, and reading those names makes one sick and dizzy. A crimson tree, in flames, follows me. On the hillocks daisies and dandelions grow. I walk and hear—I am disintegrating. On the way out of that victims' cemetery shackles snap round my ankles and I understand, from now on I must drag all this after me, all these Muslim gravestones, and one Christian cross (for Rudolf Hren), these tombs and the secret stories buried beneath them, the trees and grass, as though I were dragging after me the cover, the face of the earth.

On the other side of the road there is a pre-fabricated kiosk, where Fazila Efendić sells flowers, books, films, and souvenirs. On a little table by the till lie Gombrowicz's stories. *Who reads Gombrowicz?* I ask. *I do,* says Fazila, offering me little biscuits, she makes me an espresso and, with a smile, tells me about a recently published novel by Hasan Nuhanović. *Read it,* she says. Fazila's smile is devastating. Fazila Efendić is known to the international and local public because of her struggle for the truth about Srebrenica. Fazila Efendić could have chosen where to live, from Sarajevo to Germany or Sweden, but Fazila Efendić went back to Srebrenica, restored her house and now tends the graves of her nineteen-year-old son Fejz and husband Hamed, which lie across the road.

Now I write less and less about the Holocaust, so people no longer ask me, *Why do you write about the Holocaust so much? Write about love and nature*, but now they say, *Why do you write about the war? Write about Sarajevo now, about life in general.* What should I tell them?

For a month I followed Bosnian and Herzegovinian political, social and cultural happenings, I watched and listened to what was going on. The obsession of homogenized Herzegovinian Croats with the legalized foundation of a third entity, a retrograde Herceg-Bosna, which would definitively destroy this country, is increasingly aggressive and fierce. Despite the judgment of the European Court of Human Rights in Strasbourg, in the "Sejdić and Finci case," for three years now the Constitution of Bosnia and Herzegovina has not changed, although the court judgment confirmed the fundamental constitutional discrimination against all who do not declare themselves members of the constitutive nations. Every Montenegrin, every Roma, every Jew, every Hungarian, and so on, everyone, regardless of intellectual abilities, of acquired knowledge, of his or her political and religious views, all those who believe that they have the right to choose and do not declare themselves Bosniak, Serb, or Croat, in this sad country become trash.

I also followed the grotesque local TV programs, ethnically disinfected, ideologically frightening, rigid and truculent, especially those from Republika Srpska, and programs about abandoned hamlets in that same Republika Srpska, through which one passes (through which I passed) as through a nightmare: locked-up butchers' shops, wrecked bakers, demolished chemists, the skeletons of burned houses on which singed lace curtains flutter.

Enough. That's the past too. They say.

In Sarajevo there's an incredible number of chemists, arranged at roughly two-hundred-meter intervals. And a lot of hotels. In the trams, young people stand for their elders. Shops selling *ćevapčići*, *burek*, and other specialties are full of local customers. And people smoke everywhere. There are confectioners and cafés that could be in the center of Paris. From the Metropolis to the Zlatna Ribica, about whose owner Slobodan Matić, a zoologist and taxidermist, a story could be told that moves from life straight into literature. It is true of the cobbler Edo who makes first-class shoes to measure in three days, about the students who edit a magazine for poet(h)ical research and action, about the qualified doctor Adnan Smajić, today owner of the little world-class Franz & Sophie tea shop, where there was once the famous Jerlagić bakery with, they say, the best pita bread in town, about General Jovan Divjak and his perfect French, about his work with children throughout Bosnia and Herzegovina whose families are victims of the war, about his role in the Association of Independent Intellectuals, "Circle 99," about Enver Kazaz and his war journey, about Nenad Veličković and his series of postcards called "Monty Dayton's Flying Circus," "Yuks by the Roadside," and "Welcome to Sarajevo," of Marko Vešović, Boro Kontić, Zdravko Grebo. One can talk and write about how the journal *Sarajevske sveske* is struggling to survive, while the Government of the Republic of Croatia does nothing to support this mission seriously. Or how the excellent editor of that journal called *Sarajevske bilježnice*, *Sarajevo Notebooks*, *Сарајевске свеске*, *Sarajevski zvezki*, *Sarajevski tetratki*, *Fletoret te Sarajevës*, *Lettere da Sarajevo*, *Les cahiers de Sarajevo*, *Sarajevos Litterära Tidskrift*, *Hefte aus Sarajevo*, *Szarjavói füzetek* and *Kirjeitä Sarajevosta*, how its editor Vojka Dikić makes her famous chicken pie, for which an old cockerel must be boiled for five hours, the egg-yolk pastry rolled and soup poured over it, how that was impossible during the war. About the wrecked windows out of which gush darkness and the warning on the first floor of the building into which my room looked and on which two old ladies had tied a string and pegged up pages and pages of their manuscripts. Various lives here could be written about in such a way that no one would ever again say what an internationally known European intellectual woman from former Yugoslavia once wrote to me, *I can't imagine how depressing your peaceful Bosnia is.*

Vojka Dikić, too, told me, *You'd do better to write about Sarajevo today.*

And I said, *What about the people who were killed?*

But Vojka said, *We've all been killed, those down below and we who are up here.*

I was living in a triangle made up of three buildings. On one side was the canton's public communal firm Pokop, which organizes and carries out burials in the city's graveyards, opposite is the firm Pozder Nekropoling, which makes gravestones, and in the middle, in the middle is the Academy of Music. Violins, pianos, drums, harps, wind instruments, exercises and compositions, harmony and disharmony, successful and less successful attempts to celebrate life through music came into my room whenever I was at home. That is Sarajevo today. Squeezed between deaths through which life penetrates. In Ulica Pehlivanuša, or the "street of playful acrobats and heroes," in the general Sarajevan playfulness, in insubordination.

When was all this? Time is getting away from me again, overflowing, it will not be tamed, insane time carries me off into the madhouse of its expanse, into the underground of its gloom.

I come home and again, as soon as I go out, someone or something assaults me. I order a drink, ask for ice in it, the waiter says, *Why do you need ice, the drink is cold.* I buy *burek*, ask the shop assistant to heat it for me, and he says, *It's warm, why should I heat it?* I go to the late-night chemist, it's Saturday, 9 p.m., I've used up all the drops for my glaucoma, the chemist says, *The system is down, I can't give you the drops, come back tomorrow.*

I say, *I can't come tomorrow.*

Why not? It's Sunday!

It was the same when the nurse at the eye clinic told me to come for an examination of my endangered macula at the beginning of August. I told her, *I'm not here in August.* And, frowning and wrinkled, she pierced me with a thunderous look, then shouted for everyone in the waiting room to hear, *What do you mean you can't? You're a pensioner!*

So, I barricaded myself again and started disentangling the files, the histories of the illnesses of Adam's and my own former patients.

IRENA BECKER goes to exhibition openings. As soon as the refreshments arrive, she approaches the table. She eats slowly, masticating, like a cow chewing the cud. Her lips shift from left to right. While her lips move, she looks straight ahead, motionless, then, first with her index finger, then with the nail of the little finger of her right hand, she picks at her teeth, then she takes the ham off sandwiches, and bananas and mandarins from the serving dish, and fills a small plastic bag with them. *The ham is for my cats*, she says, *the bananas are for me, because I've mislaid my teeth somewhere*, she says, and then she leaves. Irena Becker can be seen strolling through the market, picking up discarded fruit and vegetables. *Where are your teeth?* the stallholder asks every time, *In the trash*, says Irena.

Irena stops going to book launches and chamber theater performances; they don't let her into the big theater anymore, because she no longer washes. So, she doesn't quarrel with writers and the audience anymore; if she does appear at some public meeting, she doesn't say anything. Then she disappears from the town.

Irena Becker was a sociologist. She studied society. People in society. Irena Becker was born into a well-off bourgeois family, which, until Irena disappeared, provided her with good-quality clothes and shoes, so that externally she didn't look unusual.

I buried all the cats in wet sand and decided to leave, said Irena

Becker. *But when I stirred up the sand,* she said, *the cats were still breathing, so I brought them back to life. It was June. The cats sniffed the air, I took them to the island and opened a new chapter.*

In the new chapter I was visited by a new, strange cat, which was like one of the previous ones, but I no longer know which. I thought, said Irena Becker, *perhaps it's one of my former cats after all, it has come back and now sleeps on the couch. I was worried, I didn't have sand for that cat, or a litter tray. Where would it do its business? I wondered. I went to the kitchen, put my hand under the shelf with books, you know, the one under the window,* said Irena Becker, *but the space was too small to place a tray there for that cat. Out of that space under the shelf there began to crawl some forms in the shape of a narrow letter "U," they were May bugs it turned out, I tried to squash one with my foot but it didn't work. In the meantime, the cat ran away. Where to? I don't know. It disappeared. Then from under the shelf, an enormous May bug peered out, first staring at me, then crawling toward me. It was covered in scales like a rhinoceros. It had armor. I once kept two wooden decorative rhinos, they had each lost a leg, they lay on the bookshelf. I could see that out of the jaws of the May bug that was walking toward me there hung a half-eaten smaller bug, waving its skinny little legs. I was really scared, I called my sister,* Irena Becker said. *My sister is called Flavija. Flavija said, Let me just have a shower and I'll be on my way, but she didn't come. In the meantime, my new cat disappeared, it must have jumped out of the window, because it was half-open. I called my neighbor. She came. We had a coffee and talked about our dead. That was when I decided once and for all that I had to leave.*

RAFAELA ARENDT was born in Vienna in 1948. She spent eighteen years in a psychiatric institution. She is of short stature. Diagnosis: mania. Under medication she is calm and submissive, but if someone or something angers or provokes her, she becomes vulgar and obscene. She takes care of her personal hygiene, perhaps excessively. She is in good physical health. She thinks all the doctors are her husbands. During the day she mumbles constantly to herself. At night she screams and slaps herself on the flanks.

Yesterday Willy Brandt was flirting with me, said Rafaela Arendt. *He telephoned me so I invited him to lunch. I didn't have any food in the fridge. I asked Willy Brandt what I should buy. What do you like to eat, I asked him, because he likes good food, sophisticated food. Don't buy anything, my chauffeur will come for you and we'll go to a restaurant, said Willy Brandt*, Rafaela Arendt says. *It was an impressive restaurant, luxurious and brilliant. Then everything suddenly became clear. What became clear? My life. I took out my long* Zigarettenspitze *and slowly blew out smoke. Then Willy said I suggest we have an* Après. *I didn't know what kind of drink that was, so I asked Willy: Is there an* Avant? *The waiter was surprised. He raised his eyebrows and looked at me scornfully. Then a woman with garishly orange hair came up to us, she whispered something to Willy, then laughed out loud and went away. Willy said, Later we'll go to my attic. When we reached his* attic, I saw that it was an enormous space filled with couples fucking, while some masturbated. I wanted to run away, but I couldn't find the way out. I asked Willy Brandt, Willy, where's the door? I think I've got lost, and he said, Dear Rafaela, the door is there, I locked it.

From the side, my father watched all of this. With restraint.

Otherwise, my father walks a lot, said Rafaela Arendt. He is always elegantly dressed. When he goes for a walk, he wears a long black coat and a black hat. He mostly walks on sandy beaches. When my father walks, I look at myself in the mirror. Then I see myself, Rafaela Arendt, very clearly. I have a small black cap on my head, as though I was a Jew. I'm always wearing a halter-neck shirt, I have big eyes and tanned shoulders, and white socks on my feet.

Today I climbed onto the bathtub to hook a chain onto a nail high above the tap. Right away, Marlon Brando climbed up after me, he came behind me to help, because the nail was high, just beneath the ceiling. Our bodies touched. It was a very close touch, something like an embrace. I stiffened and said, Not yet, and Brando asked, Why not? Then he kissed me. My heart almost leapt out of me. Then something snapped in my lungs. What could that mean?

BARBARA BUSS collects junk. She walks around town with little bags full of rubbish. She is untidy, her hair is unbrushed and unwashed. She doesn't speak, but she sings. Opera arias. She spent nineteen years in the psychiatric hospital. She knows Rafaela Arendt. *Rafaela used to walk about naked*, said Barbara Buss. *She would sit on a pile of dirty laundry, so the cleaners couldn't take it away to be washed. I'm looking for a white T-shirt, Rafaela Arendt used to shout*, said Barbara Buss. *Then they'd give her an injection, and she'd calm down, she didn't wear panties*, said Barbara Buss.

As she is no danger to the public, Barbara Buss is finally released from hospital. She lives in the attic of a dilapidated stone house. Barbara Buss is an older woman, around sixty. Well built, with a large stomach, as though pregnant. Barbara Buss is lively and energetic, she walks fast, jerkily.

My grandson tried to kill me, says Barbara Buss. *He said I had cut his duck's throat, that the duck had been his pet, which isn't remotely true. He maintained that his father had bought the duck for him, but his father died before he was born. My grandson, he's called Bernard, Bernard accused me of killing the duck, cooking it and putting it on the table for lunch. It's true that I never liked that duck, nor did my daughter, Bernard's mother Šarlota. The duck waddled around the apartment and shat everywhere. One day Šarlota said, Listen, Bernard, this duck is too big for our apartment, now it's an adult duck, it needs more space.*

Granny has a garden, your duck will be happy there. That's right, I had a garden then, I don't anymore. But Bernard couldn't understand, he kept saying, Bela, that was the name of the duck, Bela, Bela is happier here with me in this little apartment, she doesn't need Granny's garden, he wailed. He became tedious, he wouldn't shut up. Bela's my best friend, he whined, you see the way she follows me everywhere. Still, we moved Bela to my place. I admit, she did pine for Bernard for a while, then one day she simply wandered off and never came back.

I've got my own version, said Bernard. *One Saturday I was sent to my Baka Barbara and I couldn't find Bela. I searched the whole garden and called her, Bela, Bela my lovely, come to your Bernard. Nothing. She must have run away, said Baka Barbara. Yes, said mother, she must have run away. Then it was quite clear. I was called in to lunch. Lunch was on the table, Baka Barbara and my mother Šarlota called me in. And, of course, in the middle of the table lay Bela, with no head, plucked and roasted. That's Bela, I said. No, it's not, the two of them said at the same time. We bought it at the butcher's. They tried to force me to eat Bela, but in the end they gave up. I was five years old then. I've never had roast duck since. Maybe once, thirty years later. I'm full of hatred for Barbara and Šarlota, but now that I am a parent myself, that hatred has diminished a bit. I never tried to kill anyone.*

Barbara Buss knows Florian Winter too. Sometimes she sings to him, to him or perhaps to his pigeons, one wouldn't know.

FLORIAN WINTER. Thirty-five. He collects pigeons and other birds, those that sing and those that do not. Florian Winter does not know the happily-unhappy Hervé Joncour, of whom it isn't known whether he is an invention of Alessandro Baricco or not, so he doesn't know that seeker, that collector of elusive passions, that Hervé who locks his longing in little specially sealed boxes so it may live forever, but it still dies. Florian Winter converts all the rooms of his apartment—four of them—into birdcages, while Hervé Joncour dreams and builds aviaries, because Hervé Joncour has a park, while Florian Winter does not. Florian Winter has an apartment into which he moved when some other people were transferred out of it, long ago. Hervé Joncour said, *First you fill your aviaries with birds, as many as you can, and then one day, when something nice happens to you, open the aviary wide and watch the birds fly away*, while Florian Winter hardly says anything, he whistles and it does not cross his mind to return his birds to the celestial spaces, because nothing nice happens to Florian Winter, and it is only the silvery twittering of his birds that keeps him alive. Florian Winter goes into the untouched countryside. He watches birds for a time, then catches some and takes them home. Some of Florian Winter's birds sing, some just look dully, turning their heads, as birds have eyes on the side of their heads, so they turn their heads to at least see something. Every morning, Florian

Winter goes into his cages and sits among his flying creatures, which in time forget how to fly, that is why Florian Winter can't let them go, even the letter-bearing carrier pigeons. As Florian Winter has no life apart from those birds, he doesn't need letters, so he doesn't see why he would send the carrier pigeons anywhere or let them go. One day Florian Winter will join his birds forever; he will close the mesh door behind him, the door will click to and Florian Winter will say, *That's the real thing.* He will be found covered in feathers, the way Oscar Wilde's shat-on statue of the Prince shivers under its covering of snow. Someone will write about Florian Winter in the *Black Chronicle*, where deaths are reported, readers adore the *Black Chronicle* because they know that all those horrors happen to people they don't know, so they needn't worry. Florian Winter will diminish, he will be reduced to his initials, F. W., and his disappearance will be quiet and painless for everyone, including himself. By the grave of the homeless, Barbara Buss will sing to Florian Winter, because she will be the only person there. Not a single bird will cross the sky. Around Florian's grave, Barbara Buss will arrange her trash in the shape of a wreath. It will rain.

JAKOB KLODEL. Both wrists deformed by breaks, long ago. Age: fifty-three. Of medium height, fragile constitution, asthmatic. Hospitalized due to hallucinations. Under medication becomes calm and compliant, but is reluctant to communicate. The fingers of the left hand are contorted, the right hand is unusable. Avoids company. Spends his time in the hospital garden, comes into the building only at meal times and when it gets dark—to go to bed. Widower. Responds to questions meaningfully and rationally, with no excessive words. Gives exact information about himself. Shows no sign of mental derangement, but does not wish to leave the hospital. Two adult children. College-trained painter.

When I look at my right hand, it's as though it's not mine. I don't recognize it. It's big. I don't have such a big hand. Everything else around me is small and far away. I sometimes have a bird's head without a beak. The left side of my body doesn't belong to me. I can't feel it. I am separated from my left side. My left side is a lot bigger than my right, where only the hand is huge. When I look at myself in the mirror, I don't recognize myself. These disproportions make it difficult for me to shave. And to go up and down steps. I could topple over, my body is unstable. When I walk in the garden, I stagger as though I'm about to fall. No, I never have fallen. I know that I'm imagining all this. I'm completely outside the left side of my body. The left side of my body lives a separate life, I watch my left side from the right, my right side, apart from the hand, is quite all right, it's with me.

Yesterday that left side was in Paris; it was hurrying to an exhibition of paintings by my friend Paul Genet. But it got lost. Yes, I know that I'm not in Paris. I missed the metro stop, that is, my left side got lost. It ended up in a street lit by a blue-neon light with a lot of elegantly appointed shop windows. Then it went down an incline and into Paul's apartment. What do you mean, who did? My left-hand body. Paul's apartment consists of a lot of small rooms painted a dirty-green color. The walls are bare, without a single picture. Where are your pictures? I asked Paul, but he didn't reply. Maybe he wasn't even there. Those rooms of Paul's are like cells. Behind the door of every room, there's a washbasin. I think it would be better if there were a desk or at least easels in the rooms. Excuse me? I can't paint, I don't have my equipment here. And my arms are broken.

Maybe this is all connected to changes in the universe. The earth is turning more slowly than before. I must measure its extent. The earth's distance from the moon is also in doubt. That's why people live longer these days. People live too long.

Magnetic resonance carried out. Blood count within the limits of normal. Endocrinological tests, no observations. EEG shows no symptoms of epilepsy. Citalopram prescribed, for two weeks. Mild symptoms of depersonalization. Then olanzapine, 10 mg daily. After three weeks, hallucinations and symptoms of depersonalization in further remission, citalopram increased to 60 mg.

Mild compulsive, repetitive actions.

MARGARETA LOPEK. Twenty-seven, unmarried, qualified psychologist. Sought help, complaining that she could not feel her body. *I'm empty*, she said. *It's as though I was hollow, as though my body was somewhere far away, with no bones or organs, just covered with skin, as though that body belonged to someone else. Excuse me? I don't know to whom. Now I wear all these gloves, about twenty on each hand, so that I can make a note of how far my arms reach. I'm dead. I can't feel anything.*

M. L. also complains of increased anxiety over social interaction. *I feel terrible with other people, I'm all tense*, she says.

Tests, laboratory and neurological, within the limits of the normal. Mild depression confirmed and occasional (mild) panic attacks.

This has been going on for four years, says M. L. *My thoughts are increasingly confused, I'm confused. I'm losing touch with reality. It's like watching my own life on TV. I don't feel any emotions. I don't recognize my voice. My voice isn't my own, the voices of my acquaintances reach me from a great distance and are completely unfamiliar to me. Sometimes my hands change size, one moment they're small, very small and short, then they grow and I levitate. I'm very light. No, I don't have suicidal thoughts. No, I don't want to kill anyone. Sometimes I have something, like, visions and then I watch myself as in a mirror. I don't feel the objects I touch, someone else is touching them. I'm outside my body. And when I move, I have no control over my movements, I feel like a robot. I have to touch myself to be sure that I exist, that I have a body. Like now, I'm following our conversation from a distance, you're here, she's opposite you, while I'm there, at the other end of the room. Sometimes I'm high up, stuck to the ceiling. To-day I'm heavy, immobile, and you're a stranger, you're sitting a long way away and you're very small. Tiny. I hear my voice, but what I'm saying is losing its sense.*

Fragmentation of the personality.

Take the family history.

ADAM MARSKI. Russian by birth. Born in 1957. Appears balanced. Until hospitalized, a conscientious and hardworking secretary in the solicitors' office Kroulek & Makela. Family history shows no mental or neurological disturbances. In his forty-eighth year, along with other eccentric behavior, began to make unusual grimaces. His jokes are inappropriate and he becomes angry without justified reason. He neglects himself—he loses two incisors, but does not see a dentist.

My incisors moved by ninety degrees, they stuck out of my mouth horizontally. I tried to put them back in their place with my fingers, to push them into their natural, vertical position, but they fell out.

He lets his hair grow for a year and in his fiftieth year starts to consume sweet things in immoderate quantities. He bathes increasingly infrequently. On April 13, 2004, he does not come to work, and appears the next day with stories about a possible suicide. Placed in the Psychiatric Department. Anxious and confused. Worried about paying a debt that his wife says he paid long ago. In hospital constantly demands, and then consumes, vast quantities of cake.

I was preparing to give a lecture in the largest hall of the Law Faculty. The lecture was supposed to be about dogs. The entire academic and legal elite had gathered. I went up to the rostrum and said: This is of no interest to you, how about some cake, and then we'll have a smoke.

With time he could no longer distinguish his belongings from those of other patients, so he appropriated them, stole them one might say, without permission. The doctors put him in isolation. He is given neuroleptics, antidepressants and lithium. The symptoms do not subside. After detailed tests—neurological, laboratory and magnetic resonance—no serious deviations from the normal are discovered. There are mild disturbances in his short-term memory, his concentration declines, as does his capacity for abstract thought: he is capable of repeating various proverbs, but not explaining their meaning. He often lies on the floor and at regular intervals raises his leg and leans his foot against the closed door of his room. He often fixes his gaze on an object, such as the pencil between a doctor's fingers or the identification label on the doctor's chest. He converses in an official tone, without emotion, even with his wife. He often asks for additional quantities of food. He enters the doctors' office, takes everything within reach and salutes as he leaves. His behavior and speech become mechanical. Expected outcome: catatonia with occasional manic-depressive attacks.

It's raining hard. I'm standing with Lidija on a narrow crossbar high, very high above the ground. Lidija jumps, I stay hanging. I shout from up there, I ask Lidija: How is it down there? How are you? A heavy fall, says Lidija. Lidija is my wife.

When did that happen?

Just now.

See the childhood and sexual life of Adam Marski.

PETAR MURAN. Forty-two, homicidal mania, but in the department he does not try to kill anyone. Under observation at night, alone in his room. He often mentions two men whom he (allegedly) killed while serving a prison sentence. Sentenced to two years for embezzlement. On his release from prison he was directed to the Psychiatric Department. He considers the murders absolutely normal. *They were perfect murders*, he often repeats. *I killed them with a wooden pole, one blow to the back, without a drop of spilled blood. I simply put them to sleep. Who? Both of them.*

He is not capable of carrying on a conversation of more than five minutes. He jumps from topic to topic. Otherwise calm and nonaggressive, occasionally even cheerful, often helping other patients. Always, day and night, he holds a bent nail in his mouth. The (imagined) murder was carried out in an uncontrollable instinctive impulse. He has hallucinations:

Last night my mother died in my arms.

Your mother died thirty-six years ago.

You're mistaken.

BREDA MARETTI. Forty-one years. Obsessive-compulsive neurosis. Spends three hours in the bathroom twice a day. Showers several times in succession, brushes her teeth for twenty minutes; after she has combed her hair and put on her makeup, she brushes her teeth again. Although she gets up early, she does not get to work before eleven. The same thing is repeated before she goes to bed. When she is under pressure, when someone hurries her, the ritual is additionally drawn out.

Examine family relationships. Suppressed hatred for a loved person? Fury and hatred redirected at her own ego. Latently suicidal (for now).

There are lots of terrible little bugs in my clothes. I try to shake them out, but they cling. They won't fall off.

Last night I was woken by a voice that kept repeating: Aurora, Aurora. Perhaps I wasn't asleep, perhaps I was awake. But around four o'clock in the morning, it was already getting light, a voice really did wake me. That is, I was woken by the ghastly screams of a woman on the street under my window. The woman was shrieking, or rather begging, I want to go home, take me home, I want to go home. I wondered whether anyone was going to help the woman. Then I thought, perhaps it's me shouting, perhaps that woman is me.

TEOFIL PAR. Sixty-eight. Brought back to the Psychiatric Department after a hernia operation. Somewhere just before midnight discovered hanging from a radiator in the Surgical Department. He had wrapped the cable of a mobile X-ray unit around his neck. After sixty minutes of resuscitation, existential functions restored to Teofil Par. He was put on a respirator, but at 1.20—*exitus.*

BREDA KUKOLA. Thirty-eight. There was a flood in the hospital's boiler room. The water was knee-deep. When the workmen came, at the end of the boiler room they saw a woman wearing nothing but blue leather gloves. The woman was floating through the room. *First we thought it was a doll*, said the workmen. The dead woman's clothes and her bag were found by the door. Her relatives were summoned, and they confirmed that she was Breda Kukola, the mother of a small child, who had disappeared four days earlier. The boiler room door was locked. It is not known how Breda Kukola got into the boiler room.

DANIEL BARTIS—in a catatonic stupor. Wherever he is put, he stays. He does not speak, he does not move, he does not look at anyone. He does not respond to questions. In spite of this, his heart rate is 100 bpm. He dies a year after being admitted to the hospital. That morning he has no issues. He sits immobile for six hours by the open window, facing the mountain in the distance. Then he gets up, lies down on the floor and dies.

VERONIKA SEL. Twenty-nine. She walks in the garden beneath the window of Sigmund Olson. Between the thumb and index finger of both hands she holds a small plastic doll on a swing. She sways the doll to the rhythm of her steps and softly sings a children's song, probably a lullaby. Sometimes, in the hospital garden, Veronika Sel walks with her palms pressed together in prayer, silently moving her lips. She goes from patient to patient, begging. *Have you got two euros?*

Her voice is the voice of a child, thin and squeaky, jerky, as though she lacks breath. She takes care of her personal hygiene, she is nicely dressed, but never puts on shoes, she always wears slippers. Her slippers are checked, felt, mouse-gray, with a metal buckle at the side. Before, just after she arrived, Veronika Sel would walk around with books in her arms, rocking them as though soothing a nursing baby. She would approach patients with a smile and offer them chocolate bananas or little tarts that she bought in the canteen. *Here, children*, she would say, *help yourselves.*

At her relatives' request she is allowed home.

Six months later Veronika Sel returns to the Clinic. The transformation of Veronika Sel is frightening. She is dressed in black rags and unwashed, on her head is a wig of long, sharp synthetic filaments, also black, which falls over half her forehead. On top of the wig she has tied a black scarf stuffed with layers of back-combed artificial hair. She smiles and walks bent over. *Veronika needs to be reset*, says Sigmund Olson. *I've bought her some Seka and Braco chocolate.* Now, instead of slippers, Veronika Sel wears black winter boots that come up to her knees, but it is summer, with temperatures of 38°C. Veronika Sel looks frightening, like a witch, but happy. *She's fallen into* bezna, says Sigmund Olson. *We must get her out.*

What's bezna? I ask.

Bezna *is darkness, gloom, blackness. It's unseeingness. In Romanian. I'm Romanian*, says Sigmund Olson.

Sigmund Olson is of Danish origin.

BENJAMIN KATT, volunteer in the War of Independence. Having had some psychological issues, and at his own request, Benjamin Katt is placed in a Dominican monastery on one of the Adriatic islands. Here Benjamin mostly walks, dives and reads. He is most impressed by Vsevolod Garšin's stories "Four Days" and "Red Flower." The inner monologue of a soldier who lies for four days beside an enemy soldier he has killed in the Russo-Turkish war of 1877 is continued in the almost identical story of Benjamin Katt in 1992, on a battlefield in Croatia. Benjamin Katt has similar obsessions to the patient in the story "Red Flower," who wants to save the world from evil. Unlike Garšin, who sees evil in three poppy flowers, Benjamin Katt dives obsessively, collecting shells, whose insides he destroys. In addition, Benjamin Katt self-harms. *I'm checking my blood,* Benjamin Katt keeps repeating to the doctors. *I think that I've been exchanged for someone else and now I don't know whether I'm alive or dead,* he says.

Benjamin Katt makes strange movements with his hands. The skin on his extremities is dry and cracked. He scratches and plucks at his skin for hours. Then he rubs thick layers of body cream over the wounds and wraps them in bandages. He has a tic in his left eye, so it looks as though he is winking. It will turn out that Vsevolod Garšin and Benjamin Katt share a distant relative, unknown to the world. Garšin killed himself by jumping from the fifth floor of the building in which he lived. Although he mirrors Vsevolod Garšin's biography, Benjamin Katt will not kill himself.

CHARLOTTA BEN. A letter from my friend the psychiatrist Armando Trevi from Pula:

On July 24, 2013, the following news item appeared in the local newspaper:

The body of an unknown woman between thirty and forty years of age was found on 23.7 around 11 a.m. in the sea on the Pula Riva, opposite the former Admiralty building. According to Pula resident Karlo Donat, who was the first to inform the emergency services, the body was floating a few meters from the shore, face immersed in the water. Unofficially, we learn that no traces of violence were detected on the body, and that it is confirmed that the cause of the woman's death was drowning.

It would never officially be established why the female person quickly identified as Charlotta Ben had drowned, *face immersed in the water.* I attended the autopsy of Charlotta Ben in my capacity as psychiatrist and forensic scientist, and therefore it was not appropriate for me to report what I knew about Charlotta Ben. Besides, that news item was already out of date, fresh dramas were arriving every moment, and few cared about Charlotta Ben, there was no longer anyone truly close to her.

Two months earlier, that is, at the beginning of May 2013, the red-haired Charlotta Ben, an unmarried sculptress, comes to my office and says, *Gertrude maintains that I need help. Two days ago,*

248

after a sudden flash of bright light, I became suddenly blind and now I can barely make out shadows.

The detailed examinations and tests I carried out on Charlotta Ben did not reveal any anomalies of the eyes or nervous system. But, the patient walked uncertainly, knocked into objects that happened to be in her path, even when she did not know that I was watching. Through conversations with Charlotta Ben over the course of our ten psychotherapeutic sessions, I discovered the following:

For six years Charlotta Ben lived with an older woman, the judge Gertrude Salaš, with whom she was in an active lesbian relationship. Recently, however, Charlotta Ben had begun to suffer from fierce jealousy, as her partner was allegedly seeing a woman who was displacing her, Charlotta Ben, from the life of Gertrude Salaš. Two days before coming to therapy, Charlotta Ben secretly followed Salaš to the home of her new girlfriend and saw them both getting into a car in the dark garage. The driver turned on the headlights, the car set off, and Charlotta Ben stumbled and fell almost under the front wheels, so that she could have been seriously hurt. The frantic women picked Charlotta Ben up and took her home, where she announced that she could see absolutely nothing. *I'm blind*, she said, *completely blind*. Persuaded by her partner, who was weighed down by guilt, Charlotta Ben came to me seeking help, although she declared that she was not at all concerned about *this new sightless state. I feel fine being blind like this*, she said, *one day everything will fall into place.*

After initial therapy, I carried out several sessions of hypnosis on Charlotta Ben, who in the meantime was reconciled with her lover and, as I had expected, her sight gradually returned. But Charlotta Ben stubbornly believed that she had begun to see through some inexplicable miracle and that her blindness had an exclusively organic origin. Evidently for Charlotta Ben, her confrontation with reality and symbolic autocastratory hysterical blindness were too disturbing for her to allow into her consciousness. (In the dreams and fantasies she related to me, her eyes symbolically took the place of testes.)

I last saw Charlotta Ben on July 20, 2013. She said, *Now everything is as it should be, it's all fallen into place. The day after tomorrow at 8:17 p.m. there will be a full moon. I shall swim toward the open sea to kiss the Moon, to embrace Gertrude Salaš.*

P.S. Come to Pula. I have some information about the life of Adam Kaplan.

ALBERT LAUBE. Thirty.

Nothing works, nothing works here, the medicines don't work, I hate this place, I've been coming here for seven years now, I've been here for seven years now, it's all useless, the medicines don't work, I hate this place, nothing works, I've been here seven years, nothing works, I hate this hospital, nothing works, it's useless, I've been here seven years.

You came yesterday.

I've been here seven years, nothing works, it's all useless, I hate this hospital, I've been here seven years, nothing works, the medicines don't work, seven years.

You were brought here yesterday.

Nothing works. On the X-ray of my chest, there's no heart! Where's my heart?!

Giuseppe Desa's father was a carpenter who went broke, lost everything and vanished. His mother, always severe and now embittered, was forced, on June 17, 1603, to give birth to her son in a stable. The boy was apparently not bright. He would sit for hours with his eyes rolled upward, gaping; the other kids called him "*bocca aperta*" open mouth. For years his body was covered with sores.

He loved the Church and everything about the Church, but his uncle, a priest, thought him unfit for the cloth. Some Capuchins took him in as a lay brother and assigned him to the kitchen, but he was hopeless: breaking dishes, knocking over pots into the fire, mistaking the rye for wheat. He was expelled after a few months, returned home in rags, and was berated by his uncle and mother.

Somehow he found work in another monastery, tending the mules, and his piety, or otherworldliness, was such that they accepted him as a novitiate. He had difficulty learning and only passed the examination by a miraculous coincidence: the Bishop happened to ask him the one question to which he knew the answer.

He spent sixteen years in the monastery in Grotella, in a cell bare of even the few things monks were allowed. His self-mortifications were extreme. Draped in chains, he would beat himself with a scourge studded with nails and star-shaped pieces of steel; the walls of his cell were sprinkled with blood. For most of the year he ate only on Thursdays and Sundays; his food was dried fruit and beans—not even bread—to which he added an unknown bitter powder. A friar once tasted Giuseppe's dinner and was so disgusted by it that he couldn't eat for days.

He didn't understand when people spoke to him. After he warmly greeted two women on the road, a companion asked Giuseppe if he knew them: *Of course. It's our Blessed Mother Mary and St. Catherine of Siena.* When he spoke at all, he would mumble bits of prayers or snatches of scripture, sing songs of his own invention, or say enigmatic things. Once, on meeting a Protestant, he exclaimed: *Be cheerful: the deer is wounded,* and the man later converted. He would often tell sinners: *Go and adjust your bow,* but no one knew what this meant. He once ran outside during a furious storm, shouting *Dragon! Dragon!* and the storm suddenly ceased. He could summon birds by calling them. He would fall into trances, and the other monks would prick him with needles, hold torches to his skin or touch his unblinking eyeballs. No reaction. Opening the door to his cell, he always invited his guardian angel to enter first.

He avoided women and loathed money. When the pious attempted to give him a donation for the monastery, he would refuse and tell them to speak to a superior. Someone once slipped a coin into his cowl. Giuseppe began to breathe heavily and sweat and finally cried out, *I can't take this anymore!* He returned to normal only when the coin was removed. He drove a flock of sheep into the chapel, recited the litany to them, and they baa-ed in unison after every *Sancta Maria*.

There was something else about Giuseppe. Devotion had reduced his body and his mind to the state of physical zero for which Gandhi, in his celebrated fasts and elaborate tests of resistance to sexual temptation, had longed. Giuseppe was barely here at all, and therefore he could fly. Twice a day at Mass, and on countless other occasions, he would suddenly shout a word or two: *Love!* or *Holy Mother!* or *Beautiful Mary!* or even *Immaculate conception!* He described those words as the gunpowder in a cannon. And then he would shoot up to the ceiling of the cathedral or church or chapel, hovering in the air, sometimes for hours, singing praises with his knees bent and arms outstretched.

Two popes, ambassadors, various government and church officials, and thousands of others saw him and have left scores of eyewitness accounts. Once he flew to the top of a tree and its branches did not bend, as though a small bird were perched on it. Once, he took the hand of a confessor, lifted him up and danced with him in the air. Once, a deranged man, the Chevalier Baldasserre, was brought to him tied to a chair. Giuseppe untied him and pulled him by his hair to the top of the cathedral altar. Upon their descent, the man was sane again.

Questioned by Cardinal Lorenzo Brancati about what exactly was happening during his flights, he replied in the third person and said that Giuseppe found himself in a great gallery filled with beautiful, rare objects. Among them was a bright mirror that Giuseppe would stare into and, in a single glance, Giuseppe could see the forms of all the things in the world and all the hidden mysteries of the universe that God had chosen to show him.

Royalty came to visit, but the Church did not know what to do with him. The Inquisition investigated; his presence was deemed to be too disruptive; he was sent to obscure monasteries, traveling by night on back roads, where he was given the most hidden of the cells, but crowds of pilgrims still found him. Toward the end of his life, under orders from the Pope, he was sent to Osimo and forbidden to see anyone outside the monastery.

On September 18, 1663, after six years of solitary confinement, Giuseppe, in a fever, whispered, *The donkey is climbing the mountain.* The next day, preparing the body for embalmment, the monks discovered that his heart was bloodless, completely shriveled and dry. He had once said of the Virgin Mary: *My mother is very strange; if I bring her flowers, she says that she does not want flowers; if I bring her cherries, she will not take them; and if I then ask her what she wants, she replies: I want your heart for I live on hearts.*

This digressionary little tale (like the other stories that fall out of the frame and upset or break the so-called "uniform flow of narration") ought to lie in a real little envelope stuck where the little tale is inserted. Then whoever holds the book in his hands could take the little tale out and read it (with the aid of a cheap plastic magnifying glass attached to the book, because the little tale would be printed in tiny letters, because of its alleged insignificance), and if he doesn't wish to—so what? The reader could take all the parenthetic fabrications scattered within the covers of this book and move them from one miniature envelope into another or simply throw them away and so alter the content, create the "story" he wishes, a course of events which would flow harmoniously and rationally, in compositional and literary terms correctly, or he could do nothing: stick the little envelopes down, seal them. But, no one wants to make such a "design," no publisher, no printer, because it's expensive and considered absurd.

Fernando, his grandmother Dionisia said to Pessoa before she died in a lunatic asylum, *Fernando, you will become like me because blood is a traitor. You will drag me with you your whole life. Life is madness and till your death you will fill your pockets with madness.*

One night, Alberto Caeiro, pale, blond and blue-eyed, spoke in Fernando's skull. *I am your father and your master*, he said. *I shall die of TB in the village of Ribatejo, in the arms of my big, fat aunt.*

Such is life, replied Pessoa, *a riddle. Everything in it is hidden, including yourself.*

When Alberto Caeiro died, Pessoa did not cry, he was making love to Ophelia Queroz, a little secretary from the company where he worked.

Here's a poem for you, said Álvaro de Campos, a decadent futurist and nihilist with whom Pessoa drank from time to time, mostly in a little restaurant called Pessoa, where Bernardo Soares secretly noted his anxieties on napkins and used bus tickets. Having listened to Álvaro de Campos's lines, Pessoa was moved.

It's a wonderful poem, he said. *There are a lot of young men who look like girls. They even use cream for wrinkles around their eyes. They are delicate and like tight clothes. And jewelry. I shall break off my relationship with Ophelia.*

The next day, Ophelia came to work in a green dress with yellow flowers on it and a yellow ribbon in her black hair.

I often pass the same beggar, Pessoa told Ophelia. *His stench follows me for a long time afterward. Farewell, dearest Ophelia. I wrote poems for all the people in the world, but only my parrot knows how to recite them.*

Had he been born deaf, Pessoa may not have quadrupled, he would have remained single. And dumb. Returning from work arm in arm with the sweet Ophelia, shivering in her mauve winter jacket, he would have watched cockroaches mating.

> *Andreas, we don't know if these feelings are some slow madness brought on by hopelessness, if they are recollections of some other world in which we've lived—confused, jumbled memories, like things glimpsed in dreams, absurd as we see them now, although not in their origin if we but knew what that was. I don't know if we were once other beings, whose greater completeness we sense only incompletely today, being mere shadows of what they were, beings that have lost their solidity in our feeble two-dimensional imaginings of them among the shadows we inhabit.*
> *Yours,*
> *Fernando Pessoa*
> *Alberto Caeiro*
> *Ricardo Reis*
> *Bernardo Soares*
> *Álvaro de Campos*

I took these stories (and I have more, hundreds of them), my stories and other people's, laid them out and a map of life opened up, where lines are definitively drawn, where everything vacillates and, as in that vacillation, alters. I tried to make a crossword puzzle and saw that many of those lives crossed one another, that many of them were like others, that they were in fact the same life, or rather, that they could have been one single life, the life of a single person, both male and female, both adult and child, the lives—or life—of one single time that both vacillates and stands still. Whose voice is this? Adam Kaplan's or mine?

Paris.

For thirty-eight years I didn't so much as flit through Paris, let alone spend any time there. I now have three Parises: the playful one of the 1970s, when I scampered through it, completely disoriented, plunging into it, wanting to embrace the whole of it (what foolishness), when I spent my days visiting museums, parks, markets and cafés, where painters, writers and philosophers had used up their lives over the centuries, walking over bridges, dreaming, and at night I drank with prostitutes, sometimes in the bars of the Latin Quarter, sometimes in their moldy little rooms on dented squeaking beds with crumpled sheets, which gave off the aroma of shallow, spent passions—spacious Paris, elusive, unconquerable; I have a Paris (the one from thirty-eight years ago), which gathered itself into a knot at the center of which was my mother's death, a little constricted Paris, confined to a few half-dark streets which, through their underground spaces, through the grilles on the pavements where the homeless sleep to keep warm, vomit the steam of effluents, the stench of millions of our innards, mystical Paris, a city which, like every last town on this planet, it is impossible to disarm, impossible to conquer, in which walkers only crawl over its outside, while it just turns lazily here and there from one side to the other, sometimes with a half-asleep smile, sometimes as though saying, leave me alone. And now I have the Paris I have come to tell that everything's all right, that I no longer dream, that I can gather up all its stories, all its phases, but only its flickers, the flakes of its being, the Paris I look at panoramically, suppressing the desire to leap into it, to drown in it. I also have a fourth Paris, the Paris of Marisa, Rudolf, and Karlo, the one from 1939, and a fifth, that sparkling, headstrong Paris from Ada's already cleansed, dried stories that we leaf through the way old people leaf through albums or the tattered and smudged pressed-flower books for children, I am full of images of Paris, like marbles of various sizes and shapes, from the clumsy homemade clay ones to the magical, brightly colored glass balls jingling in my embrace and now, when I raise my arms in a gesture of surrender, I will allow them to roll away into their own life or their own death.

So, in 2013, I came to gather oblivion.

It is 1977. In New Belgrade, on the sixth floor of one of the "Six Corporals," as you look at them from the bridge, a retired officer of the Yugoslav Army sells processed aloe vera in green Fruška Gora Riesling bottles, from which he does not have time to remove the labels; there is great demand, but also great mortality. The thick gray liquid is applied to radiation burns, today no one mentions those terrible radiation burns, oncology has improved. Marisa's skin is falling off in strips. The officer calls the liquid "balm." We rub Marisa with balm. We make a tincture of aloe vera, which is taken by mouth. I go with Ada to Kisvárda, a village on the Hungarian–Russian border where in winter tears freeze. Marisa is young. In the train the attendants are Russian, in blue homespun uniforms with short skirts, everyone with swollen knees, everyone fat. The uniforms have gold buttons, like the dress coats of captains on long-haul ships. The attendants are Russian because the train continues on to Moscow, it only passes through Kisvárda. The attendants sell weak Russian tea in glasses, boiling hot, and they don't sleep at all.

Kisvárda is a village like those in the Banat region of Serbia. It has an inn and good goulash. It has farms. It has frozen mud. In Kisvárda, Dr. Baross sells anticancer drops in a little room with a low ceiling. There are rugs all over the room, on the floor and on the walls and covering the armchairs because the armchairs are shabby. There's also a microscope, old-fashioned. One enters the "clinic" through the kitchen, where the doctor's wife sits in a blue fustian housecoat; the doctor's wife sits at a wooden table and waits, there are small plastic snowdrops in a vase. There is a cabinet, reseda green, glass-fronted, and behind the glass lie upturned coffee cups. People come in droves, people come from all over Yugoslavia, because this is the day for Yugoslavia, other countries have their days. Tito is still alive, my mother Marisa dies before Tito. We get back toward morning, our mother Marisa, Marisa the doctor, psychiatrist, expert diagnostician, is waiting for us with a smile and hope for Dr. Baross' small, pointless, deceitful drops, which, of course, do not help.

We tried everything. Including Paris.

Professor Merkaš said, *There's no salvation, the richest and the poorest die of cancer*, and later he himself died of cancer. In Paris I converse with tramps and sleep in cheap brothels, the sky is clear, Parisian-blue and it is winter again, probably the same as the Hungarian winter. Marisa is bleeding everywhere. Her blood soaks through the mattress and drips onto the polished floor of the Institut d'Oncologie, within the complex of the Paris Faculté de Médecine, or perhaps it does not happen within the complex of the Paris Faculté de Médecine at all, although there are indications that this is precisely where our mother is lying, because they are trying out new medicines, carrying out trials on her (our mother— a submissive half-dead rabbit, still beautiful—*We're experimenting*, they say, *we're testing*, they say, *we've got nothing to lose*); maybe our mother is falling apart and bleeding in the Hôpital de l'Institut

Curie, because the Hôpital de l'Institut Curie specializes in treating malignant diseases, or perhaps in the Val-de-Grâce military hospital, although I don't know why our mother would be in the military hospital Val-de-Grâce given that our family has never had any connection with the army, particularly the French Army, for a long time now, for generations, our family has been an ordinary civilian, urban family. Perhaps our mother is lying (and draining away) in Hôpital Cochin. Near the Panthéon, they tell me, there is also the Hôpital Laennec, and the Maternité Port-Royal, I don't remember, I remember only the proximity of the Panthéon, where Voltaire and Victor Hugo and Zola lie, and the spry Jean Jaurès and that tame Rousseau, who all, to a man, unlike my young and beautiful mother, mean absolutely nothing to me and without them my life is perfectly possible. In Paris I see Bergman's *The Serpent's Egg* and, with Adam's brother Alvaro Kaplan, I eat steak tartare out of a soup plate, with a spoon, in the stuffy apartment belonging to the gallery owner and antiquarian Bojon. In Paris I buy crepes at an open market, fill them with raspberry ice cream, which melts completely on the way to the hospital, leaving dark-red traces on the pavement behind me, a circus troupe is dancing, and the sky is alarmingly blue.

When she bleeds, her mucous membrane falls away, Marisa is peeling in layers, from inside, disintegrating. I buy her shoes, but she can no longer walk. *I'd like burgundy ones, with thin leather straps*, says Marisa, smiling. Later I give the shoes to Katja, who is also dying of cancer. The stockings are burgundy too. I give them to Ada.

They're here, Ada said recently. *They surface from time to time.*

Thirty-eight years had passed.

You can throw them away now, I told her.

These are not my recollections, these are little images, notes written long ago, dead sketches outside myself, words pressed into paper, which watch me, which I watch until they turn into blotches, a smudge, a bloodless scribble, which doesn't make my heart tighten or my stomach clench. This is one of those stale, definitive deaths, which I collect, this death of my mother, who had been transformed into a state, into nonexistence, who had abandoned me. That's why I went to Paris in 2013, to bring Marisa's death to life, not to die completely myself, not to be extinguished.

For three months, three winter months, like a truffle-hunting dog I search through Paris, back and forth, walk then sit, look down so as not to fall, look up and find nothing, just that winter sky, a pure laundry blue, as Marisa used to say. I limp, my lower back hurts, my neck hurts, my eyes hurt, from one circle to another, from one urban, Parisian ring to another, in the hope that the links will not break and the hoop will tighten. I, flaneur, lost in memories with no reflection.

Where is the brothel-hotel I stayed in in 1977? It was not far from the hospital, I remember that, because it took me about ten minutes to get from there to Marisa on foot, but I no longer remember which hospital she was in. Not a single image flickers, glimmers. I walk around the district, the Latin Quarter, 5th arrondissement, I look at the façades, there are almost none that are dilapidated, like mine. I go into inner courtyards in the hope of finding the external staircase from which one entered rooms with no toilet or washroom. *Have a shower here*, said Marisa, *clean up, bring your dirty laundry*, I'll *wash it for you*, she said, with her withered veins they could no longer get needles into, there was no longer anywhere to prick her. *Don't worry*, she said, *there is, my ankles*. So they pricked her ankles.

Before me is a Paris I don't know. In which Paris had I stayed back then? Am I looking for a city that does not exist? Am I seeking a time that has vanished, or a vanished time that is coming back? I stand on the corner of rue du Pot-de-Fer and rue Tournefort, by the former convent for girls named after Saint Aurea, protector of Paris and prioress of the Benedictine monastery Solignac near Limoges, who died overnight of the plague in 666, along with a hundred and sixty nuns. Saint Aurea, the story goes, performed miracles. Through her prayers, she brought an abbess back to life after she had lain dead for three days. I don't know a single prayer, and the plague is, they say, more or less eradicated.

Under the recently affixed street name "rue Tournefort" one can see traces cut into the façade of the name of the former, old rue Neuve-Sainte-Geneviève. On rue Neuve-Sainte-Geneviève, lived Balzac, at number 24, or perhaps the young Rastignac, their biographies have got mixed up, they merge with one another, as do the centuries, and the years, mine and the historical ones, they flow into one another, but no longer in playful curves, just in one tedious line that, like a worn string, emits one monotonous note. Here, not far from the place where I am standing, the comédie humaine acquired its outlines.

I go to 24 rue Tournefort. The building is not like Madame Vauquer's boarding house where, in a humble little room, the ambitious young Rastignac shivered and planned his rise to high society.

On the small, out-of-the-way rue Victor Cousin I come across a little hotel, the Hôtel Cluny Sorbonne, I go in, I climb the wooden stairs to the fifth floor, open the door of a poorly furnished little room with no heating and see Lucien Rubempré, né Chardon, bent over a heap of papers. *What are you doing?* I ask. *I'm losing my illusions*, says Lucien, *et j'ai faim*. I take an open packet of peanuts from my pocket, I always have some sort of seeds with me, or grains, so that my stomach doesn't go berserk and start secreting acid, *Tu veux des cacahuètes?* I ask, and I put the little packet on the edge of the table and leave. I reach Marisa in eight minutes, I reach the Hôpital de l'Institut Curie, 26 rue d'Ulm, which means that is the hospital in which she fades away, I finally settle for that hospital, that hospital advertises, in two languages: *Ensemble, prenons le cancer de vitesse* and for the tourists, *Together, let's beat cancer*, so that all those foreigners who swarm along the beautiful boulevards of Paris, who visit picturesque shops and flea markets, who sample expensive and less expensive cheeses, first-class or diluted wines, who stand for hours outside museums in queues for exhibitions, sometimes excellent, sometimes phony, who go to theater performances by famous international artists, likewise sometimes fake and sometimes brilliant, just as that one I myself saw by Robert Wilson, in which Mikhail Baryshnikov and Willem Dafoe sing and shout, whisper and dance Daniil Kharms a little too passionately, and I laughed in horror to watch ineptly knocked-together, crooked window frames filled with darkness falling from the sky, and hideous, stinking old women just refusing to fall out of them, I saw beds (prison beds?) slinking onto the stage, swallowing their sleepers, little (harmless?) drones, like children's toys, flying up, wooden clocks ticking away the last days, huge two-dimensional cockerels, in rainbow colors, as though they had stepped out of a naïve Yugoslav painting, announcing the arrival of (a new) day, a blessed dawn, and all of this was observed by Estragon and Vladimir swinging, small, lost in space, cheerfully waiting for God, so that all these foreigners who swarm through the beautiful Paris boulevards, so that we all, staring at that bilingual advertisement of a vast smiling face bursting with health, so that we should believe that there is hope for us, that every illness, even the worst, can be defeated if we only step bravely onto the battlefield.

Kika, my patient companion on this pointless search for a lost time, says, *Andreas*, les maisons closes *no longer exist, at least not in this district, while* table d'hôte *restaurants, those from your youth, like Flicoteaux* à prix fixe, *are now frequented by working people with not exactly shallow pockets.*

And I stop looking for the room, which I don't remember in any case.

So, the Hôpital de l'Institut Curie. Rue Mouffetard is nearby, the shop selling Marisa's raspberries and warm crepes is nearby, the Panthéon is nearby, and the Sorbonne, and the botanical garden, which I only glimpsed. The retail shops (with burgundy shoes) aren't far away either.

It looks like a prison. A complex of brick buildings like those in a ghetto. Was it through this entrance that I came in the morning and left at night, thirty-eight years ago? Was it through this same entrance that my father and Ada came, because on our trips for Parisian experimentation on Marisa we took it in turns? What hotels they stayed in, how they felt, I don't know, we never talked about it, because there wasn't time. Afterward, there was no point.

Was it in this building, in one of these buildings (which?) that I jabbered nonsense to Marisa, with a lump in my throat, while she twittered, bluffing, as she performed the last act of the comedy of dying? Short-term sentences are served here. All the windows are closed, lifeless. There's nothing inside them, no bottles of juice, no jam jars, no biscuits, no coffeepots, not a single face appears in them to open the window and breathe in the autumn chill. People lie attached to drips, cytostatics make them vomit their innards or they die, just then, when *together we are beating cancer*. Kika and I stand there, not speaking, then Kika looks at me and says, *Well?* and I say, *Nothing*.

Then Kika says, *Let's at least look for that square where the circus troupe dance.*

We found the square. I don't know whether it was that square, but it would do. That square lay in the embrace of neglected buildings with crumbling façades, this one was bounded by chains and flowerbeds, in its center there was a sprinkling water feature, it's hard to get to, it's not easy to occupy it, circus acts don't take place on it, it's a tidy little square that does not tolerate acrobatic feats. It's where nomads, wanderers, played music, *les Bohémiens, les Manush, les Gitanes*, handsome and cheerful, while Kika and I sat in a bistro opposite, drinking *calvados* and nibbling on fresh *cacahuètes*.

And to console myself I said to Kika: *Listen, to prevent the battle being lost, to transform its loss into gain, maybe that battle should be left to lie in oblivion, in a cocoon of absence, in a shield of nonexistence.*

Kika said, *Tomorrow I'm taking you for fresh oysters.*

And the next day we ate fresh oysters, outside, standing and leaning on tall barrels, surrounded by noisy Frenchmen.

There was a word Daniil Kharms had forgotten, he simply couldn't remember what word it was, but it seemed to him so important to remember that word, so important, as though his life depended on it.

Beginning with M?

With R?

Yes, with R.

I said: Reason.

Kharms said: It's driving me mad.

I said: Radiance.

He said: I'm going to cry!

I said: Frame.

He threw the picture onto the ground.

I said: Reins.

He took the bridle off, leaped onto the horse and rode off bareback.

But I do remember. I remember the whole of Marisa's three-year illness, whenever I wish I can summon images, in color and movement, I see her face, I hear her voice and follow our conversations. Outings from her room in a new black skirt, made up, her hair short, grown back again, *How does it suit me?* she asks and laughs wickedly, I find her in the kitchen in an aquamarine housecoat, she is using a knife to scrape off burnt matter from the tiles around the stovetop, I have come back to Rovinj from some journey or other, it is winter, she lights the oil stove in the cellar and greets me with squid and chard and first-class Malvasia wine, bald, smiling and baked from cobalt radiation, *You see these little knots on my neck*, she says, leaning her head to the right, *they are metastases on the lungs. How do you sleep? Take care of your health*, she says as we sip cognac into the small hours, until early morning, *I'd like to sing*, she says, she tries, but it doesn't work, a thin thread winds out of her throat, jerkily, cracked, she shrugs her shoulders, I think I see a tear, but there's a smile on her lips that breaks my heart. In the hospital, when we came back from Paris, she had said, *I'm seeing double, metastases on my brain, peripheral collapse, call Dr. Škokljev to give me an injection of dexamethasone*, and she died in my arms half an hour later. In the basement of the Oncological Department where she waits her turn for radiation with the theater director Marko Fotez, and advises him in connection with his carcinoma. My mother's illness fits entirely harmoniously into the story on the huge canvas of my life, of my days with a cast of thousands, lesser and greater, close and distant, it is only Paris that floats, *sfumato*, rocks in the background, threatening to fly entirely out of the frame.

Then came the epiphany. A small, insignificant image surfaced from nowhere, in an instant. Now it glimmers, stuck to the front of my brain, and accompanies me: roofs, a view of roofs in the Latin Quarter, the view through the open window of the attic room in the brothel where I sleep while Marisa lies in the Hôpital de l'Institut Curie. And the pure, blue sky. That's all.

In this last Paris, I got lost. My purpose frayed. My focus misted over. It's cold in my room, I have no power socket in the bathroom—I shave with no mirror, blindly. When it rains, the roof leaks. I wander about and come across closed bookshops, their windows covered in sheets of brown paper, and, every so often, buyers of gold—*achat d'or*. The streets are full of dog shit, men piss at the corners, both those in expensive suits and the homeless, but there are too many homeless, so as soon as the sun warms up or the wind blows, the urine evaporates. One homeless man has set up camp in front of the building where I'm staying; I circle around him, wonder whether to join him, then he says, *Take my photo, as a memento*, and tells me his life story. I go down "my" rue du Faubourg Saint-Martin and in a side street, rue de Nancy, I "capture" two more homeless men preparing for the night. One, in rags, curls up beside the wall and immediately falls asleep, the other assembles a small tent he has just bought, he does it briskly, jerkily, checking the sketch on the instruction sheet every few minutes. Then he takes a new bed, or rather a blow-up mattress, out of a box with inflatable bed written on it, and blows. He throws his bed into his "little room." He does it all with concentration, as if in a trance. He takes a lot of tiny steps, but doesn't go anywhere. He's wearing an ironed beige raincoat and winter shoes with rubber soles, new. Later, in front of his "little house," he spreads out a red and black checkered rug, sits down on it, places a clean tea towel over his knees, and from a canvas bag he takes a piece of cheese, a wilted, squashed baguette and half a liter of wine in a carton. He "dines" slowly and ritually. As he drinks the wine (from the carton), he raises the little finger of his right hand, his nails are clean and trimmed. Then he withdraws into his bedroom, his shelter, and disappears. It is a cold and wet winter evening, half-dark. I stand leaning against the wall of the building opposite, still watching the homeless men, whom I can no longer see as they are sleeping, I fiddle with my phone, waiting for Marisa to call me. We've arranged to meet at Chartier at eight. Marisa doesn't call, so I go back to my castle. As I climb up toward Gare de l'Est, my mother finally calls. *I can't go to Chartier tonight*, she says. *I have to go to Lola's to see how she is.*

It's the Day of the Dead. The streets are as empty as the Day. Saturday.

At midnight Marisa knocks on my door. In one hand she has warm croissants, in the other a small blue thermos. *It's my birthday*, she says. *Are you hungry?*

Now, as I write, it's Mental Health Month. I don't know what that means. Is it only in this month, May, that mental health is celebrated, while in the other months it isn't, because only in May are people mentally well, and in June and beyond they aren't, which would mean that people are always mentally ill (apart from in May), or it is only in May, when everything is burgeoning and there is a lot of pollen, that people are mentally ill, and then become problematic for society, and therefore in May their incapacity and their mental illness have to be brought under control. I don't even know what mental health is. I don't know who decides or whether it hurts.

In Paris I meet Didi. Didi lives in the same complex as I do. Didi is a graphic artist.

I've got some fine wine, says Didi, taking a swig from the bottle. *I can drink again*, she says, *for years I wasn't able to. Because of an allergy. I came out in blotches all over my face and body and I couldn't breathe. Wine could have killed me. Now it's okay, the allergy has gone*, says Didi, then she adds, *My mother was an alcoholic, perhaps there's a connection.*

I said, *Your mother died.*

Yes, she died, says Didi.

In fact, in Paris at that time I was living in a castle. The square on which Gare de l'Est also stands, in that tenth arrondissement, was dominated by a castle, a former Franciscan Récollets cloister built in 1603. But, two hundred years later, the monks had presumably done what they had to do, and they headed off to Canada for a bit, and the castle is now inhabited by those who leave it feet first. They've opened a similar hospice in Rijeka as well, and in Rijeka too it is run by those who think they are close to God, and, I hear, the waiting list is quite long.

Then, in 1862, the castle-cloister is taken over by another rigorously strict order—military—and refurbished as a military hospital, the Hôpital Saint Martin; there is a French campaign against Korea in 1866, then a French raid on Tunis in 1881, then the Franco-Siamese War of 1893, and Gare de l'Est is right here, on the doorstep, so to speak, so the transport of the wounded is swift and effective. Then comes that Great War in which around one million four hundred thousand French soldiers and civilians perish and four times that number are wounded, then the hospital changes its holy name to a secular one and is renamed the Hôpital Jean-Antoine Villemin, but it remains military; military hospitals are essential.

Then, in 1913, Jean-Antoine Villemin was, of course, already long dead. Jean-Antoine Villemin had been a military doctor in the famous military hospital Val-de-Grâce in which until recently the corrupt international elite was treated. Today treatment in that hospital is rapidly eluding them, as there is ever less money for its maintenance, so the Val-de-Grâce will probably soon re-emerge as a luxury hotel complex, owned by a sheikh. It is only in the middle of the twentieth century that Jean-Antoine Villemin acquires a city plaque on which it says that, through his research into consumption and his experimentation with tuberculosis bacilli on rabbits and other small animals, he finally proved that

TB is a dangerous infectious disease, although his work remained unacknowledged for many years, Jean-Antoine was posthumously awarded a prize of 50,000 French francs.

It is important to have military hospitals; wars keep happening, bloody young men emerge from them with their lives hanging by a thread, some without arms, some without legs, some even without faces, urgent cases which would need to wait in a queue in a civil hospital, but in their hospitals they are the bosses, the doctors endeavor immediately to patch them up somehow, although the majority, if they don't die, remain until their deaths maimed in one way or another.

Today the rooms of the Récollets castle are home to an architectural school, and scientists, artists and writers from all over the world stay there.

Once in the course of my three-month Parisian stay I found myself with other inhabitants of the castle. I was told there was a meeting in the piano room. This was a hall, an unheated long narrow room with two conference tables and some fifty cheap folding chairs, to say nothing of the nonexistent piano. The light was neon, like in a deserted train station. Of the eighty or so people who stay in the castle, about a dozen had turned up, mostly young scientists in training, paid to work in laboratories and presumably renting rooms in the castle for little money. Four physicists, two technicians, two architects and a few heavily made-up Parisian shop assistants came. One had been in Paris already for a year and didn't know three words of French. Two were from Italy—from Rome and Milan—one woman was from India, and there were some Greeks. I asked them what they did after five and at the weekend, did they go to the cinema, to the theater, to exhibitions, to bookshops, to concerts, to discos. Silence. I didn't know what to talk about. They mentioned wires and currents, chemical experiments, laboratory analyses, I didn't understand a thing. On the conference table there were wrapped cheeses, bread you broke with your hands, all the wine was cheap (except mine), there were no glasses or knives. I stayed for half an hour, because I was beginning to feel cold (and we were sitting in our coats), not to say sad. What world did I belong to? I went to put antiglaucoma drops in my eyes, which often water. Still, I had discovered what *liquid solids* were, that glass is in fact liquid, fluid, although I didn't know, and still don't, what to do with this knowledge.

An Albanian painter, Edi Hila, was staying in the room next to mine, and unlike most of the French people I met at that time he seemed somehow close, I wanted to ask him all kinds of things, about Enver Hoxha's bunkers, about Skënderbe cognac, which I hadn't tasted for more than three decades but had heard that it was no longer what it once was, about cleaned mussels in jars which were imported into Yugoslavia from his country, cheap, perfect for risotto, about persecuted writers and painters who for years, right up until 1991, had been savagely tortured in prison-for-tresses scattered through the mountains, not even reachable by goat track, let alone by road, and who had written their books and poems on remnants of toilet and cigarette paper, noting or sketching their frozen dreams; I wanted to ask him about Kadare, had he really been Enver's spy, there were all kinds of questions I wanted to ask Edi Hila about the country which had walled itself in, about its forty-year whispering, about the fear that makes a human voice break, and the throat gape like a dumb black hole, I wanted to ask the Albanian painter Edi Hila all that and lots more, because I had long wanted to visit that country, that country of dignified, proud people (*besa*), where only the eagles were free and at times not even they. But I communicated with the Albanian painter Edi Hila with difficulty, although we both spoke French, because the Albanian painter Edi Hila painted the whole time, and he was also driven crazy by mice, he hadn't been able to get rid of the mice in his room and they got everywhere, into his clothes, his food, even into empty plastic bags where they rustled all night long, and so, in passing, we talked about mice. I went to the opening of his exhibition, but there Edi Hila was surrounded by invited guests and the media, so it was not exactly conducive to a tête-à-tête. Then I went back to one country, and Edi Hila to another.

Two years later I wound up in Albania, and in Tirana I unlocked Edi Hila's story. Otherwise, I didn't get at all upset in Tirana. Nothing bothered me, no one ran into me, people walked *normally*, on the right, penetrating voices didn't hammer at my brain, the sky was blue and there were no (or not many) Americans. I was afraid only that some vehicle might run me over, because there were few cars there and no one gave a fuck about traffic lights, neither pedestrians nor drivers, and the pavements were abnormally high, almost half a meter. The city looks, roughly, like the center of Berlin, because in Berlin too there are broad boulevards that stretch out of sight, and gleaming shop windows with expensive goods. The cafés in Tirana are full, the young people are fashionably dressed, they smile and peck at their iPhones. There are shopping centers, supermarkets with every conceivable alimentary product, there are many large, luxurious hotels and small, private ones, there are parks, and there is the Lana river. And, wherever I drank it, the macchiato was first class, better than in Italy. There were birds, both in cages and in the sky, and every morning I was woken up by the crowing of a cockerel.

So, although it was terrible, Edi Hila's story turned out not to be appalling compared to the ten, twenty or thirty years of monstrous torture suffered by writers such as Fatos Lubonja (b. 1951), the poet Visar Zhiti (b. 1952), or the architect and painter Maks Velo (b. 1935) and the painter Edison Gjergo (1939–89), who died in a prison for political prisoners, one of the three most dreadful in Albania, Spaç Prison. Then, in Tirana, I sat in cafés renovated in

a West European style, drinking either Albanian brandy or Skënderbe cognac and listening to Fatos Lubonja and Visar Zhiti, or
leafing through the powerful and painful portfolios shown to me
by the smiling eighty-year-old Maks Velo. About them and about
much else I shall write on another occasion, probably when (if) I
decide to relate what I now know about Adam Kaplan.

In Tirana I don't talk with Edi Hila (b. 1949) about mice, in
Tirana I look at catalogues of his old and new paintings, many
of which are now hanging in museums and galleries all over the
world, and (as though) incidentally, I hear about what was for him
the disastrous canvas commissioned by the government in 1971
(large format—it's in the National Art Gallery here in Tirana). In
the painting joyful young people with red scarves around their
necks dig holes and plant what were for the Communist Party
of Albania unacceptably impressionistic seedlings. In the picture,
young men and women bend in a furious rhythm, giddily, with
no order or discipline, carving out their future. Although at the
beginning of the 1970s the Party loosened the reins a little, just
enough to give the people the illusion that better days were on
their way—men were allowed to wear sunglasses and jeans and
grow beards, while rock music made its way timidly into homes,
and households turned their television aerials toward Italy and
Yugoslavia—after the IV (so-called "Black") Plenum of the Central Committee of his Workers' (Communist) Party, in 1973, Enver Hoxha changed his mind and walled up the country again,
filling it with new camps, new prisons, new bunkers to which he
consigned the democratically inclined artistic and intellectual
elite, and this time wrapped Albania in even heavier chains and
Shqipëria devoured itself, sinking into terrible, painful invisibility.

Because of this insufficiently socialist-realist painting ("Tree
Planting") with its exaggeratedly joyful, disobedient youth bathed
in a gentle golden light, which could have borne it upward toward

the sky (and in the sky strange, suspect shapes flutter), far from the pits which it is "voluntarily" digging for itself, in 1974, Edi Hila, on his return to Tirana after a three-month stay in Florence, where Albanian state television *in statu nascendi* sent him for "training," was arrested and sentenced to six years of forced labor on a remote chicken farm, where he dragged sacks of grain around all day and night. After he was "given his freedom," for as long as Enver Hoxha's regime lasted, right up until 1991, Edi Hila was unable to exhibit (and his earlier works were "bunkerized"). In double isolation, both personal and that into which reality nailed him, for two decades Edi Hila created his sometimes hideous, sometimes dreamy worlds. My friend the poet Arian Leka said of Edi Hila, *During the night, he dreamed of the sun and that was a crime.*

After 1974, when I came back from Florence, Edi Hila told me, *I wondered for a long time what my life was, what kind of a life was it without freedom, without artistic freedom. Florence was my first encounter with real art; for the first time I had the opportunity to see the original works of great masters, great art. Then it all sank, I looked at the world again from a distance, like a memory that has been transformed into the vestiges of reality. I thought that I would never again step into living, illuminated reality. Those were the conditions in which I had to exist and survive.*

Today Edi Hila teaches painting at the Academy of Art in Tirana. He has no wish to recall those Parisian mice.

At that time, Tomaž Šalamun and Marko Sosič came to Paris. They read their poems in a small café-bookshop, now in French, now in Slovene, then we got together on a human, not scholarly level. Then Tomaž died.

I didn't write anything in Paris, in that castle/monastery. The internet was no good, the radiators were small and lukewarm, the electric heater kept going off and, toward the end, I had that disaster with my eyes.

As in Brussels, in Paris too there was a school near the castle, and beneath my windows there stretched a park, which had presumably once belonged to the Jean-Antoine Villemin military hospital, because it was called Villemin Park. I lived in the attic and looked out at the park and the school. Unlike the one in Brussels, this was a primary school, and at break the squeals and uproar coming from it were at times too loud. I could hear the school bell as well. To my great surprise that didn't bother me at all, in Rijeka I would have been tearing my hair out. During break and after school the children swarmed through the park, which had fountains and an incredible variety of trees and plants, and also some fifty beds in which the local community grew flowers and fruit.

At the entrance to the park there was a metal notice, and in the park a stone post, a pillar, and they both say: let the children be, let them run, let them jump, let them shout, let them chase balls, let them cultivate their own flowerbeds, because once, from 1942 to 1944, the silence, the hush and the nausea must have been so enormous and terrifying, so petrifying, that they could not fit even into a child's shriek, let alone into crying.

The notices under my windows say that from 1942 to 1944, from this arrondissement, the tenth, more than seven hundred Jewish children were deported to death camps, and seventy-five very little ones wrenched from their families, killed and never buried.

There is a notice like this in every Paris arrondissement. From 1942 to 1944, the Nazis, with the wholehearted and active support of the Vichy authorities, deported a whole children's town, a town of children—11,000 youngsters—out of France to concentration camps, mostly to Auschwitz-Birkenau. I took a photograph of this notice, in passing, as I went down "my" rue du Faubourg Saint-Martin toward the Seine.

That rue du Faubourg Saint-Martin, in addition to the fact that there are rough-sleepers living in its side streets, has a history, every street has a history, every house has a story, it's just that we don't have time, and when we do have time, something to do with our eyes, our sight gets snagged.

The tenth arrondissement was once known as the warehouse district, arrondissement de l'Entrepôt. The tenth arrondissement was where the working class lived. Today various classes live there, classified and unclassified, belonging and not belonging, of various colors.

So, I go down rue du Faubourg Saint-Martin and examine the buildings, I am forever looking at buildings, wherever I happen to be, I am charmed by some façade, and even in places which I apparently know I will come across seductive architectural faces, façades which offer me new (secret) stories, and now, like Borislav Pekić's poor Arsenije Njegovan, about whom few in Croatia know anything and who, after, as he puts it, "an autotrophic way of life," with the sorrow of a man lost in time, doggedly insists that buildings are like people, with which I would not entirely agree, people forget, buildings remember, and as I look at the structures I am walking past I collide with a reality that I can sometimes no longer distinguish from what has passed.

I stop. The edifice is impressive. At the top, but under the attic gables, so that it should be seen and heard from the street, this evidently recently renovated building with huge upper windows and three broad shop fronts, which invite one into its interior, but which in turn offer an open view of the world, of what is outside, of what is happening outside, at the top, on a mosaic background of blue and gold ceramic tiles, that building proclaims to passersby that it is here, that it is ready to devote itself to the working class. In large letters, the palace at 85–87 rue du Faubourg Saint-Martin proclaims AUX CLASSES LABORIEUSES.

Then I catch sight of a plaque, a memorial plaque at eye level for the average pedestrian:

During the Occupation and with the help of the Vichy regime, this building, at the time the Lévitan furniture shop, served as an annex of the Drancy deportation camp. Here, between July 1943 and August 1944, hundreds of Jews, of whom many were later deported to Auschwitz and Bergen-Belsen, were forced to sort through the furniture and objects that the Nazis had stolen from the apartments of Jewish families.

May this never be forgotten.

That day I lost the will to go for a walk. Three memorial plaques in one half of one street, in a small urban space within an hour's walk. How many of them are then nailed into other parts of this city? That is not why I came to Paris, but again, as several times in the course of my roaming round Europe, History had grabbed me by the throat and clouded my already problematic vision. And now, perversely angry that in Croatia I don't come across so many plaques, and that if I do happen across some, they are small, almost invisible, placed high up, their letters fading, or else they are desecrated, chipped by the mallet of a passerby of unsound mind, in comparison with whom my former patients are like the lost, invisible souls of good, or else, instead of those former plaques, on the walls there are only marks, the outline of their erstwhile frames, dried mortar, flaking, and the holes of the screws by which they were once attached to the buildings and, because the National Liberation Movement was the fourth member, the fourth member of the International Antifascist Coalition, ahead of France, I decided to set about photographing memorial plaques put up to remember the victims of Fascism and Nazism wherever I happened to be. A colleague of mine is putting together a "gallery" of Ustasha "U" signs. For enraged fanatics, for genuine lunatics with bloodshot eyes, it will be an irritating monograph, if my colleague ever manages to find a publisher for it and manages to emerge from his "project" in Croatia with his life. I thought, for fun, of making a list of all the hotel rooms in which I had slept, with their numbers, but the activity with the plaques now seems healthier for my compressed spine, because it demands movement. Between 1945 and 1990 in Croatia alone around 6,000 monuments, busts, sculptures and memorial plaques were produced, dedicated to events and people connected with the National Liberation Movement of Croatia and Yugoslavia, and between 1990 and 2000 precisely 2,964 memorial signs, 731 monuments, and 2,233 other kinds of memorial signs were destroyed or damaged (*by whom? name and surname, by whom?*). By 2012 around 400 antifascist monuments of lesser artistic worth had been restored, and only a few of the most significant ones. People who presumably count them say that altogether in the Socialist Federal Republic of Yugoslavia some 15,000 monuments were erected, dedicated to the National Liberation War. Then, recently, the Belgian artistic photographer Jan Kempenaers came to Croatia and said that those monuments (erected at the time of socialist Yugoslavia, and some less than ten years after the end of the war) were magnificent (the ones he found), that with their abstract and futuristic appearance they could be considered the best of international monumental architecture.

Then, standing in front of numbers 85–87 rue du Faubourg Saint-Martin, Arsenije Njegovan came back to me, he sat on my shoulder and whispered:

But when did great passions
care about small considerations?

I leaned against that building as if it were a human being, to touch it, to have it touch me, but instead of warmth, a chill ran through my body. I stroked the plaque and continued to the river, but it, that former furniture store for the working class, monumental and brilliant, dragged itself after me, panting.

In the course of the war, in France, 71,619 Jewish apartments were confiscated (38,000 in Paris alone), from which were stolen 1,079,373 cubic meters of "goods," loaded onto 26,984 railway wagons, along with money and bonds with an estimated value of 11,695,516 Reichsmarks. That and many other dire operations of plunder throughout the German-occupied territories were orchestrated by that same Alfred Rosenberg who, at the time of the disappearance of Frida Landsberg, the violinist from Latvia, was strolling round Riga, and as he requisitioned the pianos and violins of Latvian musicians, he nostalgically evoked memories of his student days. This, this plunder in France, was undertaken by a branch of Rosenberg's special organization *Einsatzstab Reichsleiter Rosenberg* (ERR), the so-called Western Agency (*Dienststelle Westen*) within which a very lively and dedicated "Furniture Campaign," the *Möbel Aktion*, was carried out, which, of course, apart from period furniture, implied not only the theft of works of fine art and jewelry, weapons, valuable porcelain, and oriental sculptures, but also worthless articles for everyday use, cups, plates, cutlery, linen, clothes, shoes, underwear, even light bulbs, nails, tools, curtains, tablecloths, blankets, pillows, frying pans, saucepans and teapots, children's toys, from dolls and balls to little cars and electric model railways, the theft in fact of everything that makes a life, the theft in fact of the lives of those whose physical lives were also taken from them. That working group of Rosenberg's was moving through France as early as mid-July 1940, appropriating "degenerate" oil paintings, rare musical instruments (Rosenberg, as I've said, adored music), archival materials and valuable libraries, and when the terrain had been more or less taken care of and all that treasure more or less catalogued, photographed, and sent to Germany, some to warehouses for Hitler's future museum in Linz, but far more directly to Göring's country villa Carinhall, situated in picturesque hunting country within reach of Berlin (in which the morphine-dependent Göring pedantically arranged his more than 1,800 stolen works of art), Rosenberg asked for and was granted permission to continue the action, for the further cleansing of "abandoned" Jewish houses and apartments in order to satisfy the needs of the German civilian population in the newly occupied eastern territories of the Reich. But these fragments of life traveled also to Germans whose homes were destroyed by the bombs of the Allied forces, to the ordinary innocent people, so that Greater Germany could soothe their war traumas and offer them hope in a better future. Today, when at flea markets all over Europe we buy a crystal glass, a silver spoon or a china cup, a "family photograph" for a trivial sum, when we stroll through elegant or modest antique shops, when we attend auctions, we can only imagine what journeys are written into this enormous movement of people and objects across a continent and further afield, into this vast planetary exchange of lives which merge into a general chaos, a commotion, a bazaar of the past and present.

I have an assortment of glasses from Berlin, Vienna, Paris, and even New York flea markets and I often say that they are my glasses. But they are not. I have a small collection of other people's days, one could say—stolen, joys and sorrows bought for a song, toasts and commemorative speeches which here, in my half-empty room, like soft bells speak of every forced relocation of existence and being, of every violent interruption of abiding, and they send out a clear but ominous crystal sound. The objects with which I am surrounded, with which I surround myself, when the air stops the breath, when not even silence quivers, transformed into fluids they begin to penetrate the armor of my skin and sneak in among my organs, already poisoned by imprints of the past.

To carry out their general European plunder, pillage and villainy, the ERR in France engaged local transport firms which provided mechanical equipment, personnel, and Baron Kurt von

Behr—who managed the whole program and later, in 1945, with his wife and the help of cyanide and champagne, parted forever from his accumulated spoils. Something of those French "goods" was stored and sorted in what had been until then the first French furniture shop at 85–87 rue du Faubourg Saint-Martin, owned by Wolf Lévitan, who, it is presumed, was taken away by the Gestapo, never to return. Then, from 1943 to 1944, in the heart of Paris, there were two other hidden satellite work camps of the Drancy transit camp: Entrepôts et Magasins Généraux, in other words state public warehouses, known also, because of their proximity to the railway station of the same name, as the Austerlitz storerooms, at 43 quai de la Gare, in the thirteenth arrondissement; and the Bassano work camp situated in the Aryanized palace of the Cahen d'Anvers family at number 2 rue Bassano, in the sixteenth arrondissement. The majority of the inhabitants of Paris know nothing or very little of the existence of these work camps in the city center, because even the survivors of the camps, those who by pure chance or thanks to spouses of Aryan blood were not transferred from Drancy to Auschwitz, were reluctant to speak about that episode in their lives, considering it a minor and inessential episode compared to the great and appalling transportation of humanity, which of course still conceals secrets. Because those camp survivors were, one way or another, after all saved, as was all that enormous property belonging to those who were not. Even Serge Klarsfeld, the famous Nazi hunter, said, *Those work camps were not a great tragedy. The tragedy is that during the war nearly 80,000 French Jews were killed and that France collaborated with the Nazis in that.*

At 85–87 rue du Faubourg Saint-Martin then, in 1942 and 1943, worked 795 prisoners of whom 164 were deported from Drancy, never to return. Sorting through those stolen belongings, the prisoners often came across items from their own apartments or those of their friends, a small inventory that they later stacked on shelves, and then, as in a large department store, that "display" area was visited by the idle wives of SS officers who came "shopping" for trifling sums, and when they had the time the SS officers themselves would call in to choose for their nearest and dearest, again for next to nothing, some charming, unique gift.

It was only sixty years later, in 2003, that two young scholars, Jean-Marc Dreyfus and Sarah Gensburger, endeavored in their thoroughly documented book (*Des camps dans Paris: Austerlitz, Lévitan, Bassano, juillet 1943–août 1944*: Fayard) to open the little chamber of forgotten collective memory, and yet another small void acquired outlines. A year later, in the German Federal Archives in Koblenz, a series of photographs was found that document this until-then hidden Parisian theft.

In those Parisian work camps stolen goods were not only stored and catalogued, they were mended or altered. Imprisoned horologists repaired clocks, cobblers shoes, seamstresses and tailors altered fur coats and dinner suits, they gave a fresher, more contemporary look to evening dresses, little fashion salons were organized at which German gentlefolk acquired clothes for their feasts and celebrations for a song. Thus, all these removed people, all these *murdered* people, already dead, left the storehouses of the Paris work camps and for a long time afterward walked in their coats, in their suits, with their hats on their heads, with their leather bags over their shoulders, in their shoes, through the streets of their Paris, only now fused with other people's bodies in which, like a requiem, there resounded their prayers—or their curse.

That ERR stretched its tentacles everywhere. In Serbia, in mid-February 1943, the ERR, known as the *Arbeitsgruppe Südost*, launched plundering campaigns coordinated first in Belgrade from 26 Gospodar Jovanova, from the office of the then Chief

Rabbi, and then from 27 Obilićev venac, while in Croatia campaigns had already been operating in Zagreb and Dubrovnik since May 1941. In less than a month, the ERR *Dienststelle*, known as *Der deutsche General in Agram*, carried out 116 raids of houses and apartments, for the most part those owned by Croatian Jews, and at the end of June Mladen Lorković, the then Minister of Interior Affairs of the Independent State of Croatia (NDH) entered into a lively correspondence with the heads of the Zagreb branch of the ERR, wholeheartedly offering his services. To Göring and Rosenberg's regret, but fortunately for the looted, the value of the Balkan booty did not even approach that of the wealthy European families and consisted mainly of some appropriated libraries, documents, carpets, the occasional sculpture or oil painting by artists almost unknown in the outside world, and a multitude of worn household items such as cheap dinner sets and anonymous furniture. In its postwar application to the Federal Republic of Germany for the return of looted property, of objects of value the Yugoslav government sought one Rembrandt, belonging to the Yugoslav royal family, a flag of Friedrich the Great, an oil painting from the school of Raphael and a Caravaggio from the Montenegrin monastery of Ostrog. All right, they did also ask for the return of the inventory books from the collections of the Historical Museum in Zagreb, but also numerous objects stolen in Bosnia and Herzegovina and Slovenia. So, Yugoslavia asked that sixty pictures taken from the Jewish cultural society La Benevolencija be returned to Sarajevo, as well as 6,500 artifacts stolen from Zagreb's Strossmayer Gallery. But the most valuable objects preserved from the gigantic bureaucracy of the Third Reich, with its perfectly functioning machinery, were the files deposited in the Russian State Military Archive (*Российский государственный военный архив*) and the copy of them in the United States Holocaust Memorial Museum in Washington DC. Everything is written in these documents: there is a record of every theft of other people's belongings carried out in Zagreb and the majority of those carried out in Dubrovnik; they record whose house was plundered, who carried out the theft and when, what was taken, and, in some cases, what fate the victims met. Here there is a detailed description of the anti-Semitic laws and anti-Semitic disposition that spread through Croatia, along with proof of the persecution of Jewish doctors, driven out of hospitals, and Jewish musicians driven from their jobs. In other words, it is all known. It is known.

Source	Looted Object (s)	Owner	Address	Date	Notes
Fond 1401, Inventory 1, Folder 5	book collection (2,434 volumes): [172 volumes German classics 57 volumes European classics 28 volumes Latin classics 107 volumes Croatian language political writtings 33 volumes "Nova Europa" 2037 volumes still not catalogued of literature in Croatian, French and for example by Jewish authors.]	Dr. Wladimir Čorović		July 1942	All books carried the stamp of the "Hohe Schule"
AGRAM (ZAGREB)					
Fond 1401, Inventory 1, Folder 27	30-40 numbers of the Freemason newsletter "Sestar"	Peter Acinger	Agram, Radićeva 26	18 July 1941	
Fond 1401, Inventory 1, Folder 27	50 books, mainly Jewish literature	David Alkalay	Agram, Heinzlova 69	8 July 1941	
Fond 1401, Inventory 1, Folder 27	27 books, mainly Jewish literature	Wladimir Altmann	Agram, Jelačićev trg 10a	4 June 1941	
Fond 1401, Inventory 1, Folder 27	book collection (21 volumes in French, 3 volumes in English, 6 volumes of Jewish authors in German, 11 volumes in Croatian or Serbian, 3 volumes in German – not of Jewish authors)	Dr Andres Ivan	Trg Kralja Tomislava 21	8 August 1941	
Fond 1401, Inventory 1, Folder 27	5 books, mainly Jewish literature	Anton Antunović	Agram, Martićeva 70/II b. Milković	16 July 1941	

Fond 1401, Inventory 1, Folder 27	25 books and leaflets (Yugoslavian and Jewish literature: 13 volumes in Croatian; 7 volumes by Jewish authors in German; 5 volumes in German, but not of Jewish authors)	Dr Branko Arko	Agram, Kaptol 2	9 August 1941	
Fond 1401, Inventory 1, Folder 27	15 books and 20 leaflets (Jewish literature)	Alexander Ausch	Agram, Ilica 232	23 July 1941	
Fond 1401, Inventory 1, Folder 27	30 books (Freemason/ Jewish and English literature)	Viktor Badalić	Agram, Gundulićeva 2	24 July 1941	
Fond 1401, Inventory 1, Folder 27	35 books (Jewish authors)	Alexander Balaš	Agram, Palmotićeva 64 a	30 July 1941	
Fond 1401, Inventory 1, Folder 27	400 books, documents and film material (210 books in Croatian – Politics, History and Freemasonry; 117 Jewish books – mostly historical; 93 German books)	Dr Hugo Bauer	Agram, Jabukovac 15	7 June 1941	Director of Pokorny company located at Wlaschka Ulica, as well as director of company Meba, Fijanova Ulica
Fond 1401, Inventory 1, Folder 27	books	Dr. Marko Bauer	Agram, Jelaćić Platz 15/III St. (earlier apartment) Keglvićev Platz 14/ II. Re (current apartment)	24 May 1941	A few books were looted (mostly Jewish authors)
Fond 1401, Inventory 1, Folder 27	40 books, mainly Jewish literature	Dr. Richard Bauer	Agram, Preradovi ćeva ulica 5/I	9 July 1941	

Fond 1401, Inventory 1, Folder 27	2 books	Felix Baum	Agram, Grahorova 3/II	16 June 1941	
Fond 1401, Inventory 1, Folder 27	125 books (101 German literature by Jewish authors; 14 Croatian literature; 2 French and 11 Jewish "Zionistic" literature)	Edmund Blühweis	Agram, Domagojeva 2	9 June 1941	
Fond 1401, Inventory 1, Folder 27	6 leaflets	Dr, Viktor Boić	Agram, Vlaška 70 b	6 August 1941	
Fond 1401, Inventory 1, Folder 27	862 books (615 Jewish authors; 168 Croatian and 79 Jewish books)	Alfred Bondi (Bondy)	apartment: Agram, Bosanska 33 (Villa) factory: Cankarova 19	12 June 1941	
Fond 1401, Inventory 1, Folder 27	24 books (23 volumes in Croatian/Serbian; 2 volumes Jewish literature; 1 newsletter in French)	Dr. Zvonimir Bratanić	Agram, Boškovićeva 42/ I	10 August 1941	
Fond 1401, Inventory 1, Folder 27	12 books (books on Freemasonry and Yugoslavian history)	Mirko Breyer	Agram, Samostanska 8 (later: Varšavska 8)	13 August 1941	
Fond 1401, Inventory 1, Folder 27	175 books and newsletters	Pavle Breyer	Agram, Frankopanska b; office: Masarikova 5		Bookshop
Fond 1401, Inventory 1, Folder 27	book collection (270 books, including: 78 German language books on the "Jewish Question", 49 Croatian language books, 12 political literature books; 14 books by Jewish authors)	Dr. Rudolf Buchwald	Agram, Palmotićeva ulica 20	18 June 1941	Dr. Rudolf Buchwald was a member of Agram's Jewish Community;

Fond 1401, Inventory 1, Folder 27	archival records, including the "Ehrenbuch", as well as paintings	Chevra Kadisa	Amruševa 8, Palmotićeva 14	21 May 1941	The document states: "Es konnten sichergestellt werden: 1. Sämtliche Aktenvorgänge über die Unterstützung der Emigranten – insd. Etwa 5000 Aktenvorgänge, 2. Das Ehrenbuch der Chevra Kadisa 3. Bildnisse der bedeutsamen Rabbiner bzw. Förderer der Chevra Kadisa.
Fond 1401, Inventory 1, Folder 27	39 books and leaflets (23 books in Croatian/ Serbian; 9 books in French; 2 German books by Jewish authors, 6 German books by non-Jewish authors)	Dr. Adolf Cuvay		12 August 1941	
Fond 1401, Inventory 1, Folder 27	12 leaflets (Jewish literature, etc)	Vilim Ćmelik	Agram, Kamaukova 13/I	7 August 1941	
Fond 1401, Inventory 1, Folder 27	book collection (57 volumes concerning the "Jewish question", 13 political volumes and newsletters; 6 volumes in German)	Albert Deutsch	Jurišićeva ulica 24, 22nd floor	19 June 1941	"Wohnung bereits einmal von der Gestapo besichtigt, Deutsch musste viele Schmucksachen, Silber und Perserteppiche abliefern."

Fond 1401, Inventory 1, Folder 27	15 books, mainly by Jewish authors	Dr. Andrija Deutsch	Agram, Vlaška 25/I.	1 August 1941	
Fond 1401, Inventory 1, Folder 27	4 books (Jewish literature)	Dr. Edo Deutsch	Agram, Masarykova 13	24 July 1941	
Fond 1401, Inventory 1, Folder 27	118 books (16 books in Croatian/Serbian; 5 volumes of a Jewish Encyclopedia; 30 Jewish authors in German; 53 Jewish non-fiction; 9 German non-Jewish books)	Dr. Samuel Deutsch	Agram, Miramarska 20	12 August 1941	
Fond 1401, Inventory 1, Folder 27	22 books and 3 leaflets	Slavko Deutsch	Agram, Miramarska 20	11 August 1941	Together with Alexander Deutsch, the following books were looted: 13 volumes in Croatian/Serbian; 33 Jewish authors in German; 2 German books by non-Jewish authors; 14 English newsletters; 5 volumes of a Jewish encyclopedia
Fond 1401, Inventory 1, Folder 27	3 books	Slavoljug Deutsch	Agram, Peradovićeva b, III	6 June 1941	
Fond 1401, Inventory 1, Folder 27	38 books (Jewish literature, 5 Jewish encyclopedias)	Šandor Deutsch	Agram, Miramraka 20	11 August 1941	

Fond 1401, Inventory 1, Folder 27	book collection (65 books and newspapers about Freemasonry in German, French and English; 5 books concerning the "Jewish question"; 15 Rotarian literature; 50 books on politics, sociology (30 of which are in German, 10 in Croatian and Serbian, 4 in French and 2 in English); 114 books on the study of religion (62 of which were in German; 33 in Croatian, 11 in French and 8 in English); 36 volumes on Yugoslavian politics and history; 24 volumes on the subject of law (in Croatian, German and French); 16 volumes on mnemonics, (11 of which are in German, 4 in French, 1 in English and 1 in French); 29 philosophical books (18 in German, 6 in French, 1 in English and 1 in Croatian); 66 literature books (16 in Croatian and Serbian, 22 in French, 4 in Russian, 8 in English and 16 in German)	Dr. Ante Dražić	Agram, Bosanska 6/II	26 July 1941
Fond 1401, Inventory 1, Folder 27	59 books	Dr David Eisenstädter	Agram, Gjorgjićeva 3b	4 June 1941
Fond 1401, Inventory 1, Folder 27	4 books	Marino Fertilio	Agram, Ksaverska 47 c	5 August 1941
Fond 1401, Inventory 1, Folder 27	26 books (about Freemasonry and by Jewish authors)	Bozidar Filipović	Agram, Palmptičeva 35/I	28 July 1941
Fond 1401, Inventory 1, Folder 27	1 painting ("Karikatur auf einen Juden")	Ignjat Fischer	Agram, Demetrova 3	23 May 1941

Fond 1401, Inventory 1, Folder 27	Book collection (Books in Croatian and Serbian: 33 volumes; German language books concerning the "Jewish Question": 135 volumes; books by Jewish authors in German: 148 volumes; non-Jewish literature: 271 volumes	Julio / Julius Fischer	Agram, Trg Kralja Petra 5	16 May 1941	Julio/Julius Fischer was the last president of B'nei B'rith
Fond 1401, Inventory 1, Folder 27	"Collection" on Freemasonry	Viktor Frank	Agram, Josipovac 11	19 May 1941	
Fond 1401, Inventory 1, Folder 27	book collection (books concerning the "Jewish Question": 30 volumes; Jewish authors in German: 9; non-Jewish literature in German: 68; French literature: 9, English literature: 3; Croatian literature: 8)	Dr. Ivo Fuchs	Agram	19 May 1941	
Fond 1401, Inventory 1, Folder 27	120 books (Jewish literature)	Dr David Furmann	apartment: Agram, Gundulićeva 4/II. (Geschäft) villa: Donji Stenjevac 83	11 July 1941	
Fond 1401, Inventory 1, Folder 27	8 books	Edo Funk	Apartment: Stan Kurdǒva 4; office: "Obnoca", Magasinsk a broj 21	19 May 1941	

Fond 1401, Inventory 1, Folder 27	31 books (Jewish and English literature); an almost complete collection of the monthly magazine "Isbor" as well as the monthly "Vidici")	Milan Glaser	Agram, Svaćićev Trg 17/I	28 July 1941	
Fond 1401, Inventory 1, Folder 27	50 books (including 42 volumes of "Judaica" and 8 volumes by Jewish authors)	Dr. Lawoslaw Glesinger	Agram, Ilica 17/III	16 June 1941	
Fond 1401, Inventory 1, Folder 27	41 books	Dr. Robert Glücksthal	Agram, Draskovice va 62/II	11 July 1941	
Fond 1401, Inventory 1, Folder 27	18 books	Dr. Karlo Goga	Agram, Herzegovacka 71	28 July 1941	
Fond 1401, Inventory 1, Folder 27	archival records	Theodor Gruenfeld	Agram, Ilica 48	17 May 1941	
Fond 1401, Inventory 1, Folder 27	30 books	Dr. Božidar Grünwald	Agram, Gundulićeva 19	17 July 1941	
Fond 1401, Inventory 1, Folder 27	21 books (Jewish authors)	Žiga Graf	Agram, Trg Kralja Tomislava 6	4 June 1941	
Fond 1401, Inventory 1, Folder 27	book collection (Books concerning the "Jewish Question": 19 volumes; Jewish authors in German: 3 volumes; non-Jewish authors in German: 28 volumes; Hungarian literature: 2 volumes; English literature: 23 volumes)	Günsberg			

Fond 1401, Inventory 1, Folder 27	157 books (23 books in Hebrew; 25 books on the topic of the "Jewish Question" in German; 6 newsletters on the topic of the "Jewish Question"; 11 "Communist Literature"; 14 "Jewish Literature", 78 "pornographic books"	Dr. Željko Hahn	Agram, Hatzova 10/I	29 July 1941	
Fond 1401, Inventory 1, Folder 27	books	Dr. Bruno Srečke	Agram, Havlikova 6	13 June 1941	
Fond 1401, Inventory 1, Folder 27	3 books	Dr. Ralph Halle	Agram, Borošina 4/1	15 June 1941	
Fond 1401, Inventory 1, Folder 27	book collection	Srećko Halle	Agram, Djordževiceva 11	9 June 1941	
Fond 1401, Inventory 1, Folder 27	book collection	David Herzog	Agram, Vončinina 8	12 June 1941	According to the archival record, there is an attached list detailing the books; however, list was not present
Fond 1401, Inventory 1, Folder 27	34 books	Dr. Ivo Herzog	Agram, Martićeva 6	30 July 1941	
Fond 1401, Inventory 1, Folder 27	40 books	Olga Hercog		16 May 1941	
Fond 1401, Inventory 1, Folder 27	35 books (Jewish authors; Hebrew books)	Dr. Bogomir Hiršl	Agram, Jurišiceva 25/II	29 July 1941	

Fond 1401, Inventory 1, Folder 27	400 books (208 German books, 40 books in Croatian and other languages, 35 books concerning the "Jewish question", 120 "Jewish" books, 34 Judaica)	Josef Hoffmann	Agram, Boškovićeva 31/II	27 May 1941	Listing includes the brother: Rudolf Rosner
Fond 1401, Inventory 1, Folder 27	30 numbers of the newsletter Šestar,10 numbers of the newsletter Historja Slobodnog zidarstva; 30 books	Radoslaw Horvat	Agram, Medulićeva 3	22 July 1941	
Fond 1401, Inventory 1, Folder 27	26 books (Jewish Literature)	Dragan Hruš	Agram, Vinkoviceva 33	30 July 1941	
Fond 1401, Inventory 1, Folder 27	4 books	Franjo Huber	Agram, Preradovićeva 5, II. Stock	8 June 1941	
Fond 1401, Inventory 1, Folder 27	21 books (Croatian literature and books concerning the "Jewish Question")	Dr. Djuro Jelinek	Agram, Marticeva 4, 3. Stock	7 June 1941	
Fond 1401, Inventory 1, Folder 27	81 books (5 volumes – Jewish lexica 1 picture album of Jewish actors 30 German books concerning the Jewish question 24 Hebrew books/leaflets 15 Croatian books/leaflets 1 Polish book 2 monthly magazines in German and Yiddish 1 volume of the "Völkermagazin")	Mavro Kandel	Agram, Boškovićeva 32	29 May 1941	
Fond 1401, Inventory 1, Folder 27	140 books	Milan Kastel	Agram, Krajiska 18	7 June 1941	

Fond 1401, Inventory 1, Folder 27	1 book and 8 leaflets	Dr. Vladimir Katićić	Agram, Vinkoviceva 11	24 July 1941	
Fond 1401, Inventory 1, Folder 27	10 books and Jewish newspapers	Alexander Klein	Agram, Bogisaceva 2/II	24 June 1941	Alexander Klein was the secretary of the Jewish Community and was, according to this index file, able to keep some of his possessions due to a protective status he apparently had with the Ustasa regime;
Fond 1401, Inventory 1, Folder 27	7 books (Jewish authors)	Stanko Kliska	Agram, Tratinska 38/II	1 August 1941	
Fond 1401, Inventory 1, Folder 27	40 books (10 German literature books, 15 Jewish History/ Zionism books)	Hermann Kraus	Agram, Strosmayerov trg II/I	9 June 1941	
Fond 1401, Inventory 1, Folder 27	5 books (Jewish authors)	Dragutin Krekovic	Agram, Dvorniciceva 10 (Villa)	30 July 1941	
Fond 1401, Inventory 1, Folder 27	book collection (37 French, English and German books; 341 books and newsletters in Croatian and Serbian; 590 books in other languages)	Dr. Juraj Krnjević	Agram, Mesinskova ulica 53	4 June 1941	
Fond 1401, Inventory 1, Folder 27	25 books (12 volumes – political/Jewish literature; remainder literature)	Ernst Kronfeld	Agram, Ilica 15/III	26 May 1941	

Fond 1401, Inventory 1, Folder 27	books	Mirko Lederer	Agram, Tuškanac-Gvost 17/ since 16 May 1941: Keglvicev Platz 14/II. Li.	21 May 1941	
Fond 1401, Inventory 1, Folder 27	books	Dr. Vladimir Leustek	Agram, Medvescak 59	30 July 1941	
Fond 1401, Inventory 1, Folder 27	26 books	Dr. Dragutin Liebermann	Agram, Meduliceva 9	21 May 1941	
Fond 1401, Inventory 1, Folder 28	460 books	Minerva "Verlags-buchhand-lung"	Agram Praška 6	29 May 1941	
Fond 1401, Inventory 1, Folder 28	30 books (Jewish literature)	Dr Armin Moskovic	Agram Mihanoviceva 14/III		
Fond 1401, Inventory 1, Folder 28	4 books by Jewish authors	Dr. Bernhard Mostar	Agram, Trg Kralja Tomislava 6	4 June 1941	
Fond 1401, Inventory 1, Folder 28	7 books (1 book in Croatian; 1 Jewish literature; 1 theological book; 1 "Communist" novel)	Herman Müller	Agram, Ilica 220	17 June 1941	
Fond 1401, Inventory 1, Folder 28	Book collection (8 volumes on the "Jewish Question"; 17 German Jewish authors; 10 Croatian Jewish authors; 103 Croatian Literature; 17 German literature)	Dr. Neuberger	Pavao, Marticeva 8/II	27 May 1941	
Fond 1401, Inventory 1, Folder 28	Book collection (40–50 books: 10 volumes by Schalom Asch, 8 volumes by Bettauer, Remarque "Im Westen nichts Neues", "Der Weg zurueck", and 16 other literature books such as Arnold Zweig "Herkunft und Zukunft", or Artur Landsberger "Das Volk des Ghetto")	Adolf Neumann	Agram, Marticeva 14 D/ 1 floor	17 May 1941	

Fond 1401, Inventory 1, Folder 28	185 books (Serbian literature)	Salamen Nevorah	Agram, Solovjeva 18	6 June 1941	
Fond 1401, Inventory 1, Folder 28	63 books, 29 leaflets and Jewish newspapers	Mr And Mrs Njemirovski	Agram, Mulica 6	16 May 1941	
Fond 1401, Inventory 1, Folder 28	5 Hebrew books	Peter Orlić	Agram, Hercegovacka 81	24 July 1941	
Fond 1401, Inventory 1, Folder 28	395 books ("propaganda material"), monthly newsletter ("Nova Europa")	Paul (Pavle) Ostović	Agram, Preradovićeva 39/III	31 July 1941	
Fond 1401, Inventory 1, Folder 28	2 books	Silvio Papo	Agram, Waashingtonov 5	12 August 1941	
Fond 1401, Inventory 1, Folder 28	46 books (Jewish literature, Yugoslavian history: German books by Jewish authors: 7 Non-Jewish literature in German: 8 Croatian-Serbian literature: 23 French literature: 7 English literature: 1)	Eugen Podaubski	Agram, Kamaufova 4/I	12 August 1941	
Fond 1401, Inventory 1, Folder 28	13 books	Dr. Sigmund Pordes	Agram, Hrvojeva 10/I	16 June 1941	
Fond 1401, Inventory 1, Folder 28	4 books (Jewish authors)	Dr. Vladimir Prelog	Agram, Novakova 26/II	2 August 1941	

Fond 1401, Inventory 1, Folder 28	14 books	Dr. Maksim Pscherhof	Agram	28 May 1941	Dr. Pscherhof was the president of the Jewish Community in 1940/41; arrested on 14 May 1941 by the SD and sent to Graz
Fond 1401, Inventory 1, Folder 47	4 books	Hermann Müller	Agram, Ilica 210		
Fond 1401, Inventory 1, Folder 28	Library: 1. Library of the head rabbi, about 1,600 volumes ("Handbücherei des Oberrabinats), 2. Library of the Jewish Community, about 300 volumes ("Jüdische Gemeindebücherei") [Midrashim, Tanach commentaries, numerous protocols of the 'Zionistenkongress']	Rabbi Dr Gavro Schwarz, chief rabbi of Agram (Oberrabinat)	Agram, Chebra Kadisha, Amruševa 8	21 May 1941	
Fond 1401, Inventory 1, Folder 28	1 leaflet	Franjo Raverta	Agram, Jurjevska 22	9 August 1941	
Fond 1401, Inventory 1, Folder 28	207 books (102 books on the "Jewish Question", of that 73 in foreign languages; 17 political books; 88 novels, by mostly Jewish authors)	Dr Rudolf Rodanic	Agram, Meduličeva 51/I	29 May 1941	

Fond 1401, Inventory 1, Folder 28	10 volumes of "Judaica"	Dragutin Rosenbaum	Agram, Maksimirska 2	20 June 1941	
Fond 1401, Inventory 1, Folder 28	24 books (2 volumes – German non-Jewish authors; 6 volumes – non-fiction on the "Jewish Question"; 12 volumes – German Jewish authors; 1 volume – Croatian literature)	Max Rosenblatt	Agram, Bosiievska 4	13 August 1941	
Fond 1401, Inventory 1, Folder 28	208 books (40 books in Croatian and other languages; 35 books on "Jewish Question"; 120 Jewish books and "Schuldliteratur"; 34 Judaica	Dr. Rudolf Rosner	Agram, Bogsicva 2	27 May 1941	
Fond 1401, Inventory 1, Folder 28	35 books (Jewish authors)	Mirko Schönberger	Agram, Marticeva 14	29 July 1941	
Fond 1401, Inventory 1, Folder 28	5 volumes, Jewish Encyclopedia	Emanuel Schotten	Agram, Starcevicev trg 4	24 June 1941	(The Wehrmacht had taken over the apartment; more confiscations were therefore not possible)

Fond 1401, Inventory 1, Folder 28	book collection (3 books on the "Jewish Question"; Judaica – 8 volumes; Jewish authors – 25 volumes in German, 1 volume in Croatian; Political Literature – 3 volumes (German), 5 volumes (Croatian)	Armin Schreiner	Agram, Deželićeva 30	28 May 1941	
Fond 1401, Inventory 1, Folder 28	45 books (books on the "Jewish Question" – 34 volumes; German Jewish authors – 6 volumes)	Alexander Schwabenitz	Agram, Varsavska 2 a/II	12 August 1941	
Fond 1401, Inventory 1, Folder 28	2 books and letters	Dr. Gavro Schwarz, head rabbi	Agram, Marticeva 14 D, 4th floor to the right	17 May 1941	(According to the document, only very few items were found since the Sicherheitspolizei had already sealed his house; most of his documents were stored at the Petrinska address)
Fond 1401, Inventory 1, Folder 28	1 book	Dr Slavisa Senoa	Agram, Heinzlova 64	5 August 1941	
Fond 1401, Inventory 1, Folder 28	18 books (English literature)	Dr Alexander Šmit	Agram, Plmoticeva 10	4 August 1941	

Fond 1401, Inventory 1, Folder 28	131 books (101 Jewish literature; 29 Jewish books in Hebrew; 3 books on Socialism in Croatian; 1 French book;)	Dr. Karlo Spiller	Agram, Kraljice Marije	16 June 1941	
Fond 1401, Inventory 1, Folder 28	10 books (Jewish literature)	Dragutin Šrepl	Agram, Pavla Radica 26	5 August 1941	
Fond 1401, Inventory 1, Folder 28/ Fond 1401, Inventory 1, Folder 47	1 book	Dr. Stanke Švrljuga	Agram, Eduarda Jalacica 2	2 August 1941	Gifted his library of about 8,000 books to the University Library;
Fond 1401, Inventory 1, Folder 28	24 books (Jewish literature)	Bozo Superina	Agram, Gunulićeva 40/II	6 August 1941	
Fond 1401, Inventory 1, Folder 28	39 books (books on the "Jewish Question", including Theodor Herzl; 7 books in Croatian; 1 book in Serbian; 1 folder of Newspaper cuttings)	Dr Benno Stein	Agram, Varšavska 8/ I. Re	17 May 1941	
Fond 1401, Inventory 1, Folder 28	104 books (Jewish literature – 74 books; non-fiction books on the "Jewish Question" – 5 books; Literature on Freemasons – 10 books; Croatian Literature – 15 books)	Maskim Stern	Vojnovicena ul. 71	26 May 1941	

Fond 1401, Inventory 1, Folder 28	3 books	Dane Singer	Agram, Marulicev trg 4, 1 floor	8 July 1941	
Fond 1401, Inventory 1, Folder 28	131 books (101 books – Jewish literature; 26 "Jewish/Hebrew" books; 3 books in Croatian; 1 in French)	Dr Karlo Schiller	Agram, Kraljice 15	16 June 1941	
Fond 1401, Inventory 1, Folder 28	book collection	Alfred Spitz	Agram, Zvonimirova 6/I	11 July 1941	book collection was first donated to the ERR, since Mr Spitz was ordered to empty his apartment within 24 hours
Fond 1401, Inventory 1, Folder 28	10 Torah scrolls 7 ceremonial objects 3 altarpieces Numerous Torah covers etc	Synagogue Agram	Agram	26./28. May 1941	
Fond 1401, Inventory 1, Folder 28	about 60 books (13 Judaica 32 German language books on the "Jewish Question" 15 Croatian language books on the "Jewish Question" 38 books Jewish literature)	Alexander Szemnitz	Agram, Zvonimirova 2	30 May 1941	
Fond 1401, Inventory 1, Folder 28	13 books	Leo Tobolski	Agram, Subiceva 28/I	24 June 1941	

Fond 1401, Inventory 1, Folder 28	book collection (collection included: Storch, Freimaurer u. Jesuit Bojnicic, Die Loge 'Ljubabkiznjega' Peregrinus 'Freimaurerei' Burckhardt, Geheimnis des Freimaurers Prigorski, Listi o zlobostnom ziolarston)	Veljko Tomic	Agram	July 1941	SD already confiscated the book collection, but handed over the listed books;
Fond 1401, Inventory 1, Folder 28	12 books (Jewish literature; monthly magazine "Vidici")	Dr. Franjo Tucan	Agram, Milinarska 49	5 August 1941	
Fond 1401, Inventory 1, Folder 28	130 books (including books on Communism and English language books)	Oskar Vadnai	Agram, Gundulićeva 19/ II B. H. Kalan	29 May 1941	
Fond 1401, Inventory 1, Folder 28	Political literature	Većeslav Vilder	Agram, Gundulićeva 35/III	18 August 1941	
Fond 1401, Inventory 1, Folder 28	25 books (Jewish authors, etc.)	Dr. Vladimir Vranić	Agram, Kralj, Maria 25/IV	August 1941	
Fond 1401, Inventory 1, Folder 28	monthly magazine "Izbor"	Jakob Vivoda	Agram, Kraiska 11/II	6 August 1941	
Fond 1401, Inventory 1, Folder 28	Book collection (8 volumes of Jewish literature; 1 German volume, non-Jewish authors, 6 volumes of Croatian language books)	Janko Zimmer-mann	Agram, Novakova 20/II	18 August 1941	

Fond 1401, Inventory 1, Folder 28	10 newsletters "Service" (English edition)	Vladimir, Žepić	Agram, Pod Zidom 3/I	11 August 1941	According to the index card, the library of the Freemason lodge "Drašković" was given to the university library; 2,000 voumes of the monthly magazine "Sestar" were seized by the Police department or were handed over to the Gestapo.
Fond 1401, Inventory 1, Folder 29	23 books and newspaper collection	Karl Ebenspanger	Agram	26 May 1941	

What happened to all these people, who now live at their own addresses, in their own apartments, what do we want to know about them and what do we want or not want to remember? Memory and space are in a permanent clinch; when space collapses, it drags memory into its underground, into its nonexistence, and without memory, the present becomes sick, mutilated, a torso with extracted organs.

From 1991 to 1992, the American photographer and visual artist Shimon Attie projected onto shops, building façades and passersby in the eastern part of Berlin, in the former Jewish quarter of Scheunenviertel near Alexanderplatz, photographs of buildings and people from the time immediately before the events of the Second World War. Attie "cast" parts of the past into the everyday life of his present, which now twenty-something years later is being transformed once again—masking encroaching danger.

And so the erased past, nonexistent buildings, nonexistent people, their activities, their faces, their clothes, their lives creep into a new age. People pass Attie's installations and observe the past adhering to the present, some in surprise, some with sadness, some with shame, some with fury. The past cannot be returned, because it does not go anywhere, one has only to find the link that connects it to what is now and what is to come.

Let us imagine a randomly chosen address in the center of Zagreb, say today's 16 Teslina, where the Vuković and Runjić bookshop is now. Let us imagine that over the shop window full of books slides an enormous projection of the "Radio" shop in the same building, in the same place, then at 16 Nikolić. Let us imagine that it is 1940. Let us imagine that through the window we see Josef Konforti, born in Travnik in 1912, talking with customers, surrounded by radio sets, bicycles, typewriters, and sewing machines, while some other customers leaf through the latest books by local and foreign writers. Josef Konforti was killed in the Jasenovac camp in 1944.

The cobbler Gabriel Kalderon, born in Bitola in 1901, lives at 94 Ulica Vlaška. He comes to Zagreb from Bitola in 1932. He lives with his wife and four children. Registering his property to the NDH authorities, he declares that in his workshop he has 120 pairs of shoes to be repaired and that his tools are worth 300 dinars. His eldest son, eighteen-year-old Jakov, is killed in the Ustasha camp of Jadovno, and in 1943 he, Gabriel Kalderon, is arrested along with the rest of his family and deported to Auschwitz. We see him on the first floor of 94 Ulica Vlaška sitting on a stool in his half-dark workshop turning a woman's shabby shoe in his hands. Beside him sits a small boy tapping at something, and through the open window on the first floor we watch his wife by the stove, stirring something with one hand, while with the other she holds on her hip a little girl who is laughing. Beneath the projection of this enormous photograph we can make out the advertising board of the Pletix shop in which swimsuits and underwear were sold, here at 94 Ulica Vlaška, and immediately beside it we see the hairdresser Trans-X, with a woman sitting under a hair dryer reading *Glorija* magazine.

Let's go to 63 Ulica Vlaška. At 63 Ulica Vlaška, Avram Levi, son of David Levi, born in Sarajevo in 1911, stands at the counter of his small shop selling clothes and shoes, he is looking out at the street, wondering whether he will sell anything to anyone that day. The aroma of freshly baked pizza comes from the Kariola pizza café beneath the projection, customers drink beer and peck at their smart phones and vacantly throw warm triangles into their mouths.

Avram Levi was killed by the Ustasha in Jasenovac in 1942.

Almost opposite, at 64 Ulica Vlaška, shines in large blue letters OPTO-CENTAR, an optician and eye clinic in which misted gazes are sharpened. On its Facebook page the Opto-Centar addresses potential users of its services with the ambiguous question *How is your outlook on the world?*

Darkness is falling, the street lights come on on Ulica Vlaška. The neon letters of the Opto-Centar flicker. At number 64, Leon Altarac, son of Avram, born in Sarajevo in 1909, locks up his artisan knitwear workshop and goes home. It is 1942, or rather 2015. The blue, sharp eye of the Opto-Centar follows Leon Altarac's supple step: as far as the killing field of Jasenovac, where for Leon Altarac the lights go out forever.

Moise D. Salom, born in Sarajevo in 1874, locks up his wholesale manufacturing business at 2 King Petar Square. He brings his palms to his temples and through the scrupulously clean glass casts a last glance into its dark interior in which, he knows, everything, all the goods, all the exclusive men's and women's clothing is tidily stored and catalogued. Moise Salom inhales deeply, puts the keys to his shop in the right-hand pocket of his trousers, does up the top button of his perfectly tailored white poplin shirt, rolls up his sleeves and goes for a glass of chilled white wine at the Esplanade Hotel. Moise Salom moved into the Esplanade Hotel a few days ago. It is the summer of 1941, let's say July. Past Moise Salom's shop cars drive, people walk, the young fiddle with their cells. Beneath the sign SALOM MANUFACTURING RETAILER, at number 2 Victims of Fascism Square, there gradually appears the name of a shop, MODERATO, on the window of which is a sloppily pasted poster: *Visit Moderato. At affordable prices we offer beautiful, sophisticated clothing for those who appreciate classical style and elegance. The comfortable, relaxing environment entices the majority of our customers to come back.* There will be no coming back for Moise Salom.

Soon after the establishment of the NDH, Moise Salom registers his property; he specifies that more than 8 million dinars of his own capital are invested in his retail business, in 1940 he achieves a turnover of around 24.5 million dinars, while in the storehouse, according to records on May 26, 1941, when he makes an inventory under police supervision, he owns goods to the value of 7 million dinars.

So Moise Salom drinks a glass of chilled white wine in the Esplanade Hotel. His family is already in Switzerland. Tomorrow, Moise Salom will withdraw all his money and close his bank account. A ticket for the night train Zagreb-Zurich and a passport in the name of Marko Salopek is lying on the bedside table in his room. The partisan attacks on the railway lines have not yet begun. Not until August 1941 will the Swiss authorities impose an absolute ban on the reception of Jewish refugees. In other words, Moise Salom, alias Marko Salopek, has a chance of life.

But that evening, Moise Salom does not manage to go up to his hotel room. Two young men from the Ustasha police approach his table and take him away. Moise Salom is killed in Jasenovac in 1942.

After the global Nazi thefts of the lives of millions had so unexpectedly ambushed me in Paris, the fact that, after the death of Ada and my father Rudolf, and in contempt of his will, his wife, the then 87-year-old insatiable, complex-ridden creature who watched soap operas for years and leafed through trashy magazines, that political convert who, having once been a member of the League of Communists of Yugoslavia, today virtually licks altars, she who in the course of the TV broadcast of the proclamation of Croatian independence, accompanied by the song "Danke Deutschland" dedicated to Hans-Dietrich Genscher, and performed by an anonymous singer dressed in a little pink dress, for that dinner she had roasted a suckling pig and opened a bottle of champagne, and in a threatening voice accused me, since I had not watched that tasteless spectacle, *You were probably with some Serbs*, she, who had once been married to a Croatian Serb who escaped from her and from Yugoslavia as soon as he had the chance even though they had a son, presumably, therefore, a little Serb, the fact that this woman stole paintings (with the artists' dedication to our parents), sculptures, carpets, ornaments with the names of Marisa and Rudolf engraved on them (she threw the books out, and I came across one, dedicated to my father, on a used bookstore website, and I called them and asked them to keep it for me, which they did), the fact that she had appropriated a good part of a life lived outside her presence, but once I learned about the global Nazi thefts of the lives of millions, everything that this woman did seemed to me fairly trivial, so I was able to take the question of inheritance, the question of theft, which my stepmother had carried out thenceforth quite calmly.

Where that woman was concerned, I had clearly failed as a psychologist. In many of her unfounded outbursts of fury and hatred, I had recognized, oh yes, pathological jealousy, the need to possess the ostensibly loved object and remove—eliminate—the rival. Hence the elimination of things that either belonged to us or that we had given to our father. The walker I had bought for Rudolf, and after consultation with an expert I bought a mechanical one, the simplest, because I was told that walkers with handbrakes for semimobile people could be fatal, and Rudolf had moved about perfectly well, until that woman took my walker away and bought him the one with handbrakes, which he once forgot to operate and fell and ended up having an operation for a broken hip at ninety-two. Or when Ada made a large Reform cake for Đoja's birthday, *It's a complicated cake*, said Ada, *it takes a lot of time*, and she carried the cake all the way from Rovinj to Zagreb so that we could celebrate his birthday together (Ðoja and Leo were still small and cheerful), that woman gave us each a thin slice and took the rest, a thirty-centimeter, magnificent cake made with chocolate and walnuts to a neighbor whom she could not stand. Leo said, *I'd like some more*, and that woman hissed, *There isn't any!*

For that woman, anyone who attempted to get close to our father was dangerous and had to be got rid of. Over time, friends, Istria, his children and grandchildren disappeared from Rudolf's life; all that remained was her, a wrecked and poisoned inner landscape echoing with the words, *You are mine, mine alone.*

The older our father got, the less he resisted.

When he came to visit us she would telephone five times a day, and should Rudolf decide to stay a day or two longer, she would go off demonstratively to a spa and on her return wouldn't speak to him for days. On the other hand, if we visited our father, she would sit us down in the kitchen, seat herself at the head of the table, occasionally saying, *All right, I'll go away so that you can talk*, and of course she didn't stir.

For the pathologically jealous, the loved one is property. Consequently, that woman appropriated objects from the time Rudolf lived with Marisa to realize some material gain, fair enough, but that plunder was also a consequence of her obsession to appropriate those four decades that preceded her life with our father so she could keep him all to herself, even when he was dead.

Jealous, envious people are skillful manipulators, often angry with no reason; which is when they can become aggressive. Then they lie. Jealous and envious liars are devoid of empathy. They are sociopaths who avoid looking their interlocutor in the eye, but are sweet-tongued. Narcissistic personalities skillfully simulate emotions. For every feast day, that woman would give Ada and me pajamas. I have more than twenty pairs of her pajamas. Manipulative narcissists can even be experienced as hospitable, agreeable.

Narcissists are abusers. They exploit others, then reject them. That woman could not retain a single home aid for more than a month. Those aids were clever (healthy) and they would bolt. They were people, not consumer goods. I won't go all the way back to her childhood to find when or why that woman developed her obsessive need to control. Fuck that woman's childhood.

Narcissus is a split personality.

Narcissistic, envious people attack those who don't recognize their superiority, who consider them "average." Which, had that woman been at least average meetings with her would not have become a nightmare. When I came back from Canada, I brought her a blouse, a sweater, or something, and an oven mitt. That mitt became the switch for an outpouring of accusations along the lines of, *Who do you think I am, a cook!*

The little plant on my bathroom windowsill has flowered. Two red blooms on little thin stems sway in the wind. But someone has cut down the huge tree, a healthy, powerful tree whose crown protected my little plant. From now on the little plant will have to look after itself.

Lonely old women like feeding pigeons. They collect leftover bread and go to the little parks in the center of town. As they feed the pigeons, these lonely old women scatter the crumbled bread around and coo. The pigeons coo with them, they turn in circles, waddling and shaking their tails from left to right. Once they have used up what they brought, the women leave, the pigeons stay. They wait for a new victim, a new provider. Pigeons are insatiable creatures; relentless and tenacious, but when they don't get what they want, they can become aggressive. Some people maintain that pigeons are among the most intelligent birds, I think that they are clever only when it suits them, only when those they wish to master, to manipulate, obey them unquestioningly; otherwise, pigeons can become foul, evil and unreasonable birds. Like some people. Such people, just like flocks of pigeons, like to parade in groups, then they become brave, they shout, threaten and generally create an unpleasant, loutish racket. When they are on their own, though, just like the pigeons, such people shrink, keep quiet, pull their heads down between their shoulders, hide, look docile.

Some people call pigeons flying rats. There are better birds than pigeons.

Julija Amati. I thought of her because there is an influx of pigeons at the moment. They have crapped all over my windows. As soon as I open the shutters, they bring twigs and make nests and sit on eggs, so I tend to sit in the dark. In summer I can't open the balcony door if I have any food left out in the kitchen, because the pigeons come in and feast. Once they tore a washing-up sponge to pieces. Whenever I go out, I return five times to make sure I have closed the doors and windows. I am terrified. I imagine coming home, entering the apartment, and clouds of pigeons swirling, flying toward me and suffocating me. Julija Amati is constantly before my eyes.

Julija Amati worked as the chief medical nurse in the Department of Psychiatry at the Belgrade clinical hospital, where I also worked. Julija Amati was my friend Adam Kaplan's right hand. She was slender, quick and smiling, she had curly brown hair, disobedient hair that escaped from any restraint. Wicked little locks kissed her neck. She had a soft voice and a silvery laugh. *She's fuckworthy*, Adam Kaplan would say. She had a cheerful energy, in her step, in her touch. Julija Amati was queen of the Department, unaware of her beauty and her powers. When I left Belgrade, Julija Amati was thirty-five.

There was a photograph of Julija Amati among the files that Adam Kaplan left me with his farewell letter. The photograph was attached to a folder bearing the name JULIJA AMATI. I thought there must have been a mistake, a swap, a joke, because, looking at the photograph of a deformed person, it was only with considerable effort that I detected some minimal similarities with the Julija Amati I remembered from the time I left the clinic in 1992. Nearly twenty-five years had passed, so in this photograph Julija was fifty-something. Inside the covers of the file lay the life of Julija Amati recorded factually, with a typewriter, while beyond that dossier, in the head and heart of Julija Amati, a tormented, painful drama was played out, about which I read in Adam's confidential, handwritten notes. I don't wish to dissect Julija Amati's story for the public, it's a complicated story, but I mention it because of the pigeons.

So, after the death of her teenage child (leukemia), virtually overnight, Julija Amati became (visibly) obsessive-compulsive. In the Clinic, she barely functioned as she spent more and more time combing her thick, wayward hair, washing her hands and dressing and came to work two to three hours late. Her relationship with the patients also became problematic: as she considered them a source of infection, she barely approached them, and if she happened to touch them (or they her), she rushed to the bathroom, where she scrubbed her hands with a nailbrush, sometimes drawing blood. In addition, Julija Amati became an obsessive collector of trash. At the end of the working day (she often stayed until last) Julija Amati shook all the trash from the Clinic into a large plastic bag and carried it home, where she arranged the items in rows of seven. These were all more or less typical, standard symptoms of obsessive-compulsive disorder, not to say stereotypical. What was not typical were the stories, the nightmares, the crushed lives, flattened as though in a press, which thrashed about beneath the symptoms trying to acquire a shape, restore their fullness and, before they crumbled, leap back into existence.

As a trained medical nurse with ten years of experience in the Department of Psychiatry, Julija Amati could have presumed that there was something wrong with her. She said to Adam Kaplan, *I have obsessive-compulsive disorder. I won't be treated, because the treatment takes a long time. My serotonin is low. I shall devote my life to pigeons.* So Julija Amati gave in her notice and set off on a mission to save the town's pigeons. She toured the parks and devotedly fattened up those insatiable flying creatures. And the pigeons, the more they ate, the more they multiplied. With time (I learned from Adam's notes), the town sky became covered with blue-black birds, the crowns of trees too, roofs and squares, everything, the whole landscape darkened and swayed as though drunk. Some pigeons even got onto trams and buses, stood by the door and got out at quite specific stops. From Adam Kaplan's notes I gathered that he had visited Julija Amati on several occasions, but also that he had met her in Belgrade parks, that he had continued to have long conversations with her, in the desire to help. That was probably when the photograph was taken. *So what*, said Julija Amati, *Tesla used to feed pigeons in American parks. He even took sick pigeons back to his New York hotel room, where he treated them. Tesla had a white pigeon he fell in love with, it stole his heart, that's what he said.* I love my pigeon the way a man loves a woman, she is my life, *said Tesla, and I love my pigeons, they know me and they wait for me*, Julija Amati told Adam. And she said, *Listen, Adam, there have been and are still lots of obsessive-compulsive people, including famous ones. They are pedantic people. I know one who checks a hundred times a day whether his heart is still beating. He is desperately frightened of death, but I'm not afraid of death, Adam, so leave me alone. I listen to my pigeons cooing, because they tell me about the torments of dead souls.* That's what Julija Amati said.

Julija Amati was found by her neighbors. She was lying on the floor of her room, surrounded by hundreds of black bags full of hospital and city trash, covered in a flock of pigeons. Waggling their tails, the pigeons were pecking Julija Amati, so that it looked as though she was breathing. Where her eyes had been, in those pecked-out hollows, two pigeons had laid eggs.

In Paris, my eye trouble exploded into a threat of blindness. Although I had checked my eye pressure every two to three weeks, and, thanks to the drops I was taking, it had lain, tamed, curled up at the bottom of my small tear duct, that python, that boa constrictor, that thief of sight, but at a certain moment, no one knows why, it moved, it stretched its snakelike body, reared up and wrapped itself around my right eye, hissing, *I'll stifle you.* Looking at the world from under the pressure of a bearable 21 mmHg, my eye was now floundering, squeezed in an embrace of 50 mmHg without my knowing, or feeling, anything. The doctors went ballistic. I was operated on the next day. From Paris I was supposed to travel to a book fair in Mexico, where there was already a team from Croatia, but the doctors said, *You can go, but you'll come back blind,* so I didn't go. I borrowed money and cashed my two thousand euros, which the Croatian Health Insurance Fund (HZZO) refused to reimburse me because they maintained that my procedure had not been urgent. I was even sent the expert opinion of an ophthalmologist, a court expert witness, a specialist, who described the state of my eye in detail in the HZZO notice of rejection even though he had never seen me, let alone peered into my organ of sight. I might as well chuck that European health card, which is claimed in Croatia to cover emergencies, because in France no one recognizes that Croatian European health card. Now I am dragging myself through the courts with the HZZO, although I know that I have lost this battle as well, because for as long as that dandy Varga, who turns up the collar of his dark coat, like a young sport, and flits about in it, and who likes nurses' tight uniforms and foreign ski resorts, for as long as he was at the head of the Croatian Health Insurance Fund, he said, *There'll be no payments, no one's expenses abroad will be covered.* That edict was probably passed on to his successor, so my chances are nil. Nor was the French operation really successful, my right eye is half-dead, it looks through tears, sees fuzzily, wavily. I feel like gouging it out.

To demonstrate that she refused to see the world around her, a schizophrenic patient of Adam Kaplan's suddenly gouged out her eye in the course of psychotherapy and, while she was being given medical assistance, she gouged out the other one as well. It's not that unusual. For instance, Jonathan Swift nearly gouged out his

317

eye because it was inflamed. Five male nurses were barely able to hold him back. When his intention was frustrated, he decided not to speak for a year.

In Paris, Kika photographed pigeons.

Jovica Aćin also had an episode with pigeons. In Croatia, of course, few have heard of Jovica Aćin, because in Croatia there is a general forgetfulness in connection with Yugoslavia, a logorrheic emptiness prevails, full of poisonous crap, and that forgetfulness, quite logically, includes literature. But I remember:

> *I sit down, almost falling backward. And then, right in front of me, a pigeon lands on the terrace railing. Another lands on my table, pecking at crumbs fearlessly, then makes for a sweet roll in the basket. Soon, on the railing and the table, quite a large one, covered with a white linen cloth, another dozen pigeons flock. I turn my gaze away from the square, for I am seeing something I have never seen before and which I do not manage to understand. All the pigeons are invalids. Every last one of them has a damaged right leg. Just the right one, not the left. Their right legs are, in fact, stumps, which, as they hop about on the tablecloth and railing, make them limp. I stayed, with my first, then second cup of tea with milk, smoking, and my sitting on the terrace drew on, while the first pigeons were replaced by others, then those by yet others, and all were lame in their right legs. Not one pigeon had an intact right leg.*

There, even invalid pigeons don't give up. Even if they limp, they attack, they are still aggressive.

Had I gone to Brancusi's studio, behind the Pompidou Center before that half-successful ophthalmological intervention, perhaps his Măiastra would have protected me, because Măiastra is a golden bird that protects the blind, restores their sight. Măiastra also prophesies the future, and might have said, *Andreas, you don't see well, and what you do see is deceitful. Nothing but a chimera.* That golden bird was once a cursed queen from another world, and now, covered in dazzling plumage, she lives in great isolation. Her eyes are bright and clear, her eyes are in fact crystal pearls that gleam. That mythological bird from Dacia changes her shape, but always protects life, she says: *Death is not the end, finality is endlessness, if the body is not free, the spirit is, even when it dies, the spirit moves.*

I visited Brancusi's birds, the gold ones and the marble ones, afraid of touching them, but my crippled eye didn't blink. Then I went with Kika for pancakes.

Later I visited Brancusi in the Montparnasse cemetery, where Sartre also lies, because it was most convenient for him to go to Montparnasse given that his apartment and the café he went down to in his slippers from his rooms were right here—near the eternal hunting grounds.

In the end, I went to Shakespeare & Co. bookshop, which has an interesting history, but there's quite a lot about that history on the internet, so whoever is interested should take a look. I was looking for Stefan Zweig, *Have you got any Zweig in English?* I asked, because at that time Zweig had settled in my head, where, like a mantra, he kept declaiming his suicidal message: *My language has gone,* said Zweig, *and Europe, my spiritual home, is destroying itself.*

In the little rue des Récollets, in which there is a coded iron door at the back entrance to "my castle," where there is neither shop nor café, where no tourists walk, nor many Parisians, there is a bookshop that specializes in selling photographs and photographic literature—Librairie Photographique Le 29. I go in as in a trance, I enter the distant days when, with a small Canon, I visited the hidden nooks of the town I grew up in, maniacally clicking; when, in my miniature, darkened kitchen at night I developed photographs, hundreds of photographs, and when I threw all that, that photographic dream, into a cardboard suitcase with developing dishes, tongs and measuring syringes, with mixers, thermometers, pegs and tanks for developing film, with papers of various thicknesses and composition, with developers and fixers, with an old-fashioned Russian Opemus 4 enlarger, with a lamp and a timer, into a suitcase which I would never open again, and now forty years have passed since then, but still, as additionally heavy but useless baggage, I drag it after me on all my house moves. Everything in that suitcase must have rotted by now. The photographic paper has probably turned to dust, the liquids evaporated, the bulbs burned out, the Opemus rusted. An old wound was opened. The first thing I came across in the Librairie Photographique Le 29 was a monograph about Tina Modotti with a series of her photographs. I can't now, nor do I wish to go into that chapter, which indirectly, through the anarchic activities of my grandfather Max Osterman and directly up to the antifascist national-liberation war of my father Rudolf Ban in Istria, catches on my life too, because it's a complicated story for a book of its own. I can't now write about the girl Tina Modotti, born in Udine, a little town virtually in my neighborhood now, about Tina Modotti, whose photographs have only recently begun to be exhibited by much vaunted international museums, about her lovers who included photographers, painter-muralists, Soviet communist agents, NKVD and GPU agents, then anti-Trotskyists, crazed political assassins, bloodthirsty murderers and their victims. These were Roubaix de l'Abrie Richey, Xavier Guerrero, Edward Weston, Julio Antonio Mella, Vittorio Vidali and some others, I can't, I don't wish to leap into the years of secret and public conflicts of the Mexican, Cuban, Soviet, Spanish, Italian and then Yugoslav Communist Parties, all that could be written about by those who like that literature known as *noir*, or those communist know-alls, there's a wealth of intriguing espionage subjects there.

In the Librarie Photographique Le 29, leafing through Tina Modotti's works, I feel out of the frame again, no longer knowing into which picture, into which model, into what range I should enter, into which time; the previous century and this one had coalesced, adhered in a squashy mass, which, like a half-dead, distended wild beast, at times powerful, at times in a state of decay, wafts around itself the stench of death and madness. I was looking for a book of photographs for the friends to whose house I was going for dinner and immediately reached for Tina Modotti, but then thought better of it. Tina Modotti is mine. One branch of Tina Modotti's life that spread over two continents, the branch named Vittorio Vidali, reaches to me. Vittorio Vidali, also known as Jacobo Hurwitz Zender, Carlos Contreras, "Comandante Carlos" and Enea Sormenti, as required, born in Muggia, the twenty-year-old founder of the Italian Communist Party, later an agent of the Comintern who, in collaboration with the Lithuanian agent of the GPU Iosif Grigulevich, planned the liquidation of Trotskyists and other anti-Stalinists, who fired with his own hand at members of the POUM, including its founder Andrés Nin and, after the war, in 1947, returned to the place from which he had been driven twenty-five years earlier, now the free territory of Trieste, where in 1954, in obscure taverns (with a pistol in his belt), he engaged in dangerous conversations about Zone A and Zone B with my father Rudolf Ban. So, I bought Tina Modotti for myself, and for my friends the monograph of another photographer, I no longer remember who.

Bernard served mackerel pâté on little blinis, dried black olives in oil flavored with herbs and garlic, tiny chanterelle sausages and first-class champagne. We talked about contemporary Russian literature. At the table we discussed religions, gods and mostly popes, because we were all atheists and Christmas was approaching. I could talk about the pope again, because this new one came to Sarajevo and for three days before his visit all the TV channels in Croatia announced his arrival with extraordinary emotion and euphoria, and when at last he came, the announcers talked about him nonstop, while the witnesses of that performance were en masse reduced to tears of exaltation. Then, as usual, there were three days of recapitulation of the visit. I took a Croatia Airlines plane, where, at the entrance, accessible to every passenger, there was a 40 x 30-cm copper plate on which it was written that it was precisely this plane on which we were flying that had carried the pope, the one who died. My books appear every two to three years, so in each there is space for a little episode about a visit of one of the Holy Fathers either to Croatia, or the "region."

Bernard also served foie gras—goose pâté in cognac—thin slices of apple in vinegar with aromatic herbs, sautéed blusher mushrooms, petits pois and fried endive. To finish, various cheeses, some with truffles, others without, and a rich chocolate mousse. The red wine was from Bernard's personal cellar in Provence, thirty-three years old. If I knew French and Russian well, I would be a translator from Russian to French, in Paris.

Then, with Bernard, Gabriel and Gojko, I at last went to Chartier, to the café of Rudolf and Marisa's youth, a café in which everything is simple and refined, as in fact all simplicity is refined. Chartier has a website with both the history of this legendary restaurant and photographs from both the past and the present, so there is no need for me to elaborate.

In Paris I dreamed too much. I dreamed in various languages, hideous scenes. For instance, that my kidneys were sucking the marrow out of my spine: *Renal suction of spinal marrow!* I cried. I dreamed that my nose had vanished, that I had a bird's head. One morning I woke up repeating, *Just feed him the branches of an uncontaminated being*, wondering what that could mean. After the operation, I was given injections in my eye. One was jabbed into me by a half-trained nurse who asked me in passing whether there were ophthalmologists in Croatia, and my eye swelled up, bled and all but fell out, plop. I shrieked with pain and fell out of a bus.

Dreams must be forgotten. That's why dreams come, to be forgotten. That's why we dream, to forget. Such dreams, the psychiatrists maintain, are in fact parasite synapses and it is best to shake them off as a matter of urgency. But what can we do if our dreams drag themselves after us like phantoms, if they come back and multiply, if they stick to us like feathers to tar, if they run around inside our heads, humming in various tones, and if we do cast them out, they come back.

In Paris I met a man, a Frenchman, who always welled up when he heard Bosnian *sevdalinke* songs. *Get me some sevdalinke,* he said. That man was convinced that he had some inexplicable connection with "that part of the world," he said. *Everything there provokes powerful emotions in me,* he said. *Everything there touches me deeply,* he said, *I'm always on the verge of tears.* He recounted that, whenever he arrived in "that part of the world," he always wore dark glasses, so that people would not see his tears. Kika got some *sevdalinke* for him after I left Paris, so I don't know whether he cried when he listened to *sevdalinke* away from "that part of the world." I had lunch with that man (who writes good books), and then, before he traveled to Jerusalem, where, he said, haircuts were expensive, I went with him for a haircut to an Indian hairdresser (for six euros) in the Passage Brady near "my castle." Paris is full of hidden arcades each of which has a story, but on the whole tourists rarely visit Parisian arcades. Walter Benjamin wrote about Parisian arcades, the nineteenth-century ones, in his unfinished texts, but then most tourists don't read Benjamin (or have heard of him), so why would they visit the arcades? I visited a dozen of them. They are not what they used to be, they have become a caricature of a world within a world, a town within a town, a one-time commercial utopia on the tenets of capitalist ideals has been transformed into a freak. Through their glazed arched roofs, the Paris arcades let in a murky light, their pavements laid with marble or ceramic tiles that echo with footsteps in the same rhythm, their shops have died. The Paris arcades no longer dream anything, their world does not offer hope. From a miniature universe of dazzle and luxury, the Paris arcades have merged with the outside world of disintegration and decay. For thirteen years Benjamin tenderly waved his little red flag, then the hand of madness hammered nails into a coffin of dreams and Benjamin killed himself.

In Paris I walked backward. And so consoled myself.

A year after Paris, I let myself be catapulted into timelessness, into outside-time, into a dead past, a deceased time in which there was no me or my memories, nor memories of my forebears, into a time so archaic and distant, so disjointed, a time through which thick, stagnant blood flows, so that its petrification, its extinguishedness, its delusive, truncated existence, its needlessness and superfluousness began to suffocate me. Here is all the preserved beauty of past centuries, natural, architectural, artistic, scattered over the hills of Tuscany, and dappled (stamped) with huge estates of fenced olive groves and vineyards in the middle of which, like plump sturdy women spread out in the sun, broad single-story or at most two-story villas lie in the embrace of immense lawns, flowerbeds, rose gardens and orchards, tended gardens with little streams and artificial lakes, with little paths leading up and down to swimming pools with loggias, in which staff from the Philippines, Ukraine, Poland and Romania, and perhaps also from Croatia, from wherever there is wretchedness and poverty, serve light afternoon snacks to their employers whom they address as *barone* and *baronessa*, *contare* and *contessa* and their guests, and in the evening dinners that often lack *un certo non so che*, glad that they have an income (sometimes even a good one), a roof over their heads and in that shithole a free Sunday when they have nowhere to go (escape) to other than perhaps the local church or the local cemetery. The cutlery is silver, the glasses are crystal, the stone floors are covered with rugs from all over the place, from Persia, China and Mexico, the walls weighed down with engravings and oil paintings by well-known and unknown artists and by rows of old and new books. All this would be all right if that world agreed to remain nestled in its illusions, in its worn-out dreams and to bask in them. But no. These people would like to stay in their cocoons, steeped in the tassels of an extinguished past, but they would also like to stroll through our contemporaneity, however painful, dark and ruined it is. They would like to peer into life, this one now, reaching right to the edge of danger, to its threshold, and then swiftly to return, which seems inarticulate, clumsy and sad. They step into the present sometimes cautiously, sometimes haughtily, dragging after them their heavy, decadent, decrepit luggage not knowing where to take it, where to put it down. They are confused, they wonder what they could do to make the time pass, to make their lives pass, but they don't do anything, or else they study forever, or they set up charities which help the hungry, they look for sponsors, they organize cultural events such as literary festivals with monetary prizes for well-known, but also for virtually unknown writers, such as myself, then they found privately funded residences where those writers write and pretend that they enjoy all this, this luxury, this convenience, as though they have come from this world, as though they were born into it, but they were not. And these writers become servile, which is disagreeable to see and hear, and in addition to constantly praising and approving something, although no one obliges them to, some of them dedicate their books even to the dogs that live (and die) on the property.

It isn't nice that, all spruced up, I am supposed to enjoy a luxury that is offered me unconditionally, I am supposed to be grateful for the fact that I have a room to work in, a whole floor to myself and airy silence dappled with little pinpricks of birdsong. I am supposed to be happy that someone prepares my meals, that every morning Nimala's husband brings fresh bread into "my" kitchen, that I have two caffettiere for espresso, skimmed milk in the fridge and jam, that Irina from Lvóv, with whom I stutter in Russian, wants to wash and iron my underwear, but I won't let her, because in that tower where I am housed there is a washing machine, there is also a sitting room, and on the floor above me they have placed the then 38-year-old Filipino writer with a Canadian address Miguel Syjuco, who won a prize for his first work *Ilustrado*, published also by the Serbian press Geopoetika, but since books from Serbia don't come to Croatia, I hadn't heard of it.

It doesn't matter how good or not so good Miguel's book is. A novel could be written about Miguel Syjuco, or if not a novel then certainly a novella, the story of his search for a space within his authoritarian family, for freedom from the intellectual and political (corrupt) elite that stomps on, stifles and punishes every attempt at rebellion, even if it is reduced to the declarative *non serviam*. The story could be told of Miguel's flights and wanderings from Australia to Canada, about how, after his father had disowned him for disobedience, Miguel worked as a bookmaker at horse races, as a barman, as an extra in order to survive, he did some other strange little jobs (a guinea pig in scientific laboratory experiments) and finally, with a doctorate in his pocket, he began to write reviews and columns for American and Canadian journals. Today, it seems, Miguel, having adopted the Anglo-American code of communication, that artificial, singsong one, full of high false tones with a lot of "oh, please" and "oh, thank you" accompanied by a half-suppressed smile, stands on the capitalist feet of mass-produced correctness.

The fashion of writing columns about restaurants and their gourmand offerings has begun in Croatia as well, but, it appears, it has not exactly taken root. In the West, this empty absurdity continues to stimulate the salivary glands of those with deep pockets. Those with shallow pockets, that is those who have no pockets at all, don't read them, instead they may sometimes walk past some brightly lit restaurant and watch the people eating inside. An American prestige magazine pays between five and ten dollars a word for a review of one or two pages. Miguel Syjuco is happy when an opportunity for a little job like this turns up, so he hopped out of our backwater to Paris for a couple of days to cover the opening of some little suburban brasserie. He came back with a stumpy little story about his brief trip, and with a bag of sliced bread over which everyone at the table had drooled, as they had over a small box of nondescript chocolates. I said nothing, gobsmacked. The bread in any Istrian village is a hundred times better, from corn bread to bread with olives or onions. Not to mention *griottesi*. Later Miguel ran off to the controversial Milan Expo 2015 and served us up imbecilic drivel about nothing, and the others listened piously, although they didn't exactly relish those little anecdotes of Miguel's. What matters to him now is being au courant. But there are other things in Miguel's life; a daughter, now grown up, born when Miguel was seventeen and when they travel together *people think she's my girlfriend*, he says; there's a mother pining for her runaway son, there are five more brothers and sisters scattered over the world and there is that Manila, those Philippines from which Miguel runs, but they follow him like a vast rolling burden, they get into his head, between his eyes, drill into his brain and leave indecipherable messages which give Miguel terrible, long-lasting migraines, and he can never make out whether they, the Philippines, are calling him back or threatening to crush him.

We know nothing about the Philippines. For us, the Philippines, with their population of almost a hundred million and eleven million more scattered over the globe, are a distant, exotic country. The Philippines, with an incomparably more tempestuous and richer history than that of little self-centered Croatia, are of no consequence to Croatia. And therefore the people who live in the Philippines (or those who run away from the Philippines) are of no consequence to Croatia, as are the books they write. Not now to go back in time, into history, let's stay in the twentieth century, perhaps we ought to know that during the Japanese massacre in 1945 in Manila, 100,000 civilians were killed and that in allied bombings Manila suffered most in the Second World War after Warsaw, that it in fact disappeared as a city. Croats, however, know only about Imelda Marcos and her three thousand pairs of shoes.

Miguel is reserved and transparent, refined and fragile as a porcelain figure through which swollen waters flow, furious waters whose glint and roar may be discerned only by an attentive observer. I won't tell his life story, it's in print, so if anyone wants it, it's there.

I also met the young Ethiopian-American writer Maaza Mengiste, sent by her parents at the age of four to the New World to save her life, and who wrote in her first book about the bloody revolution in Ethiopia, about the civil war that lasted from the 1970s until 1991, in which members of her family died and who got upset, *I was so angry* she told me, when in a prominent place on the walls of this villa she noticed photographs of the former barons in the service of Mussolini's army in Abyssinia. That invasion of Mussolini's into Ethiopia in October 1935 was unexpected and brutal, involving the use of a combat poison similar to mustard gas. Between 1936 and 1937 Mussolini's Blackshirts carried out a series of appalling massacres against the Ethiopian population, and then plundered and torched their houses. During the Italian occupation, around 275,000 Ethiopians, and altogether 670,000, lost their lives. For these and other atrocities carried out by the

Fascist military hordes in Africa and in the Balkans, not one Italian has ever been taken to court, never even accused, let alone sentenced for war crimes. When the British troops in Africa defeated the Fascists, they interned many soldiers in camps, some of which were set up in Kenya. There, in those Kenyan camps, individual members of the Italian aristocracy lived, but that was never mentioned on this estate, so I asked. My questions did not provoke discomfort, only contempt for the effrontery of a *Schiavone* with no noble pedigree sticking his nose into other people's family relations. So, on that aristocratic estate, on which, in addition to people and dogs, secrets were buried, it occasionally seemed to me that life, that instinctive, dark life was pulsating under the earth, while outside life flowed calmly on, cleansed and painless, illuminated by an opaque glow of tedium.

Now, about that, about that imperialist dream of conquest of the elevated fop Benito who adored bowler hats, small airplanes, chamomile, pedicures and his body, about that monstrous dream of his of the integration of Africa and the Balkans in a New Roman Empire, Maaza Mengiste is writing a new book.

Nevertheless, that Tuscan estate, that refuge for writers, offered little sparks of fun. Those sparks illuminated the small obstinacies of this world, the threadbare everyday, which (perhaps because of a lack of funds, perhaps because of fatigue with the false luster) crept into our days. The curtain in my bathroom was old, spotted with mold, and some of the hooks holding it up had fallen off, so it drooped untidily. In some places the ceiling was crumbling, the plaster between the beams had fractured and cracks had appeared. The wooden garden chairs needed to be varnished and possibly lacquered; the bottom of the Teflon pan was scratched and the handle loose, so the pan "wandered" over the heat, the dishes could have been newer and there could have been more kitchen utensils. Nobody changed the burned-out light bulbs. In some rooms the electrical sockets had come off the wall and hung by bare wires. Oh joy! I imagined that this now empty empire of blurred sheen was gradually falling apart, that mirage, that shabby, worn-out dreamcatcher, as I had imagined and dreamed of the day (which I shall not live to see) when the roots of everything we live through will begin to get entangled and gradually dry out or rot, no matter, together with those circus-like royal families and the cardinals and all those bishops dressed up in gold-studded robes scattered across the globe.

I could have enjoyed my time on that Tuscan estate, but I didn't. At least not the first ten days or so. All of it, that pointless luxury garnished with hollow, Emmentaler conversations reserved for the evening hours, conversationlets, became a murderer of thought, a leech of the spirit, a thief of worlds and dreams. Conversations over dinner began with exclamations of gratitude; like that TV cook Ana, every single one cheered *mmmmm*, after which they asked each other (and me) *Whose cuisine do you like? Do you know how to cook? What do you cook? What do people eat in your country?* (I felt like saying *Shit, we all eat shit*, which would have been taken as unforgiveable vulgarity.) Then they'd start gossiping, then a euphoric exchange about the latest episode of *Game of Thrones*, where I was completely handicapped. *Roy Andersson*, I said, A Pigeon Sat on a Branch Reflecting on Existence. *Has anyone seen that?* Silence thudded into the risotto and the Tuscan red wine, hogwash remained on the table.

One evening we went to the next-door villa for a garden party. I walk along the woodland path accompanied by the future owner of the estate on which I am staying and ask him who we're going to visit, who are these people?

She's a wonderful person, says the forty-year-old Italian with a Brooklyn address and a barely explicable occupation.

What does she do?

She's a great mother.

I'm a great father, as well, I say, *a single parent.*

The wonderful person and great mother did turn out to be a pleasant hostess, only she was a little anxious that her daughter would soon be coming from London (where she had just finished school) with eighteen friends, and she wondered whether she had eighteen sets of bed linen and towels. *But when I've welcomed them all, I'll escape to a spa, even if it's not at all cheap, three and a half thousand euros for a week, no matter, I have to protect my nerves,* said the wonderful person and great mother, *then I'll come home when the servants have cleaned the house up.* The brother of the hospitable hostess, who otherwise lives in Naples, did the cooking that evening, and afterward everyone again went *mmmmm*, and while he was cooking, I helped, so we talked, and he told me, because I asked him, I asked them all how they spent their time, what they did, to hear whether these people did anything at all, did they earn their living, and he said *I'm an artist.*

What's your medium? I asked, *oil, water color, drawing?*

Oh no, I process my photographs on a computer, I have gallery owners and I exhibit, said the brother of the hospitable hostess, skillfully placing mozzarella and chopped tomatoes onto his bruschetta, then he took out his iPhone and showed me his works, and finally, when we had become sort of close, he complained that he couldn't find people to cultivate his vineyards on some southern Italian island so I suggested that he should go to the refuge on Lampedusa and employ some of those traumatized, half-dead rescued souls.

The husband of the agreeable hostess is a lawyer in London, where that Italian-French-Spanish family presumably lives for the rest of the year, but the husband of the agreeable hostess does not spend his time in his legal profession, but surfing, because he's crazy about surfing and surfs all the time, in any water he happens to be near, or to which he travels. Maybe that's why the husband doesn't like coming to his Tuscan villa, to his Tuscan olive groves and Tuscan vineyards, but still, that evening it was the most cheering thing I heard, as, even if indirectly, it confirmed that I was not entirely insane. The agreeable hostess and good mother of two twenty-year-olds, who, to my surprise, could cook, was somewhat weaker on literature, because a few days later, when the conversation turned to the Nobel Prize winner Saul Bellow, she asked *Who's that?* And when that middle-aged woman lacked for a topic of conversation, she went back to already used-up ones, in other words, she repeated herself quite a lot.

I also talked to a middle-aged woman of unspecified origin who lived in Paris. *You're a writer?* I asked, because where I was staying there were writers, mostly American, among whom there were some pleasant ones, *Oh no,* she said, *I just have a published collection of interviews with well-known people.* I asked this lady which well-known figures had wandered into her book, I've forgotten what she said because I hadn't heard of a single one of those well-known people, which could mean that from a Parisian perspective, and also a global one, I am uninformed. The lady talked to me about some former Yugoslav émigrés, political, it seemed to me, her acquaintances, who were spreading around Paris some fairly controversial, not to say false information about socialist Yugoslavia, *Have you met Kiš?* I interrupted her, and she asked, *Who's that?*

I also met an architect, you could see at once he was a dandy and womanizer, who lived in New York too (Tuscan Italians seem to be mad about the Big Apple, just as Americans are mad about Tuscany), and that architect was then working on the restoration of an Italian castle belonging to an American millionaire, *Have you been to Tirana?* I asked, *No,* he said, *but I've been to Ljubljana and seen Plečnik's library, fascinating,* here he rose a little in my estimation, but he had with him an apparently submissive young Russian woman, forty years younger, although a lover with a mission, a program, a *project*, that was clear, *I'm an architect*, she said, *but now I'm studying design in Florence, otherwise I live in Moscow*, she said. I couldn't work out how she lived in Moscow, because the snappily dressed architect (68), in an open linen shirt with rolled-up sleeves, listed the virtually uninhabited little Greek islands he had been visiting for several years with that young Russian lover of his and where the two of them bathed naked in blessed quiet, under the Greek sun. *Is there any news about Tsipras' negotiations with the IMF and Central Bank?* I asked, and he said, *Greece is a beautiful country*.

I met a pair of brothers who don't come into this story, although they live in Tuscany, which could mean, as I know, that there are also people from the present day living in Tuscany. One of the brothers is a well-known (and good) musician and composer, the other is an excellent photographer. Conversation with them, on their Tuscan estate, flowed cheerfully, without misunderstandings, because although the lawns were tended and the little hills green, a provocative chaos reigned all around, someone was baking pizzas, people ate in passing, we were barefoot and the mosquitoes were going nuts.

During the Second World War, Nazis lived in some of the villas belonging to the Italian aristocracy. (*They weren't Nazis, but soldiers of the Wehrmacht*, said some former and current owners of those villas, with a dose of irritation in their voices.) Then, during the Second World War, good wine was poured in those villas, people cooked with olive oil, and some staff had managed to stay. Relative calm reigned and undesecrated nature bloomed; members of partisan "bands" attacked SS personnel in little Renaissance towns, they didn't touch the aristocracy, this was told to me in a steady voice by former landowners, that is, the descendants of former barons and dukes, entirely cynically, without comment. Some of the owners of Tuscan and other Italian villas "found themselves" involved in the humane task of saving Ethiopian cultural treasures during Mussolini's campaign in Abyssinia, but those times were long since past, so there was no point in wasting words on them. Only, here and there in an album or on a wall, one could see small black-and-white, already yellowing photographs which preserved the memory of the beginning of the decline of the Italian bourgeoisie, whose epigones stubbornly relate fairy tales from a long since buried age.

It was as though, during my stay in Tuscany, I had ended up in an American period drama, but there is no drama. I floated on great, terrifying beauty (*la grande bellezza*) and cursed Sorrentino and his ghastly film.

Then again I was amused to be a participant in an operetta, whose music I imagined, could hear, but that was inaudible to the people on the estate. Secretly I spent time with Gombrowicz, watching the actors of the Tuscan vaudeville changing their costumes and masks as they acted in the grotesque tragicomedy of the present, like characters from Gombrowicz's *Operetta*, those not exactly frivolous entertainments for the mannequin dolls of the past. I observed the way this little closed society did not see the signals being sent to it by a distant lighthouse, or the angel of history, that *Angelus Novus* of Klee's, the way they did not know that their operetta was sending out the first (or last) notes of Europe's funeral march as it is laid to rest.

I brought to the owner of the estate where I was staying, the founder of that altruistic refuge for writers—otherwise well known in Italy as the former owner of one of the most famous Milan galleries of the mid-twentieth century—a Vlado Kristl monograph. And before she had peered into the linen bag of the museum where the book was printed, she asked me, *Is it something to eat?*

VLADO KRISTL (Zagreb, January 24, 1923–Munich, August 7, 2004) is considered one of the fathers of Croatian abstract art. Kristl's filmography and biography are well known, but less is known about his painting, particularly after 1962, when Kristl left Croatia (Yugoslavia). Hence it was at the Rijeka exhibition that works from the artistic opus of Vlado Kristl from the period 1959 to 2004 were shown for the first time.

Working in two cultural centers, from the beginning of the 1950s to the beginning of the 1960s in Croatia, and after that for several decades in Germany, a magisterial place for Vlado Kristl has been incontestably established in the art of the second half of the twentieth century. First it was Kristl as a film-maker, whether his animated, experimental, short and feature-length films or video works. Then it was Kristl the painter, poet, man of the theater, writer, thinker, but also typographer and designer. But regardless of the fact that a lot has been written about him as a complete and multifaceted person, Kristl remains an illegal immigrant of European art, an artist always here—present, but not fully discovered, unidentified, understated.

(Jerica Ziherl, from the introduction to the catalogue)

At first, I slept badly. One night I dreamed about a small black horse, rocking in a net hung between two trees. When it stood up, I saw that it was barely fifty centimeters high and about a meter long. I wanted to take that miniature horse in my arms, but I didn't. I just gazed at it, completely enchanted. Both Jung and Freud had all sorts of things to say about horses that enter dreams. Then I dreamed someone told me my sister Ada had been diagnosed with carcinoma of the kidney, which is known as *sedia Turca*, and *sedia Turca*, in addition to being a comfortable seat, *à la chaise longue*, can also be a squatting place, that is, somewhere to shit.

The tower in which I was staying was some distance from the main building—the villa—about two hundred meters, across a large (tended) lawn with shrub roses and lavender, some yellow flowers, walnut and olive trees, five dogs that run riot on the meadow, and when they are not running, they're crapping, which can be awkward when one is returning to the tower at night, because the field is not lit, and the dogs hover around the table at dinner time and nuzzle between one's legs. Two of the dogs are pugs, pugs have trouble breathing, they have squashed faces, short noses, they wheeze, at some point in the course of several centuries of breeding something interfered with their breathing organs and they sound like asthmatics, and since I am asthmatic, and the Tuscan climate is fairly damp, the three of us produced strange noises, the only difference being that I could alleviate my rattling with little pumps, while the pugs couldn't. When they sleep, pugs snore. They have sensitive, bulging eyes, and if their collar is pulled too tight or they raise their heads too high, their eyes can pop out, then their eyes have to be put back in their sockets, where they belong. So, I found two similarities between myself and the pugs, respiratory and ophthalmological, although pugs are small and I am big. One of them, Lauretta, was thirteen years old, blind and, it seemed to me, senile, because she kept talking to herself, producing terrifying atonal sounds as she roamed the estate. During dinner Lauretta would stick to my leg, snuffling madly. There were also two shaggy mongrels, very distrustful of people, I managed to befriend one of them, Achilleo, because I told him all kinds of things in Croatian, I told him everything that was bothering me, and when he caught sight of me, he would run across the lawn to greet me, he would smile and his ears flapped in the air. With the other shaggy one, Ermelinda, I couldn't get anywhere. Later I was told that Ermelinda had had a traumatic life, that she was fearful, that she didn't come near anyone, especially not men, that she never ran, that nothing in life interested or pleased her apart from staring fixedly at the six cats that appeared at the window during dinner. Ermelinda watched them in a trance, fixed them with her big yellow eyes framed by black eyelashes, staring in such a way that some of the household believed she intended to butcher them.

As far as the tower was concerned, until Miguel moved into the attic, it was somewhat spooky to live in it alone, because the tower had a lot of entrances, main and secondary, which weren't locked, and on the façade were nailed marble memorial plaques dedicated to long and recently departed members of that baronial family, along with two additional plaques for departed dogs, although in the small copse leading toward the swimming pool there is a little obelisk with about twenty names engraved on it. *Whose are those names?* I asked the baronessa, *They're the names of dogs that lived and died on the estate*, she said, and as far as my stay in the tower was concerned, I was not certain whether, beneath the plaques on its façade, they too, those people and those dogs, were buried at the foot of the tower, but even if they weren't, I somehow felt their presence as though I was among the dead, as though I was in a kind of tomb, even though the tower was airy and spacious. Later, I got used to it.

I got used to all of it. I was tamed.

I began to look into the life of the owner of the estate, and the landowner herself, a well-groomed and well-preserved ninety-year-old, who prided herself on her excellent vision (she'd had cataract operations, which of course she didn't mention), straight back, so a spine in better shape than mine, with a set of her own teeth, admittedly with slightly impaired hearing and pains in her neck, but, thanks to operations on both knees, of firm and brisk step, I began to see her in a soft light that spread warmth through the end of my stay. From its beginning, wars, murders and persecutions had roared through that life, and of them the Armenian genocide had determined, that is, marked the lives of many families, including, on her mother's side, her own. Here was a solitary childhood buried in the protocols (and shackles) of the Italian aristocracy, with a certain confusion in connection with her comprehension of the horrors brought by Fascism, there was, later, revolt and a leap, more an attempt at a leap into real life, but in fact flight into a life bounded by high art and members of the upper class. Nevertheless, through that life, through the life of that one-time baroness, walked an army of internationally well-known painters and writers, some of them excellent, and I thought that for some readers, those who were not so preoccupied with the horrors of the present, it would be good if someone, some ghostwriter, could help that woman to collect her recollections, impressions and meetings from the times when capitalism was somewhat healthier and buoyant. Then she, this already fragile woman of still steel will and sharp eye, would be able to consider her past, her life, from the outside, not exactly as a complete, compact work, but as time that keeps flowing and, like everything that moves, bears with it deposits of clean water and silt. So, as I was leaving, with an empathy that surprised me, tinged with sadness even, I embraced and kissed the former baroness.

Then a red light came on in me. Before me stood Luciana Castellina (b. 1929), three years younger than our baronessa, Luciana Castellina with whom, before coming to Tuscany, I had had dinner in Rome, in the ordinary, virtually proletarian trattoria Settimio all'Arancio and, until the wee hours, completely entranced, I listened to the story of a life that was all giving, and still is, which was an idea, a dream, a vision of clear outlines for which it was worth existing. And so, leaving the romantic Tuscan oasis for writers of varied origins and worldviews, I was suddenly overcome by a wave of my politely suppressed irritation, my intolerance burst through, I was overwhelmed by the anger that grows in me when I listen to stubborn denials of what is obvious, unconvincing tales and anecdotes relativizing wars and the horrors wars brought (and still bring) and it all came back to me and swirled up and at least for a moment I breathed, I breathed steadily, deeply and well, driving my asthma into the background. I was going back to my fucking poverty-stricken, unjust world.

LUCIANA CASTELLINA—writer and political journalist, author of numerous publications, long-term member of the Italian parliament as well as that of the European Union, tireless activist— is one of the most prominent Italian intellectuals of left-wing provenance. The daughter of a highly regarded Milanese businessman and a Jewess from Trieste, Luciana Castellina was educated in Rome and studied law at Sapienza. In 1947 she participated in the First World Festival of Youth and Students in Prague, became a member of the Communist Party of Italy (PCI) and came to Yugoslavia with the International Brigades to work on building the Šamac-Sarajevo railway line. There, in that Roman trattoria Settimio all'Arancio, in January 2015, Luciana Castellina took out her badge from that action, laughed, then placed the small object on the table, everyone at the table got up, came round, bent down and touched that forgotten artifact from a buried age. Luciana then talked about

Zenica, about Sarajevo during this recent war, and about much else—her life in Rome under Fascism, about the yellow stars on her clothes—Luciana talked firmly, clearly, without pathos, and I felt like stealing her and taking her home. Luciana Castellina, arrested several times for political activities: in 1948, during demonstrations protesting at the failed attempt on the life of Palmiro Togliatti; in 1950 and 1956 in similar circumstances: then in 1963 during a protest connected with Operation Gladio run by the CIA, after which she spent two months in Rome's Regina Coeli prison. She was driven out of Greece during the military coup there in 1967. Three years later, together with the founders of the monthly magazine *Il manifesto*, she was expelled from the Communist Party of Italy, after which she participated in founding the Socialist Party of Proletarian Unity. Contributors to *Il manifesto* were left-oriented journalists ready for a critical evaluation of the Italian Left. In 1971 *Il manifesto* became and is still today a daily newspaper. Critical of the Communist Party of Italy, *Il manifesto* had many followers; it was livelier, more vital and more independent than the Party paper *L'unità*.

I shall not now sketch the political biography of Luciana Castellina, whoever is interested can look it up and study it. But here, for a start, a conversation with her in 1985, published in the magazine *New Left Review*: https://www.jacobinmag.com/2014/03/italian-communism-remembered/

Politics was not Luciana Castellina's only world. Students, young people, film, art, gender equality, human and civil rights, wherever there was injustice, Luciana was there, loud, passionate and argumentative. Here are her books too: in 2011 she published *La scoperta del mondo* (*The Discovery of the World*), in which she describes growing up in Fascist Italy from her fourteenth to her eighteenth year and how she decided to step into the world of politics. It is a book about war, anti-Semitism, resistance to Fascism and belief in social justice. In 2012 she published *Siberiana*, the mental journey of a stormy political epoch in which she was an active participant.

In April 2015 (aged 85), Luciana Castellina became a member of the National Committee for Another Europe with Tsipras, a coalition of the Italian Left in the European Parliament. With the communist leader Alfredo Reichlin, she has a son and a daughter, both teachers at universities in London and Rome.

I asked our baronessa, of course I did, whether she knew Luciana Castellina. *She was very beautiful,* said the baronessa, *and her husband cheated on her with the mother of my neighbor here. Italy is small,* said the baronessa, *we all know each other, although we don't need to think the same way.*

✉

Yes, I got used to the servants, to the conversational and mealtime rituals (the shared dinner was compulsory, with a semiformal dress code), to the silverware, the works of art, to the fact that I had nowhere to escape to, that it was two hours' walk to the nearest village, to being the prisoner of glaring, voracious beauty. And then, when I had got used to all that, I stopped writing.

A few months later I spent four weeks in Tirana. I walked, I observed, I listened and I sorrowed. In Tirana I wrote.

In Paris I almost always visit Café Tournon, where I sit for hours because of Joseph Roth. I reread Joseph Roth's books, the ones about drunkenness, literal, alcoholic, and the one about the delirium of the dead age of a dead empire (Austro-Hungarian), listening to the way Roth's works emit a doleful lament that warns of looming catastrophe. I sit in Café Tournon also because of Roth's fucked-up life, because of his homelessness, trying to grasp how and why the whole civilizational nausea drags after us like a slimy trail or blocks our way. How and why the excellent journalist— "Red Roth," "Red Joseph"—writing superb texts in Austria, Germany and France, in Holland, the Soviet Union, Poland, Albania and Italy, ends up in the corner of a small Parisian bar in which, with a cognac in one hand and a pen in the other, working for up to eight hours a day, he creates some of his best works. Roth and Zweig were friends, perhaps that's why I look for Zweig in Paris. With Hitler's coming to power and shortly before his annexation of Austria to Germany, in February 1933 Roth leaves Berlin and goes to Paris, from where he writes to Zweig in Vienna:

Now you can already see that we are drifting toward catastrophe. Apart from our personal existence, our literary and financial existence too have been destroyed; all this is leading to a new war. I wouldn't bet on our lives. They have succeeded in bringing in the domination of barbarism. Don't be deceived. Hell reigns.

I tried to understand how Roth, and not only Roth, as early as 1933 saw all that was happening, what was coming, although for many nothing was happening, and now again the trumpets of Jericho sound while we blissfully roll our tiny barren days along. I thought of Roth also because today Croatia is basking in a swamp of historical revisionism that is becoming fascistized and Ustashaized, all around us dark figures leap out, violent and inarticulate, crazy, mental invalids maddened by abstractions that conceal the disastrous concept of the destruction of all this world's joys and freedoms, entranced by abstractions such as the homeland and the Church, abstractions too big to nest in my small heart. I thought about Roth because, in addition to the hooked cross on that Croatian football stadium that has mysteriously surfaced from the depths of Croatian soil, and which I see as the subversion of the overwrought, helpless libertine who says, *There you are, look, this is who you are*, little Croatia has now also dug in its heels in its hysterical defense of a beatified archbishop and cardinal, in a pathetic campaign to proclaim him a saint. An incomprehensible autistic blindness reigns over the question of the clerical-political-moral activities of this archbishop and cardinal, disgusting lies are proclaimed truths, this refusal to see the way certain dignitaries of the Catholic Church walk on tiptoe in the dark, in its catacombs, *Hush, hush, sweet Charlotte*, frightened, cowardly, sunk in the stagnant waters of their imaginary power; their inactivity is terrifying, in the way, as in horror films, it metamorphoses into a misdeed, a pathetic endeavor to serve two contradictory ideas at the same time, one of freedom and the other of submission and servility, so that life is being reduced to "both … and …," to "but" when "and" means the eradication of the human race, before which every "but," including God's, must give way, because there is no faith that is greater than the life of one innocent person. That military vicar of the Independent State of Croatia could have not offered comfort to the future butchers, he could have said that the NDH, Independent State of Croatia, was not at all a work of God, but hell, the essence of human evil, the creation of morbid dreams, extirpated intelligence, eclipsed reason, just as back in 1934 the Lion of Münster, Bishop Clemens August von Galen, roared when he publicly attacked the Nazi ideology of blood and soil, when he said that unconditional loyalty to the Third Reich was becoming slavery, when he led protest groups against Nazi euthanizer rampaging, and was quite justifiably beatified. As far as open, uncompromising concrete anti-Nazi struggle goes, here is the Berlin Bishop and Cardinal Konrad von Preysing, a German prelate of the Roman Catholic Church. As far as I know, Konrad von Preysing was not beatified (he died in 1950) and there was never any discussion of his being proclaimed a saint.

That Croatian archbishop and cardinal could have not accepted, that is refused the Poglavnik Pavelić's decoration "Order for services rendered—Supreme Order with Star," that archbishop and cardinal, instead of directing anemic appeals for improving living conditions, or rather dying conditions in the Jasenovac concentration camp, could have gone to that lively camp and he would not, oh irony, oh sarcasm, have *heard from various sources that here and there some behave inhumanely and cruelly with non-Aryans as they are deported to collection camps, and also in those same camps; what is more, that such behavior does not spare either children, or the old, or the sick*, he would perhaps have been able to *see* what he had heard, although it is debatable whether even then he would have done anything about it. So, the deportation of non-Aryans—oh, how graphically the archbishop accepts the Nazi terminology—is all right, by the book, except that the delivery of parcels of food and clean clothes might have been more effective and better organized (insofar as there remained relatives who could prepare and send such parcels).

I "kept company" in Paris with Joseph Roth, also because, while he was despairing about the fate of Europe, his private life was disintegrating into chaos and pain. After five or six years of a relatively harmonious marriage, his wife Friederike Reichler Roth, known as Friedl, was diagnosed with schizophrenia, and at the end of the 1920s placed in the famous Viennese Steinhof sanatorium, then the most state-of-the-art European psychiatric hospital. When Hitler came to power, Steinhof became a lair of arrogant and disgraceful figures who, through their experiments, exterminated those who were undesirable to the Reich, including many children. While in the 1930s, and up until the end of the war, "specialists" in the brain dug around in the cerebral mass of their patients, the park of the Steinhof hospital, a lovely spacious park dominated by the famous white church with its golden cupola, masterpiece of the architect Otto Wagner, remained untouched; what is more, an army of trained horticultural workers tended to the preservation of its luxuriant beauty. Otherwise, which is completely morbid, psychiatric hospitals are by default surrounded by elegant and heavenly parks, as are the majority of the former concentration camps.

But in mid-1940, Roth's Friedl was moved by the Nazi experimenter-exterminators to the splendid Renaissance castle Schloss Hartheim, not far from Linz, expressly transformed into a Nazi euthanasia center that functioned according to the guidelines of the Aktion T4 Program. The castle had already been adapted as a psychiatric hospital at the beginning of the twentieth century, when it was known as the *Psychiatrische Anstalt*, later popularly cruelly renamed *Idioten-Anstalt*.

In Hartheim, between May 1940 and December 1944, 18,269 physically and mentally handicapped people were killed by carbon monoxide and lethal injection, plus more than 10,000 camp inmates, exhausted by labor and hunger, sick and suffering from tuberculosis, brought from Dachau, Mauthausen and Ravensbrück. Hartheim was the only killing center in the Second World War from which not a single person emerged alive.

When in June 1945 members of the American armed forces began to investigate Schloss Hartheim, they found a steel safe in which the Nazis had stored statistical data about the killings carried out. A brochure of some forty pages contains monthly reports of the killings, which they called "disinfection." Among the statistical data found at Hartheim, there is a note with the estimate that through the "disinfection of 70,273 people with a possible life span of another ten years," food was saved to the value of 141,775,573.80 Reichsmarks.

First phase of extermination:

1940							
month 5	month 6	month 7	month 8	month 9	month 10	month 11	month 12
633	982	1449	1740	1123	1400	1396	947

1941							
month 1	month 2	month 3	month 4	month 5	month 6	month 7	month 8
943	1178	974	1123	1106	1364	735	1176

Total number killed
18,269

Trial for the killings at Hartheim:

In the main trial for the murders in Hartheim, sixty-one people were accused, including the doctors in charge of the program, Georg Renno and Rudolf Lonauer.

	M.	F.	Total
Doctors	3	0	3
Nurses	15	8	23
Administrative personnel	9	7	16
Drivers	4	0	4
'Stokers'	6	0	6
Unknown occupation	6	3	9
Total	43	18	61

Judicial proceedings:

The accusations against thirteen people were withdrawn, and the trial of twenty-two people was postponed because they could not be traced. The accusations against seven people were thrown out because the accused had died. Two of the accused were given prison sentences, and the trial of thirteen of the accused was postponed to a later date. The fate of three of the accused remains unknown.

Sentencing:

The sentences were handed down on July 7, 1947. The state prosecution sought the death penalty for nine of the accused, but only two of the sentences were carried out. The sentences for nurses were more lenient than had been requested. The death sentences were carried out in Dresden in March

1948. Those who were sentenced to long-term imprisonment were amnestied in 1956 and freed.

Friederike Reichler Roth disappeared in Hartheim, but Joseph Roth would never know that. At the news that his friend, the playwright and poet Ernst Toller, had killed himself in a New York hotel in May 1939, Roth's contracted heart burst and his cirrhosis-riddled liver disintegrated, and four days after Toller's death, with pneumonia, in delirium tremens, he sailed into memory.

So I remembered Joseph Roth also because of Friedl, because along with Friederike Reichler Roth, these people vanished in Hartheim:

JAN MARIA MICHAŁ KOWALSKI (1871–1942), Polish priest and first *Minister Generalis* of the Mariavitski Order;

BERNHARD HEINZMANN (1903–42), German priest of the Roman Catholic Church, proclaimed a martyr. He publicly opposed Hitler's frenetic drivel about the superiority of the Aryan race. In 1941, he was arrested by the Gestapo and transported to Dachau. Prisoner number 24433. He was killed in Hartheim with carbon monoxide, then burned;

FRIEDRICH KARAS (1895–1942), Austrian Roman Catholic priest. In 1942, arrested by the Gestapo and sent to Dachau. Killed in Hartheim;

WERNER SYLTEN (1893–1942), Evangelical theologian. Arrested in February 1941 and sent to Dachau. Seriously ill, he was transferred to Hartheim in 1942, in a "contingent of invalids."

Several other concentration camp inmates were transferred from Dachau to Hartheim (and killed): three hundred and thirty

(330) Polish, seven German, six Czech, four Luxembourgian, three Dutch, and two Belgian priests. I won't think about the Istrian priests, men of the people, who with a partisan cap on their heads joined the National Liberation Movement and fought against Fascism, that upsets me even more because of all the hysterical propaganda in the name of the canonization of a long since dead bishop and cardinal who was beatified twenty years ago, because of so much senseless fanaticism, so much virulence, the sick obsession that one controversial figure of this world should be placed on the throne of the saintly. There are no saints and it's good that there aren't. Who has been given the task of judging the sinlessness of some and the sinfulness of others?

In January 2013 a European Union directive came into force whereby pig farmers had to ensure that their pigs had manipulative objects to make them happy, so as to satisfy their need for rooting and stop them chewing their own tails or those of other pigs. Among the various toys on offer, little balls were favored, yellow ones. The design of this yellow toy for local pigs (which the pigs were able to chew) was developed by a research team at the Faculty of Organic Production at the University of Kassel, Germany, over eight years. As far as the choice of color was concerned, victory went to yellow because, the scientists affirmed, pigs immediately notice anything yellow, given that in their porcine world the color yellow is a rarity, so little yellow balls attract their attention, which would not be the case if the balls were red, because, the experts say, pigs are somehow blind to everything red. After the pig-entertainment law was passed, farmers were given three months to implement it—they had to throw several toys, preferably little yellow balls, into every sty. Failure to comply with the law on the wellbeing of pigs entailed financial and custodial sanctions. Later research has shown that, today, European domesticated pigs, piglets, sows, boars and farrows are merry and carefree animals and, thanks to the little yellow balls, entirely free of stress.

I don't know what compelled me to offer the story of the yellow balls for European pigs to a Goethe Institute director at a literary gathering abroad, because the story had no connection whatsoever with the mostly empty literary-philosophical presentations. I blathered on, partly as a joke, partly with irritation in my voice, about the Orwellian undertaking of the present-day European Police, and at the end of my tirade the Goethe Institute director said, with a polite smile, *Oh, no. I have a pig farm, and now that they have their yellow balls, my pigs are happy and relaxed.*

So, yellow is in again. Stray dogs are marked with a yellow chip in their left ear (just as under the Third Reich they identified Jews in passport photographs by obligating them to have their left ear exposed), and smoking zones are marked with a yellow geometric shape on the pavement.

Some ten years ago, in a psychiatric hospital in France, a double murder occurred. Arriving for work one morning, staff saw that the head of the nurse on duty that night had been placed on the TV set in the hospital day room; the nurse's body was found by the door leading to the fire escape. Another nurse lay in a pool of blood, her throat slit, butchered, with multiple stab wounds to her body and neck. Both victims were around forty years of age, married, and mothers to small children. The weapon with which the murders had been carried out was not found in the hospital. It was presumed to be a sabre or a machete.

The hospital building is set in well-tended parkland of some forty hectares, in a forest at the foot of the Pyrenees.

On the cover of the first issue of the magazine *Acéphale* (1936, edited by Georges Bataille) there is a drawing by André Masson inspired by da Vinci's *Vitruvian Man*. The drawing shows a naked but headless human figure holding in his raised right hand a flaming heart, in his left, a dagger, and in his groin sits his skull. Under the title *Acéphale* are the words *Religion • Sociologie • Philosophie • and the statement: LA CONJURATION SACRÉE*, in other words "sacred conspiracy."

> Man has escaped from his head just as the condemned
> man has escaped from his prison. He has found beyond
> himself not God, who is the prohibition against crime,

but a being who is unaware of prohibition. Beyond what I am, I meet a being who makes me laugh because he is headless; this fills me with dread because he is made of innocence and crime; he holds a steel weapon in his left hand, flames like those of a Sacred Heart in his right. He reunites in the same eruption Birth and Death. He is not a man. He is not a god either. He is not me but he is more than me: his stomach is the labyrinth in which he has lost himself, loses me with him, and in which I discover myself as him, in other words, as a monster.

Georges Bataille

To minimize the possibilities of such outbursts by psychiatric patients, psychiatric patients are pacified with medication and occupational therapy. Occupational therapy consists of physical work—which can be creative, but generally is not. Occupational therapy for psychiatric patients might be collecting withered leaves in the hospital garden, washing floors and so on, but also drawing, painting, making little clay sculptures (work that can be done by hand), through which the psychoanalysts try to penetrate the underground of the human soul. Sometimes, along with physical therapy, they throw in musical exercises, listening to music and singing. A fairly common therapy for psychiatric patients is dramatic performance, which does not require the mental engagement of the "sick," because their engagement frequently amounts to being obedient, that is, to taking direction from those who dream up the performances. Nevertheless, occupational therapy is more a passive than an active pastime. Does this mean that intellectual work leads to madness or that the "mad" are not in a state to form judgments independently, that is, that even the attempt at independent reasoning and individual action excludes a person (the madman) from the group, which then proclaims him trash, that is, a "case," and places him in an isolation cell, prison, psychiatric, social, whatever?

A few years ago, the staff of the psychiatric hospital in Popovača brought its charges to the island of Ugljan to show their "peers" their production, "Hedgehog's Home." The press release said that the patients had rehearsed diligently to demonstrate that what was best for them after leaving the hospital was to continue the treatment at home, with prescribed therapy. The director of the production was a nurse, and the costume designer was her colleague, also a nurse. The press release said that the show's producers "had visited many hospitals in Croatia with their little acting company." It is enough to look at photographs from that melancholy, dilettante carnival, that hideous manipulation of human pain, that empty, shabby entertainment, that eerily bounded existence, that little, submissive, disciplined company, that world at the end of the world, to see a copy of one's own existence, here, allegedly—from the outside.

With the decapitation of those nurses, the perpetrator had crossed the threshold that protects the boundaries of the body. The body disintegrates, fragments, bursts, and its parts float through despair, suffering, agony and sorrow, through waters without embankments or dams, through barely navigable waters, muddy and destructive. The body no longer has borders, it is dismembered, scattered, wild, but again, preserved in pieces.

I have a collection of the dreams of Adam's and my patients, the majority of whom were not seriously ill. Many of these dreams (like some of my own) are about precisely that, about the fear that we are going to disintegrate, fall apart, burst, break, that we will no longer be whole, that we are reverting to a mirror from which we are observed only by little pieces of what we believe is our self, our shattered "I."

LINA:

I have to collect my laptop from the repairman. I'm in a hurry, but obstacles keep getting in the way. A friend I haven't seen for ages suddenly appears in front of me, now in a wheelchair, with no left leg, just a long metal spike in its place. An open wound, swollen and bloody, gapes on her right forearm. I ask her, Why haven't they cleaned and sewn up that wound? It's nothing, she says. I push her in that wheelchair and smell a sour odor emanating from her body that makes me feel sick.

DORA:

After an argument with my daughter, who maintained that I am not a good person, I dreamed that she had locked me in a little room like a prison cell and slid home the bolt on the outside. In my dream I called for my mother and my voice woke me. The same night I was out walking with my grandmother, we were looking for shoes, everything around us was very quiet. Then my father appeared, alive, although he had been dead for a long time.

BREDA:

I go out of the hotel room, the door automatically locks behind me, I don't have a key, I can't go back. At the end of the corridor, in the half-dark, I see David. Sorry? David is dead. David is my unended love.

So, I see David. I call him, I tell him, I can't get in. A blonde woman appears, she takes me to a different room, David is there. Then, with two children, with my hands on their shoulders, I walk to that woman who is dressed like a witch.

RUBEN:

I have a white sock over my head. Under the cloth, two large coins press into my eyes.

EDA:

My daughter has to have an operation on her heart. We are in a shack with a lot of people. I enquire about the best cardiologist. Someone suggests Karlo. Karlo is my former husband, a dentist, but he's not my

daughter's father. Someone else suggests the cardiologist Ida Brun. I don't
know who Ida Brun is. I ask the people there, Are we in Macedonia?

ALBERT:

I go to take a shower, the bath is full of fat women squeezed into one
end of the tub. I get in, but I can't stretch out my legs, which annoys me.
What's more, someone has hung their clothes on the rail for the shower
curtain, so I can't pull the curtain, I'm afraid I'll splash the bathroom.
But there's no way I'll splash anything given that the bath is full of
women. Then suddenly everything and everyone disappears, even the
water. I'm left sitting in the empty tub.

ESTER:

My daughter is going for a walk with Boris Gomel. Boris Gomel was
my first boyfriend, I didn't sleep with him. Then I don't know whether
my daughter is going off with Boris Gomel or with Karlo Richter, the
painter and fascist. One of them, I can't see his face, comes back without
my daughter. We've broken up, he says. He sits down on a deckchair
behind thick glass, and I watch him from behind.

PETAR:

I went to a brothel and I couldn't find my way out again. Two weeks
later, I died. When I was dead, I thought, brothels are like graveyards.
What could that mean?

We dream so as to forget. So that we don't fall into nonexistence.

All of that exists, the disorder, the fragmentation, the din, in
reality and in dreams, but in literature and in life, the public and
the market want order, harmony and a (logical) flow, *simplicity*, so
that the little gray cells empty tidily and painlessly.

In a different psychiatric institution in France, the famous La
Borde Clinic, also situated in a wooded valley, but this time that of
the Loire—oh, those woods, those parks, with camps and lunatics—
of which some fool wrote that it is in the true sense of the word a
refuge, a sanctuary where patients find peace and rest, in that clinic
they didn't put on an amateur sketch like the nurses' production of

"Hedgehog's Home," but rather a properly rehearsed *Operetta* by Gombrowicz. Today it is perhaps no longer interesting to speak about the significance of the La Borde Clinic, about its founder Jean Oury and his colleagues, the antipsychiatric movement that included Gilles Deleuze, Félix Guattari, Frantz Fanon, Georges Canguilhem, François Tosquelles and many other left-oriented intellectuals of the 1960s and '70s, a movement which (like that of Franco Basaglia in Italy) combines Marxist philosophy, educational reform and psychoanalysis, a movement according to which patients freely and actively participate in running the institution (self-management?), and where neither the doctors nor the nurses wear uniforms, in which there are clubs and workshops, in which the hospital ramparts are broken down and the doors thrown open, so it may no longer be of interest to talk about the significance of the La Borde Clinic, psychiatry, they say, has become more or less accepted, internationally equalized, globalized—with the significant help and support of the pharmaceutical industry. But then, antipsychiatric movements redefined the relationship between psychoanalysis and politics, laid bare moral lunacy and psychiatric racism. Clinics such as La Borde were small societies in constant flux, clinics that shunned stagnation, stability, that bigoted untouchable rigidity where the rules are always firm and stifling.

It is no coincidence that in the La Borde Clinic there was a performance, along with many other dramas, of Gombrowicz's *Operetta*, about which Nicolas Philibert made an excellent documentary *La Moindre des choses* (*Every Little Thing*). Patients and hospital staff participated in rehearsals and in the final production, and the audience could barely tell who was who. At first glance, Gombrowicz's dialogues appear absurd, the characters change roles, costumes (and masks), and watching the way patients and staff do the same things, we see that the border between what we call *mens sana* and *mens insana* is permeable. Are the patients (and the staff) playing themselves, or characters from Gombrowicz's grotesque?

This is what Operetta *is about*, says Gombrowicz, because he knows that the human eye either does not see well or sees what is not there, or does not see anything at all; that the human ear either does not hear well, or hears what is not there, or does not hear anything at all; that the human mind comprehends with difficulty what exists, that it threshes and crushes what exists, sometimes submissively, sometimes violently, in the name of a peaceful dream that is then masked as ominous reality.

Here's a certain Potkoff, a duke and horse lover, says Gombrowicz,

and he advises Fior, a world master and dictator of men's and women's fashion: Let us invite ... guests to cooperate, says Potkoff, let it be a masquerade, and those who wish to take part in a fashion competition, let them throw sacks over the clothes of the future which they have themselves created. At a certain sign, the sacks will fall, and the jury will give prizes for the best concept, while Maestro Fior, enriched by these ideas, will announce the fashion for the year to come.

But, Potkoff is not Potkoff, neither a duke nor a horse lover!

says Gombrowicz.

No, that's Josip, the prince's former manservant, dismissed from service some time before, and now an agitator and revolutionary activist! Human clothing has gone mad ... In a whirlwind, in a flash of lightning,

the strangest changes of clothes can be seen: a prince/
torch, a priest/woman, Hitler's room, a gas mask ...
Everyone covers themselves up and no one knows who
is who ...

In *Operetta*, fashion (trendiness) devours the past, but the unstoppable past (History) penetrates through the trendy, masked rags and then all hell is let loose. *Revolution!* exclaims Gombrowicz, hoping too soon, because social life, political life, personal life, all those lives, big and small, still breathe behind masks; hammed up, they are woven into an existence that does not let them go into an age that grips and spins us around like tops.

And no one knows who is who.

I suddenly think of the jolly title of a theatrical production (for children and adults) on the repertoire in my neighborhood when I was living in Skopje: *Snow White and the Seven Dwarves.* I walked around Skopje saying "you dwarf" in Macedonian. Otherwise, that one-month stay in Skopje was therapeutic; there was a nearby milk bar called Venus and a shop with a sign: *STOP! Buy cheap.* But that Skopje of mine is (in part) outside this story because, like hardly any other city, it brought me peace, a total absence of anxiety, through which I slid as in a dream.

An autumn afternoon, around half past four. The little town has grown dark, it is raining hysterically, torrentially, menacingly, there are no passersby, no one on the street, just cars hurtling by. I'm sitting by the road under the yellow awning of a café, the air is damp and warm, I'm drinking freshly squeezed orange juice, there are no voices around me, no footsteps, only the blurred outlines of vehicles and the celestial cascade through which one can glimpse distant, locked lives silent, out of reach. Emptiness and a protective downpour.

This morning I've been summoned by the tax office "to clarify some matters."

You mean, you earn money abroad, so, you work abroad, says the fat official not looking at me, so she can continue undisturbed with a game of patience on her computer.

I don't work abroad, you can see that I'm here. Those are author's royalties.

That's the same thing.

No. They're fees for writing. They're called author's royalties.

Even so, you work for foreign countries.

I don't work for foreign countries.

So how do you get money, if you don't work?

I write. Here.

What do you write?

Books.

What kind of books?

Thick ones.

What about?

I don't get a chance to reply.

Hey, Olga, the official shouts across the room, *there's a man here says he writes some kind of books!*

Afterward I go to Željko's secondhand bookshop to calm down. *It's going to rain,* I say as I leave, *I'm going to Terazije to get some cigarettes.*

And I'm going later to the Karaburma market for some eggs, laughs Željko.

It's twenty-four years since I left. Belgrade still crouches in my brain.

The next day I set off from Rijeka to see Armando Trevi, my friend and a psychiatrist from Pula, who "has some information about Adam Kaplan's family."

On the bus a man spends the whole journey talking to a nonexistent (perhaps?) Anita. I listen and don't listen. At the same time. I'm tired of other people's pain. Sick of other people's worm-eaten, corroded lives.

But I keep looking, following and trying to recognize those little sparks of suffering that flit all around me, to avoid the glimmers of my own madness.

Another man sits with his arms crossed, without stirring, for the entire two-and-a-half-hour journey. Close-cropped hair, shirt with narrow blue and white stripes, hand-knitted gray cardigan (rice-grain pattern) and linen trousers. A well turned-out man with gray hair and a gray moustache. A cemented man, buried in a stupor.

The image shatters. Broken by the driver's voice, *He's polluted, polluted. He's not clean, he's polluted, he's not clean.* It's 2015.

Beside me sits a woman in a red knitted dress, blonde hair pulled back in a greasy ponytail, around forty years old. On her lap she's holding a tattered little teddy bear made of rags with splayed paws, and squeezing it. Behind me is an old couple, they yell as they talk, but at least they talk. Somewhere in the middle of the bus two men are discussing some dramatic event, for them at least, one of them keeps interjecting *How can I put it?* Not to look at the woman squeezing the flattened teddy bear and her filthy nails, I count the number of times the man says *How can I put it?* Five. The journey from Rijeka to Pula, by a roundabout way, is full of bends and makes one nauseous.

Armando Trevi has a private psychiatric clinic and sometimes works in a "Home for Adults with Mental Disorders." In that home (which the psychiatrists visit once a week for an hour or two), those who need to can also stay—and they do—with no time limit, or until their death. The home is now called Vila Marija. Once, the Vila Marija was the Vila Rizzi, but as a comparatively more convenient building for housing the inconvenient has recently been built next to the Vila Rizzi, which is in fact a family house, the whole complex is now called the Vila Marija, after one of the daughters of Lodovico Rizzi (1859–1945), former mayor of Austro-Hungarian Pula (five mandates, from 1889 to 1904). A fair number of old people reside in the home, but there are also younger patients. I doubt that its residents perform anything like Gombrowicz's plays, although it is surrounded by an extensive park, a wood known as the Bosco Rizzi, where the autumns are full of autumn colors. And birdsong. Lodovico Rizzi has been given back his name in the form of a hill called Monte Rizzi, admittedly on a smaller scale, as the rest of the hill is, I believe, called Vidikovac, or "Outlook Hill." It's not important. Armando Trevi is fascinated by Lodovico Rizzi and as we sit in the restaurant of the Hotel Scaletta, Armando tells me that Lodovico Rizzi has, finally, and he hopes definitively, *acquired his own street, called Rizzijeva, quite a long street today*, he says, *and not as short as in the days of*

Empire. When the Fascists came, Armando continues, *Rizzi became Claudia, then D'Annunzio, and in the time of Yugoslavia, Partisan Marko Orešković. Now Rizzi has come back, but as you can see the sparkle Pula had in those days has not.*

The Hotel Scaletta is still there, I say, *although there are often no shadows on the other side of the road anymore. In the summer, in that shade, we used to sit and drink wine until dawn.*

When Armando had listed everything that the Rizzi family had given Pula, starting with Lodovico's father, who, before his son, in 1864, had become its mayor, down to Lodovico himself, *Listen, when he died he left a gasworks, a water-supply system, sewers, a hospital, a telephone exchange, a market hall, a bank, a secondary school for girls, a town museum, an electric tram system, Pula at that time had four pharmacies, did you know that? It had three bookshops and seventy-five inns and restaurants, it had twelve clocks*, after Armando Trevi had listed it all, with picturesque descriptions and a wealth of detail, which took some time, he ended his tirade with an apparently significant crescendo: *At the beginning of the 1900s Pula had six hotels too, including Scaletta, and that is where the story of your Adam Kaplan begins.*

But I already knew that. That, and much more besides. Adam had written the history of his family in the "legacy" in the form of a letter I had been given before his funeral by Dominik Marengo. I mention this so it doesn't appear that the story of Adam Kaplan is incomplete in a literary sense, that the "bait has been thrown" but the situation left "unresolved." It's a complicated and lengthy story that merits particular attention; this isn't the place for it.

But there were things I hadn't known, something had been "left out" of Adam's letter.

Lodovico Rizzi was buried in 1945 in the town cemetery in Pula, and at the end of the 1940s his villa was redeveloped as a *manicomio*, a not at all sophisticated mental hospital. There, in the Vila

Rizzi asylum, in 1995, among some old health cards, the then fifty-year-old Adam Kaplan found the file of a woman by the name of Alba Kaplan. And his search began.

When the new section of the Vila Marija was opened, a process of tidying up the archives began, that is, transferring information about old, very old patients, onto computers, destroying the files, said Armando Trevi. *That was when I found the photograph of a woman called Alba Kaplan, and I thought that this woman might have been in some way related to your friend Adam. Here, this is her. Long since discharged from the Vila Rizzi.*

I looked at the bony face with dead eyes, an expressionless face of a small woman of roughly sixty. That photograph had not been in Adam's "letter."

I think Alba Kaplan was moved from the Vila Rizzi to Lopača some time toward the end of the sixties, said Armando Trevi.

Lopača is a psychiatric hospital on the edge of the town where I now live. I knew that she was there, in the hospital to which there is no public transportation, so it is difficult to get there, I knew that this was where Adam had finally found Alba Kaplan—his mother. He had found her just before she died, when Yugoslavia had already fallen apart, and Alba Kaplan had stopped talking. *She looked through me,* Adam wrote, *she didn't say a word, she didn't stir, I don't know whether she was breathing. I had to go on searching.*

And that's enough for now. Adam's family story branches into several countries, from Croatia through Italy, Albania and Africa, up to him, Adam's adoption in Zagreb and his move to Belgrade. I leave that for another occasion, if and when I feel like it.

In my practice I came across two cases of sexual self-harm. A few hours after his attempt to circumcise himself with scissors, a 24-year-old man, L. B., was brought to the first-aid surgery of the psychiatric clinic. He worked as a teller in a bank. The examination found, on his penis and mucous membrane, three lacerations of around four centimeters in length, which, under general anesthetic, were cleaned and sewn up. L. B. recovered quickly and before he was discharged he came to me for a conversation. His father had died a week earlier. *My father's death depressed me a lot,* said L. B., *and I thought that this act would help clear my mind.* In the medical history of the patient L. B., apart from an appendectomy, there is no mention of any other surgical intervention, serious trauma, nor any indication of psychiatric troubles. Nonsmoker. Doesn't drink or use drugs. Free from hallucinations. Concrete and abstract thought, sound reasoning—all normal. He sees himself as a practical, sensible and rational person. He refuses further psychiatric or psychological support.

While we were on night duty, Adam Kaplan and I, an ambulance brought to the surgery of the psychiatric clinic a 35-year-old unemployed, unmarried man. R. N. was in a state of shock. Three hours earlier, he attempted autocastration. Resuscitation was carried out with an infusion of colloidal solution, after which R. N. became agitated and refused a blood transfusion, maintaining that this was an "inadmissible attack on his privacy." During his psychological-psychiatric treatment, R. N. talked about his previous incarnation in the eighteenth century, when he was persecuted in Russia as the leader of a great religious movement and when he castrated himself with a red-hot poker. In his medical history there is no mention of psychiatric illnesses in the family; there is mention, as possibly relevant, of the patient's father's death three days before his self-castration. Adam Kaplan concluded that the patient R. N. was in a state of acute reactive psychosis and prescribed him a sedative administered by drip, after which R. N. received a blood transfusion and his wound was treated under general anesthetic—a ten-centimeter-long scrotal laceration with which R. N. had succeeded in removing his left and the lower part of his right testicle. R. N. recovered, and after another conversation with him, Adam concluded that R. N. was lucid and rational. Prescribing him more sedatives, he let him go home with a follow-up meeting arranged for ten days hence. In the meantime, R. N. killed himself by swallowing a large quantity of herbicide. Afterward, Adam told me, *These two cases are unusual, because most men who genitally self-harm are already psychotic. Most have a longish history of sexual self-harming and are permanent psychiatric patients. With the patients L. B. and R. N. their autocastration was the first indication of psychiatric disorder. Those are the only two cases in the history of this department,* said Adam, *and they both happened after the recent deaths of their fathers. Although,* Adam added, *I remember a case of autocastration in a man who had lost first his dog, and then his canary.*

Theoretically, genital self-harm after the death of a parent can happen because of an unresolved Oedipus complex. I shall not elaborate on that theory, because it is fairly straightforward and familiar to most people. When the death of someone close occurs, in some people the sense of guilt (because of anger) blossoms to unbearable dimensions and does not permit grief to creep into the small baggage whose place is on the upper (or lower) shelf of our inner storeroom. The sense of guilt then feeds the already poisonously swollen sorrow and seeks a way out. And there are various ways out: from autocastration, self-harm, mania or depression, suicide, or murder, or writing.

Father died is a famous, quasi-striking literary opening. If *Father died* (or, *Mother died*) isn't an opening, then it is an ending, the packaging and sealing of an ostensibly resolved guilt, a final leap into the waters of spiritual purification. Everything in between, in the book, in the confession, in the story, is the drawing of that road, the winding path that has to soar into a celestial choral symphony.

But that is an illusion. There is no spiritual purification, nor does anything fly off into the sky, or if it does take off, it comes back. This settling of accounts with fathers and mothers is not a conversation, but an invented, imagined dialogue with ghosts, with the dead, in fact the monologues of spoiled, infantile sons and daughters who either stamp their feet and scream, or wail: *You are to blame for my suffering, for my failures and this is my charge against you—je vous accuse.*

That's not fair. That cowardly settling of accounts with those who are no longer here. But, if the knots of our fears and hates could be disentangled by the two or three people involved, face to face, while the fathers (and mothers) were still alive, then so many self-pitying stories would remain unwritten, so much (poetic?) fury and so many one-sided accusations unexpressed, so much false solace denied to readers.

After the death of my father, what is left are film clips, little moving pictures, some cheerful, some less so, little pieces of his life that please or sadden me, which, when I wish, I look at and follow the way a reader follows episodes from the life of fictional or less fictional characters, then closes the book and goes for a walk. My father and I have ended our story together. With a lot of shouting, quarrelling, and reconciliation, our accounts are now clear. When Rudolf shrank (with age), the space around him became light, cleansed and open. I entered that space without fear, making in it a new niche for my son Leo, while my father, tiny at the end, watched our existence from where he was crouching in a corner, his arms open for an embrace and a smile on his face.

Perhaps I am writing a book about my father, not a book about *myself* and my father, but a book about his undreamed dreams, about his visions, which, fifty years later (when he was no longer there) became reality, about his loves, about his partisan fighting, about his enduring antifascism and obsession with the idea of *fratellanze* and *convivenze*, about his political battles, about his Party disobedience and Party punishment, expulsion from the Communist Party of Yugoslavia, sheepishly withdrawn by that same Party two decades later, licking their own shit, and his friends and political enemies (Ranković, Špiljak, Blažević, Bakarić, et al.) who bugged him from a position of strength when his life was at stake, about his travels, about the food he liked, the books he read, the painters and writers he spent time with, his games of chess and preferans, the languages he spoke, the humility with which he lived, the poverty in which he died.

When Milošević stole money from the National Bank of Yugoslavia, and Rudolf had already retired and married that shrew, that moral cripple and physical harpy (how could he have been so blind?), he handed Ada and me an account book from the Beogradska Banka with a deposit of fifteen thousand American dollars that no longer existed. *Here you are*, he said, *this is all that your mother Marisa and I saved.* The checkbook is here somewhere, twenty or so years have passed, it's all written down properly, except that the Beogradska Banka no longer exists.

It is not yet known, although one can guess, and more than seventy years later, by whose directive Rudolf's brother brought his comrades his own death sentence during the war (in Istria), not knowing what was written in it, and it concerned Rudolf as well, but it is known that at that time within the Party the conflict between the dogmatists and liberals was growing, a conflict that would last until the Party's collapse and from its center poisonous arrows would fly, "killing" some and inspiring others to defiance and disobedience.

I haven't written much about Rudolf. *You write about your mother*, he used to say, *write something about me*, he said, opening a recently published book of mine and with a pencil in hand began to read in the hope of finding himself in at least one paragraph. He cut out what was published about my books, whatever he came across, and catalogued it all, organized it, stuck it onto sheets of white paper and placed them in folders, without my having any idea about it. Unlike his other writings, the political ones that had disappeared, I found this insignificant little file tossed in among the small stained blankets that his crazed wife generously gave us.

I could write about how Rudolf, along with his brother, in 1943, founds and edits the *Voice of Istria*, whose wartime issues were printed on illegal presses between northern Istria and Gorski Kotar; I could write about his Proclamation to the people of Istria on September 13, 1943: *Istria is joining the motherland and proclaims its unification with our other Croatian brothers. Long live Croatian Istria!* and here he sponsored the people of Istria, and not the Communist Party of Yugoslavia, which individual political bigwigs found then, and later, extremely irritating; I could write about the way, even as early as 1945, totalitarian minds engaged in orgies, *while I couldn't attack our war comrades, landowners, local leaders and priests, or Italians who had fought with us in large numbers*, and the local Party heavyweights, carpetbaggers who sent the

"top brass" to Istria to muddy the waters, launched a filthy, viru-
lent campaign laden with fabrication and threats; I could write
about the falsified election in the constituency of Poreč-Buzet in
November 1953, about which I have already written in one of my
books, an election in which, as was rarely the case in the then state,
there were as many as three candidates on the list for Istria, one of
whom was Rudolf, who, because of his respect for the authority of
argument rather than the arguments of authority (the Party) was a
nuisance, and so, as later during Milošević's "people's happening,"
or recently in Croatia during the nationalist demonstration of
tent-dwellers and all kinds of ustashoid-fascistic-clerical figures in
front of theaters, in squares, outside state institutions or through
internet portals, the people were bribed with small change, free
transport, food vouchers and barren promises of a better life to
persuade them to yell inarticulately, foaming at the mouth. For
decades afterward, Rudolf received private letters of repentance,
begging forgiveness. I've got them, those letters. I could write
about how and where we lived in Zagreb in 1948, when Rudolf
was an editor with Naprijed Publishers, or how we came back
from America in 1953 on the cargo ship *Montenegro*, while other
Yugoslav diplomats sailed on the two queens, *Mary* and *Elizabeth*,
how we later made furniture out of wooden packing crates (chip-
board), which we painted with olive-green oil paint, the way snow
fell into our rooms and Ada and I were treated for the first stage of
tuberculosis. I could write about Rudolf's other battles within the
League of Communists of Yugoslavia (SK), Federal Committee,
*I had a lot of struggles within the SK, I was expelled from the Party,
then taken back, and twenty years later received written confirmation
that I had been right, and the leadership of the infallible Party was
wrong. Few people in Yugoslavia received such confirmation.* I could
write about the way, when he was removed from their immediate
high-political proximity, kicking him into the benign sphere of

tourism (*That'll shut him up!*), he realized his dream of an open Yugoslavia, and within a year visas for all foreign citizens were abolished and real, serious tourism began; I could write about the way, when he was "sent out of sight" for a second time, while the submissive were sent to diplomatic offices in Paris, London or Washington, Rudolf was posted to Sudan, where in the Nubian desert Yugoslav firms soon began to drill wells and where thousands of lives were saved from hunger and thirst; there is more, but that one life was too small for historical remembrance, however defiant and visionary it was, so not even public television, Croatian Radio Television, deemed it necessary to mark Rudolf's death.

There was almost nothing that could get him down. Not war, not Stalin, not Tito, not the Party, because in his battles he was not alone, he had friends, he had Marisa and he had us. And then the woman did it for him, that pathologically jealous shallow bourgeoisie for whom "Istria was far away," and Zagreb's Dolac Market close by. And so in the end Rudolf said, *All right, what's done is done, at least I'll go back when I'm dead.* Perhaps that's the origin of the image that occasionally comes to me before I fall asleep: Rudolf, freshly shaved, in the room with three beds at the old people's home, sitting on the edge of his bed and greeting me with a smile, his arms wide open.

Living with Rudolf was stressful. Until we left home, and later to a degree, Ada and I seemed to be in a film with elements of a political thriller, full of terror and horror. A film in which the hero fell into a trap, pulled himself out, only to be ambushed again.

He died alone, and he was afraid of solitude.

He approached death in that state-run old people's home, in a three-bed room where one could only lie, as there was no room even for a chair for visitors. But he would get up, lame as he was, with a barely healed, shoddily operated-on hip, with open wounds from bedsores, he would drop into his wheelchair, roll himself to the elevator and into a communal space where he played chess, and in group therapy sessions made roses and narcissi out of crêpe paper and little drawings of boats on choppy seas. He gave these to us later, because he loved giving, all his life he gave us small gifts, pointless, but in fact with a point, chocolates, keyrings, scarves, caps, badges, and he kept all of that, those little bits and pieces, in the drawers of his desk, and on feast days and birthdays he would ceremoniously hand us books, and shirts and ties for me, I can't remember what he gave Ada, wrapped in gift paper, excitedly, as though he was the one receiving the presents and not giving them. He also gave us the occasional relatively modest sum of money and then, in the home, we (Ada and I) left him money so that he would at least have some for coffee from the machine, because he had said to us, just once, *I've never been so poor.* As I was leaving, to go back to this place here where I have no one close, not truly close, he would get junk for me from the machine, biscuits and savory snacks for the journey. He also gave me some of the unused disposable hospital scrubs in which they washed him, he had collected a heap of them and gave them away because he had nothing else to give.

His books vanished. His correspondence vanished. Political and intimate correspondence, and that from friends. I have Rudolf's letters to me, but that's not important now, and I have a postcard found long ago (while we were still a family) with Lenin's portrait, which Rudolf had sent in 1948, from the Fifth Congress of the Communist Party of Yugoslavia in Belgrade, to his by then wife Marisa in Zagreb, with "comradely greetings."

During the bad times, immediately after Stalin's Resolution of the *Informbiro* and Tito's "No!" when Rudolf was running the information center in New York, he visited American universities and tried to explain the outlines of a visionary path, open, although utopian, which ultimately collapsed, only for a septic pit to be revealed today beneath its ashes. By night he learned English, by day he practiced it; globally speaking, postwar Yugoslav diplomacy was in the first league in contrast to Croatia at the beginning of the 1990s, when for instance the ambassador (a nationalist HDZ Party cadre) held court in Rome for seven years, a man followed on tiptoe by a ghostly interpreter who whispered answers to His Excellency's anxious question, *What did they say, what did they say?* when virtually no contacts were made in that neighboring country, apart from its small and insignificant diaspora.

In New York, our apartment was visited by Earl Browder, Alexander Kerensky, Lillian Hellman, Dashiell Hammett, Louis Adamič (and many others), bringing their (intimate and political) stories and their books, which later, many years later, I leafed through, although they weren't among my books of choice. (Borges was becoming fashionable.) But Rudolf would say, *Read, it could be useful to you*, so I found myself torn between Kafka and Sartre, between Thomas Paine and Dostoevsky, and later, utterly confused, between Lacan gazing at Freud, and Breton and Bataille. Lujo and Zlata Goranin came as well (a small black dog and Zlata's spaghetti *al pomodoro* with hard-boiled eggs on top), and there was singing and music. Nothing has remained of those times. That woman, she who like a boa constrictor sucked up Rudolf's will and everything he left to us—his life before her—that woman cleared away; she threw out his books and his writings, because those times were too large and expansive for her cowardly little patch, and because, right up until Rudolf's death, they were infused with the breath of beautiful, playful, and to her inaccessible Marisa.

In the old people's home, Rudolf did not give up straight away. To begin with he was lively, he had company, and he had rid himself of the idiocies of that virago. *These bedsores won't go away, I'll have them all my life*, he said when he was ninety-two. They separated him from his books, from his writings, from his stamp collections (which they stole after his death, sending us a suitcase full of empty albums), from small decorative objects about which, imagining them, he could have written something during his peaceful days in the old people's home, they separated him from his pictures, from sculptures by his artist friends, from his clothes, they unhooked him from his life, they took his oxygen, that woman and her son, while he, squinting in one eye (because no one bothered to call in an ophthalmologist or take him to one), he read whatever I brought him—papers, essays, philosophy and the occasional novel. When I arrived, and I came for a day every other week (alternating with Ada), because I had nowhere to spend the night, because I couldn't afford a hotel, he was waiting for me in a clean tracksuit (he had never worn a tracksuit in his life), sitting on the edge of his bed, shaved and smiling. He would throw himself into his wheelchair and we would leave that house of death at great speed.

Rudolf didn't have his own apartment. He didn't have the money to pay for home care in an apartment that was not his own. Rudolf's apartment in Rijeka had been sold and he moved into his stepson's apartment, having previously signed a statement to the effect that, should he one day begin to lose his grip, they, the woman and her son, had the right to put him away, I don't remember where, somewhere they chose, where people presumably cared for lost souls. Half the money from the sale of Rudolf's apartment (acquired during his life with Marisa) was in that woman's account, the other half in Rudolf's and he used that money until he had used it all up (his pension was less than five hundred euros a month, so then the woman and her son decided that Rudolf really had lost his grip and had to be put away. *My dignity has been a bit fucked up, I've fucked it up a bit*, he told me then, in that home, as we smoked and drank beer in the little café on the ground floor. At the reading of his will, the woman just lied, claimed that Rudolf had sold his apartment and given us the money. Now I'm trying to get access to all payments into her bank accounts, and we'll see.

Rudolf remained lucid to the end, he was not losing his grip, and he never lost it. He was just mislaid, they mislaid him. His French was still good, his English excellent, not to mention his Italian. He didn't have false teeth, or those bridges, or any kind of implant. He was missing one of his fifth and both of his sixth and seventh teeth, but his front teeth, admittedly a bit loose and no longer white, were all there.

I didn't like going to the care home because I would run into the sons and daughters of old and infirm residents, some of whom knew neither who they were or where they were, they lay like corpses and opened their mouths mechanically while the staff fed them gruel from little spoons. And that frightened me.

In the bed next to Rudolf lay a former Ustasha whose surname was Boban, he was ninety-seven, presumably he's dead as well by now. After the war, Boban scarpered to France, and in the 1990s he came back to die on the breast of his motherland. He was a cousin of Rafael Boban, that semiliterate lout and cutthroat, commander of the Black League, which used to go around fairs before the war selling spangles and tobacco. The Boban lying beside Rudolf stole other people's possessions—candy, sugar, tea bags, tissues, and sometimes also money. Taking small steps, dragging his feet, he would creep into the neighboring rooms, thinking that people couldn't hear him, because he was deaf. When the nurses caught him stealing, they would just say *tsk tsk tsk* and turn away their heads. And so, willy-nilly, there was a "reconciliation" between the Partisan and the Ustasha. In the old people's home. In silence. And impotence.

There was also an old woman, a long-term resident, who used to visit Rudolf's room, she would dig herself in beside the door and wail, *Take me home, please, take me home.* There was another woman, quite refined, but with empty eyes. She would come in, turn to Rudolf, and say nothing. I would ask her, *Do you need anything?* and after a long pause she would say *Closeness.* Every time. As though she had stepped out of a Beckett play. I would ask her, *How old are you?* She would just stand there saying nothing, then whisper: *Very.* In the dayroom I would always find an old man with a small, dilapidated address book, crossing out the names of those who were no more. Then he'd say, *I must call him.* In the end he could have thrown the address book away. There was no one left.

There was often the stench of urine in Rudolf's room.

In the home I heard sons and daughters frantically calling the staff, *Please come, nurse, father has soiled himself, mother has soiled herself,* at which Rudolf would say, *I didn't pass a stool for three days, then I crapped on Christmas Day.* One day he told me, *Our third preferans player has died,* so I filled the breach, we played until midnight, I got to Rijeka at four in the morning.

I brought him the strongest combinations of vitamins and minerals so that he'd hang onto life for a little longer, but toward the end he lost interest. To start with, we went to nearby restaurants for lunch, we drank good wine, ate salted cod and laughed. I pushed him in his wheelchair so he'd breathe in the fresh air, because in the home it was doled out to them in droplets. We moved from café to café ad nauseam, so as to go back as late as possible. Sometimes our hands would be cold. Sometimes we would place our hands on each other's hands and talk, knitted together like that. About the past. About the future, about what music would be played at his funeral, *"Beautiful land, beloved Istria," play that for me,* he said, and Elis Lovrić did it magnificently, first at the crematorium in Zagreb, where some people looked at each other in surprise, and then in his Istria, where some people wept. Rudolf's last interview for an Istrian newspaper bore the title "Good luck, Istria of mine!" In Zagreb, the cremation was a caricature. All right, a delegation of Istrians came, Zvonko, his other roommate from the home, came, Buda Lončar came and bowed to him, my heart broke, afterward, in the cold, Buda waited for a taxi but none came, either for him or for us, it was cold, it was February. There was no wake, as Ada and I had nowhere to invite people, and we didn't know most of those people, I don't think that Rudolf had invited them either, most of them were friends of the "grieving" widow and her latest home-help, because she kept having new ones. The Istrians went straight back, so that Ada and I, our children and Jadranka from our childhood went to eat lamb and potatoes baked under a lid in a quiet restaurant where there was a fire burning in the grate. Then we parted.

But the wake in Karojba was festive. Rudolf sat nearby, "his" Malvasia wine was drunk, "his" prosciutto and goat's cheese, crostini and fritters were eaten, his people proposed toasts. Half of Istria came to the funeral in Karojba. I brought Rudolf from Zagreb to Rijeka. I let him spend the night in the living room, where there were books, a Turkmen carpet and souvenirs which he had given me. The next day I took the bus that goes around Istria, I put my father on the seat beside me (the urn was wrapped in maroon corrugated paper, as though I was carrying a panettone) and took him for a drive, his last sightseeing tour of the towns, villages and hamlets he had visited on foot who knows how many times during the war, whose people he loved, to bid them farewell.

The woman didn't come to the real funeral, the Istrian one, of course. *What?* she said, *Get my shoes dirty in that mud!* Now she wants some kind of share in the ownership of the grave in which my great-grandfather, my great-grandmother, my grandfather, my grandmother and my father, with their long and painful Istrian stories, lie. She says that half the grave belongs to her, but the grave isn't ours at all, it is Istrian, protected, because after the war

381

Rudolf, his brother, and my grandfather made a gift of the land in Karojba where there is now a school and a basketball court, and their family home in Pazin, around which a wallpaper factory was built, and so on, and in return dead Rudolf acquired 2x1 meters of red Istrian earth in which he could disintegrate. The woman also generously declared that she was willing to come to an agreement with us over the ownership of the Karojba grave, but I don't know how she'll negotiate over something she says doesn't exist. I told her that she could jump straight into that grave if she wished, although I might, I said, bring Marisa from Belgrade to lay her beside Rudolf, because that was love, and then in court that woman feigned a heart attack, which was in fact an ordinary hysterical attack, and even though she was ninety years old, unfortunately she didn't drop dead.

She also wanted to come to an agreement about the pictures she had stolen, only I don't know how because she didn't intend to give them back, not even the one that Rudolf gave me for my birthday when he was in the home. *Go and take Božena Vilhar's carnations*, he said. Of course I didn't go, that's not my style, and it's debatable whether that woman would have let me into her son's apartment, because when we came for what belonged to us by order of the court (and which she gave us), she had placed her son and her nephew at the door like Cerberuses and had thrown Rudolf's old suits into the hallway, not, of course, his evening attire, his dinner jacket, nor his winter coat (which I could have used), she had shoved into cardboard boxes the moldy pillows and blankets which Rudolf had put over his knees in the home, all with the sticky remnants of food that had fallen out of his hands toward the end. I immediately sent Rudolf's clothes to flooded regions, I washed the blankets, which I now use to cover my knees in winter when I sit in my tenement, often in the half dark.

What will she do with Božena Vilhar? She has no idea who Božena Vilhar is, she certainly doesn't know who her husband, Janez Žirovnik, was, known as Osman in the partisans. I've known Božena and Osman since my childhood, I've been to see them in Opatija countless times, I've listened to Osman and Rudolf's partisan stories, once when I got lost in Trieste and didn't have any money (I was eighteen), Osman came to get me and took me for *melanzane alla parmigiana*. He gave Ada a gold brooch for her wedding. I know where, in which building, Božena Vilhar, then Ružić, was living in Sušak in the 1930s. I remember happy evenings spent as Marisa and Rudolf, Božena and Osman rummaged through their past, when they sang and danced, both here and there. I could say things about more or less every oil painting that now hangs on the wall of that virago's apartment. For instance, about

Joza Janda, Vilko Šeferov, Bata Protić, Beba Galović, Šana Šotra, Mirko Počuč, Franc Slana and Dora Plestenjak, Sabahudin Hodžić, Ivan Radović, I knew them all, they all sat at our table, I went to all their exhibitions, I was in their studios, in their apartments, I knew what kind of clothes they wore, the way they laughed and what angered them, while, at the discussion of the will, that harridan announced that those paintings were all stolen Jewish property, which left Ada and me speechless, astounded, so stunned, flabbergasted, appalled at the dark mind of a grasping hysterical old woman that we didn't say a word. When we came to our senses and decided to sue the bitch, the lawyers told us, *It's too late now. Let it go, the woman's mad.* She's not mad, she's loathsome, because later, when I told all this to the judge at the hearing, she addressed Ada and me in that shrill voice of hers, *Vermin, Serbian vermin!*

There's a story about a certain Frau Kutowski who was placed in a Berlin asylum in 1987, believing that she was Anita Berber (the Anita Berber on the painting by Otto Dix), that notorious Anita Berber (later she had a plaque dedicated to her on the building in which she lived), a nude dancer, drug addict, scandalmonger of Weimar Germany, who after the Great War became world famous and who, in 1928, aged twenty-nine died of tuberculosis. Through her delusions, Frau Kutowski, fat, ugly and old, in her interactions with the hospital staff and other mentally ill patients, stole someone else's life, wormed her way into the subversive pulsing, into the defiance and self-destructive revolt of Anita Berber, disturbing her surroundings anew. Frau Kutowski was the actress Lotti Huber in Rosa von Praunheim's film *Anita: Tänze des Lasters* (*Anita: Dances of Vice*). There, that's Rudolf's widow losing the plot, imagining that she is Marisa, that before her no one had shared any kind of life with Rudolf, except that Frau Kutowski's mission was to expose human depravities, while she, that real-life, not cinematic fiend, in the madhouse of our age, had no such mission.

For Rudolf's funeral in Istria, someone had made little cushions on which we were supposed to lay his medals. *What medals!* screeched that woman, *There aren't any medals. Whoever saw medals being placed on a coffin!* she yelled. There, in that Zagreb crematorium, there were no little cushions or medals, while in Karojba there were only little cushions. The medals were later miraculously discovered, allegedly in the attic: those from the National Liberation War (Commemorative), those from subsequent services to the Federal National Republic of Yugoslavia and the Socialist Federal Republic of Yugoslavia, of the first and second order, one from the Presidents of Egypt (Nasser), Sudan (Nimeiry) and Finland (Kekkonen), from the Prime Ministers of Sweden (Palme), Italy (Pertini) and so on. I shall sell them, I'll sell them all abroad, to collectors, because no one here in Croatia needs them, no one cares. (I'll keep the Commemorative medal.)

In the home, Rudolf had no clothes to go out in, only those rags to wear in the house: pajamas, two tracksuits, a cardigan, and slippers. They thought, presumably, that woman and her son, that Rudolf wouldn't be going out anymore, out of that home, that bed, that waiting room. He had no shoes, no winter jacket, no cap, no gloves, no scarf, so I brought him all of those things, my own, so that he'd have them for our "walks." Toward the end he became thin and fragile. I wanted to move him to my place, or into a home in Pula or Rovinj, he would have been near us there, near his Istrians, one summer I organized a stay for him in the Rovinj home—in our old house he would have been imprisoned again—it's a humane home in the center, with beautiful grounds, on the way to the wood and the sea, and I imagined myself taking him in his wheelchair to see his friends, to the shore, to the swimming pool where he would swim again, because nothing hurts in water, in water one is light and blessed, I imagined us sitting on a terrace, in a tavern, eating squid, black risotto, polenta or *fuži*, offering him a last shred of life, that still undamaged (but suppressed) little island of happiness. He didn't want to come. Perhaps he was afraid of that woman's hysterical scenes, perhaps he didn't want to be a burden to us, perhaps he wanted to wallow masochistically in his own foolishness.

From the outside it wasn't possible to see or hear what was happening in our father's chest. But Ada and I knew. What was happening was pain, pressure. In his chest, it seems, Rudolf was again carrying a pneumatic chamber, a small space with doors and windows through which he watched the air in it becoming thin and stifling. He'd had enough.

He couldn't kill himself with his pistol, because his war pistol was at first at my place and is now in the museum in Pula. He couldn't throw himself out of the window, that would have been unnecessarily dramatic and created all kinds of complications for others. He opted for pneumonia.

Two weeks before he died, we went out to lunch, he crumbled bread and collected the crumbs on the table. Recently he had been collecting crumbs, scraps of paper, any little bit of rubbish he noticed, then he would start straightening crooked objects, coasters, notebooks, newspapers, putting things in order, keeping things under control. I watched with surprise and unease. Two weeks before he died, as I was leaving, he said, *We won't see each other again.* A tear glistened in an eye, I no longer remember whose, his or mine, we hugged and I left.

A week later I got a telephone call: *Rudolf has a high temperature and pneumonia.* His roommate, Zvonko, the one who came to the Zagreb funeral, told me, *He sat in the cold bathroom, wet after being showered. He didn't want to dry himself. Leave me alone, he kept saying.*

I went back to Rijeka to collect some things, some clothes, with the intention of going to Zagreb the next day. I had a fever that climbed up to 41 degrees Celsius. I lay in bed, unable to get up for a week. I called Rudolf every two hours, he spoke less and less, I asked the staff at the home to take him to hospital, they said, *He won't let us, he won't go.* Ada went and moved Rudolf to the Pulmonary Department.

On February 20, 2013, Rudolf called me. He said, *Andreas.* I asked questions, I talked, I spoke: nothing, silence at the other end. And heavy breathing. I caught the next bus to Zagreb. *He died ten minutes ago,* said the doctor.

It's all okay. I'm sorry that I didn't keep him company as he went, that I didn't stroke his forehead, his cheek, that I didn't say anything to him. I did to Marisa. I talked to Marisa and she heard me. I held Marisa's hand when her head drooped. I'm sorry that I didn't get to say "Tata" to Rudolf. For decades I hadn't called him Tata, just Rudolf or, in moments of suppressed tenderness, Rudi. Old as he was, and in a bad way, I just found it grotesque to call him Tata, but now I miss that, which is all the more pathetic.

I recently read Dragan Velikić's *Islednik* (*The Investigator*). In this excellent book, the middle-aged narrator talks about his mother angrily, sometimes almost accusingly, but the whole time calling her Mama, which bothered me at first, from a literary point of view, it seemed somehow soft to me, exaggeratedly tender, too sentimental, then I shuddered.

The book is also about Istria and some houses in Pula, so it is all the closer to me. Because I too have a building in Pula (that asylum), about which I might say more at some stage. In Velikić's book, the narrator says that *when she moved into a home, Mama imagined that she was no longer in Belgrade. She began to speak in the Croatian variant. Often during my visits she would hurry me to leave so as not to miss my train. In her head she moved from town to town.*

The last time I saw her, she was living in Rijeka. She had partially adopted the Fiume dialect. She asked me when I was going back to Belgrade. Which hotel I was staying in. As we parted, she took me by the hand and said, in dialect: When you come again, don't forget to bring my notebook. It's got the addresses of hotels in it. Without it I can't travel anywhere.

I shuddered (frightened?), because I understood that in this book the narrator is investigating other people's lives, those close to him and not so close, to reach his own, and that in every search facts are not enough, facts are dead without compassion, without feeling and a bit of personal suffering. And, again, I saw that our umbilical cord wraps around this planet on which we walk, thinking that we are alone and abandoned.

Dear Mama, concludes the hero of Velikić's novel, *soon I'll be speaking the Fiume dialect.*

And, like Rudolf before his death, I collect crumbs. Scraps of paper, small coins, shreds. My gaze is constantly drawn to the ground, as soon as I catch sight of anything I get up, stop what I'm doing and pick up the grains, the fragments, the slivers and lay them on my palm. I straighten objects, bring them under control—crooked chairs and tables, mats, plastic and cane blinds. I create order.

Marina Tsvetaeva said: *How did the heart break and how was it that*

It didn't break.

Now I have time at a time when I don't have any time.

I want to have my eyelids lifted to see better. I'm only half looking. But if such an undertaking entails a general anesthetic, I'll have to wait. That carcinoma of the breast operation was a walk in the park compared to when my appendix burst and its rotten contents spilled through my insides. I should have died, but, there, I didn't. In hospital, on drips and intravenous injections of antibiotics, I lasted ten days, it was summer and the mercury soared to 40° Celsius, we didn't get clean sheets because, they said, the woman who worked in the laundry had gone on holiday, only one shower in the department functioned, the one in the women's bathroom, maybe they thought men didn't wash. After that operation I puffed up, I was like a clown, I almost took off.

Then everything settled down, came back to normal. I deflated to a decent static state. Sometimes I even hear my heart beating.

I swapped places with Ada. I said, *You miss the city, you go there, you'll have my books and memories of a previous life.* Ada said, *I don't need memories*, but she went. Just like that. That city holds nothing for us, no recollections, no old images, no joys and no sorrows. We can read its history, we can sometimes study it, we can hear about it and watch the inhabitants of that city falling into a trance over their own memories. In that city we wear ready-made clothes, new, ironed, that never fit the way they should, they rub like newly bought shoes or starched shirts.

I buried myself in Ada's Rovinj cellar. I painted the walls, made a new bathroom, changed the windows, threw out the old furniture, I'm gradually settling in. I go for walks. The woods are full of pines, I collect pine nuts. I pick mushrooms and asparagus. I have (old) friends, I play preferans, I play chess. A few days ago I caught myself singing. Occasionally Leo and Đoja come, Ada comes as well, we sit in the garden and laugh. We are together, the remnants of the Ban clan. Then I cook for all of them, that makes me happy; I grill little gilthead fish, I fry squid, we eat maneštre and chard, I make pesto from my pine nuts; I get Teran wine from Tonije from Motovun, Malvasia from Franc from Poreč, Ricardo brings me grappa.

When I moved, I sat on the seashore and gazed into the distance. I didn't weep like that phony, that mellifluous Coelho, who talks drivel. I opened my backpack, which I had been hauling with me for two and a half decades, and which had reached the end of its road. In the bottom rolled a few old mislaid trivialities, incidentals, trifles, trinkets that rang like little bells, fading away.

The sea glittered, little silver arrows like acupuncture needles flew through the air and pierced my arms, my chest, my legs, my eyes, and for an instant I saw nothing, no blueness, no infinity. I heard (again) Cioran whispering:

> To an extent I acknowledged my country, which had given me such a significant opportunity for suffering, I loved it because it could not respond to my expectations.

which was additionally soothing.

Then Dom Sebastian, King of Portugal, crept up, sat down beside me, put his arm around my shoulder and said:

> Others take my madness away
> with all that took place in it.
> Without madness what is man

391

> *more than the healthy beast,*
> *corpse adjourned that procreates?*

Then I leapt up and swam.

I'm an excellent swimmer. Strong and graceful.

(That day) the soft, seductive and tranquil sea rolled over my back until it had wrapped around me, embraced me, whispering *Now you are mine, imprisoned and secure in my depths ... I am your master.* But, with each of my movements, Dom Sebastian became ever quieter; I speeded up the movement of my legs and arms, I breathed steadily, I cut through the water, wounded it, and the sea softened. I swam for hours, that was my last marathon of account-settling, I swam, and alongside me, like a support crew, slid Kierkegaard, multiplied a hundredfold, repeating with me, like a mantra, with each stroke, rhythmically (to that water): *My misery is my castle, which is set, like an eagle's nest, among the clouds on top of the mountain. No one can conquer it. From it I fly down into reality and snatch my prey.*

In *EEG*, Daša Drndić has incorporated or quoted the words of a number of writers. If there is any writer whose work has not been acknowledged here, we will make due reference in any future edition.

Lines from E. M. Cioran's *Cahiers 1957–1972* © Editions Gallimard, Paris, 1997.

A line adapted from an interview of Milan Kundera by Philip Roth on November 30, 1980, printed in the *New York Times*.

Lines from Ludwig Wittgenstein's *Tractatus Logico-Philosophicus*, 6.431, translated by C. K. Ogden, published in the United States by Harcourt, Brace & Company, Inc. in 1921.

Excerpt from "On Noise" in *Essays by Arthur Schopenhauer*, selected and translated by T. Bailey Saunders, published in New York by A. L. Burt Company in 1902.

Lines from *Jean le bleu* by Jean Giono © Editions Grasset & Fasquelle, 1995.

Excerpt from *The Sickness Unto Death* by Søren Kierkegaard, edited and translated by Edna H. Hong & Howard V. Hong. Published by Princeton University Press, Princeton, New Jersey, 1941.

Excerpt from *The Luzhin Defense* by Vladimir Nabokov, copyright © 1990 by the Estate of Vladimir Nabokov. Used by permission of Alfred A. Knopf, an imprint of the Knopf Doubleday Publishing Group, a division of Penguin Random House LLC. All rights reserved.

Lines adapted from *Die Schachnovelle* by Stefan Zweig, first published in 1942 in Buenos Aires and in Europe by Gottfried Bermann Fischer in 1943.

Lines from "Optical Illusion" (1934) in *Today I Wrote Nothing* by Daniil Kharms, English translation copyright © 2007, 2009 by Matvei Yankelevich. Used by permission of The Overlook Press, an imprint of Harry N. Abrams, Inc., New York. All rights reserved.